Praise for other novels by
Kim Iverson Headlee

Dawnflight
"Intense."
~ USA Today

Morning's Journey
"Compelling."
~ CS Fantasy Reviews

King Arthur's Sister in Washington's Court
"Entertaining."
~Publishers Weekly

Liberty
"Epic."
~ Drew's Random Chatter

Raging Sea

To Chris
with all my best wishes!
Kim
Iverson
Headlee
The Story tells us.

KIM IVERSON

HEADLEE

PENDRAGON
COVE PRESS

Published by
Pendragon Cove Press

Raging Sea by Kim Iverson Headlee
Copyright ©2018 by Kim Headlee

http://kimheadlee.com
https://twitter.com/KimHeadlee
http://www.facebook.com/KimIversonHeadlee

Publication History
Paperback, 2019
ISBN: 978-1-949997-01-9
Library binding, 2019
ISBN: 978-0-9971202-9-5
E-book, 2019
ISBN: 978-1-949997-04-0

Bear's Head line art Copyright ©2014 by Jessica Headlee
All other interior line art Copyright ©2018 by Kim Headlee
Cover Art Copyright ©2019 by Natasha Brown
Cover photo:
"Portrait of a handsome muscular bodybuilder posing over black background"
©2013 by prometeus, ID 27755689 Depositphotos.com
Photo of Kim Iverson Headlee Copyright ©2006 by Chris Headlee
Fonts, public domain: Cambria, Lightfoot Narrow, and Neverwinter

Raging Sea

by Kim Iverson Headlee

The Dragon's Dove Chronicles, Book 3

FUATH CHÌ LEÌS AN SÙILEAN.
GRÀDH CHÌ LEÌS AN CRÌDHE.
GRÀDH NAOMH CHÌ LEÌS AN DEÒ.

CALEDONIAN PROVERB

"HATRED SEES WITH THE EYES.
LOVE SEES WITH THE HEART.
HOLY LOVE SEES WITH THE SOUL."

Contents

CHAPTER 1

THE FORMER EXALTED Heir of Clan Alban of Caledon was dead.

He was certain of it.

There existed no light, no pain, no smells, no heat, no chill, no sensation of any kind save the most beautiful strains of harp music he'd ever heard. The images it evoked bespoke love in its many incarnations: the frenzied passion of the Belteine fire dance, the soaring joy of two souls bonded by desire, a mother's fierce protectiveness of her children, the lament of a bereaved spouse, a lullaby for a newborn, the rapture of a long-delayed reunion. The Otherworld wasn't like what he had been taught—he saw no eternal battlefield where Lord Annaomh's Army of the Blest fought Lord Annàm's Samhraidhean minions. None of the ancient tales mentioned music in the Otherworld, but he supposed the Old Ones could have whatever they liked.

Comforted by the melody, which was jaunty and lilting and mournful and jaunty again, he wasn't about to complain to his sithichean hosts.

The final notes thrummed into silence. "Well done, Eileann," spoke a nearby male voice in Caledonaiche. "I'll wager the Old Ones themselves are pleased by your harping." This won the murmured assent of other Caledonach men.

"Thank you, Tavyn." The female Caledonach voice sounded demure, as though unaccustomed to hearing such praise.

He was about to add his lauds to Tavyn's when pain battered his head and chest. Apparently, the gods weren't done tormenting him. He had been housed with his people—his former people. If this group had recognized him, they never would have allowed him into their company.

Caledonaich did not associate with those who had been stripped of honor.

Dragging a hand across his eyes, though unwilling to open them, he encountered the folds of a bandage swathing his brow. His hand dropped to his chest, and he found another bandage where his battle-tunic and undertunic should have been. He probed the ache's source and winced. Half a handspan farther down, and the wound would have gifted him one-way passage to the Otherworld.

Where am I?

"Rest easy, brave one." He must have uttered the question aloud, and the lady harper sounded much closer than before. "You're in the field hospital at Port Dhoo-Glass."

The Caledonach ward.

He groaned.

Someone pressed a cool, damp cloth to his cheeks and neck. He had to admit it did feel good.

"Medics found you with a gash on your forehead and a spear in your chest," the woman continued. "If you hadn't moved when you did, they would have left you for dead. You're lucky to be here."

Some luck. He wished the medics had left him to the ravens.

Worse, his pain-fogged brain at last attached meaning to the names Eileann and Tavyn. They belonged to the daughter and son of Chieftainess Dynann of Clan Tarsuinn, his dead father's clan. Tavyn was commander of Second Turma, Manx Cohort, the unit that had charged the Sasunach line beside his. He turned his head onto one cheek and tried not to groan louder.

A hand slipped under his head to lift it a bit. Keeping his eyes closed, he didn't resist. No sense in rushing the inevitable.

A cup touched his lips, brimming with a warm, honey-scented liquid.

He flickered open his eyes and gazed past the cup's rim into the face of the most beautiful woman he had ever seen, save one. Lustrous black hair tumbled past her shoulders to sweep toward his chest. Graceful eyebrows accented brown eyes that glimmered with more compassion than he deserved. The light flush of her cheeks made him think of roses beneath a dusting of snow.

Her berry-red lips gave him the gift of a genuine smile.

He swallowed a mouthful of the liquid and grimaced, its bitterness a fitting reminder of the state of his soul.

"Valerian." Her smile adopted an apologetic cast. "For your pain. Does it need more honey?"

"Nay." Was his voice as harsh as it sounded? He couldn't help it; his worst pain, valerian couldn't cure. He grasped the hand cradling his head and moved it so he could lie flat. To his surprise, he found it difficult to let go. He did his best to return her smile, though it had been moons since his facial muscles had moved in that direction. "Thank you, my lady."

Nodding, she disengaged her hand and rose, leaving the cup on the stool beside his cot. She bent to dab his cheeks with the damp cloth and placed it beside the cup. "I'll be staying at the fortress until my brother is well enough to travel. Send for me if you need anything," she whispered. Her kind smile inflicted the anguish of a hundred spear thrusts. "My name is Eileann."

He knew; gods, how he knew. If he had never heard her speak, he'd have known from the blue woad Tarsuinnach falcon tattoo spread-winged and screeching across her right forearm, symbol of her status as their àrd-banoigin. Chieftainess Dynann would retain clan leadership for as long as she remained fit for the task, but Eileann carried the responsibility for continuing the line of succession. By Caledonach law, Eileann was free to choose her consort. That her left arm bore no tattoo meant she hadn't exercised that choice.

Mayhap he could . . . nay; he was forgetting himself. Or rather, what he had become.

Eileann nic Dynann probably had suitors lined up from one shore of Caledon to the other. If she didn't, the likelihood of her choosing an outcast was less than the sun changing its course at zenith to set in the east. Best to put her out of his mind. Best for him—and for her.

As she glided to her brother's cot and reached for her harp, he found he could no sooner forget her than forget the shameful events of his past that prevented him from ever trying to woo her.

He groaned into the pillow.

Seated on the stool beside Tavyn, Eileann picked up her lap-size traveling harp. She plucked a few chords but couldn't decide what to play.

What a strange young man, whose pain runs deeper than the wounds of his flesh.

Other men, those not wounded past caring, lavished upon her their smiles and winks and words. That one didn't appear to want her ministrations, yet he'd clung to her hand as though it were a lifeline. A lifeline to what, Eileann couldn't fathom.

Nor could she fathom how she might comfort him, but the thrumming of her heart commanded her to try.

"Well, dear sister, are you going to play something else for us? Or do you intend to daydream the hours away?" Tavyn's tone carried its usual hint of affectionate mockery.

She smiled. Play something . . . yes, of course. The injured men enjoyed her harping, but that one in particular—the one with a hole in his chest and a hole in his soul—had appeared to be entranced by the music. As her fingers found the correct strings, she slid a glance at him. The warrior's eyes were closed, but a faint smile lingered on his lips. She poured her heart into her playing, hoping she could coax that smile to strengthen.

The next time she chanced to look his way, he had turned from her.

She finished to greater applause and spoken praise than before. Yesterday, that would have pleased her beyond measure. Today, the person whose response mattered—and it was strange to think of anyone outside her clan in those terms—remained silent.

So did her harp's strings.

"Daydreaming again?"

Leave it to Tavyn to drag her into reality. She nodded at the mysterious warrior. "Who is he? Do you recognize him?"

Tavyn's face tensed. "No, I don't—wait." He lowered his eyebrows. "Angusel mac Alayna." The name sounded like poison on Tavyn's lips. "Now he calls himself Aonar."

Aonar. Alone.

Then Eileann recalled why: Angusel mac Alayna of Clan Alban had tried to rescue Chieftainess Gyanhumara's bairn, and his failure had resulted in the bairn's murder. Gyanhumara had dissolved his Oath of Fealty to her and banished him from Clan Argyll lands. Clan Alban considered him a disgrace, as well. By extension, so did all of Caledon. No wonder his pain had seemed so deep.

As she gazed at his sad and vulnerable face, she could find in her heart no hatred or disgust or contempt or even pity, just profound sympathy.

"Medics!"

Tavyn's shout broke her reverie. He had sat up and was waving an arm. "Tavyn, what's wrong? Are you all right?"

He gave her an annoyed look. "Of course." A pair of medics scurried over to his cot, and Tavyn regarded them. "Move that soldier out of this ward. Now." He jabbed his thumb in Angusel's direction. "The one who owns the legion officer's cloak."

Eileann scanned the ward, but every other cloak displayed a Caledonach clan's pattern. Angusel's was plain scarlet.

Angusel pushed himself to a sitting position. As she watched in shocked silence, he swung his legs over the cot's side and bent to reach for his boots, reeling and gritting his teeth.

Shaking her head, Eileann gripped Tavyn's forearm. "You can't! He's too badly hurt!"

"He doesn't belong with us." The alien sternness of his stare made her gasp. She released his arm. He glared at the medics. "You have your orders, men."

"Aye, Decurion Tavyn," they replied, saluting.

The medics gathered Angusel's few belongings and got him to his feet for the walk to the Breatanach ward, and Eileann's heart went out to him. She couldn't debate her brother's logic or military authority. Angusel no longer held a place in Caledonach society, including the portion of it that resided within the Pendragon's mostly Breatanach army.

Supported by the medics, Angusel shuffled toward the door. Except for a warrior's occasional moan and the footfalls of Angusel and his escorts, the converted barracks room lay silent. Men able to watch the scene trained their gazes upon the departing trio. Angusel ignored them, his head hung low. Eileann ached to play him one last song.

In her mind she played that tune for him, a rousing warrior's send-off, and prayed for his recovery.

THEY PAUSED at the ward's outer door, and he looked up. One of the medics proffered the iron dragon brooch and cloak that had betrayed his identity to Decurion Tavyn. Not that his identity mattered; he was but one of Arthur's soldiers, duty bound to go where ordered.

If that meant crawling elsewhere to die, then so be it.

The other medic helped him don his rent battle-gear and handed him his sheathed sword. He took the cloak from the man's companion and pinned it in place. His helmet he'd lost in the battle, yanked off by a Sasun who didn't live long enough to regret the mistake.

As the first medic opened the door, a gust bullied its way inside, unfurling his cloak, guttering the oil lamps, and stirring the rushes. The wind bore the clean scent of the outdoors. It heightened the lingering stench of injury and death. The cold air braced him.

Across the compound, heading his way, shadowed by a dark billow that resolved into an Argaillanach-patterned cloak, strode . . . *her*.

He exited the Caledonach ward. As he turned to his sword side, a hand gripped his uninjured shoulder.

"The Brytoni ward is this way, Optio," said the first medic, in Breatanaiche.

He shrugged the man off. "I have business elsewhere. Dismissed, both of you." He needed no help for what he had in mind.

They exchanged a glance, shrugged, saluted him, and reentered the ward. He headed toward the fort's gates and away from *her* as fast as his pain and the ragged remains of his dignity would permit.

HE STOOD on the bluff, staring at the gray-green sea pummeling the Manx beach a score of paces below. The Sasunach funeral pyre at his back belched draconic heat and eye-stinging smoke and gut-wrenching stench. As dizziness washed over him, the sandy ground felt as insubstantial as the cloud-laced sky. Palm to sweating temple, he tossed off the surreal sensation with a shake.

Earth, sky, fire, water . . . as if he were a god imprisoned at the convergence of the elements.

He snorted.

No longer did anyone address him by his given name, which meant "raging sea." The official duty roster listed him as Optio Aonar, a junior officer not of command rank. No matronymic, no clan, no country; physically, emotionally, spiritually alone.

Uttering a dry chuckle, he gave himself a nickname: "a Dubh Loch," a poetic description of the condition of his soul.

He drew his sword. The blade bore mute testimony in myriad notches and scratches to the Sasunaich he'd consigned to today's pyre during last night's battle, but it gave him no satisfaction. He had prevented the death of the most important person in his life, and she had displayed more care for that thrice-cursed battle trophy he had helped her capture.

If not for him, it would have been her head gracing a Sasunach spear, and yet she had rejected him. Again.

Rage made his hands shake. Tightening his grip, he lowered the sword to heart height, as though she were standing captive before him, but he couldn't enjoy that fantasy. She had stripped him of his place, his kin, his clan, his country, his very identity, but he could no sooner harm her than cut off his hand. His oath forbade it.

But the gods alone knew how much longer it would restrain him.

The soldiers moved on to build a new pyre, leaving him, indeed, alone.

Aonar.

He studied his sword. A smith could hone it for someone else's use. Too bad his life couldn't be salvaged as easily.

As he considered dropping the sword, the thunder of the sea gave him an idea.

The warrior who had named himself Aonar a Dubh Loch cocked his sword arm and launched the weapon into the heavens. He tracked its progress toward an outcropping of boulders near the water's edge and swore.

"You, down there!" he shouted in Breatanaiche, hands cupped to his mouth. "Watch out!"

Cursing his ill luck, he summoned strength he didn't realize he possessed and hurried for the path leading down to the beach.

"Prioress, duck!"

Through Niniane's fatigue-dimmed senses, Sister Willa's warning sounded muffled and remote. A whirring noise intruded. She glanced up to see an object streaking toward her. Gasping, she flung herself from the donkey's back, hit the sand, and rolled. Her braying mount bolted. In which direction and how far, Niniane could but guess. She stretched facedown, arms over her head, grimacing as pain jolted her left shoulder. The object struck nearby with a resounding *thwack*.

A gentle hand came to rest upon her uninjured shoulder. "Are you hurt?" Willa's voice trembled.

Swatting sand from her face, chest, and arms, Niniane sat up. She massaged her sore shoulder, thankful it had not been dislocated. "I'm fine, Willa." She studied the sword. Its sweat-whitened leather grip, dried bloodstains, and nicks along the blade's edge proclaimed recent use. The sword had embedded, point down, at the base of a rock, quivering as the waves baptized it in sea foam. "Where in heaven's name did that come from?"

"From me, Prioress."

Niniane whipped her head around to see Angusel finish sliding down the embankment. The still-gangly youth regained his footing and staggered toward her, grimacing.

"I'm so sorry, my lady," he said between rasping breaths. "I hope I didn't hurt you."

Merciful God, glistening blood soaked his bandages, and he was worried about her? She scrambled to her feet. "No! I—"

Willa stepped forward, finger wagging. "And a good thing for you, lad. I ought to—"

Groaning, Angusel collapsed onto the sand.

"Oh! Prioress, he needs help!"

No lie. "I will assist him, Sister." As Niniane drew abreast of her would-be protectress, she laid one hand on Willa's arm and pointed at the receding equine form. "Please see Heather home and tell the sisters to expect me soon. I can ride Ironwort." Niniane glanced toward their pack animal. Ironwort was pulling wisps of salty sea grass from the nearby embankment.

While Willa retrieved Ironwort's pack frame and empty baskets and strode down the beach, Angusel tried to stand but sank to his knees. He swatted away Niniane's attempts to examine his wounds, though she ascertained that they weren't life-threatening.

His spirits, however, required drastic therapy.

Niniane hitched up her skirts and waded through the chilly late-September surf to the sword. It took several twists and tugs to free it, as if the sand and water were too greedy to surrender their treasure.

She approached him. He had managed to stand, and the rising tide was licking his booted feet. Holding the sword by the pommel, point down, she stretched her arm toward him. "Yours?"

"Not anymore." An ocean of anguish resounded in those two whispered words.

Her arm aching from having spent too many hours, too recently, tending too many wounded soldiers, she lowered the sword's point to the sand and leaned on the pommel, as old Sister Octavia would use her cane. She prayed for the right words. None came except, "What will you do?"

"What I must." He raised his head, clenched his fists, brushed past her, and strode into the water.

"Angusel, no—wait!"

Surf breaking around his knees, he stopped and turned. "I am

Aonar a Dubh Loch." She must have looked as puzzled as she felt, for he added, "Alone from the Black Lake."

"Black Lake?" The Isle of Maun had a Black River, called the Dhoo in the Manx variant of the Brytoni tongue, one of two rivers that gave Port Dhoo-Glass its name, where together they fed the Hibernian Sea. But Maun had no natural lakes of any great size, black or otherwise. She followed the line of his gaze and felt her eyes widen. "You don't mean—"

He nodded once. "I must return to it."

The force of his despair smote her.

"You are not alone, Angusel! I am with you." She drew a breath. "So is God."

"*Faugh!*" Twisting toward her, he made a chopping and sweeping motion. "Keep your god, Prioress, and I will keep mine." He faced the sea, his shoulders shifting in a sigh. "For all the good they do me."

"Killing yourself is not the answer."

A sneer marred his lips. "What do you, a dweller in the shadow of cloistered walls, know of answers?"

She thrust out her chin. "I know that wherever there is life, there should be hope. Where there is hope, courage. And where there is courage, strength." She lifted the sword in both fists and leveled it at him. "What I hear from you, Angusel of Caledonia, is that you lack the strength to take this weapon and improve your life." Shrugging, she lowered the sword. "Perhaps killing yourself will be better." She stalked toward the dunes. "For everyone."

A noise between a gasp and a sob floated above the waves' lull. The splashing told her he was following, but she didn't stop. They won free of the water, and he dropped to his knees in the damp sand, head bowed, at her feet.

"I cannot deny your wisdom." The golden-brown eyes that met hers glistened with unshed tears. "Please forgive me, my lady."

"I will, Angusel, on two conditions." His upraised eyebrow inquired them of her. "Stop calling yourself Aonar."

"But I—"

"But you will never see that you're not alone until you forgive yourself. That is my second condition."

"Forgive myself?" Confusion and hope warred across his face. "How?"

How, indeed? No two people trudged the same road. Helping Chieftainess Gyanhumara to confront her grief over Loholt's loss had proved to be Niniane's key to forgiving herself for her ineffectual role in the tragedy, but she'd had to discover it for herself, as would Angusel.

Lord willing, she could guide him onto the best path.

For the present, however, his path needed to divert him as far from Gyanhumara as possible. Ironwort wandered over to nuzzle Niniane's arm. She grabbed his lead rope. "Return to the priory with me."

"What?" Surprise forced Angusel to rise. "How will that help?"

She gave the warrior a frank appraisal. "First, those wounds need tending."

"These?" He gazed at the bloody bandages bulging through the rends in his battle-tunic and shrugged. "These will mend."

"Yes, with proper care and rest," she insisted. "Quiet contemplation too. It has wrought many a miracle."

"I am a warrior, not a priest." Angusel thumbed the unadorned iron dragon pinned to his short scarlet cloak. "Arthur's warrior."

"And Gyanhumara's," she reminded him. His eyelids twitched. "So you shall remain while your body and spirit heal in my care." Tendering a smile, she arched an eyebrow. "Physician's orders. I shall inform them."

"No!" He sighed. "I'm sorry, my lady. Please tell only the Pendragon."

"As you wish."

He looked at the sword she held, then at her face, bewilderment dominating his expression. "Your god is not mine. What shall I do at the priory?"

"Those who aspire to greatness must first learn servanthood." Her gaze captured his. "No matter which god one follows, much good can result when one focuses upon serving others."

A flock of curlews caught his attention, and his head seemed to track them as they scurried to pace the ebb and flow of each wavelet, poking their long, curved beaks into the brackish mud. "I thought I knew the meaning of service," he whispered. Something startled the birds, and they rose in a feathered cloud to skim the wave crests. He regarded her. "If there is aught you might teach me, I am willing to learn."

She pressed the sword's hilt into his palm. "One day, you shall forge your anger and guilt and pain into something far better." This she had Seen often: Angusel as an older man in battle, felling foes like deadwood. She might be bereft of the Sight, but the only way to erase past visions was their collision with present reality. "Something," she said, confidence strengthening her smile, "the likes of which the world has never known."

His fingers convulsed around the hilt, and he took the weapon from her. He regarded it for a long time before lifting it to his face in salute.

The set of his jaw and fierce glitter in his eyes promised that this prophecy would come to fruition.

CHAPTER 2

ADIM AL-ISKANDAR PUFFED along behind the pair of guards as they escorted him to the audience hall. More guards followed him, bearing the chests containing his most expensive wares. He tried not to think about the sealed gilt trunk made of fragrant pine, the contents of which he dared not guess.

His Saxon escorts halted at the huge double doors to utter the watchwords to the soldiers on duty. Palm pressed to his silk-wrapped head, he took several deep breaths. The guardsmen swung open the oaken doors. Giving a final tug to his best green-and-red brocaded honey-gold robe and crafting his most genial smile, Adim Al-Iskandar of Constantinopolis entered the presence of the overlord of the West Saxons.

In his travels, from Alexandria to Tarabrogh, Al-Iskandar had seen few sights to compare to this throne room.

Light cascaded into the vaulted chamber from clusters of burnished gold lamps suspended on thick chains fastened to the ceiling. Dozens bracketed to the walls washed the white limestone in a golden glow.

Though he was no stranger to Wintaceaster Palace, his breath caught as he took in the pairs of tall, fluted, snowy marble columns that marched the length of the hall. Their heads and feet bore the intricate art of a master stonemason, and from each column hung the banners of the lesser kings, princes, and nobles owing fealty to the hall's builder.

Arched recesses interrupted the two longest walls at regular intervals. Within each recess stood a soldier of the royal guard in an iron-linked hauberk and purple surcoat displaying the crowned White Horse. Each man had a seax and longsword hanging from his belt and gripped a spear. Al-Iskandar had sold their liege the shields, ash ovals with pointed iron bosses, three years earlier.

A magnificent tapestry smothered the wall between each guard post. Here was the crossing of the first Saxons from the Continent to the Isle of Brydein at the invitation of the Brytoni King Vortigern, half a century earlier. Over there was a bloody scene from Liberation Night—which the Brytons had dubbed Night of the Long Knives— when the Saxons had rebelled against Brytoni authority by killing scores of nobles during a feast.

Al-Iskandar rubbed his arm where a gold torc pinched, reminding himself to have the bauble lengthened. His benefactress had made this journey quite worth his while.

Several tapestries portrayed hunts whose quarries ran the gamut of the factual to the fantastic. The fleet stag raced beside the elusive unicorn; the quail covey fluttered toward the soaring phoenix; the fierce boar charged the ravening dragon.

Overcoming the temptation to admire these priceless treasures at greater length, he continued striding across the polished cream-and-jet marble floor crowded with Saxon nobility, dancing attendance upon their king. The men, tall and blond and robust, swaggered about attired in surcoats that matched the columns' banners. Their ladies were blushing flowers of womanhood, lavishly perfumed, gracefully gowned, and bejeweled to earn the envy of Queen Cleopatra. Feeling the lightheadedness return, he pressed fingertips to the silks covering his temple.

At the far end of the audience chamber, on a raised white marble platform, stood the gilt throne. Overhead, the crowned White Horse pranced across a deep purple field. Behind and to either side of the platform stood a dozen royal guards. The mountain-size warrior standing to the throne's left had to be their new captain. His predecessor had fallen in battle through no fault of Al-Iskandar's wares.

King Cissa sat his throne in gold-crowned, ermine-robed, amethyst-sceptered majesty.

As Al-Iskandar jostled through the throng, he squinted to discern the identity of the middle-aged man and the younger warrior-woman chatting with the king. They reclined on oaken chairs to either side of the throne, flanked by retainers whose black surcoats bore the Gold Hammer and Fist of the South Saxon king, Ælle.

Like Cissa, Ælle was crowned and robed in ermine. It stood to reason that the woman must be Ælle's daughter, Princess Camilla. She wore a hauberk of exquisite silver links; ceremonial, Al-Iskandar recognized, since unalloyed silver was too soft to deflect the bite of iron and steel. The scabbard strapped to her right hip was made of garnet-studded silver. A pity that the scabbard was empty, in deference to her host, for Al-Iskandar would have traded half his possessions for a glimpse of the weapon housed by such sumptuous furnishings. A slim silver circlet bound the princess's long golden hair.

This had to be a state visit, then, perhaps to discuss trade agreements. He congratulated himself on his timing.

As gracefully as his bulk would permit, he went to one knee before the dais. "Your Majesties," he greeted the monarchs in fluent Saxon, bowing and tapping fingers to chest and head. He repeated the gesture to the princess. "Your Highness."

"Well met, Master Adim Al-Iskandar." Beaming, Cissa rubbed his bejeweled hands together. "What fine weapons and armor have you to show us today?"

As news of the merchant's wares flew from mouth to mouth, most noblemen approached for a closer look.

Instinct warned him to transact his regular business first. While he displayed his costliest swords, daggers, greaves, belts, breastplates, and helmets, the gilt chest remained sealed. He politely but firmly sidestepped queries about its contents.

Upon stowing the transactions' jewelry and gold in the pouch slung across his chest, Al-Iskandar cleared his throat and called for the last chest to be brought forward.

"King Cissa, I present to you a gift from"—the guttural Saxon tongue lacked certain sounds for the proper pronunciation of the Picti name, forcing Al-Iskandar to improvise—"Queen Guenevara of Caledonia." As for making Chieftainess Gyanhumara appear as if she ruled her entire nation, well. At the rate she was slashing through her enemies, aided by the man the Saxons and Eingels had dubbed the "Dragon King," she would earn the title soon enough.

He bid a guard to sever the thick wax seals. Grunting, Al-Iskandar struggled to lift the massive lid. He was not unprepared for the sight within, or the pungent burst of preserving spices, but it made him blanch.

Camilla gasped, wide-eyed as her left hand clutched her ivory throat. The men nearest the chest, including the two kings, fought to suppress similar reactions. Those who found their view blocked pressed forward.

Inside lay the body of a warrior dressed for battle. The bronze-linked hauberk was not torn anywhere that Al-Iskandar could discern and bore not a single fleck of blood. The green-and-gold surcoat likewise appeared intact and clean. A garnet-inlaid gold buckle gleamed from the sword belt. The fingers of the right hand were frozen around the hilt of a naked seax. The left arm was bent, hand to chest. In the elbow's crook nestled a bronze helmet. The griffin perched on its peak glared through baleful emerald eyes.

The part of the body the helmet had been designed to protect was gone.

King Cissa stared at the corpse, his jaw tightening, though whether from grief or anger, Al-Iskandar couldn't discern. "Merchant, who is this Queen Guenevara of Caledonia? And what," he demanded, his eyebrows lowering, "happened to my brother's son?"

Wringing his hands and trembling in what he hoped was a convincing show of fear, Al-Iskandar related what he'd heard about the land and naval battles that had occurred on and around the Isle of Maun and of the demon-fierce woman warrior who had defeated Prince Ælferd. He remained alert on this precarious ground. An ill-chosen word could get him killed.

Worse, he'd have his gold and jewelry confiscated and be thrown out to beg his way home.

During his tale, a hush blanketed the hall. Al-Iskandar's words trailed away to make the silence complete.

King Cissa beckoned to the guard captain and whispered into the man's ear. The captain bowed and strode to one of the closer columns. All eyes watched him tear down the Green Griffin, face about, and march to the dais. On bended knee, he offered the banner to his king.

The king rose, accepted the proffered standard, and laid it over the mutilated body of his nephew. Princess Camilla walked to the coffin, kissed her palm, and pressed it to Prince Ælferd's chest, tears streaking her cheeks. After she withdrew, King Cissa yanked the lid down. He kept his palm upon the lid while its dull thump echoed around the chamber and died.

"Merchant, I have a message for Queen Guenevara of Caledonia. Tell her she shall answer to me." Grief twisted Princess Camilla's lovely face. After she dashed away the tears, her gray eyes glittered with diamond-hard hatred. "I shall not rest until I have taken her life."

"As you will, Your Highness." Al-Iskandar summoned his sincerest smile and rendered the traditional bow of his people.

Upon receiving King Cissa's assent, he quit the throne room as fast as decorum permitted. His every step became a silent prayer thanking Al-Ilyah for his good fortune.

Never mind that the princess had tendered no payment for the service. Were he to deliver such a message to the mercurial Chieftainess Gyanhumara, he would need the protection of Al-Ilyah's three hundred fifty-nine companion deities too.

GAWAIN MAP Loth, former heir to the chieftainship of Clan Lothian of Brydein—a destiny he'd raced to abandon for enlistment in Uncle Arthur's army—stood in the Tanroc garrison formation, watching Aunt Gyan award members of the Port Dhoo-Glass garrison accolades earned during the "Second Battle of Port Dhoo-Glass, on Ninth Calends October, in the Year of Our Lord 492."

Commander Gyan, Gawain corrected himself with an inward grin, the military title she preferred to the standard—and Roman—prefect. Under either designation, she was the Dragon Legion officer in command of the forces assigned to the Isle of Maun, which included the smaller units stationed at Ayr Point and Caer Rushen. Caer Rushen couldn't mobilize because there had been no way to summon them without alerting the Saxons, and the Ayr Point men had to keep guarding that fort's signal beacon. Both units had lent assistance in the thwarted invasion's aftermath at Port Dhoo-Glass as well as at the Saxons' beachhead near Caer Rushen; necessary duties, if not glorious ones.

His aunt looked magnificent dressed in Caledonian ebony leather armor and boots, in contrast to Arthur's gold-and-white Roman parade uniform, the sword riding her left hip second to the famous Caleberyllus in length and to Gawain's father's sword, Llafnyrarth, in breadth. Her short-cropped hair, whipped by the stiff sea breeze, framed her head like tongues of flame.

The reason for its shortness revived Gawain's hatred for Angusel. But this was a time to celebrate the honors being bestowed upon Gawain's brothers-in-arms. He banished that fatherless whelp from his mind.

"Centurion Peredur mac Hymar, front and center!" Gyan ordered.

This is it! Her brother, commander of Gawain's unit, strode onto the platform and saluted Gyan and Arthur. *Tanroc's citations are next!* Gawain counted it an honor to have fought in the battle; he had drawn guard duty the night of September twenty-third, "ninth calends October" on the Roman calendar.

Aunt Gyan presented to Uncle Peredur the unit award, a large gold disc embossed with the three-legged symbol of the Manx Cohort, to be affixed to the shaft beneath the award won last year, after the First Battle of Port Dhoo-Glass. While Tanroc soldiers were called forward to receive smaller bronze versions to be worn on their parade harness, Gawain relived the most recent battle in its confusing, exhilarating, painful, terrifying detail. He felt the ache in spirit as well as foot of the midnight march across the island, culminating in a post-midnight sprint to arrive as the Dhoo-Glass line crumbled under the ferocious blond Saxon onslaught, the shock of seeing Gyan unhorsed by the Saxons' leader, and the gut-churning determination to fight his way to her side. Gawain had saved Angusel's life in the process, though that was unintentional. Rumor had it the whore-spawn had taken a spear to the chest later in the battle. If there existed justice in this life, that wound would prove to be Angusel's last.

The gaze of every officer on the platform seemed to impale Gawain, and he squelched his hatred for the young man whose failure had inflicted fathomless sorrow upon Gawain's family.

"Soldier Gawain map Loth," Gyan said, her lips twitching into the barest of smiles, "front and center!"

He squared his shoulders, puffed his chest, lifted his chin, and obeyed.

As with the earlier award recipients, Arthur's aide, Centurion Marcus, passed the ornament to Gyan while Centurion Rhys, Gyan's clansman and aide, read the citation aloud in his lilting Caledonian accent:

"Soldier Gawain map Loth of Clan Lothian, Gododdin, Brydein is hereby awarded the Phalera Draconis for conspicuous bravery in battle to save the lives of Prefect Gyanhumara nic Hymar, Clan Argyll, Caledonia, and Optio Aonar, Third Turma, Manx Cohort. Without regard for his own safety, Soldier Gawain led a charge to engage a squad of Saxon royal bodyguards. His actions as a warrior and leader bought time for Optio Aonar to reenter the fray, and for Prefect Gyanhumara to kill Prince Ælferd, the Saxons' leader, thus reversing the tide of battle."

"You have my everlasting gratitude, nephew," Gyan murmured beneath the troops' cheers as she pinned the bronze, dragon-embossed disc to the center strap of his harness. One of the highest decorations in the army . . . he swallowed hard.

"I had help," he whispered. Angusel—Optio Aonar's—well-timed leap had prevented Prince Ælferd's seax from gouging Gyan's throat. Gawain had only kept a horrible situation from getting worse.

Sadness eclipsed her face. "I know."

"I don't deserve this." Gawain tugged at the disc.

She stilled his hand. "Arthur and I disagree with you. And I do hope to bestow that other phalera someday. Perhaps you might assist me?" She must have seen an expression brewing on his face that she didn't like, for her gaze sharpened to a glare. "We shall discuss this another time."

Her glare schooled into a neutral expression, and she looked past him toward the assembly. "Soldier Gawain map Loth's exemplary battle performance has earned him a promotion to the rank of decu-rion"—Centurion Marcus passed her a folded scarlet officer's cloak upon which gleamed a dragon-shaped iron brooch with an amber chip for its eye—"as well as his choice of postings."

Gawain's eyes widened as he accepted the symbols of his new rank. The brooch's ring bore no enamel, indicating his freedom to stay in the infantry, transfer to the navy, or return to the cavalry. He thumped fist to chest. "It matters not where I'm posted, so long as I may serve you, Commander Gyan!"

She answered his salute in the Caledonian way: upraised right hand clenched, splayed, and clenched. "Well spoken, Decurion, but I urge caution in considering your decision. Such postings have not ended well for some." Her steady gaze swept the assembly. "I refer, of course, to our honored dead, whose sacrifices we shall glorify with each bow shot, spear cast, and sword thrust for the rest of our lives!"

The cheers, shouts of agreement, and pounding of spear butts on the market square's cobblestones continued as Gawain saluted. He spun about, quit the platform, and rejoined his unit. As he faced forward, he was heartened to see Uncle Arthur regard his wife with undisguised admiration.

Uncle Peredur prepared to take his leave, but Arthur ordered his brother-by-marriage to wait.

"Your commander has finished presenting her awards," Arthur said, using battlefield timbre, "and a most impressive array it was. I speak for all Brydein and Caledonia in commending you for your bravery and skill, your loyalty and selflessness. I am proud of you, whether you have earned the privilege of wearing an ornament during parades or not."

Arthur glanced at Centurion Marcus, who withdrew an object from his sack. It couldn't be a phalera, Gawain realized, because the centurion hid it in his fist.

"I have two well-deserved promotions to bestow," Arthur an-nounced. "Centurion Peredur mac Hymar of Clan Argyll of Caledo-nia is recalled to legion headquarters, effective immediately, to begin duty as Tribune Peredur, Praefectus Cohortis Equitum."

Gawain blew a relieved sigh to see Peredur accept the red-ringed bronze dragon with the sapphire eye to replace his red-and-green-ringed copper one. Gawain's uncle-by-marriage had given up command of the Horse Cohort to accompany Gyan to Maun after Loholt's death. Gawain hoped this was a sign that Peredur, at least, had moved past the tragedy. The tribune's Caledonian salute seemed to radiate pride and promise.

At Arthur's signal, Centurion Marcus passed him another small object. Arthur held it aloft: a sapphire-eyed gold dragon encircled by a braided band of green, red, and blue. Gawain's mouth fell open as recognition dawned. He closed it, but not before Arthur noticed and gave him a short nod.

"I presented this brooch to my bride on our wedding day last year," began the Dux Britanniarum of the Dragon Legion of Brydein, "with the implication that she would stand at my side as honorary second-in-command. Her leadership of the Manx Cohort, on the battlefield as well as off, has proven to me that she deserves far more than an honorary position.

"Therefore, on this the second calends October in the year of Our Lord 492, I revive the Roman office of Comes Britanniarum, second in military authority to the Dux Britanniarum, and bestow that office, with all its duties and responsibilities, upon Gyanhumara nic Hymar of Clan Argyll of Caledonia." He removed Gyan's bronze dragon brooch. While she kept her cloak from slipping, he pinned the gold brooch in place. "*Comitissa* Gyan shall appoint officers to the posts of Tanroc Garrison Commander and Manx Cohort Prefect, and she is recalled to legion headquarters, effective immediately."

Gyan gave Arthur a sharp Caledonian salute, and he answered, fist to heart, with a Roman one. She faced the assembly and brandished a Caledonian salute for the troops.

"It has been my highest honor and privilege to serve with you, Brytoni and Caledonian alike. If but half of you feel a tenth as much for me, then I count myself blessed. I shall miss you until next we may serve together. May your gods strengthen you for that day." A sudden grin split her face. "But regardless of what *he* says"—she jerked a nod over her shoulder at Arthur, who beamed at her—"it will always be 'Commander Gyan' to you. Consider that a standing order!"

"Aye, Commander Gyan!" came the thunderous reply. Gawain hoped his shout rang loudest.

CHAPTER 3

THE BEGGAR SAT in the dust, his back propped against the rough-planked wall and a dry flagon in his grip as the tavern's patrons swaggered into and staggered out of the nearby door. Now and then, someone would toss a mite his way. The kinder men aimed for his cup. Most coin fragments landed paces beyond reach, forcing him to use his crutch like an oar to pull his maimed body to them, driven by his desperate need and his benefactors' guffaws.

His tremors caused the mites inside the flagon to jump and jingle. A half dozen more and he could drag himself inside for a draught, perhaps even a crust of bread and a rasher of bacon, if the tavern-keeper's profits had been good.

He squinted toward the setting sun and sighed. It would take till near closing to collect that many coins. Business had slowed to a crawl since the Pendragon's reinforcements had departed Maun—when? A week ago? A fortnight, a month?

So much for that crust and rasher.

Grief over his lost vocation crippled his soul as he knuckled his grumbling gut and shook his head with another sigh. Days had become meaningless.

God, how his head ached.

That pain he could drown in ale. Nothing could erase the phantom agony shooting through his body from his missing leg.

Grinding his teeth, he screwed his eyes shut and braced his head on the wall.

"I ken ye need a draught, auld boar."

He opened his eyes to find himself staring into the hazel gaze of a man he knew as Gull. Though Gull kept to himself, he bought him a drink no matter how many coins the beggar had managed to collect.

His smile felt thin as he lifted his flagon before his face to parody a salute. "Many thanks, friend."

Gull took the cup, emptied the coins into his fist, and stashed them in a fur pouch chained to his belt. The beggar's hand closed over the black leather forearm guard that covered Gull's right arm from wrist to elbow. Gull gave a reciprocal squeeze and disappeared into the tavern.

He massaged his stump, wondering about the exchange that had repeated so often, in words as well as gestures, that it had become almost ritualistic.

Mayhap Gull recognized a kindred spirit. He and Gull were of an age, with the gray hair and sun-weathered faces to show for it. Like him, Gull had the broad back, deep chest, powerful arms, and callused, scarred hands of a warrior—though Gull could get about on two legs, damn him.

Bitterness rose like bile in his throat, and he drew a long breath. Gull's accented Brytonic marked him as a Pict, but he was the lone soul on Maun who cared about the beggar's plight, and he hated himself for thinking ill of the man.

He shut his eyes and settled in for the wait, serenaded by the off-key singing and raucous laughter and vulgar jests emanating from the tavern.

"Centurion."

He opened his eyes, heart thrashing. The Dhoo-Glass commander, here? Impossible; he'd overheard talk about her promotion, and that she'd assigned one of her clansmen to lead the Manx Cohort in her stead.

The new prefect disdained beggars, regardless of their former station, and probably had sent a female subordinate to roust him. Picti warrior-women had to be common enough, if their two most powerful chieftainesses were any example. He grabbed his crutch for the arduous process of levering himself to stand on his remaining leg, praying Gull would return soon.

He didn't see anyone of command rank in the alley, just a trio of enlistees leaning upon each other, weaving and giggling toward the main thoroughfare. Mayhap he'd dreamed the soft, pleasant, female voice. He could use that draught.

As he concentrated on establishing his balance, he heard the swish of robes and glanced up to see the prioress of Rushen Priory standing before him, a serene expression upon her face in spite of the crude surroundings. She had no escort, though she seemed so ethereal and untouchable that perhaps God's angels warded her steps.

She extended a hand. "May I assist you, Centurion Elian?"

He grunted. "There's a title I've not heard in more than a year."

"It's yours again, by the Pendragon's command, with full pay and privileges."

Surprise made him recoil, and he almost fell. She hurried forward to support his right side. Shame scorching his cheeks, he shrugged her arm off and hopped backward to lean on the tavern's wall. "Look at me, Prioress. Take a good, hard look." He didn't bleed the self-loathing from his tone. Rag-padded crutch wedged under his armpit, he folded his arms. "How can I be of use to anyone, to say nothing of the Pendragon himself?"

"There is a warrior he wishes you to train." A smile bent her lips.

He pursed his lips and blew out his disdain. "My training days are done. Arthur knows this. I could no sooner train the sea to lap at my feet—foot." He glared at his remaining limb and laughed.

"Ye belittle yourself overmuch, lad."

Elian glanced over his left shoulder to see Gull exiting the tavern. Gull thrust Elian's flagon toward him. He thanked the Pict and downed half of it in one pull.

After using his knuckles to wipe foam from his lips, he asked, "How long have you been standing there?"

"Long enough." Gull faced the prioress. "Who be this warrior, my lady?"

"He says that in his own tongue, his name means 'Raging Sea.'"

Elian had never heard the phrase. Gull stroked his close-cropped, gray-streaked black beard.

"Why would the Pendragon send you to deliver this order, Prioress? Why not one of his own men?" Elian asked. "And why appoint me to the task, of all people?" *Why me and not someone who isn't half a man?*

"Because I requested it—and you." From a pocket of her robe she withdrew a parchment leaf. "If you doubt your reinstatement, Centurion, here is the Pendragon's writ."

Not that the hen-scratching would have meant anything to Elian, but the Scarlet Dragon seal and Arthur's mark inside appeared real. He'd seen both, often, when he'd served as Tanroc's garrison commander on the other side of Maun. On the other side of his life.

He thrust the parchment at her. Beggars had no need for such things. She shrugged and tucked it into her pocket.

"This is madness. Warriors need sparring partners." He slapped his stump. "I would have better success hobbling to the moon." Her benign expression seemed to challenge the truth of his assessment. Exasperation mounting, he looked to his friend. "Explain it to her, Gull."

"I shall be his legs, Prioress."

"What? You?" Elian's eyebrows shot up. He lowered them notch by notch as he voiced each key issue: "You're not a Bryton. You might have been a warrior, but you owe no allegiance to the Pendragon or to anyone else, as far as I know. Why should you deign to involve yourself in this matter? What do you gain by it?"

"This warrior named Raging Sea intrigues me."

The prioress chewed her lip. "Two men at the priory, I was prepared to accept. Not three."

"The priory?" Elian asked. "Not the fort?"

She shook her head. "Your student still recovers under my care."

"*My* student." Elian worked up a mouthful of spittle, recalled his manners, and swallowed it.

"*Still* recovers?" Concern clouded Gull's face.

"His story is his to share." She drew a slow breath, fingering the delicate silver cross at her bosom. "I must refuse your kind offer to help Centurion Elian. Our guesthouse barely has room for two people." Her expression turned frank. "The centurion and his student are well known to me. You, good sir, are not. I intend no offense, but I cannot put my sisters at risk from a stranger."

"Aye, for sooth. 'Tis a fair wise lady ye are." He swept her a deep bow. "I call myself Gull, and Elian has the right of it: I was a warrior and lann-seolta master."

Lann-seolta, Elian recalled, was a Picti term that meant "blade-cunning." His eyebrows hitched upward as Gull continued. "Now I earn my bed and board wielding mallet and saw. With your leave, Prioress, we shall build our own wee house for to live in whilst we train Ainchis Sàl."

The prioress gave Gull a questioning look.

"'We?' Who is this 'we' you speak of so glibly, man?"

Gull's was the merriest—and soberest—laugh Elian had heard in many a moon. "I might teach yon prickly auld boar a thing or two, as well." He laid his hand upon his heart. "If ye be willing to accept me, I shall not disturb you or the other womenfolk. Ye have my word. And if your word be nay, my lady, then ye shall hear naught else from me."

She regarded Gull for a long time. What she saw in his gaze Elian couldn't begin to guess. "I believe you, Gull," she said. Her smile shaded to enigmatic. "Raging Sea will benefit from your teachings as well as Elian's."

"Come, auld boar." Gull grabbed Elian's arm, stooped to adjust it across his shoulders, and stood to bear the weight of Elian's legless, useless side. "We have a warrior to train."

"Again with the 'we,'" Elian grumbled. He drained the flagon and tucked it into his belt. Who was he to disobey the Pendragon, no matter how mad the command? "So be it, then. Let us go to this man called Raging Sea and see what sort of warrior we can make of him."

The prioress led them toward a donkey-drawn cart positioned in the intersecting street, but before they had taken a dozen steps, Elian halted. "What did you call him, Gull? Ainchis Sàl?" When Gull nodded, Elian asked the prioress, "Do you mean Angusel?"

"You knew him by that name," said the renowned healer of bodies and souls. "What he calls himself today is a measure of how much he has healed—and of how much healing he must endure."

ANGUSEL A Dubh Loch sweated and grunted under the weight of the timber he'd been ordered to carry from the dwindling pile. Since the arrival of Centurion Elian and the Caledonach called Gull, and Prioress Niniane's pronouncement that Angusel's shoulder and head were healed, the autumn days had become a blur of backbreaking effort: cutting wood, toting water, and performing other heavy chores for the nuns each morning and toiling over this cottage in the afternoon. The tasks were punctuated by brief periods to care for and exercise his warhorse, Stonn, drink, eat, and rest. In that order.

The work blessed him with dreamless nights and by day kept him from dwelling upon . . . *her*. Upon how he had failed her, how often she had rejected him, and how, as impossible as it seemed, he might earn her forgiveness.

The beam teetering on his sword-side shoulder, he trudged past Stonn's corral and the accompanying whicker to the building site, where Elian sat astride a stool, hammering treenails into the lower portion of the wall. The centurion preferred to leave his new wooden leg off while he performed stationary tasks. It still unnerved Angusel to see the linen-wrapped stump twitch as if the rest of the flesh weren't missing. The crutch and leather-capped oaken leg leaned at the table that held an ale skin and bucket of treenails, close enough for Elian to press either walking tool into service.

Gull stood perched on a ladder, working on framing the roof. At Angusel's approach, Gull climbed down to help him. Hoisting the beam between them, they ascended separate ladders and wrestled it into the notches. Then they drew out their mallets and treenails to secure it to the supports.

Angusel dashed sweat from his eyes and glanced over to find Gull regarding him. The Caledonach seemed familiar. Surely he'd have recalled a man who wore black leather bracers up to the elbow on both forearms even though the elder's days of waging war had to be long since done.

But he had not asked Gull about his past; he hadn't dared, for Gull would expect the same of him. That would mean having to admit that he'd been outcast from Caledon and risk being rejected by Gull too. Worse, he would have to admit why.

He buried the chilling memories, holstered his mallet, and descended the ladder to join Gull, who had beaten him to the ground. "What next, sir?" Angusel asked Elian, flexing his arms and dreading the answer. He was still rebuilding strength in his shoulder, and the day's work had left him more fatigued than he'd expected. "Thatching?"

The centurion surveyed the completed roof frame. "Tomorrow you lay the wattles and thatch." Elian exchanged a glance with Gull, who strode toward the tent where they had stowed their supplies and weapons. The Caledonach returned, carrying two long, wooden practice swords. "Today," Elian said as Gull tossed Angusel one of the swords, "we see how much work is needed to finish building you."

He would have preferred to conduct this test when he felt better rested, but he suppressed his protest.

Cowards and incompetents spouted excuses.

While Elian grabbed his crutch and hopped over to perch on a log, the combatants kicked aside construction debris near the cottage to clear a larger area. By tacit agreement they met at the center and lifted their swords in salute.

As Angusel adopted an attack posture and circled his opponent, the familiar heat of battle frenzy banished the fatigue. The clatter of sword on sword revived battle memories, and Gull became the despised foe.

However, this foe proved far cannier than most. Grace and precision marked his style as he thwarted Angusel's attacks. When Angusel quickened the pace, Gull matched it blow for blow and countered with unexpected twists, feints, kicks, and lunges.

Angusel's frustration mounted, and he unleashed the full fury of his assault.

GULL PARRIED a long, swift series of Angusel's blows, kicks, and body blocks. Some moves could have killed a lesser opponent.

Sweet Nemetona, my brogach can fight!

It took his last dollop of shrewdness and skill to stay ahead of the merciless advance. But Gull saw mistakes aplenty in Angusel's tactics and form: lunging too far, overbalancing, revealing his intentions with his eyes, relying too much on his sword, too often failing to resume the correct position of readiness following a thrust. Doubtless, Elian saw the same flaws.

Time to put an end to this.

Gull disengaged and spun away. When Angusel charged, Gull stuck out a foot. Angusel failed to adjust his stride. He tripped and went sprawling. Before he could recover, Gull rushed in to pin him to the ground beneath his sword.

Angusel's heavy panting hissed out between gritted teeth. The golden-brown eyes that glared at Gull seethed hatred.

Gull drew several deep breaths. He couldn't remember the last time he'd gotten so winded in a practice bout. He smiled, affection surging through his breast for the talented young man. "Enough, lad." He spoke in Breatanaiche for Elian's benefit.

"Why did you do that?" The battle flush faded from Angusel's cheeks, but his gaze had lost none of its intensity. "It was not honorable."

"Honor." Gull raised the sword and offered his hand. "Honor has nae place on the battlefield." True enough for most circumstances.

Angusel batted Gull away and stood. After flinging down his sword, he stalked toward the beach.

"Gull's right," Elian called to the receding form. "Kill or be killed, simple as that."

Not that there was anything simple about the son of Alayna.

Elian bade Gull to follow Angusel. Gull wasn't altogether sure how much good he could accomplish, but he strode after him anyway.

He caught up after Angusel had scrambled atop a rock that became a wee island at high tide, dislodging seagulls. They flapped off, scolding. Gull splashed through the wavelets to make the climb.

"Leave me alone," Angusel muttered in Caledonaiche.

"I don't see your name carved here," Gull retorted in the same tongue. "I like to brood in this spot too."

"You? Hah. What could you brood about, old man? You haven't lost kin and clan and country."

Gull glared, but Angusel was gazing seaward. The seagulls bobbed atop the waves, preening, napping, or keeping watch.

"Do not presume to know what I have and have not lost, Raging Sea from the Black Lake. Add a wife and son, and your list will be as long as mine."

Angusel's arrogance crumbled. "I'm sorry, sir. Truly. It's just that I—" A growl rumbled deep in his throat, and he pounded the rock. "I want to reclaim my honor! My place!" The fist unclenched. He rubbed it on his thigh, brushing off bits of rock and dried bird dung, and sighed. "My life."

Gull had not wrestled such issues in years. Seeing those same struggles reflected on a face so full of youthful manhood and promise goaded his guilt—and infused him with purpose. The obstacle course for recovering what had been lost might be twisty and steep, but it had to begin with the first step.

He loosened the thongs of his shield-side bracer.

"What are you doing?" Angusel asked.

"Preparing to answer your questions about my past."

"By showing me, what? A scar?"

"Aye."

Gull tugged off the sheath. The sea breeze felt wonderful on his sweaty skin, cool and liberating.

Beside him, Angusel gasped. His gaze shifted from Gull's arm to his face and back to his arm. He reached toward the skin that had become so pale, the design it bore stood out in stark contrast in spite of its age.

Before Angusel's fingertips could make contact, they contracted into a fist, and he pulled it back. Angusel's chin trembled, and he gritted his teeth.

Gull flexed his forearm, making the woad lion appear to prowl for the first time in far too long. "'Gull' is short for Guilbach, my birth name," he murmured. "For my deeds in battle, Uther the Pendragon and his men called me—"

"Gwalchafed. 'Falcon of Summer.' A Breatanach name bestowed by the enemy upon an honored adversary. The name I heard most Caledonach warriors call you too." As Angusel spoke, rage built upon his face like a thunderstorm. His eyes glittered as if they might shoot lightning bolts. "Father." He spat the word like an epithet.

Angusel jumped into the swelling surf, waded onto the beach, and strode toward their camp. The ache wrought by his son's departure smote Gull harder than any battle wound he had ever suffered.

CHAPTER 4

EILEANN NIC DYNANN watched from her seat on the dais in Dùn Fàradhlann's feast hall as servants delivered brimming pitchers of heather beer and platters of Samhainn cakes to the lower tables. Each fist-size cake had a core of sweet apple mush, and their appearance on this, the final night of Samhainn, heralded the people's favorite annual rite: the Dance of the Summer Wraiths.

Symbolic of the eternal struggle between the Army of the Blest and the cruel Samhraidhean, this dance represented a young warrior's first opportunity to earn the privilege of joining the Army of the Blest in the Otherworld, should it befall him—or her—to die before experiencing combat on this side of the veil. The unblooded dead were consigned to the ranks of the Samhraidhean, doomed to suffer the ravages of blazing eternal summer without hope of receiving the succor of autumn's bounty, winter's rest, or spring's rebirth.

Outcasts shared that fate, blooded or not.

Unbidden surged the memory of Angusel trudging from the field hospital's Caledonach ward, and unbidden sprang Eileann's tears.

She blotted them with a fingertip on the pretense of scratching an itch.

"An itchy eye means you've seen your future mate." Her mother, Chieftainess Dynann, grinned at her. "Coileach, or perhaps Iomar?"

A fortnight earlier, Eileann had bidden farewell to those men, Coileach mac Airde of Clan Alban and Iomar mac Morra of Clan Rioghail, the latest in a suitor parade that had begun at Belteine. The visits had gone as well as could be expected—a feast of awkward with a heaping side dish of embarrassment—leaving Eileann no closer to choosing a consort than swimming to the Isle of Maun by way of the ice-shrouded Orkneys.

"We"—Dynann nodded toward her consort and Eileann's father, Chieftain Rionnach—"favor Chieftain Ogryvan's cousin Iomar. Ogryvan's daughter had the wisdom to marry an army."

Forcing a smile, Eileann whispered, "Mother!"

Dynann shrugged and regarded the pieces of roasted venison and carrots on her platter. She used her meat knife to spear one of each, popped them into her mouth, chewed, and swallowed. "I cannot see why the Tarsuinnaich shouldn't benefit from Argyll's closer alliance with the Pendragon."

"The way I understand it," Eileann said, "the Pendragon promised to aid the Caledonaich as the need arises. Did he not?"

Rionnach canted past Dynann to give Eileann a long appraisal. She resisted the urge to squirm. "Aye, lass, that he did. But tell me who will be first in line for that aid." Eileann twitched a shrug. "His kin-by-law, that's who. Stands to reason. No man in his position would do one whit differently."

Eileann thought about quipping that the Pendragon seemed to be a different sort of man, based on tales Tavyn had shared since returning home for the winter, but she refrained. Sometimes there was no arguing with her parents.

Most times, in fact.

"You cannot postpone your choice forever," Dynann said. "Our Ab Fhorchu ferry business shrinks by the day because of the thrice-cursed Angalaranach hold upon Dùn Éideann. Next year they will be menacing other launch points along the south bank, sure as we're sitting here. Having extra incentive for the Pendragon to help us would be a tremendous boon to the clan."

"I know, Mother." First Eileann had to figure out how to stop thinking about the one who could never become her consort. Sighing, she chafed her falcon tattoo and closed her eyes.

"Patience, Dyn," she heard her father whisper. "Nothing good comes of a rush to judgment."

"Nothing good comes from doing nothing," Dynann murmured.

Eileann couldn't bear to admit they were both right. Another sigh escaped.

The boom of oak hitting stone captured her attention. Dread of her future fled. The Dance of the Summer Wraiths had begun! Two-score Samhraidhean, portrayed by veteran warriors wearing black armor and animal skulls smeared with fresh blood, and wielding blood-dipped cudgels, poured into the hall through the double doors. They leaped and lunged, sidled and spun amid the audience, whining for Samhainn cakes. Those feasters who obliged their entreaties, they left in peace for a while.

When the pleas shifted to screeching demands, the feasters retaliated by throwing the cakes. Much beer-soaked laughter ensued to see apple mush spattered across a gruesome face, or a cake stuck to an antler only to be plucked off and eaten by the "wounded" Samhradh.

The low, loud notes of aurochs horns announced the arrival of Lord Annàm, the Adversary. The accursed brother of the blessed Lord Annaomh was portrayed as a hideous specter wearing an ox head with bloody teeth and eye sockets. The identity of the warrior dancing the part of Lord Annàm was a secret guarded by the high priest, lest evil befall the chosen warrior. For it was the eternal role of the Adversary to incite his Samhraidhean to inflict cruelty upon mortal kind.

Lord Annàm stalked toward the dais, swinging two bloody cudgels, which he knocked together in time to the music, creating a ferocious clatter. The Samhraidhean lunged and jumped and swiped at their victims, growling and howling to raise the dead. Roaring, Lord Annàm leaped toward Eileann, making her squeal. She pelted him with cake after cake, but he kept surging toward her and her parents, his cudgels' rhythm beating faster, like the rhythm of Eileann's heart.

"Who shall save us?" wailed Dynann, Rionnach, and Eileann.

"Who shall save us?" became the constant chorus of the oppressed feasters.

"None shall save you from Lord Annàm and his Samhraidhean!" chanted the Summer Wraiths in malicious, gleeful response.

At the height of the verbal frenzy, the high priest thumped his staff on the slate floor. "Behold Lord Annaomh! He hears our cries! He sees our plight! Praise be to the Lord of Light!"

In charged Lord Annaomh, wielding a flaming spear that glowed golden upon his whitewashed armor, face, gloves, boots, and helmet. The Army of the Blest, similarly painted but armed with torches, sprinted into the hall behind him. They fanned out to engage the Samhraidhean, drawing the spirits' attacks upon themselves and prompting heartfelt cheers of, "Praise be to our Chief Savior, Lord Annaomh! Praise be to the Blest!"

One of the Blest was Eileann's younger sister, Rionnag, who had completed her trial-of-blood rite during the moon's past cycle. Grinning fiercely, her new bian-sporan bouncing against her leather battle-kilt, Rionnag bounded toward the dais, swinging her torch and scattering Samhraidhean to scurry, wailing and cringing, into the shadows.

When Lord Annaomh raced over to assist Rionnag against Lord Annàm, Eileann gasped.

Tavyn was portraying the blessed Lord Annaomh!

Eileann's surprise vanished with her next breath. Tavyn's cavalry squad had been instrumental in piercing the Sasunach line during the attempted invasion of Maun, and Tavyn's javelin had drawn first blood, earning him a special army accolade. Of course such battle keenness carried a price, but Eileann was relieved to note that his healing leg wound didn't seem to be troubling him as he and Rionnag chased off Lord Annàm and the Samhraidhean closest to the dais.

As Lord Annàm followed the last of the Summer Wraiths from the hall to the jeers of the "rescued" feasters, servants marched in bearing platters of beer flagons and fresh-picked apples for rewarding the Blest. By tradition, peeled apples were bestowed upon the saviors.

Tavyn was receiving his Samhainn reward from their parents. Eileann grabbed an apple and her knife and chatted with a panting but happy Rionnag as the peels pattered onto the table between them.

When she was almost ready to present her offering, she noticed Rionnag's eyes widen and dart from the apple peels to Eileann and back to the peels. An ancient belief stated that an apple peeled on Samhainn would spell the letter signifying one's destined spouse. Eileann had viewed that method of prophecy as a jest . . . until this night.

The peels from Eileann's apple had fallen into two piles. One pile suggested the triangular outline of a harp. Its neighbor spelled the letter *A*. Eileann touched the peel forming the sound board of the harp-shaped pile. The peel sprang under her fingernail to make a sideways *A*.

"None of your suitors has a name that starts with that letter," whispered Rionnag, glancing at their parents. Eileann felt thankful that their attention remained fixed upon Tavyn. Dynann was presenting him a frothy flagon. "Know you another man—"

"Nay. No one." Her heart thudding like a war drum, Eileann swept the peels to the floor.

She sucked in a breath and touched her mother's arm. "Iomar," she said.

"What's that, dear?" Dynann watched Tavyn accept the ritual apple from Rionnach and take a bite.

Eileann pressed her fingers into Dynann's tattoo of the wave-shaped serpent that symbolized Rionnach's clan, Uisnathrean. Her mother looked more annoyed than curious, and Eileann almost changed her mind. But Clan Tarsuinn couldn't afford for her to. She cleared her throat and swallowed her trepidation.

"At Belteine, I will marry Iomar mac Morra of Clan Rioghail."

THE CHIMNEY'S stones scraped Angusel's tunic-clad shoulders. Behind him lay the completed cottage. He called it a prison for his having no choice but to work, train, drink, eat, and sleep so close to the man who had sired and abandoned him.

Elian was standing near enough that he could have counted the centurion's nose hairs, had Angusel not grown a handspan since the last full moon. That prospect might have been funny, if not for the reason-robbing rage coursing through his veins. Elian's fury seethed in his sharp glare and clenched jaw.

It was nearing the fourth market day since Gull—and he'd sooner chop off his sword hand than call that man "Father" again—had revealed his identity. Elian seemed to be aware of their changed relationship and of Gull's past, but the old centurion cared for naught beyond Angusel's hard work, improving combat skills, and absolute obedience.

Samhainn had come and gone three market days ago, unremarked by the cottage's residents save for the bonfires Angusel had chanced to notice blazing across the countryside. Not that it mattered. He saw no point in celebrating an eternal reward to which he would never be entitled.

Though late November by Ròmanach reckoning, the winter gales had begun to blow often enough to force the trio to work inside most days. Conversations with his sire were curt, awkward, and far too frequent for Angusel's liking. He couldn't trust himself to keep a civil tongue.

Gull never volunteered an explanation for faking his death and Angusel refused to ask. When a man walked out on wife, son, kin, clan, and country, reasons mattered less than a wagonload of dog vomit. Such a man stood so far beneath contempt that Angusel couldn't imagine a worse deed. In comparison, his failure to rescue Loholt seemed like stellar heroism.

After enduring a long string of commands from Gull this morning to fetch and sweep and wash and chop and stack and do just about everything else short of draining the sea, Angusel had decided that enough was damned well enough. He had suggested where Gull could stack the wood—a dark, tight, stinking place—and stalked off.

Elian had overheard and ordered him into the compound.

"I don't care if he's your great-great-aunt Alisa, back from spending one night in the Otherworld to find that fifty years had passed in this one." Bracing both hands on the chimney, Elian kicked it. The wooden leg produced a loud *thock*. "I especially don't care if he works you each minute of each day until the Last Judgment. You answer to me, and I order you to obey him." He jerked a nod toward Gull, who stood near their supply shed.

"Aye, Centurion." Angusel submerged his anger to keep his tone even. He would obey both men as duty demanded, but bestowing respect upon one of them was another issue altogether.

Elian scrutinized Angusel for what seemed like an eon. What he sought, Angusel hadn't a clue. Nor did he care. Finally, Elian uttered a snort and glared at Gull.

"And you, dead Pict who seems to have made a miraculous recovery." Gull grimaced but held his ground. "Explain yourself."

The "dead Pict" drew a deep breath and let it out slowly. "This matter be between my son and me."

"Vacca cac. Any matter that degrades the performance of my trainee is by definition not a private one. For weeks, the unanswered question of what happened in your past has hung like a double-edged sword between you two."

"Centurion Elian, I don't want—"

Elian's upraised fist cut off Angusel. "To hell with what he wants. You will give me that answer," the centurion ordered Gull.

"As ye will, Elian." Rubbing the Albanach Lion on his shield arm, Gull gazed skyward as if expecting the words to be etched in the heavens. He leveled his gaze at Angusel. "Ye know how your mother can be. Flirtatious, I mean."

Who knew better than Angusel? He had watched her throw herself at eligible men of Breatein as well as Caledon after her consort, his father, had been declared dead. The list included Arthur the Pendragon at the treaty-signing feast, and what an embarrassing display that had been. Not that the man who had caused her to sob over his mangled "corpse" for half a sennight deserved the insight.

"Wait," Elian said as Angusel debated how to reply. "His mother is—"

"Alayna nic Agarra, chieftainess and exalted heir-bearer of Clan Alban. I was chieftain and her consort," Gull said.

"You still are, you maggot-riddled armpit of a dead, rotting mongrel!"

"Ainchis Sàl! Guard your tongue!" Elian snapped.

"I am?" Sheer astonishment dominated Gull's tone.

"She never chose anyone else after you. You! Not that she'd take you back after the suffering you caused her." *Us.* Angusel clenched his fists, shouldered past Elian, and stalked closer to Gull, regretting that his battle-sword lay in the building behind the man. "If she did entertain the idea, it would be over my corpse." He faced the sea, fists on hips, face tilted skyward, eyes screwed shut, and shouted, "I apologize to all dead dogs! This worthless excuse of a man isn't even fit for your company!"

A fist caught him under the jaw, sending him staggering. He flailed his arms, but he couldn't get his legs under him. He fell. His battle-ravaged shoulder crashed into the shed, sending needles of light splintering across his vision. He tasted the metallic tang of blood and spat. It strengthened his urge to kill.

Gull flexed his fist a time or two. "How many times do we have to tell ye to ne'er take your eyes from your opponent?"

Working his sore jaw, Angusel righted his stance. "Give me a sword, and I'll show you how well I've learned that lesson."

"Will ye now? That, I should like to see." He strode for the shed.

"Gull, wait," Elian called. Gull disappeared into the shed. When he emerged, carrying two naked battle-swords and no shields, Elian blanched. "No! I forbid this!"

"I told ye this is between the lad and me." Gull tossed Angusel a sword and assumed a combat stance. He grinned. "Or should I say 'my wee little lassie' here?"

Growling, Angusel charged. He unleashed a swift series of slashes and thrusts, hoping—nay, praying he would catch Gull unprepared. No such luck. Gull dodged or parried each blow. Despite the twists and tricks and spins and kicks and lunges and charges he tried, Angusel couldn't score a single hit on anything other than his opponent's sword.

Gull made it look so gods-damned easy.

Strike that. Gull wasn't making any offensive moves, only defensive, as if he didn't care enough to deliver a satisfying fight.

"That's it, isn't it?" he gasped out between attacks. "You don't care! That's why you left us." A low lunge, blocked. Recoil, slash high. Blocked again. "You don't care about Mother or me! Why?" Midsection thrust, dodged. "Why?"

As Gull spun clear, Angusel readied his next strike. And froze.

Gull had dropped to his knees, head bowed and sword on the ground. The hilt lay close enough for Gull to grab, so Angusel approached him sword first, inching toward Gull's weapon until he could kick it away. With his sword's point pricking Gull's throat, he raised the man's head. Gull cracked a smile of . . . approval?

"Ye attacked in rage but didna let it master you. Nor did ye lose sight of your adversary, e'en at the end. Your lann-seolta needs a woeful lot of practice, but Elian can find someone else for that. I can die content." He closed his eyes. "Finish your work, then."

"Answers first." Angusel drew a deep breath, held it, and hissed it out. "Father."

Gull snapped his eyes open. "Oho. 'Father,' now, is it?"

"What, is that a lie too?"

"Ye saw a body like unto my size and shape and coloring, dressed in my armor, holding my sword, wearing my gold torcs, his face a bloody pulp where a horse had trampled it, and his shield-side fore-arm hacked off but showing enough woad to suggest the Albanach Lion. What ye didna see, lad," he murmured, "was that the dye had been painted on the flesh's surface."

"I saw Mother sob over that body for days! The whole clan did! I—" Into his mind's eye sprang his four-year-old self, toddling toward the corpse to pet the remains of the beloved tattoo, only to shrink at the bloody horror. He sucked in a breath. "The priests had to restrain her at the funeral, or she'd have thrown herself onto the pyre."

The memory's weight crashed upon him. He lowered his sword and sank to his knees, chin to chest as he fought for control. Gripping the hilt helped. When at last he could look at his father, compassion dominated the older man's gaze.

He asked in a hoarse whisper, "How do you know what I did and didn't see?"

CHAPTER 5

TEARS BLURRED GULL'S vision. He blinked hard. "Nae one noticed an extra priest that day."

"Why?" Angusel's pain-wracked outcry echoed through the draw, startling a flock of doves from a nearby tree and making Stonn stamp at the corral rail. The knuckles of the fist gripping the sword had gone white. Anguish contorted his face.

Gull wrenched his gaze from his son to regard Elian, who was leaning on the cottage's wall and appearing by turns worried and relieved. They shared a nod, and the centurion thumped into the cottage.

The Exalted Heir-begetter of Clan Alban—and it astounded him that he had never lost the status—leaned forward to grip Angusel's shoulder. He said in Caledonaiche, "Your mother was planning to replace me."

Angusel's eyes and mouth rounded. He jerked back, and Gull's hand fell away. "What? Nay!"

"Oh, aye. She was flirting with Ogryvan of Argyll at the gathering of the Confederacy before my last battle."

"So Mother would have made you fight a black-blade challenge. You would have beaten him!"

"Mayhap. But I had no wish to risk killing a fr—"

"You took the coward's path."

Gull narrowed his eyes. "What I took, Angusel mac Alayna, was an opportunity to help my son fulfill his prophesied destiny without my having to murder a string of good men."

Angusel blew his derision through pursed lips and stood. "That, for prophecies. And opportunities." He hocked and spat. The bubbling glob landed in the dirt between Gull's knees. "*That*, for dead men who return to life after ten years and expect to be treated as if naught were amiss." Clutching his sword, he stalked into the shed.

Gull retrieved his sword, stood, and followed. He found his son inside the door, facing the weapons rack. Angusel had stowed his sheathed sword and was holding Gull's empty scabbard, tracing the lion design that ramped and roared across its bronze face.

The bonding-day gift from Alayna was the sole item of his past that he'd dared to keep.

He lowered his sword's point to the floor.

"What I expect is for you to master everything I teach you." He held out his hand, palm up, and Angusel surrendered the scabbard. Gull slid the sword home but didn't place it on the rack. "If you want me to go, I will. I've become adept at watching you from afar."

That got Angusel's attention. "When I lived at Arbroch too?"

"A Caledonach not of Clan Argyll caught living on Argaillanach lands? No bloody chance. I'd have been imprisoned or executed as a spy, given the fears about Chieftainess Gyanhumara and her bairn. I stayed close to the border, avoided the occasional Móranach patrol, and kept my ears and eyes open."

Angusel looked away, but not before Gull saw the grimace. "So... you know."

"I know that you did your absolute utmost—"

"My utmost wasn't good enough! It should have been. Now," Angusel dropped his voice to a whisper, "I don't know if it ever will be."

"Nor can you, until you face another trial that taxes your skill and your strength and your soul as that one did. But if you hear nothing else from me, hear this, Angusel, and hear it well: your utmost is all anyone can ask of you. Blaming yourself for failing to thwart the consequences of people's evil choices is a fast path to madness."

"Arthur the Pendragon said as much to me . . . after . . ." Angusel sucked in a breath, held it, and slowly blew it out.

"Wise man. Heed him, then, if you cannot bring yourself to heed me."

His son didn't move.

Neither did Gull, drawing upon his warrior's patience to give Angusel the time he needed. The boy—and he was but a hurting child, Gull realized, despite the strength most men would kill to possess—made as if to take a step toward him, then clenched his fists and stayed rooted in place.

Hefting the sheathed sword, which didn't feel half as heavy as his heart, Gull girded his mind to depart.

Fingers dug into his forearm. "Don't go. Please, Father." As Gull faced around, Angusel launched himself into Gull's arms. "I can't lose you again!" Momentum carried them out of the shed, and Gull dropped the sword to complete the embrace. "I—I just can't."

"I'm so sorry I made it seem that way." The words sounded worse than inadequate, but Gull meant them to the core of his soul. He let Angusel vent the wet remnants of his anger against his shoulder. If Elian had asked which of them was holding on tighter, Gull would have been sore pressed to deliver an accurate answer. After his own churning emotions crested and ebbed to a manageable level, he whispered, "Son, I pray you never shall."

He hoped with the last shred of his being that the Old Ones would grant his plea.

The sound of an impatient throat-clearing cut short his prayer. He and Angusel parted. Elian stood in the cottage's doorway, arms folded, though Gull could have sworn the man's sternness was feigned.

"If you two are quite finished," growled the centurion, "I'd like to remind our trainee there's wood to stack."

Wiping his eyes, Angusel glanced at the jumble of split logs and colored. "I'm sorry, sir, truly." He faced Gull, his flush deepening. "And you, Father—oh, gods. How can I ever—?"

Gull ruffled his son's hair. "Nae need, son." He gave Angusel a measuring stare, glanced at the skies—which had remained calm, and the temperature was behaving itself for once—and reached a decision. "Elian, the wood shall keep. Our wee lion cub needs a woman. So do I, truth be told." He picked up his sword.

Over Angusel's embarrassed, *"What!"* soared Elian's hearty laughter. "I suppose you know a place," said the centurion, grinning.

"Of course. Don't you?" When that yielded no response, Gull continued, "How long has it been for ye, auld boar?"

Elian's grin soured. He pivoted on his wooden leg and stomped toward the cottage. "None of your cac-licking business. Take him, then. Just don't be all day about it." The words faded until the last few were almost inaudible.

"Hear that, lad?" Gull said to Angusel, looking toward the cottage. A pity Elian didn't want to participate, but it meant an extra choice for them. He regarded his son, expecting to see gratitude for the reprieve from chores.

Angusel's countenance showed naught but disapproval.

"Father," he said, "we—that is, Caledonaich don't—use—our women like that."

"Of course not. Why do you think so many of our foreign slaves were women?" That was how it used to be, Gull thought with a wistful pang as he ducked into the shed to replace his sheathed sword on the rack. In the better days, before Arthur the Pendragon had conquered the Confederacy and abolished the practice in Caledon—while hypocritically retaining captured Scáthinach and Sasunach warriors as legion drudges. Probably legion sods too, the poor michaoduin.

Emerging from the shed, Gull shrugged. He set a brisk pace toward the path that led inland, plucking his black cloak off the corral fence from beside Angusel's as he passed. He secured it without breaking stride. Anybody could justify anything, he supposed, given enough motivation.

When he realized his son wasn't keeping pace, he stopped and looked back.

"You heard your commander. Fetch your cloak. We need to hurry."

When his son didn't respond, Gull beckoned. Angusel retrieved his legion cloak, gave Stonn a pat, and joined him.

"These are not sailors' whores who carry every disease known to every man of every land touching the seven seas, if that's the rock stopping your plow," Gull said. "They are clean and kind and know their craft. I hear they're good with first-timers. Far more expensive than most, but you let me worry about that. This time."

Angusel shook his head as he wrestled with the unadorned iron dragon cloak-pin. "That's not it, Father. I can't—that is, I don't think I could—be—with a woman unless I love her." He got it fastened to his liking and gave Gull a level stare. "It wouldn't be honorable."

"Honorable?" Gull snorted. "This has naught to do with honor, my lad. Or love. You're wound tighter than a spearhead, plain and simple, and have been for weeks. Months, I'll wager. You need to learn to let go. Cast that shaft now and then. What kind of father would I be if I failed to teach you that?"

Angusel's mouth twitched into a lopsided grin, and they resumed course. "These—women, are they . . . pretty?"

"Pretty enough." In truth, Gull never remembered that detail. The face he saw belonged to the woman who had borne him the fine lad striding at his side.

THE TINY chamber was lit by a pair of candles sitting atop a low, square table. Their tendrils of smoke—one yielding the scent of lavender and its companion giving an earthy-sweet aroma unfamiliar to Angusel—framed a platter-size mosaic of a gods-blessed goat-man capering amid scantily dressed dancing women.

Angusel stood naked near the narrow bed while Gwelda knelt, performing oblations upon him with her fingers and mouth and tongue. His breath came in husky pants as he tilted back his head, closed his eyes, and surrendered to the blissful sensations.

His father had been right. He could get used to this.

At Angusel's request, Gwelda did not speak as she worked. His father occupied the adjacent chamber, and the thumps and groans and exclamations seeping through the wall proclaimed that Gull and his partner, Lili, lay engrossed in the spirited rite. Angusel wanted to learn by doing: not just what pleased him, though that was the focus of Gwelda's present ministrations, but what would please . . . another woman.

A divinely beautiful face shimmered in his mind. He snapped his eyes open and stared at the mousy top of Gwelda's head. That helped. He grasped her lavender-scented hands and tugged. She undulated, skimming a tithe of her flesh against his as she stood. A close look at her nut-brown eyes and spice-dusted cheeks and berry-painted lips rooted his reality.

Her hands clasped to his buttocks, Gwelda took a step backward. He wrapped his arms around her, fastened his hungry mouth to hers, and bore her onto the bed.

He knew what to do, of course; his main questions revolved around his strength. How little force would make him seem ineffectual? How much force would be welcome? How much would hurt her? He had no idea, but he was desperate to learn. He never wanted to hurt ... another woman.

So he kept his gaze transfixed upon Gwelda's face and let her disciple him, guide him, show him with her lips and her hands and the hitching of her hips. She showed his tongue how to caress her nipples to transform her breath from puffs to gasps. She guided his fingers where to touch her—slowly at first and light as a butterfly's wings, then faster and firmer and deeper—to release the flood of her warmth and coax ecstatic little moans and escalate her hips' rocking.

She taught him when to cast his spear.

A feeling akin to battle frenzy enraptured him as he buried himself in her slick, hot depths. But unlike battle frenzy, which ignited him like an oil-soaked torch and scorched to ash all senses and emotions save the ravening lust to kill and kill and kill, this sensation kept building and teasing and taunting and tormenting him until he knew he'd go mad.

He shut his eyes and quickened his thrusts.

She appeared.

He opened his eyes, looked down upon her face ... and despaired.

She remained: her eternal flaming, short-cropped hair framing sea-green, half-lidded eyes, complementing full, red, moist, passion-parted lips. Smiling a benediction, those sweet lips conceived his name but birthed no sound, save the gasps and moans her priestess had taught him to elicit from her.

Horror twisted his gut. He pushed up and struggled to free himself before he could profane her sacred temple with his unholy offering.

She was not done with her terrified acolyte.

She dug her nails into his buttocks, locked her legs around him, and held him captive inside her sanctum with her almighty strength as they bucked and bucked and bucked.

The dam of his devotion burst. The frenzy catapulted him past rational limits. The curse far beyond mere guilt branded his soul.

The goddess smote madness upon him with one vengeful word: "Gheeeeeeeeeeeee-aaaaaaaaaaaaaannnnnnnnnnnnnn!"

He rolled off her, sank to his knees on the cold stone floor, buried his face in his hands, and sobbed.

GULL HAD finished with Lili, his favorite woman of this enclave for her resemblance to Alayna in nimbleness as well as looks, when they heard the keening outcry. They exchanged a glance. Then the voice registered—as did the implication of the utterance—and he couldn't jump into his trews fast enough.

He grabbed his bian-sporan and dashed from the chamber, almost colliding in the hallway with one very frightened Gwelda. She clutched a plain-spun, ankle-length underdress to her front.

Grimacing, Gull asked, "Did he hurt you?"

She shook her head, more of a spasm than anything else. He accepted that as answer enough and pulled coins from the bian-sporan that doubled her usual rate. She snatched the coins, dipped him a curtsey, and dashed down the hall. Without sparing the briefest glance at her bare backside, Gull ducked into the chamber she'd vacated and pulled the door shut behind him.

The abject misery in which he found his son, huddled on hands and knees, his forehead to the floor like the most wretched of penitents to be damned by a god—or goddess—wrenched his heart.

Gull squatted and laid an arm across the trembling shoulders. He could think of no words except, "I'm sorry, son."

Those broad young shoulders heaved as Angusel drew a deep, shuddering breath. He puffed his cheeks and released the air as he pushed himself onto his knees. His next breath he expelled as a halting sigh, and he pressed his hands' heels to his eyes. When Gull raised his arm, Angusel looked at him. His sword hand moved to cover his fealty-mark. The depth of sorrow in those golden-brown eyes defied measure. His son seemed to have aged ten years in ten minutes.

"I am so, so sorry."

Angusel twitched an eyebrow and lowered the hand. "For what? Letting me discover the truth about myself?" Shaking his head, he pulled his tunic from the tangle of clothing beside him, shrugged into it, and met Gull's gaze. "I thank the gods Centurion Elian wasn't here. Please don't tell him, Father. She . . . can't ever know."

Indeed. Her consort would eat Angusel's ballocks for breakfast and use the rest of him for target practice after supper. "No soul will hear a word of this from me," he promised.

Gull rose and turned so Angusel could finish dressing, recalling that he needed to retrieve the rest of his gear. As he eased the door open, a whispered question halted him:

"Am I—allowed—to return?"

"Coin is always welcome here, if that's what you're asking." The faint sound of supple leather on leather told Gull that his son had pulled up his trews. He faced about to find the lad tying the cords. "I paid Gwelda well. But if she is too—that is, if she doesn't wish to entertain you, I'm sure her companions will." He chided himself for his curiosity, but he had to know: "Does this mean you enjoyed it?"

"Mostly." Angusel uttered a short, mirthless laugh. "In truth, all but the last bit." He bent to pick up his boots and cloak. He sat on the bed, boots beside him, and pulled the scarlet wool through his fingers until he got to the dragon pin. "I want—I *need* to find out if it gets easier. It does, doesn't it?" Raw hope and yearning bled through his tone as he clutched the cloak and dragon.

"It does, son."

Gull smiled to mask the lie.

FERGUS OG RÓIG and his men led their captives—*honored guests*, he corrected himself, suppressing a grin—down the considerable length of Tarabrogh Hall. The fact that the Bhratan emissary and his troops had remained alive long enough to beach their warship owed to the fact that they'd arrived on Eireann's sacred shores under the banner of the Black Boar. If they'd flown the Scarlet Dragon, their flesh would be fattening the fish.

How long these men remained honored guests stood in direct relation to how interested Fergus's foster brother was in the message the Black Boar's emissary bore. The Black Boar had fought under the Pendragon's orders to help destroy the Scáthaichean war-fleet, but that was last year—and the Pendragon and his she-demon of a wife wore the most Scáthaichean blood. Now, the Black Boar was giving his own orders.

The political shift was keeping his men alive—that, and their bearing.

Cuchullain had devised a modest test of Bhratan nerves. At regular intervals, between the huge Silver Wolf banners, stood naked Aítachasan warriors selected for their crimes against Scáthaichean women. Each chained Aítachait had had his rìbhinn-crann hacked off at the root and sewn into his mouth. Their blood complemented the berries of the holly swags festooning the hall, and the profusion of pine boughs and braziers of smoldering cones battled the stench. December's bite had killed most of the flies, but the hardiest feasted upon bloody groins and faces that could no longer twitch.

The closer Fergus, his men, and the Bratan got to the massive carved Great Seat, where Cuchullain sat watching their approach, the more alive stood the Aítachasan captives, evidenced by the escalating concert of chains and gagged, pathetic cries. Fergus and his men had standing orders to slay the Bhratan company at the first display of womanish weakness.

Thus far, these Bratan seemed to have iron ballocks. Every underling kept his gaze riveted to the man marching in front of him, and their leader gazed at Cuchullain. That too engendered subtle advantages.

Fist upraised, Cuchullain halted them beyond the outermost course of hammered-copper sheets covering the flagstones that defined how close anyone could approach the Laird of the Scáthaichean. The perimeter marked the distance of a remarkable dagger throw. The inner circle, wide enough to thwart a traitor's lunge, was paved with silver.

As foster brother, Fergus had held silver-circle privilege for as many years as Cuchullain had ruled, but this day's proceedings were not about him. He remained near the Bhratan guests and his men, flanked on both sides by dozens of the laird's household guards.

At present, the only persons standing with Cuchullain were his intimidating sword-brother Firduar, his charioteer Lagan, and his wife, the gorgeous Lady Dierda. The finest battle-gear armed the three warriors, and Cuchullain wore his ceremonial white wolfskin cloak; no surprises there. Lady Dierda wore a pine-green gown embroidered at the hem and sleeves and neckline with parades of loping, snarling silver wolves. Its bodice enhanced her breasts, revealing the creamy tops. She never attired herself in such an alluring manner.

Fergus realized that was part of the test.

Iron could melt. These Bhratan ballocks had better be made of granite.

Cuchullain clasped Lady Dierda's hand and rose. "The honored wife of the Silver Wolf shall greet the emissary of the Black Boar." He gave her hand a lavish, lingering kiss and nudged her forward.

All smiles, she approached the Bhratan troop's leader, her sheathed, emerald-hilted dagger swinging from her belt. Before she stepped off the copper plating, she executed a neat little pivot, hitching her bare shoulder and winking at the emissary. She angled toward the last—very much alive and unmaimed—Aítachasan captive.

Courtesy demanded that the Bratan watch her. Cuchullain, Firduar, Lagan, Fergus, and every other Scáthaichean warrior watched the Bratan.

And what a show she performed, murmuring to the terrified Aítachait, stroking his hair, his cheek, his chest, his gut—slowly, lightly, inexorably inching down toward her target. When she pressed her lips to his, caressing his rìbhinn-crann and coaxing it forth, the poor aífhein didn't stand a chance. He had to know his fate but closed his eyes and accepted the gift of her mouth, returning an echo of that reward and choosing not to see her draw the dagger.

A deft slice, and the deed was done. Lady Dierda avoided the spurting blood and used the captive's shock to stuff his dismembered flesh down his throat. His gagged agony and the frantic rattling of his chains reverberated throughout the hall.

She must have taken pity upon him; she slashed his throat and wiped the blood on the captive's arm. The noise died.

Not a man in the hall, Fergus included, he wasn't ashamed to admit, could suppress the inevitable shudder—except Cuchullain and the Bhratan leader.

"Emissary of the Black Boar," said Cuchullain, beaming and signaling her to approach the man, "I present the Lady Dierda."

Clasping the dagger, she swayed up to the Brat and launched into a similar routine. The Bratan carried no weapons but wore their battle-gear, so she had to work a wee bit harder between their leader's legs. The effort showed on his face in the form of an occasional long blink or soft expulsion of breath, but he remained stoic while she played her dagger against his leathers.

She gave her husband a satisfied smile. "This Brat be a man, my lord, and no mistake, brave and loyal to his chieftain beyond all doubting. If it pleases you, my lord, it pleases me to learn how he may be so resistant to my"—she gave his sheathed rìbhinn-crann a firm caress—"charms."

Cuchullain inclined his head. "The Black Boar's emissary has leave to address us."

The Brat pressed his fist over his heart and bowed to Cuchullain. "My deepest thanks, Laird Cuchullain." He saluted Lady Dierda in an abbreviated manner. She remained standing so close that Fergus could smell the clouds of roses scenting her hair. So could the Brat, to judge by the twitching of his nostrils and lips. Said the Brat with a ghost smile, "Lady Dierda, I do commend you for your charms." Her delighted laughter prompted the same from Cuchullain, Fergus, and the other Scáthaichean warriors. A few Bratan uttered brave chuckles, but most exchanged quick looks. Into the lull, their leader continued, "But I must confess, my lady, that I've had practice. The woman to whom my lord chieftain is betrothed is nigh as beautiful, beguiling—and dangerous—as you are."

"Ha! My husband, this Brat be a golden-tongued demon!" She kissed the emissary's cheek and reclaimed her place at Cuchullain's side. "I like him."

"As do I, my wife." They enjoyed a long, deep kiss. "Give us your name, honored emissary, and the nature of the business the Black Boar wishes to discuss with the Silver Wolf."

Again the emissary bowed. "I am Accolon map Anwas, and the business is simplicity itself, Laird Cuchullain: land deeded to Scáthaichean"—his use of the proper word rather than its Rhòmanaich-corrupted form, *Scotti*, raised eyebrows across Tarabrogh Hall—"settlers in Dalriada, in exchange for the Silver Wolf's alliance against the Pendragon."

CHAPTER 6

THE MESSENGER ARRIVED at vespers on the calends of April. Niniane was a prayer shy of completing the worship service when she noticed him and his taller companion. Neither man carried weapons. They remained standing near the doors, well away from the sisters, heads bowed and hands clasped, though not as supplicants. The messenger wore a plain, if well-made, blue tunic and leather leggings, boots of the same hue, and a grass-green cloak crossed by gray and black. His blue-ringed silver dragon badge showed the sole indication of his legion affiliation. His companion stood dressed in a standard legion cavalry officer's scale-armor tunic, undyed undertunic and leggings, and scarlet cloak. His black boots were not the typical footgear for a Brytoni soldier.

She wondered less about that oddity than about what message could be so important that Arthur had sent his fleet commander to deliver it.

For Bedwyr's benefit, she added: "Lord God, we humbly beseech Your divine mercy for those whose work sends them onto the sea to guard us from raiders and invaders. Please grant these brave men the shelter of Your mighty wings from storms and rocks and enemies. Keep them safe, we pray, so that they may return to their homes and loved ones when their work is done. Lord, in Your mercy . . ."

"Hear our prayer," chanted the sisters. Bedwyr mouthed the response. Whether he uttered the words aloud, Niniane couldn't tell.

She intoned the benediction to conclude worship. The elder sisters remained kneeling for private prayer while the rest rose to attend to their duties, which at this time of day related to the preparation and serving of the evening meal.

Several sisters greeted Bedwyr with gratitude-laced smiles. This didn't surprise Niniane. In the past two years, the priory had seen twice the terrors that any woman deserved to experience in her lifetime. A man known to be a proven bulwark against the chaos—especially when he didn't appear to be battling said chaos—was a welcome sight.

Bedwyr's companion raised his head at Niniane's approach. She stifled a gasp.

"Angusel?" He had arrived at the priory last year in a ruined ebony battle-tunic of the style favored by his people. His boots, it seemed, forged the final link to his past, and Niniane dared not broach that subject lest it reopen a wound that might never close. "Your new uniform becomes you," she said. Working for the sisters and training with Elian and Gull had caused him to fill it out well, but she kept that observation to herself.

"Thank you, Prioress." It grieved her to see the gratitude in his golden-brown eyes eroded by the undertow of sadness. She wished she could do more for him but knew he would have to deal with the sorrow on his own terms. "For the healing and for your faith in me."

"Always, my son. Always. You resume your legion duties, then." She glanced at Bedwyr as the three of them walked toward the chapel's door. "At headquarters? Or a different posting?"

While Angusel held open the door, Bedwyr shook his head. "He stays to help defend Maun, along with the extra troops I've brought from their winter homes."

Niniane held her reply until they had stepped outside, out of earshot of the praying sisters. She shut the door and leaned against it, whispering, "Arthur expects trouble here?"

Bedwyr too kept his voice low. "Arthur is being cautious. We have confirmed that Cuchullain is rebuilding his fleet." He rubbed his lip. "Where he will send it, and when, is anyone's guess."

Sighing, Niniane closed her eyes and tilted her head till it contacted the chapel's door. "Dear Lord, defend us." She smiled at her visitors. "And in Your mercy, defend those who defend us."

Bedwyr returned her smile, but Angusel did not. The young man laid his fist over his heart and bowed his head. Upon completing the salute, his eyes glittered with renewed purpose. "Prioress, I promise to continue helping you and the sisters as often as my duties permit."

"I appreciate that, Angusel. We all do."

"Ainchis Sàl, my lady. Optio Ainchis Sàl a Dubh Loch, Third Turma, Manx Cohort. That is how the duty roster reads."

Niniane wished that the path to healing didn't have to switch back upon itself, and she knew that wish's futility. The deeper the pain, the more convoluted the journey.

"If you don't collect the rest of your gear and leave soon, lad, you're going to get the lash for being late." Bedwyr's tone was not unkind. "Report to my ship at dawn if you change your mind."

Angusel gave him a sharp legion salute. "Aye, Fleet Commander."

"Go with God, Angusel—Ainchis Sàl, my son," Niniane said. "And with my blessing."

He nodded, faced about, and descended the steps.

After he disappeared from view, Niniane regarded Bedwyr. "Change his mind about what?"

Lying prone, Angusel wriggled under his cot, reaching for the undertunic that had been kicked there during the past several months and forgotten. Last year he could have finished this task in a thrice. Now, between the thicker armor and the muscles that armor protected, the damned thing lay beyond his fingertips.

"You're being an amadan," said his father behind him.

"If that means 'bloody fool,' then I agree," Elian said. Angusel heard the step-thump of the centurion's tread as he moved closer.

"Refusing such a prestigious posting is foolish enough, but you and she were inseparable."

Angusel stretched but couldn't quite hook the fabric. Sighing, he scooted from beneath the cot, stood, and faced his mentors. "I don't need her charity."

"Charity!" Gull bellowed.

"What you need is to avail yourself of this opportunity." Elian's eyes narrowed. "Or are you a puling boy, afraid to face the consequences of your actions?"

Angusel balled his sword hand and dug it into his thigh to keep from swinging at his soon-to-be-ex-commanding officer. "Centurion Elian, I have been facing those consequences since the day that whole sorry business happened. Failure, disgrace, humiliation, banishment, rejection . . . what else would you have me face, sir?"

"What every warrior must learn to face: fear."

Angusel snorted.

"Has it ne'er occurred to ye," Gull said, "that she offered this posting because she has forgiven ye?"

Aye, though he couldn't afford to indulge in that hope.

He dragged the cot away from the wall. The errant undertunic was a ruin of dust-encrusted cobwebs and dried sweat, and no time to wash it. After shaking it out as best he could, he stuffed it into the canvas sack that held the possessions he wasn't wearing, save one item. His fist closed around the gold lion brooch, another man's payment for treason and the symbol of Angusel's freedom from being the Pendragon's hostage. He pressed the brooch into Gull's palm. "You should understand why I cannot do this, Father."

"Nay, lad. I only understand why ye must."

Angusel used the motion of tying shut his sack to mentally tie down the spiking anger. "Why? You didn't."

"That be why I know ye must accept the posting."

Elian's brow furrows had been deepening during the exchange. "What in hell are you two talking about?" When neither Angusel nor his father offered an answer, he held up his hands. "Never mind. In any event, Gull is correct." Fists on hips, he thinned his lips. "Ainchis Sàl a Dubh Loch, Third Turma, Manx Cohort, I order you to accept the invitation of the Comitissa Britanniam to join the new unit called the Comites Praetorii."

"You can't! It's—" Angusel hated how shrill he must sound. He cleared his throat. "Fleet Commander Bedwyr said it's a volunteer posting, sir."

"Yes. And I order you to volunteer."

THE CHAMBER served by the outer door to Niniane's cottage featured a raised central firepit vented through the thatch by a tin chimney. Until Christmas she had slept in this chamber too, and worked in the adjoining chamber. Thanks to Angusel and his mentors, she enjoyed a separate bedchamber accessible through the workroom and heated by its own hearth, leaving the main chamber free for hosting visitors. She invited Bedwyr to sit while she stirred the firepit's embers, added a split log from the stack, and settled into the other chair. Upon their arrival, Sister Marcia had brought wine and a platter of roasted venison morsels, cheese, and fresh-baked bread, and Niniane bade Bedwyr to refresh himself.

"Thank you for your prayers," he said before sampling the hospitality. "They are most welcome."

"And necessary?"

"For the vagaries of winds and waves and rocks and rains, aye." He gazed toward the firepit. "For the vagaries of men too, but no specific threats that we're aware of." A smile underscored the assurance, but she couldn't help sensing his implied "yet."

"I will continue praying for you and your men, of course." At this rate, she would achieve the Apostle Paul's goal to "pray without ceasing" soon. She felt honored to do so, especially for Arthur's close friend and those under his command. "I'm grateful for your visit, Bedwyr, but troop transport and courier duties stand several ranks beneath the Navarchus Classis Britannia." Her smile softened the tease.

He laughed, poured wine for them, and saluted her with his goblet. "Believe it or not, I am using that title now. On Arthur's reports, anyway. Keeps him happy and me away from the barber." Arthur's threat to have Bedwyr's long brown hair cropped in the Roman style

Arthur preferred for his soldiers was a well-known joke throughout the army and fleet. His jest, however, left her no closer to an answer.

"So. You came to evaluate Angusel for him?"

"He'll get that report too. He's right fond of the lad."

"What of Gyanhumara? Do you think she will forgive him?"

"Aye, we've talked about it, Gyan and Arthur and I. Publicly, though . . ." Bedwyr stared into his goblet before taking a swig. "From what she's told me of her people's ways, I'm not sure she can."

And no public forgiveness meant there could be no restoration of Angusel's honor, kin, clan, or country, Niniane surmised. "I'll pray for a happier resolution." This left the painful item on her list of possible reasons for Bedwyr's visit. "If Arthur has sent you to inquire whether I have Seen anything, please give him my regrets." She strove to keep her tone brisk.

Bedwyr's gaze became sympathetic. "I will tell him, but—I'm sorry, Niniane."

"Don't be. Please. What I See and do not See is part of God's plan." Her frustration that the Almighty had stopped sharing fragments of His plan with her she dared not mention. "What will you tell Arthur about Angusel?"

"That I'm glad he's on our side." Bedwyr ate a mouthful of venison and chased it with a swallow of wine.

She lifted an eyebrow. "Meaning?"

"I saw him and that older Caledonian practicing. When Gyan asked me to deliver her invitation, I thought she was being charitable, but—gods! Angusel is, what? Fourteen?"

"Fifteen. His natal day was last week."

Niniane felt her cheeks heat to recall how Angusel had celebrated the occasion, and she busied herself with her drink. Her visitation rounds for dispensing medical supplies, wisdom, and prayers included a certain women's enclave where the vocations were carnal rather than spiritual. While speaking to one of the residents, she'd noticed Angusel leaving another woman's chamber. His face was flushed, but he had seemed subdued, pensive. She was thankful she hadn't let him see her.

Bedwyr was chuckling. "Fourteen, fifteen. Doesn't matter. At that age, Cai and I didn't have half Angusel's swordsmanship talent. Or strength."

"Did Arthur?"

"He was always besting both of us, so maybe." Bedwyr looked down to retrieve a rolled parchment leaf from his pouch. He passed it to her, seal up. The scarlet wax bore the imprint of a cross fashioned of three intertwined strands. "Gyan wasn't the only one at headquarters to give me a message bound for Maun."

It took her last mote of will to curb her fingers' trembling as she broke Mer—Bishop Dubricius's seal. The words seemed harmless, an invitation to accompany him at Morghe and Urien's wedding.

The way the bishop had ended the message, however, rocked her heart to its foundation:

As you ponder your decision regarding whether or not to accept, I commend to your attention the Apostle Paul's first letter to the believers at Corinth. Without you, my dearest Niniane, I am nothing.

"Niniane? What's wrong?"

Bedwyr's quiet but urgent tone startled her, and she didn't realize she had closed her eyes. She looked down to see her right fist clutching her robe over her heart, which was hammering like the hooves of a stampeding herd. Relaxing the fist and drawing a deep breath, she did her best to smile at Arthur's fleet commander.

"Might you be willing to return to Maun in a fortnight to retrieve a passenger?"

GULL STOOD beside Elian on the dock, facing Angusel. Behind the lad, whose sack was slung over an armored shoulder and featured a smooth bulge where his helmet lodged, the Breatanach fleet commander's vessel swarmed with crewmen adjusting the rigging, stowing the last crates and barrels, manning the oars, and preparing to cast off. A blindfolded Stonn had been loaded and secured to the rail amidships, with a crewman stationed at his head. The fleet commander and his steersman conversed astern. The rising sun bathed the warship and its occupants in a hopeful glow.

Stonn whinnied, and Angusel glanced over his shoulder.

This was it.

"I'm surprised you're not coming with me," Angusel said.

Gull grunted. His decision had surprised him a mite too. But it had been the best one. He glanced at Elian, resplendent in spotless legion battle-gear for the first time on an oaken leg, and grinned. "The auld boar needs me more than ye do now."

"Right," Elian said, moving his head as if to measure the sun's position. "And our new recruits need both of us to whip their soft, sorry arses into a force Arthur can use." He thrust out his sword hand, and he and Angusel grasped forearms. "God's speed and strength to you, son."

After giving the centurion's arm a squeeze, Angusel released it and rendered the legion salute. "And you, sir."

Pride dominated the centurion's expression as he mirrored the gesture.

Blinking, Angusel stepped in to touch the gold lion brooch where it held Gull's new scarlet cloak in place. Being Elian's civilian assistant for troop training did not entitle Gull to wear the legion's dragon badge—not that he had wanted to—but the Manx Cohort commander had given him an officer's cloak to signify that his orders carried full authority.

"I'll keep the wee golden beastie safe for ye, lad." Gull yearned to embrace his son, but the openness of their surroundings constrained him to offering his arm. Angusel gripped it with strength that no longer surprised his father. As they parted, Gull couldn't resist adding, "Donna forget to keep eyes on your opponent."

Angusel swiped his cheek and grinned. "Fight me, sir, and see if you need to remind me."

"Ye can count on it, mo brogach."

His son gave a brave nod to him and Elian, spun, and mounted the gangplank, his legion officer's cloak swirling behind him.

Gull sensed the centurion depart and knew he must follow, but he couldn't bring himself to leave the dock until after the ship had cast off and his son's receding form, partway eclipsed by the rail and his warhorse, had become naught but a sparkling speck upon the deep blue sea.

IT HAD been a year and more since Angusel had set foot inside the praetorium at Caer Lugubalion, but his memories of its doors and corridors, columns and tiles, steps and statues surged forth with heart-rending intensity. Nothing about this opulent Ròmanach palace had changed.

Everything about himself and his relationship to its primary residents had.

Clenching fists and jaw, he lengthened his stride.

Two blue-cloaked guards flanked the door leading into the workroom of the Comitissa Britanniam. They saluted him, and one requested the purpose of his visit. Angusel's answer satisfied them. The guards motioned him to enter while they remained in the corridor.

Four pairs of eyes stared at him. The mouths beneath two of those pairs no longer possessed the ability to voice a comment. Below the shelf displaying the embalmed heads of Niall the Scáth and Ælferd the Sasun stood . . . *her*, beside her clansman and aide, Rhys. Angusel grieved to see her hair cropped as short as ever. He chewed the inside of his lip. It appeared that she and Rhys had been discussing something Rhys had written; parchments and quills and nibs lay scattered across his worktable amid pots of different colored inks. They straightened upon Angusel's entrance. Their intense scrutiny made his face heat and his pulse pound. To keep from retreating, he raised the shield of military protocol with a sharp Ròmanach salute.

"Optio Ainchis Sàl a Dubh Loch reporting, Comitissa." He lowered his fist but didn't relax it. "As ordered."

She cocked an eyebrow and glanced at Rhys. The centurion departed. She beckoned Angusel into her private workroom. He mentally girded himself as though entering a lioness's den.

And what a den it was, its Caledonach furnishings carved with symbols of the gods, the shelves overflowing with scrolls, three of the walls covered with swaths of wool woven of the various Caledonach and Breatanach clans' patterns. The Albanach and Móranach colors were conspicuously but not surprisingly absent. Two embroidered dragons faced off between the windows behind her worktable, each ramping across a field of gold: one scarlet and the other midnight blue. Surmounting the banners, her battle-sword, Braonshaffir, gleamed from polished pewter hooks shaped like a dragon's talons.

Arms crossed and expression crosser, she regarded him for what felt like an eternity.

"Visit the quartermaster before you report to Centurion Cato of First Ala. You are out of uniform."

He gave his head a slight shake. "My lady?"

"Trade your Caledonach boots for Breatanach ones. Then begin your duties as optio for First Ala. You did bring Stonn, I trust?"

"Aye, my lady, but I thought—that is, your invitation to join the new unit—" Gods, he felt like a dithering fool before her darkening scowl. He clamped his mouth shut.

"The Comites Praetorii needs men who will not hesitate to lay down their lives for me." Her upraised palm stilled his protest. "That is why I requested volunteers. I had hoped that you—" She chafed her arms, her expression softening a wee bit. "Since you say you were ordered to answer my invitation, I must conclude that you are not ready to join my unit."

He wanted to disagree but couldn't voice a lie.

"I cannot pretend to understand how you feel about being here," she continued. "Though I can guess. Trust between warriors must flow both ways. Last year I betrayed your trust in the worst way imaginable, and I am so sorry." Her gaze became hooded, and she bowed her head. "If I could change the past . . ." She closed her eyes in a long blink. Tears glistened upon the lashes. Blinking twice, she regarded him. "I pray that you might choose to forgive me one day."

Forgive her? For meting the punishment he deserved for failing her and her son?

Yet as her words settled into his mind, he realized that she was right. He couldn't die for someone he couldn't forgive.

And he couldn't make a promise that he might never fulfill.

He gave her another Ròmanach salute. "I shall correct my uniform and report to Centurion Cato at once, Comitissa."

"A moment, Optio."

From a nearby shelf she retrieved a linen pouch that was a wee bit smaller than his bian-sporan. Curiosity conquered his anxiousness to escape. She tugged on the pouch's cords, widened its mouth, and pulled out a bronze disc embossed with the legion's dragon.

"This phalera is yours. For saving my life." She sighed. "I stood no more deserving of your selfless bravery that night than any convicted traitor."

Again he yearned to disagree, but again he couldn't.

Her nod looked sad as she strode forward to press the phalera into his upraised palm. In letting go, her fingertips chanced to brush his. He clenched his fist over the disc to stem the tingle shooting up his arm. Mayhap she had felt it too, if her flash of surprise was an indication.

The memory of that look dragged on his heart. He sought a way to change their circumstances, but the words she needed most to hear lodged in his throat.

He rendered a final salute and waited in silence to be dismissed.

CHAPTER 7

THE SAFFRON, WOAD, crimson, and purple dyed clothing sported by the wealthier visitors rippled among the earthy, plain-spun garb of the clergy and common folk thronging the parade viewing area at Caer Lugubalion. Men and women selling meat, bread, and drink circulated among the people like little eddies in the human current.

The crowd's size appeared almost as large to Gawain as that of Uncle Arthur's wedding to Aunt Gyan, and it included his aunt Morghe, his aunt Yglais and her husband, Alain, his grandmother Chieftainess Ygraine, other Brytoni and Caledonian rulers and their families and retinues, high-ranking clergy, and a host of worthies Gawain couldn't identify.

His parents and younger siblings had not made the sixty-mile trek from Dunpeldyr, which was disappointing but understandable: the annual Angli cattle raids would begin soon, if not already. An uptick of pride conquered the disappointment. His father might have ended their estrangement in honor of today's occasion.

He hoped so.

Blinking, he wished Loth Godspeed in combating the Angli threat, and he prayed that his new legion duties would give him a way to help.

His horse, Arddwyn, tried prancing in place. The movement shattered Gawain's reverie, and he brought Arddwyn under control. His cloak slipped, and he adjusted it to better conceal the rest of his new uniform, as ordered.

The infantry cohorts finished marching onto the field. They completed a circuit of the parade ground and halted encircling the perimeter, leaving an avenue for the day's central attraction, bisected by a shorter avenue leading to the viewing platform. This wasn't a typical parade, starting with the fact that Uncle Arthur and Aunt Gyan were not leading it. General Cai had led the infantry onto the parade ground while Arthur and Gyan waited beside Uncle Peredur and the Horse Cohort. Gawain squinted to make out the gold-tipped crests—Gyan's blue and Arthur's red—of their parade helmets from his place as decurion of Sixth Ala's fifth turma, five alae behind where they sat mounted with the First.

Arddwyn snorted, champed the bit, and pawed the ground. Gawain whispered calming words and stroked his neck; he could sympathize. Every soldier had been drilling for—and grumbling about—this day for the past week, though he for one had been glad of the practice, since he would be part of the primary deviation.

The last infantry cohort marched to its place and halted. General Cai shouted the order for all units to face the long aisle; another deviation, since the troops usually faced the viewing platform.

First Ala's signifer raised his unit's banner, prompting the signifers of the remaining alae to do the same. A horn blew, the banners canted forward, and the Horse Cohort surged ahead. They guided their horses between the infantry units down the long aisle and maneuvered them to face the platform. By the time Gawain's unit reached the aisle, Arthur, Gyan, and Peredur had split from the Horse Cohort to ride partway down the bisecting aisle, and they were positioned to watch the horsemen. A fourth, Centurion Bohort, accompanied them, carrying a furled blue banner. When the last ala—the Eighth—had completed its maneuvers, the four commanders wheeled their mounts to face the platform.

"On this day my sister, the Lady Morghe, departs for her wedding to Chieftain Urien of Clan Moray of Dalriada." Arthur pitched his voice for a battlefield.

The crowd cheered, and heads swiveled toward Morghe, where she sat on the viewing platform. She rose and waved, executing a slow pivot. Odd; the graceful maneuver stuttered midway. She had to be looking toward First Ala, but before Gawain could determine what might have affected her, she recovered her composure.

Arthur murmured to her. She gave a tight shake of her head, waved to the rest of the crowd, and resumed her seat.

Her brother squared his shoulders. "In honor of this auspicious occasion, the Comitissa Britanniam has created a special cavalry unit."

Straightening in the saddle, Gawain chewed his lip to contain the grin.

Gyan said in her Caledonian-accented but excellent Latin, "This unit contains the best horse-warriors of the legion. By this time next year it will be a full ala, and the Pendragon and I will host annual cavalry competitions as needed to replace members. Since the unit's first duty is to escort Lady Morghe and her party, Tribune Peredur mac Hymar, prefect of the Horse Cohort, will serve as temporary commander." She gave her brother a brief smile.

Centurion Bohort raised the unit's standard: a dark blue dragon on a gold field.

"Comites Praetorii," shouted Peredur, "front and center!"

Gawain flung back his cloak and nudged Arddwyn out of formation, joining the twoscore and two men riding at a slow canter around the Horse Cohort to the crowd's sustained roar.

His inward grin died as he passed First Ala and saw Angusel mounted beside that unit's commander, Centurion Cato. Angusel wore a bronze Phalera Draconis identical to Gawain's, and for the identical reason. That disc might proclaim he and the whelp as being part of a military brotherhood more exclusive than Gawain's new squad, but there was no way on this side of hell that he'd ever acknowledge such a kinship. He fought down the disgust that threatened to shudder through his soul; this day belonged to Gawain's kin by blood and by marriage, and hatred deserved no place here.

From the corner of his eye he saw Angusel glance down and away, and Gawain's heart made a short lurch.

HE KNEW he should remain stoic, as he'd been drilled countless times, but he couldn't help averting his gaze as Gawain rode by. Emotions that had to remain hidden assaulted him: grief, of course, mixed with anger and unworthiness and regret, bound by a taut cord of sadness. The determination not to be overwhelmed by the taunts and pranks of First Ala men had kept that sadness from veering into despair.

She had posted him to the First, and he would sooner die than fail her again.

Her words today had bestowed a glimmer of hope that he might earn a place in her "Count's Guards" elite unit. He nurtured that hope as a freezing man feeds an infant flame dry grass and twigs lest it die before it gains the strength to save his life.

He looked up as the last of the Comites Praetorii members approached First Ala on their way toward the central aisle. Through the rising dust clouds, he gazed over the heads of the nearest infantry century toward the crowd and blinked, hard.

An absolute vision of loveliness stood near the rail, bedecked in an overdress dyed an exquisite shade of azure, embroidered with a gold falcon. The same design, in woad, decorated her right forearm. Eileann's rich brown tresses were plaited with gold and blue ribbons and wrapped around her head. Her cloak, the Tarsuinnach pattern of saffron crossed with blue and red, was edged in gold, her due as àrd-banoigin.

The only missing details: her harp and her smile.

He surmised she was attending this event to honor her brother, Tavyn mac Dynann, one of the Comites Praetorii inductees who had cantered past them among the transfers from units other than the Horse Cohort. Angusel wondered who had replaced Tavyn as commander of Second Turma, Manx Cohort, and whether he might have stood a chance at the promotion had he stayed.

Nay. A weanling would make a better a squad leader.

A stolen glance at Eileann banished his discouragement. She seemed to be looking straight at him and smiling. Mayhap 'twas sheer happenstance, but his lips tugged into a half smile. Hers deepened.

His spirits felt lighter than they had in too many sennights.

Then he realized that she was standing next to the man to whom, come Belteine, she would be married. Iomar glowered at Angusel.

Heart plummeting, Angusel fastened his gaze upon the Pendragon, who had stepped forward.

RATHER THAN individual oath swearing, which would have tried the patience of people and animals alike, Uncle Arthur addressed the assembled troop:

"Do you swear by all that is holy to protect Gyanhumara nic Hymar, Comitissa Britanniam, on and off the battlefield and to obey all lawful orders given by her either directly or through your superior officers, even unto death?"

"Even unto death!" chorused the Comites Praetorii, Gawain included.

The trouble was, he mused days later as the procession plodded at the pace of the horse-drawn litters carrying Ygraine and Morghe toward the Clan Moray stronghold of Dunadd, no one had warned about the possibility of dying of boredom.

That changed in a blink as they neared a fork in the road to find a band of mounted Scotti warriors approaching them on the intersecting trail, which originated at the seacoast.

"Praetorii, alert!" ordered Gyan in Latin, sword in fist.

Arthur drew Caleberyllus. The Comites Praetorii freed their swords and closed ranks around the litters.

The Scots halted and fixed their attention upon Morghe's escort but seemed otherwise unperturbed.

Gyan and Arthur nudged their mounts forward, as did the Scotti leader. A second Scot detached himself from their formation, a spear clutched in his left fist. From its shaft rippled an undyed, unadorned linen flag.

Gawain's aunt and uncle sheathed their swords, but neither relaxed in the saddle.

"Commander Fergus," said Gyan, switching to Brytonic with a dip of her head. "You survived."

"As did ye, Chieftainess, but ye both"—he jerked a contemptuous nod toward Arthur—"made it damned hard for me sword-brethren and me."

They were referring, Gawain realized, to the First Battle of Port Dhoo-Glass, after which a few Scots escaped by stealing Brytoni fishing boats two nights after the battle.

"Next time, we'll make it easier for you to meet your gods." The Scotti would be fools not to believe Arthur's promise. "What business brings you onto Brytoni lands under the banner of truce?"

"Business that be none of yours, Scarlet Dragon." On the Scot's lips, the title became an insult.

Arthur scowled. Gyan shot him a look. He remained wary. She smiled at the Scot named Fergus. "It appears that your party and ours are bound for the same destination." She tilted her chin and moved her head in a slow sweep. "With your womenfolk?"

Gawain eyed the Scots closer. True enough, as many women rode in their ranks as men, and not so much as a dirk in the lot. Each woman, he noted, shifting in the saddle to relieve the sudden pressure, was prettier than the last. At danger's first whiff, Gawain had seen naught but spears and swords.

"It seems my brother-by-law has invited you to attend his wedding." Gyan's eyes narrowed to slits. "Why would he do that, I wonder?"

"Urien's counsel is his to keep," Arthur said. "The fact remains that these folk are here, and so are we." He turned a predatory grin upon Fergus. "And I imagine that Urien's—guests—shall not mind the added protection as they travel to Dunadd. Attacks can be ever so unpredictable at this time of year."

Fergus had the ballocks to laugh, as did some of his men. "We shall aye rest softer knowing that the great Scarlet Dragon guards our backs." His upraised fist signaled his party forward.

And as we gag on their dust and tread through their cac, Gawain grumbled to himself, stifling a cough as Gyan gave a similar order to her men. White flag or no, Gawain would not have changed a thing.

He could well imagine that everyone else on his side of the cac piles felt the same.

WHAT A disappointment.

The litter resumed its lurching, swaying gait. Morghe closed the curtains and nestled into the cushions, holding a lavender-scented cloth over her nose to counter the horses' stench. As entertaining as she expected the meeting of Arthur and Gyanhumara with Urien to be, she would have liked to have seen her brother and sister-by-marriage bloodied by those Scots, despite Fergus and his men having terrified her half out of her wits the summer before last.

But Gyanhumara had made a valid observation: Why were they here?

Morghe resolved to find out. As Urien's wife, she deserved to know what transpired inside Clan Moray's borders. And if Urien didn't agree, she had a plan for changing that too.

ANGUSEL, CLAD in a clean tunic beneath his practice gear after having discovered that the tunic he'd planned to wear for the drill session had been fouled by one of the stray cats that lived behind the barracks—the fouling arranged by a fellow ala member, no doubt—hefted Stonn's saddle and bridle off their pegs in the storage room and hustled toward the stables. Tardiness was punished by three stripes, regardless of the reason's validity.

"Damn!" came a muffled outburst from inside a stall, followed by a wet thud and ungodly clatter.

Clenching his teeth, Angusel quickened his pace. The gouges from his latest punishment had healed, but its memory hadn't.

Banging echoed against the stall's walls as Angusel drew closer, chorused by a string of Breatanach oaths. An ala groomsman, he guessed, had fallen victim of a soldier's prank.

The stall was Stonn's.

Battle frenzy boiled up inside him. He dropped Stonn's gear and sprinted to assist the unfortunate soul.

He didn't have to kill anybody, thanks be to all the gods. Stonn was fine, mouthing wisps of hay and gazing at Angusel as if to inquire about the fuss. The same could not be said for the young man who sat in the muck, his buried pitchfork's tines thrusting through it like defiant islands. The disgusting stuff covered him from the crown down. Angusel wondered at that strangeness, until he glanced up and saw the tilted bucket, dripping gooey gray-green ooze, which had been perched above the stall's door.

That muck bucket had been meant for Angusel.

He clamped off his anger, entered the stall, and offered his hand. "I'm so sorry," he said in Breatanaiche. The lad looked at Angusel's hand as if it were an alien thing. "Come, let me help you."

"You, sir? You're an officer. Why should you bother with the likes of me?"

"Nobody deserves this." He thrust his hand closer. "Must I make it an order? And don't call me sir. I may be an officer, but only just."

"Yes—Optio?" The young man grasped Angusel's forearm and hauled himself up. Angusel shook his head. "What, then?"

"What the duty roster reads, Ainchis Sàl. And your name is—?"

"Drustanus." He retrieved his pitchfork. They departed the stall but paused at the saddle and bridle lying slumped in the trampled dirt of the stableyard where Angusel had dropped them. "I'll put away Stonn's gear and clean his stall for you after, well, after I'm not part of the problem." A rueful grin accompanied the promise.

"Drustanus—Centurion Marcus's nephew?" Angusel had failed to recognize him under the filth. "You should be in the ala too; we're of an age, you and I, and you look plenty strong. What did you do to draw this thankless duty?"

Drustanus shrugged and peeled off the tunic, which had begun to dry. The action showered the ground with smelly bits, revealing a muscular chest that confirmed Angusel's assessment. "Uncle Marcus says I should earn my place based on my own merits, not upon family connections."

Angusel gave a noncommittal grunt. He'd lived in the Pendragon's legion long enough to keep his opinions about the decisions of his superiors to himself. However, that didn't mean he couldn't attempt to influence changing them.

"I'll see you in the old training ring after supper." His choice was dictated by the likelihood of their not being seen; no sense in angering a superior who stood several ranks higher, even if the officer was Drustanus's kin. "Borrow a practice sword from the armory, and tell the soldier on duty that I ordered it." He glanced toward the field where First Ala had gathered, his mood souring. "And let me have your tunic."

"What? Like this?" Drustanus held it out by a muck-free patch of fabric, the garment pinched between thumb and forefinger.

Angusel snatched it from him. "It should help me settle other business. Go visit the baths and don fresh clothes. I expect Stonn's gear oiled and his stall spotless before afternoon drills are done."

Drustanus grinned and saluted. "Yes, sir!" The grin widened. "Sorry—Ainchis Sàl!"

Angusel felt his answering grin form as he watched his new friend hurry away. A whiff of this latest fouled tunic killed the grin.

He left Stonn in his stall and stalked off to join his unit.

The most frustrating thing about the pranks—the humiliation and stripes aside—was that Angusel had no clue who was responsible. He would have preferred to have confronted the man or men privately; soldiers caught brawling could expect ten stripes and ten days' confinement to barracks at half pay. However, confrontation provided no guarantee that the pranks would stop.

After what had happened to Drustanus, Angusel didn't care what anybody thought of his actions.

"You're late again, Optio. And this time you have forgotten your horse." Several of the horse-warriors snickered. Centurion Cato silenced them with his glare, but a few continued smirking. Cato dismounted, gave the reins to the soldier beside him, and removed the whip from his belt. "Ten stripes." He started closing the gap.

"As you will, sir." Angusel flung the tunic at Cato's feet, halting the centurion's advance.

"What in hell is this piece of filth?"

"When you report my punishment, you can add that the nephew of Centurion Marcus slipped and fell in my horse's stall because of a muck bucket that had been rigged to fall on me."

"What!" Cato rounded on the others. The smirking men, too slow to amend their demeanors, got summoned out of formation, beginning with Dunaidan, whose snickers, in Angusel's opinion, had sounded the loudest. They dismounted and hastened to line up before the fuming centurion while the closest soldiers held their horses' reins. "This foolishness ends here. Ten stripes for each of you." Cato brandished the coiled whip. "I don't give a bloody damn if you are responsible or not." He leveled his glare on the unit. "Another incident like this, and the entire ala gets the lash and ten days at half pay. Understood?"

After a resounding chorus of, "Yes, sir!" Cato ordered the chosen men to strip to the waist and kneel. Angusel joined them.

"Optio, what are you doing?"

"I was late, and not mounted. I deserve ten lashes too, sir." In spite of the cost, Angusel needed the favoritism far less than he needed those damned pranks. He'd grab the whip and flay himself if the centurion wouldn't wield it on him.

"So be it. Strip and kneel." Respect colored Centurion Cato's order.

Twisting to wrestle out of the clean tunic, Angusel chanced to notice the same sentiment in the upraised eyebrows of Dunaidan and several other ala members.

CHAPTER 8

CCOLON MAP ANWAS tugged at the hem of his bronze-studded battle-tunic. This marked his first time being garbed in anything other than a legion uniform to meet the Pendragon.

It had been almost a year since he had followed his longtime friend and commander into a new life as Urien's chief adviser, a post which now included diplomat, the last bloody thing he'd ever expected. But it had given him ample opportunities to become accustomed to wearing the Clan Moray gold-crossed black cloak, rather than legion scarlet.

He caught himself giving his jerkin another tug, gripped his sword's hilt, and chided his foolishness.

A pair of glances affirmed that the soldiers flanking him atop Dunadd's gate tower either had not noticed the lapse or possessed wit enough not to react.

Drawing his cloak tighter to ward off the chilly April breeze that swooped in from the coast, heralding spring with a reminder that winter wasn't quite done, Accolon shifted his gaze to the farm-marbled distance and the approaching band winding its way alongside the pale blue ribbon that was the River Add.

Neither cold nor distance could stem his reaction to the prospect of whom the Pendragon and his men were escorting to establish permanent residence here.

Tightening his jaw, he used the excuse of leaning over the platform's rail to mask that reaction, damn her.

After what Urien had endured because of another woman, Accolon would sooner eviscerate himself than jeopardize this relationship or the fragile peace it promised for everyone—except Accolon.

He stilled the grinding of his teeth.

As the minutes marched by and the company's members grew larger, their count appeared double what Arthur had said it would be. Accolon was about to send one of his men to alert Urien when a flash of white caught his eye. Squinting, he leaned farther forward.

"Sir? Is aught amiss?" asked Lucius, his second-in-command. It hadn't been easy convincing Lucius to quit the legion, since he remained sympathetic toward the Pendragon, but it had been essential: Lucius had been privy to Urien's deception during the cavalry games that had been staged for the Pendragon's nuptials, and he needed to be kept close. Harder was Accolon's task to dissuade Urien from staging a convenient accident.

Accolon hated to waste good officer material.

He glowered at the man, who straightened and swallowed. "Were your scouts in error about the size of the Pendragon's unit?"

"No, sir. Lady Morghe's escort met another band of wedding guests yestermorn." Lucius jutted his chin. "The guests that Chieftain Urien had ordered to be informed about directly."

"Ah. Of course." And Urien hadn't seen fit to mention it to Accolon. No surprise there. The chieftain's drumbeat was often a solitary one.

Thinking about those other guests revived uncomfortable memories. To dispel them, Accolon stared at the approaching companies. The Scots' white flag was unmistakable now, and he could see Arthur halfway back in the pack, distinguished by the brush on his helmet's crest and the scarlet cloak billowing above the white flanks of his stallion.

That the officers riding in a box formation surrounding the litters belonging to Lady Morghe, Chieftainess Ygraine, and Prioress Niniane were wearing blue cloaks rather than the standard legion scarlet, however, was a mystery that would have to wait.

"Permit them entry with but a token challenge," he said to the guard captain, who saluted.

Accolon quit the tower, ordering Lucius to accompany him, and prepared to welcome the woman slated on the morrow to become the wife of his best friend.

He derived a mote of comfort from the fact that Lucius had tugged on his own battle-tunic too.

An hour later, standing beside Urien's immense chair on the dais of Dunadd's hall as the Pendragon strode toward them beside his mother and sister, Accolon had to force himself to keep his fists relaxed. Urien, to judge by the slow, rhythmic way his fingers straightened and curled around the boar-headed knobs of his chair's armrests, was fighting a similar battle—as were the Moray soldiers of Urien's personal guard, arrayed at strategic points about the hall. The Scotti contingent's meeting, a few minutes earlier, had progressed as smoothly as could be expected, and those men and their wives were being shown their quarters, but trust between former enemies was a hard prize to win in spite of what their leaders might wish.

Urien's decision to permit the presence of his mother, Lady Wreigdda, and the other Moray noblewomen had to be helping to dispel the tension; fear-bred hostility was the last thing any man wanted to show in front of his woman.

Accolon hoped the women's silent influence would prove to be deterrent enough.

"Chieftain Urien," said Arthur's mother with a short but graceful nod. Her utterance didn't cause Clan Moray fits of scandalized gasps because Ygraine was a chieftainess in her own right. As such, she outranked her son, but he appeared to have buried his resentment regarding that vagary of his life's circumstances. "We thank you—and your lady mother, Wreigdda—for your gracious invitation to your home."

Wreigdda, standing foremost among the ladies clustered near the dais, smiled at Ygraine. Her black gown was embroidered with the Boar of Moray in gold thread, but her plain widow's headdress displayed a poignant reminder that she continued to mourn Dumarec nigh on a year after his passing.

Arthur drew a breath, but Ygraine regarded him sharply. She returned her gaze to Urien, sharpening it further. "We could not help but notice, however, that you greeted your foreign guests before greeting your wife-to-be and her kin."

"A precaution I took for your safety, of course." Urien's smile did not encompass his eyes. "You are ever well come to the seat of Moray as a valued ally, Chieftainess Ygraine." His gaze shifted and softened. "I thank you for this opportunity to strengthen our alliance through marriage to your daughter."

Rising from the chair, Urien extended his hand, smile broadening. Morghe, her smile hinting an emotion Accolon couldn't identify and therefore didn't trust, stepped forward to clasp it.

"And I'll thank you to remember, Chieftain Urien," Arthur said in a low, measured, dangerous tone, "whose protection Lady Morghe shall always enjoy, regardless of whom she marries."

Ygraine gave Arthur an annoyed glance that went unseen. Morghe grinned.

Urien arched an eyebrow, wrapping his arm about the waist of his wife-to-be, and she leaned into his embrace. "Ah, Lord Pendragon. A pleasure, as always." The Chieftain of Clan Moray made a show of scanning the hall. "But it appears that you have forgotten to bring the woman you should be most concerned about protecting." Of course Urien knew that Arthur had forgotten no one; the scouting report Accolon had read had been quite clear on that point. Before anyone could react to Urien's implied threat, he ambled on with, "Where is Chieftainess Gyanhumara? Have you managed to saddle her at your hearth, where she belongs?"

Morghe's grin widened.

"The Comitissa Britanniam," Arthur said through clenched teeth, "is where she belongs: in the Add Valley at the base of Dunadd, setting up camp alongside her men."

Ygraine touched Arthur's arm, and his posture relaxed a little. "Gyanhumara appreciates your invitation too, Chieftain Urien," she said. "But she did not wish to overburden your hospitality, what with so many . . . other guests lodged under your roof."

Accolon didn't miss Ygraine's subtle emphasis; doubtless, Urien didn't either.

"What my mother is too politic to ask, Urien, is why have you invited my former captors to be honored guests at our wedding?"

Morghe's utterance caused most onlookers to erupt into exclamations of scandal and shock. Accolon couldn't quite suppress the laugh that exploded from the depths of his gut.

MORGHE HAD never been hustled out of a public chamber that fast. It would have been aggravating if it hadn't been so comical. Urien had flushed such a bright shade of red, she'd expected him to fall dead at her feet.

He might have too, if Accolon's choked-off laugh hadn't snapped the spell cast by Morghe's question, and Urien had dragged her into the hall's private audience chamber before she could gauge the reactions of her mother or brother or anyone else.

No, not dragged. Urien still had his head attached. For how much longer would depend upon this conversation's outcome.

"I suppose I shouldn't be surprised." He circled the snug but luxuriously furnished chamber like a caged lion as Morghe stood in the middle of its slate floor, which had been etched with the Boar of Moray. She didn't bother to keep him in sight. Her brother stood a shout away; she could hear his muted tones, as well as her mother's and Accolon's, seeping through the oaken door. "You are your mother's daughter."

Morghe judged the timing and put out a hand, allowing his chest to collide with it. His surprise let her shift closer, sliding that hand toward his face while the other slid in the opposite direction. When it found its target and began caressing, his breathing grew husky, and he lowered his ravenous lips upon hers.

Thank God men were so easy to manipulate.

"And my father's," she reminded him as he broke off to feather kisses across her throat toward an earlobe. "Both have taught me much about what it means to rule." Urien straightened, eyebrows knotting. "And my brother taught me that it's a waste of resources to ignore perfectly good counsel because one fails to esteem the counselor."

He glared toward the door and then at her. "What are you imply-ing, Morghe?"

"Isn't it obvious? Make me chieftainess to rule Moray jointly with you."

"What!" He reined the word to a raw whisper, but she detected escalation in the conversation outside the chamber. "And halve my power?" She saw the end of that question—*with a woman*—in the curl of his lip. "Never."

She pressed a fingertip to that curl, smoothing it. "Don't be so quick to assume your calculations are correct." In response to the skepticism forged between the wrinkles of his brow, she asked, "How many votes can Clan Moray cast among the Council of Chieftains?"

"One, of course, unless I cannot be present."

"Of course. And how many votes has Clan Cwrnwyll?"

The skepticism yielded to dawning recognition. "Chieftainess Ygraine's and, when she is absent, Chieftain Alain's."

"Indeed. My half-brother-by-marriage, appointed by the clan's el-ders and ratified by the council as a nonvoting member except when Ygraine does not attend a gathering because, whether my mother likes it or not, some governing decisions are best suited for men to make. The wars of which your lot are so fond, for example. And does the clan of my other half-brother-by-marriage, Lothian, possess an extra council seat?"

She knew the answer was no, and so did he.

"What you ask is so . . . so . . ."

Morghe smiled and resumed her attention upon his quickening nethers. Before his mouth could descend upon hers, she said, "The word you are looking for is *logical*. There is much good I can perform for Clan Moray as chieftainess, beyond giving you another council seat."

Urien snorted but didn't disagree.

"So, as chieftainess," she murmured as his fingers danced across her heightened vulnerabilities, "I must again ask why the Scotti con-tingent is here."

"Because"—he pulled her closer so she could feel between her thighs the effect she was having upon him—"I do enjoy baiting your brother."

That much was no state secret. Nor was it a state secret what her brother would do if he could see them, since their union was not yet legal in the eyes of the Church. Urien had to possess another reason. Curbing her grin, she initiated a slow slide against the man who would offer her a share in as much of the world as he controlled. "And?"

He increased the pace and pressure of their slide, to her escalating delight.

"And I have decided to permit the Scots to settle on Moray land as a buffer against the Picts along the Argyll border."

If he hadn't decided to kiss her just then, he'd have seen panic flare in her eyes.

As she responded to his kiss, stroke for passionate tongue stroke, she banished the panic to mull where the baby known as Eoghann and his guardians could be relocated.

No child deserved to grow up in fear of falling afoul of the merciless Scots.

URIEN MAP Dumarec stood atop Chieftain's Rock, dressed in his ceremonial battle-gear and bathed in dawn's strengthening light, surveying the crowd that surged through the wall's side gate following the conclusion of prime mass on this holiest of days—for those to whom such things mattered—the Feast of Christ's Passion. The Scots had declined to attend the religious service and occupied the far side of the courtyard. Gyanhumara and those of her men who had not gone to mass had formed up near the section of wall protecting the chapel.

Gyanhumara . . .

She stood garbed in gleaming bronze and gilded-leather armor, her shorn, flame-red hair stiffened with white lime streaks and twisted into spikes. Gold, dove-headed torcs encircled her neck and bare biceps. Her gold dragon brooch glittered from its perch, fastening her gold-hemmed, dark blue cloak. A dragon ramped across the great bronze buckle of her sword belt. No scabbard hung there, in deference to the purpose of this day.

All Urien could think about was the day he would strip off those armaments and adornments, the day he would take that which she had dared to deny him.

Her glare warned him not to raise his hopes. The lowered eyebrows framing his gaze delivered a challenge of their own.

Abrupt cessation of activity at the gate drew his attention.

After the last of the worshipers had taken their positions facing Urien, the elegantly robed and coifed Ygraine and Wreigdda processed through the gate, followed by Arthur escorting Morghe. Gyanhumara stepped from the formation to join them.

As prearranged, Urien had not attended mass at prime, owing to the ancient tradition that kept the bride hidden from the groom on their wedding day. As the mothers glided into the assembly's front row, Urien received this morning's first clear view of his bride.

God, what a vision!

Morghe stood swathed in gold fabric embroidered front and back with the Boar of Moray in ebony thread. Her auburn hair lay piled atop her head and was decorated with ropes of black pearls that must have cost a fortune. A delicate cap of cream-colored lace, its gold threads highlighting the boar design, framed but did not obscure her face. Morghe was everything Gyanhumara was not: soft, gentle, refined, wise, willing . . .

He wondered how willing she would be after he refused to grant her the privilege of reigning as chieftainess.

Morghe's gaze met Urien's, and her lips curved into the sultry smile that made his blood heat. He couldn't help but return it.

Arthur placed her hand into Urien's, gave a sharp nod to both of them, and withdrew to stand between his wife and mother.

The priest rambled on about the sanctity of marriage, and then bade Urien and Morghe recite vows to honor and cherish and respect each other. Urien mouthed his way through the affirmations while silently urging time to speed ahead to the ceremonial kiss.

"Do you, Chieftain Urien map Dumarec, vow to protect your lady wife, Morghe, from all hurt and harm?" asked the priest.

"Of course I do." To have said anything else in front of Arthur, his mother, and their allies would have been gross stupidity.

The holy man faced Morghe. "And do you, Lady Morghe, vow to obey your lord husband, Urien, in all things?"

"I will," she said in a tone worthy of a battlefield commander, "as

Chieftainess of Clan Moray." Into the crowd's shocked silence, she reached up and laid her hand on Urien's cheek. It was warm and had a fragrant, earthy scent. His flesh tingled under her touch, and his lust flared. "Isn't that right, my love?"

His emotional self screamed that this foolish move would lead to chaos. His logical half recalled the points she had made about the Council of Chieftains and other ways she could assist him as chieftainess that would never be permitted her otherwise.

He surveyed his clan and the guests, all of whom were regarding him with varying degrees of confusion, expectation, curiosity, skepticism, or encouragement.

Inhaling Morghe's tantalizing scent, Urien reached a decision. He unpinned his boar brooch, removed his black clan mantle, and draped it around Morghe's shoulders. Its lower hem pooled across the rock.

The silence was broken by the sound of one pair of gloved hands clapping; Gyanhumara's, he realized. He cocked an eyebrow at her, and she gave him a respectful nod.

The applause swelled as her men, Arthur, Ygraine, and others added their accolades. Urien glanced at Morghe. Her smile was radiant.

"We have completed our vows. Have you not a proclamation to make?" Urien asked the priest, who was not clapping and appeared to be half a breath from a dead faint.

"A proclamation? Oh—of course, my lord." The man raised his arms. "In the sight of God and all you honored witnesses, I proclaim the lawful wedded union of Urien map Dumarec and Morghe ferch Uther, Chieftain . . . and Chieftainess of Clan Moray. May your union be fruitful and may your days be forever blessed."

The cheers faded to naught in Urien's mind as his lips met Morghe's for the first time as husband and wife. She gave his lower lip a playful nibble. He grinned his surprise and nibbled back, earning him a demure giggle from his wife.

Their days—and nights—might be blessed indeed.

They parted, and he treasured her smile, which hinted at those blessings to come. Hand in hand they beheld the sea of smiling faces. Together he and his wife announced, "Let the festivities commence!"

CHAPTER 9

ALF CROUCHING AND half lying across his supine opponent, pinning the man's arms and immobilizing his legs, Gawain struggled to regain his breath. Fergus had fought a hard wrestling match. They might be yet grappling had the Scot avoided a tactical error that gave Gawain the opportunity he needed to secure the win.

Listening to the whistles and claps and hoots of the feasters, he could imagine how he and Fergus must look: shirtless, sweating, panting, and sprawled across the slate and rushes, body to body like a pair of spent lovers.

Gawain grinned. "I thank you for the fine tumble," he murmured to his opponent. "It was most satisfying."

Fergus's answering grin seemed to carry a sly undercurrent. Gawain could have sworn that the man spoke a phrase that sounded like, "Good luck." Since that made no sense, he decided the Scot must have said, "Good bout."

"Well done, Gawain map Loth, my new sister's son by marriage!" boomed Urien from his place at the high table. "Rise and claim the hero's portion."

The disappointed groans uttered by the Scotti contingent were drowned by the accolades of Gawain's kin and companions-at-arms and the other Brytoni guests. Gawain rolled to his feet and helped Fergus stand. While Gawain donned his tunic and cloak with assistance from the servant who had been holding the items for him, the Scot addressed his countrymen.

"Nae need for that noise, me brave sword-brothers! I shall be having me way with yon bonnie lass ere long."

"Name the day!" Gawain swatted Fergus on the backside, and the Scot jumped like a startled maiden. "Or night."

Amid the roar of mirth, as Gawain stepped up to the dais to claim the traditional victor's meal of honey mead and the boar's haunch, a Scotti woman joined him. Her beauty—in particular, the way her full breasts strained the fabric of her silver-embroidered black bodice, bulging above it as if they might win free in the next instant—made him forget what questions he might have had about her intent.

"My lady?" asked Urien. "How may we be of service to you?"

Gawain marveled at that response; three days of feasting and bedding his wife seemed to have done much to mellow the chieftain's humor. A good thing, he mused, since he would gut Urien if a jot of harm came to his aunt at her husband's hands. Then Arthur could mangle what was left.

The Scotti woman opened her stance and pitched her voice to carry to the crowd. "I be called Caitleen, and this fine lad"—she glided her fingertips down Gawain's arm, igniting a trail of tingles—"has bested me husband in a fair match. According to the traditions of our people the Scáthaichean, Chieftain Urien, I request the boon of presenting his victory meal."

Urien appeared to ponder her request as he took a pull from his gold-embossed silver goblet. He commanded a refill from the maidservant standing behind his chair, and saluted Fergus's wife with the full goblet. "Fairly spoken, Lady Caitleen. I am pleased to grant this request to the wife of Clan Moray's newest ally. And neighbor."

The guests seated at the high table snapped their heads toward Urien. All but Morghe wore frowns. A glance at the feasters sitting at the lower tables revealed their abrupt disinterest in the food.

Arthur's sharp, "Ally?" was almost drowned by Gyan's quarrelsome, "Neighbor?"

Urien laughed. Morghe beamed. Merlin and Ygraine exchanged glances. Niniane, seated beside Merlin, closed her eyes and tilted her face heavenward.

"Ceding a few hundred hides of Moray land to Fergus's clan is an excellent bargain for lasting peace with the Scots," Urien said to Gyan and Arthur. He smiled at Lady Caitleen. "That is to say, the Scáthaichean." Her smile broadened.

Gawain couldn't miss the emphasis Urien had placed upon the word *lasting*. To judge by the deeper frowns, neither had anyone else.

"Who shall pay that price when these . . . Scáthinaich"—Gyan used what Gawain guessed was the Caledonian equivalent rather defiantly—"outgrow their few hundred hides?" She lowered her eyebrows. "Argyll?"

Urien slapped his chest. "Chieftainess Gyanhumara, you wound me. I possess their profound assurances that they shall be model tenants. Don't I, good my lord Fergus?"

"Aye!" thundered the foster brother to one of Arthur's most dangerous enemies. Fergus, who had donned his fine tunic while his wife had been presenting her request, grinned at Gyan. "The chieftainess should well recall that I be a man of me word."

"I pray that your word has gained in value since the last time I encountered it," she said. Arthur's consternation-laden stare went ignored as she busied herself with her goblet. Gawain bit his lip to hide his grin.

Morghe gave an exaggerated groan. "Please, my lords and ladies. This is a wedding, not a council chamber. My wedding, for those of you who seem to have forgotten that fact." Goblet in hand, she stood, beckoned to the servant bearing the victor's haunch, and instructed him to deliver it to Lady Caitleen.

"Brave warrior, accept this gift as but a token of my esteem." Lady Caitleen hefted the haunch from the servant's platter and deposited it into Gawain's outstretched hands. Her tongue flicked from between lush lips to taste her fingers.

The political sword-rattling had not dampened his appetite, and he tore off a generous mouthful. The salty skin crackled, and the flesh beneath was tender and juicy and hot, just as he preferred it. He closed his eyes for a moment of pure appreciation as he chewed and swallowed.

He inhaled Caitleen's earthy-sweet scent as she sidled closer to him, and he opened his eyes. A soft smile adorned her lips. He abandoned the boar's haunch on the table.

Expression intense, Morghe leaned across the table to pass her goblet to the Scotti woman.

Caitleen's smile widened as she pressed the goblet into Gawain's hand. His fingers brushed hers. He felt a lower part of him stir awake.

"May this victor's cup refresh ye as nae thing ever could," she said.

God, she was so very beautiful . . . and so very married.

Gawain murmured his thanks. Normal mead was not potent enough to kill his lust. He prayed that the brewer had made an error in the recipe and drained the goblet in one pull.

She moistened her lips. Her smile shaded from radiant to sultry. She glanced at Fergus, who returned her look with a smoldering one. "And may this kiss remind me husband to compete harder."

No stranger to a woman's mouth, Gawain had never experienced such an arousing kiss. She nibbled his lower lip. When his mouth widened, she slid in her tongue to caress his. She molded her body to him, shifting her hips in a tantalizing rhythm.

Reason fled. He enveloped her in a crushing embrace and deepened the kiss, matching her rhythm and reveling in the mounting ache that would soon find release . . .

A woman's scream confused him. Rough male hands dragged him back. Chest heaving and hair swirling about her head like a flame unbound, Caitleen glared at him while trying to hold closed her torn bodice.

Gawain blinked. Her appearance made no sense. *What in hell did I do?*

"Ye attacked me, monster!" she shrieked.

Did I speak those words aloud?

He shook his head, as much to clear it as to deny her claim. The room wouldn't quit spinning. He wanted to bend over, but the Scotti warriors held him fast. Nausea clawed at his stomach. The feast hall had erupted into a cacophony of shouts directed against him.

"I'm sorry, my lady! I didn't mean to—"

Fergus hammered an uppercut to his jaw. Gawain stumbled into the warriors, who tightened their grips. His vision fractured into needles of light, and the hall spun faster. Acute pain twisted his gut. He felt hot and cold at once. Gasping and heaving, he choked down the burning bile. The Scots clutched his arms harder. He closed his eyes and would have sagged to his knees if his captors had let him.

"Chieftain Urien, you and your guests be witness to this heinous assault upon me innocent lady wife," Fergus stated. "I demand his head."

"No!" shouted Gyan and Morghe together. They shared a look.

"No," Morghe repeated at Gyan's nod. "This action is so unlike my nephew's normal behavior that it deserves further investigation to determine a just punishment." She smiled at Urien. "What says my lord husband?"

Urien directed his gaze toward the end of the dais. "Prioress Niniane, please examine Gawain and his food and mead."

The renowned healer murmured her assent and placed both palms upon the table.

"Thanks to my excellent mentor," Morghe said with a glance toward the prioress, who kept seated, "my herbal and leechcraft skills should prove equal to this task."

Urien waved his approval. Morghe navigated from behind the table, stopping first to sniff the haunch. After running a forefinger across Gawain's bite mark, she touched the finger to her tongue. She performed a similar examination of the cup. Her expression conveyed no conclusions.

Eyebrows knotted, she approached Gawain and felt his forehead and neck. Her hand was an icicle, and he gritted his teeth. When she probed his jaw where Fergus had struck him, he couldn't stop the wince. His knees wobbled. He locked them. She ordered the Scotti warriors to release him and step back. They complied upon receiving affirmation from their lord. She bade Gawain to raise one arm parallel with the floor. Embarrassing tremors shook his hand. Clenching it didn't help. When she pressed down on the fist, he couldn't summon the strength to resist her, and the arm fell to his side like a deadweight. He rubbed it, his heart thrashing in double time to the strokes.

"You found nothing on the cup or meat?" Gawain whispered, despising his failure to prevent panic from bleeding into his tone.

His aunt gave him a sympathetic smile and faced Urien.

"Gawain has a fever and—"

"Aye, the fever bred of lust." Fergus hugged his wife.

Morghe shot him an annoyed look. "When was the last time lust robbed your husband of strength, Lady Caitleen?" When that netted glares from both of them, she addressed Urien. "Something Gawain ate or drank made him lose control over his baser urges. I propose—"

"'Twas your selfsame cup he drank from!" Caitleen shrieked.

"Perhaps traditions are different among your people. I do not poison my blood kin." Gawain couldn't figure out why discomfiture flickered across Urien's face; his head ached too much. "Furthermore," Morghe continued, "what reason could I possibly possess to disrupt my own festivities in this deplorable manner?"

"I do hope, Chieftainess Morghe, that ye are not suggesting that me wife did aught to bring this upon herself. 'Twould be most unfortunate for our alliance."

"Executing my sister's son for an act committed while he was not in control of his faculties would be equally unfortunate." Morghe wore a half smile; shrewdness dominated her expression.

Urien rose. "No one is suggesting anything of the kind, Lord Fergus. Neither is anyone denying the harm done to your lady wife. What may appease you, other than Gawain's death?"

Fergus ran his tongue across his bottom lip, shaping it into a grin. "What says the Scarlet Dragon? The man be one of your soldiers," he said to Arthur, "and ye've been strangely silent."

Arthur took that as his cue to stand, and he looked none too happy to do so. "In the Dragon Legion, a soldier's punishment is meted by his unit commander." Gyan accepted his proffered hand for as long as it took to rise beside him.

Even in the throes of battle, Gawain had never seen her look so stern.

She drew a long breath and expelled it. "Since there was no commission of rape—"

"By Scáthach, he intended to!" Caitleen wailed. Fergus shushed her, stroking her cheek.

"Only the gods may judge a man's intent, if there exists no action to demonstrate it," Gyan stated. "Gawain's actions demonstrated lewdness and a breach of self-discipline. Therefore, his punishment is the legion standard ten lashes."

Fergus released his wife, stalked to the dais, and smacked the table. Utensils jumped. Their users scowled. "Not good enough! Not by half!"

Urien raised his hands. "I agree." He faced Arthur and Gyan. "Gawain attacked an honored, highborn lady in front of scores of honored, highborn witnesses. That demands special consideration."

For a long time Gyan regarded the first man to whom she had been betrothed. Finally, she faced Gawain and extended her hand, palm up. His eyes widened as the implication dawned. Her nod confirmed it. His fumbling fingers unfastened his legion badge, and he let his blue Comites Praetorii cloak slip to pool at his feet. The pit in his gut suggested how long he would be forbidden to wear it.

"Forever, Commander Gyan?" he dared to whisper as he surrendered the badge. The tremors got worse, and his self-loathing deepened.

"Comitissa."

In one word she had banished him from that brotherhood too. His gut ached.

Her fingers eclipsed the dragon brooch. "Prefect Peredur," she said to her brother while pinning Gawain under her steady but sad gaze, "arrange to have this soldier escorted to camp and confined, under guard and permitted no visitors except yourself, Arthur, Merlin, and me, for the duration of this mission."

As Peredur joined Gawain, the Scotti warriors returned to their places. Gyan said to Fergus and Caitleen, "I am sorry for my soldier's behavior. I appoint my second-in-command to deliver the physical portion of his punishment"—she glanced at Peredur—"to commence after my duties here are concluded so that I may be present."

"We demand to be present too. Else how would we know—"

If Gyan's glare had been any colder, Fergus and his wife would have frozen into ice pillars. "You shall be informed. My lord."

Peredur clamped Gawain's arm. Gawain flinched, wanting to protest, to scream that he'd been targeted and manipulated, that it wasn't his fault. One glance at the countless hostile faces—even among his own kin—convinced him of that plan's futility.

He hung his head, and his march into disgrace began.

Chapter 10

SWORD AT THE ready, Angusel circled his opponent, inviting attack. Drustanus's thrusts and slashes were improving, if predictable, but his footwork was atrocious. One quick lunge or twist and he'd go down every time. But he kept getting up, eager for the next round.

Their wooden practice weapons clattered together. Angusel's sword almost slipped from his grip. He grinned.

"That's the way! Now follow it with a body block." He demonstrated at full force, and Drustanus yelped as he sprawled, kicking up a dust cloud that made them cough.

Waving his sword to part the cloud, Angusel bent to offer his shield hand, which Drustanus grasped to haul himself up.

"I think I have the right of it, Ainchis Sàl." Sword cocked, Drustanus adopted a fair attack stance. "Let's have another go."

They never got the chance.

Angusel had moved their training sessions to the main ring near the fort's north gate upon receiving Centurion Marcus's approval to practice there after supper so this activity wouldn't interfere with their regular legion duties. This evening, the double gates had swung open to admit a large mounted unit.

The last ala had returned from maneuvers hours ago.

He lifted a finger to signal Drustanus to pause, and together they watched the Comites Praetorii parade toward the barracks.

Nay, "parade" was not the word for it. The horsemen—and woman—looked dust covered, bone weary, and dispirited.

What in the name of all the gods had happened?

Drustanus whispered the same question.

The Pendragon and . . . *she* rode past them. Drustanus and Angusel rendered the expected legion salutes. The company's members kept their forlorn gazes trained upon the road before their horses' hooves as if to do aught else would invite scorn.

"Wasn't he in that unit too?" Drustanus dropped his unacknowledged salute.

Angusel, who had been watching *her*, followed the line of Drustanus's gaze toward the procession's tail to discover the *he* to whom his student had referred. His heart lurched.

Gawain map Loth, clad in a plain cloak and traveling clothes, was riding between two uniformed guardsmen—if in fact "riding" could describe someone with bound wrists astride a mount being led.

As Gawain passed the enclosure, a gust of wind flipped aside his cloak, exposing his back. The tunic's undyed linen displayed splotchy red stripes.

One explanation fit these facts.

Angusel threw down his sword, sprinted to the rail, and vaulted it. The guardsmen tried to block his approach, but he dodged between their horses and dragged Gawain from the saddle.

"You! You disgraced yourself, and all of them!" Angusel's fists vented his fury. "Machaoduin! You disgraced *her*!"

Gawain tried to protect his face, but he did not disagree. Angusel struck harder.

"Optio Ainchis Sàl a Dubh Loch, desist at once!"

She had ordered it.

He obeyed.

While the Pendragon and all the Comites Praetorii save the two men guarding Gawain continued toward the barracks, she had reined

Macmuir about and was thundering toward them, her eyes blazing and her lime-spiked hair quivering as if readying barbs to launch an attack. She slowed her stallion and maneuvered him in a tight circle to bleed off his unspent energy.

"You," she said to Drustanus, who had run to the rail holding Angusel's practice sword as well as his own. "Barracks."

"Aye, Comitissa Gyan." He thumped his chest and quit the ring at a dead run.

"You and you," she addressed the guards, "Infirmary. Get his wounds dressed, let him change clothes, and escort him to my workroom. You"—Angusel's heart squirmed its response to her glare—"make yourself presentable for an audience with me. Immediately."

CAMILLA ÆLLESDOTTR sat in Ælferd's chair, behind his worktable, which she had placed in her private chambers of the fortress overlooking the rocky beachhead of Cymensora, fingering one of his precious blue glass goblets and trying to make sense of the scribblings scattered across the parchment. They were purported to represent enemy troop deployments and patrol patterns on sea as well as on land, but this evening she stood a better chance of solving one of Loki's impossible riddles.

Some days she wondered why she'd petitioned Ælferd's uncle, King Cissa, to move Ælferd's personal effects here from his final posting at Anderceaster. Every day she wondered why it had become her wyrd to die a ringless widow.

She used that naked hand to clutch Ælferd's goblet and drained the wine it held, knowing he had liked that vintage as much as she did.

Every day, she never believed that she could miss Ælferd more acutely than the last. And every day, she proved herself wrong.

She balled a fist to support her forehead, blinking hard to check the tears and wondering when they would stop springing forth unbidden. The pain lancing her chest she could do nothing about.

A knock rattled her door. She blinked twice and straightened.

"Enter."

Hador, the warrior whom her father had designated as captain of the guard at Cymensora and therefore her chief protector and adviser, answered her summons. An atypical grin leavened his war-chiseled but handsome features. Fist to chest, he gave her a deep bow.

"Welcome news, Captain Hador?"

"Yes, Princess. The harbormaster and I have spoken to a certain Manx fisherman of your acquaintance."

Camilla felt her lips twitch upward. "Ah, what does that old salt swiller report this day?"

"Port Dhoo-Glass is increasing security measures to prepare for the arrival of a . . . how did Ymyl term it?" Hador stroked his thick golden beard. "A woman of eminence."

Her elation slid as a realization dawned. "No name?"

"Oh, he gave a name. Ghee—something. You know how thick Ymyl's accent is."

She knew. "Ghee-ann, perhaps?" The few Saxons who had survived the clash that had killed Ælferd and nigh on a thousand of his men had reported that as being the name of the enemy commander, the shortened, foreign form of the name by which Camilla knew the whore who had murdered and mutilated her beloved Ælferd: Guenevara.

"I shall dispatch a man to obtain confirmation, Your Highness. The port is not closed; its residents won't pay heed to a new trader." He must have seen an expression on her face that compelled him to add, "It would be madness to act on such scanty information."

The news's nature let her forgive him for not answering her question directly. Guenevara might fall into her grasp! That would yield ever so many choices for exacting revenge.

She rose from behind the desk, trailing her fingers across wood Ælferd had touched, and approached Hador. "It would be madness not to act if the opportunity presents itself. Do I make myself clear?"

"Perfectly, my lady."

Camilla extended her ringless hand. "Please bid your man good hunting for me, Captain."

As he clasped that hand and bent over it, he didn't see her eyebrows lift in response to the tingling sparked by his lips brushing the backs of her knuckles.

ONE PERFUNCTORY bath later, Angusel stood in front of the shelf beside his cot in the First Ala barracks, naked save for the towel he'd girded about his loins, contemplating what she might have meant by "presentable."

His status as one of the legion's lowest-ranking officers and no longer possessing noble privileges had left him two choices: either his parade uniform or clean sparring gear. He opted for the crisp red linen tunic worn under his parade armor—the armor itself was stored in the armory, which was locked before supper each evening—and best leggings, his officer's cloak, and legion boots, the latter bearing the training ring's dust and scuffs.

The scuffs he could not address lest he incur her wrath for taking too long to report to her workroom, but he used the damp towel to wipe off the dust.

After he was admitted into the lioness's den, she studied him long enough for his head to start feeling light. He recalled an infantry parade trick and loosened his knees.

"Explain yourself," she said in Caledonaiche.

He decided that she meant his earlier behavior rather than his choice of dress, and drew a deep breath. "I was defending your honor."

Her eyebrows shot up so fast that if their relationship had remained on its old footing, he'd have laughed. "Indeed! How do you justify defending honor with dishonor?"

"I—" His eyes widened. "I cannot. I'm sorry, my lady." He averted his gaze, despising the too-familiar flush of shame. Behind him the door creaked open, and he heard the heavy, unison tread of soldiers marching toward the chamber. He stood past caring who listened to this confession and switched to Ròmanaiche to make it. "I was angry beyond the capacity for reason. I chose to act while in that state, and that was wrong of me."

Please forgive me!

When he dared to look up, her countenance had lightened. He mustered his last drop of sincerity to add, "I vow that it shall never happen again, Comitissa."

Her lips curved into a faint smile. It surprised him to realize how much he'd missed seeing it, and he fixed his gaze to the red and blue dragons on the wall behind her to avoid making a greater fool of himself for staring at her.

"I trust that you will exclude battle frenzy from that vow, Ainchis Sàl," she answered in Ròmanaiche. "There will come a day when your unit will need that unbridled . . . passion."

What an odd choice of words, he thought, and blinked. The smile had gone and she appeared to be looking past his shoulder. He turned.

Gawain map Loth, damp haired and swathed in clean bandages, tunic, and breeches, stood outside the open door between his two guards. The guards rendered smart legion salutes, pivoted, and withdrew. Angusel, anger flaring, resisted the temptation to shoulder-check Gawain on his way to following the guards.

"Optio, stay," she commanded, and Angusel faced her. "Soldier Gawain, enter."

As Gawain shut the door and took position beside Angusel, who wanted to sidle away but held his ground as ordered, she folded her arms. "Optio Ainchis Sàl, your assumption was correct. Soldier Gawain did disgrace himself and, by extension—"

"We've been over and over this, Commander Gyan!" Gawain sighed at her warning hum. "I'm sorry. *Comitissa*, I swear by God that I don't—"

She flicked a finger. Gawain pursed his lips.

"Gawain, there is something Arthur and I could not tell you until now, scores of miles from—unfriendly ears. We believe Fergus used you to cause an incident calculated to provoke us."

"What? Why?" Gawain shook his head. "And why me?"

"Our theory is that he had decided to involve whoever won the match, and he made certain that he would be the other competitor."

Gawain's short chuckle sounded rueful. "I knew my win came too easily at the end." His eyebrows lowered. "But that doesn't explain how it happened, or why it had to be me."

"Win?" asked Angusel. "What sort of win? Against Fergus—the Scot? The man who held you captive, Comitissa? *That* Fergus? He attended Morghe's wedding?" He shook his reeling head.

"His wife must have placed whatever substance affected you on her lips," she said, electing to answer Gawain first. "The fragile political situation may have convinced Morghe to forego examining the woman. As for the Scots targeting you, that was bad luck. Or perhaps good luck. If you had not been family, we would have had no choice but to execute you. So be grateful for that mercy."

Gawain grunted.

She regarded Angusel. "Urien has forged a personal alliance with the Scots. Arthur and I recognized the trap Fergus had set for Gawain, but if we had protested, Urien might have chosen to side with his new allies. We couldn't take that risk." Her gaze, directed at Gawain, softened. "I'm sorry your career became a casualty of our political decision, but for the sake of honor, the demotion must stand. For now."

"Understood, Comitissa Gyan." Disappointment dragged at the corners of Gawain's mouth, but not for long. "I'll have a chance to earn a place at your side?"

"Of course, with hard work and worthy deeds. I expect not a drop of sweat less." The smile she directed at Angusel sent an unexpected thrill through his soul.

One thing puzzled him, however.

"Alliances aside, why would Urien invite Fergus and that lot to his wedding?"

Her smile vanished. "Urien deeded Fergus land near the Argyll–Moray border."

"Gods, no!" Angusel clamped his mouth shut.

"Of course we have implemented plans to be extra vigilant. We shall try the economic angle too; trading partners go to war less often. Meantime, if Gawain wants to tell you the details of his bout and what happened afterward, he will." She leveled her gaze at Gawain. "And you will tell him."

Over Gawain's panicked, "What!" Angusel said, "Comitissa, I don't have to know—"

She knotted her fists and stalked to within a pace of them. "You two have shown nothing but animosity toward each other for months. Ever since . . ." Sighing, she rubbed her arms. She crossed them, and her glare returned. "Ever since Loholt. Arthur has noticed too. This ends here.

"Gawain, I am assigning you to First Ala. Optio Ainchis Sàl a Dubh Loch is your commanding officer. If he orders you to spit and you don't, I assure you that you will regret it. Understood?"

"Yes, Comitissa." The sigh and eye roll made it the most sullen agreement Angusel had ever witnessed by a subordinate addressing a superior officer.

Her scowl deepened. "If you expect to regain your place in the Comites Praetorii, it begins with how you handle this posting."

The defiance leeched from Gawain's expression, replaced by humility and a thread of hope. "Understood, Comitissa Gyan."

A hundred questions spun in Angusel's mind, led by, "Does this mean—that is, my lady, the legion's command structure does not place any men under the optio. Do I have to order Gawain around?" The commands he issued to Drustanus did not represent official legion business except in the broadest sense. To contemplate commanding someone who had outranked him bordered on the ludicrous. To say naught of the fact that Gawain was several years his senior, though that show of disrespect tempted Angusel to ask about being issued a whip.

"The Pendragon has given dispensation for First Ala's optio to have an assistant. You may do with Soldier Gawain as you see fit. Dismissed."

Gods.

Angusel could not have fathomed a less helpful response.

"As you will, my lady." He pointed a stern look at his subordinate that he hoped would keep him quiet. "Soldier Gawain, come with me."

The silence lasted for as long as it took for them to salute the Comitissa Britanniam, depart her workroom, and leave the praetorium. On its black-veined marble steps, prancing up and down and around Angusel like a moon-mad maiden, Gawain chanted:

"What is *your* will, sir? Repair your armor? Mend your tunic? Shine your shield? Muck your horse?" He looked at Angusel's scuffed footgear. When his gaze rebounded, his lips had curved into a wicked grin. "Lick your boots?"

"Just shut your gob." Angusel understood Gawain's lightened mood, but seeing no end to his own exile, he couldn't muster one jot of jubilation. "That's an order."

"Shutting up, sir!" Gawain gave an exaggerated salute, biting his lips but failing to stunt another grin.

"And stop being an ass." As if there was much hope of that happening. Angusel careened down the rest of the steps and into the main thoroughfare.

"Right, sir. Because that's the one thing that you do not need an assistant for."

Angusel gazed at the darkening twilight sky, clenching his teeth and fists, thankful that none of the fort's other residents were abroad at this hour. Her summons, which he'd mentioned beforehand to Centurion Cato, would prevent him and Gawain from getting the lash for reporting late to barracks, but Angusel had no desire to test the limits of that reprieve. He veered onto the first cross street of the barracks complex and kept walking.

When he could muster a mote of civility, he asked, "What in the name of all the gods is that supposed to mean?"

"What does 'Ainchis Sàl a Dubh Loch' mean?"

"It's my name." First Ala's barracks building was not far, and neither was the end of his patience.

Gawain moved into step beside him. "Stupid self-indulgence is what it is. Angusel. Sir."

That whip option was looking better by the syllable.

Growling, he hustled Gawain into the nearest alley, which separated the kitchens and mess hall, and shoved him against the wall. "She took kin, clan, country, privilege, purpose—everything from me! I am nobody. Less than nobody. I—" He sucked in a ragged breath, released the neckline of Gawain's tunic, and braced his back on the rough, cold stone, eyes closed. "I don't deserve my name," he whispered, sighing. "And I especially do not deserve to hear it from a member of the family I failed in the worst way imaginable." Pursing his lips, he shut his eyes tighter to trap the welling moisture.

When Gawain didn't answer, Angusel blinked them open, expecting to be alone. A bigger surprise than the fact that he wasn't alone: Gawain was regarding him with compassion.

"If you had said that to me a fortnight ago, I would have agreed with you." Gawain offered his sword arm. "Aunt Gyan was right to pair us. My name has become like a stench to people; perhaps I need a new one too." He gave his hand a slight shake, extending it further, and smiled. "Suggestions, sir?"

"Amadan." Cracking a lopsided grin, Angusel clasped Gawain's forearm.

"And that's Caledonian for—?"

"Ass. The animal, not the anatomy." Angusel let go and chafed his arms, glancing down and away, the grin crushed under resurging guilt. "I meant no offense by it."

"None taken. Angusel."

He nodded at Gawain and pushed away from the wall. "Summons or no summons, Centurion Cato is going to spit our heads on pikes if we don't hurry." He broke into a jog, and Gawain kept pace. "And it's Optio Ainchis Sàl when we're in public," he said between breaths. "That is an order, Soldier Gawain."

"Until the duty roster changes, sir."

They charged toward the door opening into the room block Angusel shared with Centurion Cato, where they would have to make space for the new unit member. Angusel resolved to petition the centurion to promote Drustanus into the ala too, since his combat skills now surpassed legion standards and the harsh winter had opened several spots on the roster.

Gawain reached the door first and yanked it open for his superior, executing a salute that held no trace of mockery.

As Angusel returned the salute, he welcomed the return of his most nonlegion grin.

CHAPTER 11

ACCOLON APPROACHED MORGHE'S workroom, fighting to bury his resentment. His being the chieftain's adviser did not give the chieftain's wife the right to put Accolon at her beck and call, especially when that meant exposing his bad shoulder—the one that had been wounded last year while conducting a covert mission for Urien—to the damned cold morning mist.

He shook his head, rubbing the shoulder under his cloak, and quickened his pace past the great hall. Of course she had every right to order him around; his best friend had ceded that right to her. And, Accolon had to admit, she was proving to be an apt ruler. Her soaring popularity as she dispensed wisdom and justice in settling the people's disputes, freeing her husband to concentrate upon the clan's weightier matters of alliances and economics, was but one example.

Her workroom was another.

Accolon reached the door and pushed it open; she had insisted from the first day to noble and commoner alike that knocking was not required here.

Unlike Urien, who had established his workroom near his—and Morghe's, Accolon reminded himself—sleeping chambers at the heart of Dunadd, she had commandeered a storage building near the kitchens. In the weeks since her arrival, it had been fitted with a hearth and chimney, a slate floor, and rare glazed windows thanks to Clan Cwrnwyll wealth she had brought to her marriage. The building still housed the herbs, cooking oil, lard, salt, flour, and other goods for which it had been built, but better organized.

The liberated space she had filled with a table for grinding herbs, mixing salves, and rolling bandages, and she had added plain but sturdy chairs for visitors as well as a tall-backed, cushioned seat for herself. Dunadd possessed a physician and infirmary, of course, but no one gainsaid the establishment of a second facility so close to the kitchens, where mishaps often occurred.

One of the visitors' chairs was occupied. Morghe was bending over the trembling hand of a kitchen maid, first slathering salve on a cut fingertip and then binding it.

She glanced up at Accolon and nodded a welcome.

"You are excused from your duties until tomorrow," Morghe told the lass. "See me first to have your wound checked and redressed. It should be fine in a day or two, but stay away from the knives for a week."

The lass rose and dipped a curtsey. "Aye, my lady. Thank'ee, my lady!" She whirled and almost bumped into Accolon. "Oh! So sorry, my lord!"

Accolon stepped aside with a smile and a sweep of his arm. "The fault was mine, good woman, for being so near. Heal yourself, and enjoy your day."

The servant bobbed another curtsey and fled the workroom. The door banged shut behind her.

"Practicing your diplomacy, I see."

Accolon turned. Morghe was wiping her hands on a cloth and grinning. She dropped the cloth onto the table and stepped around it to within an arm's length of him. Dressed in the plain-spun garb she favored while working inside this chamber, she looked like a nun. It heightened her allure.

To rein in his emotions, he pictured her kneeling with hands clasped and head bowed. That made it worse.

He cleared his throat. "As are you, my lady." To her raised eyebrow, he added, "Excusing a servant from duty because of a mere cut."

"Not so 'mere' as you might think. You didn't see how long it took me to stanch the blood. Any deeper and she'd have lost the tip." Not one trace of defensiveness marred her tone.

She undulated closer; he bridled the instinct to retreat. Nothing was happening between them, and nothing ever would.

"You summoned me, Chieftainess?"

"How is your shoulder?" She laid a hand upon the exact spot she had field-dressed last year despite the fact that he would have killed her if he hadn't been hit by that damned spear. "I've noticed how you rub it." The pressure of her circling motions increased. The shoulder did feel better.

He shrugged her away. "It is well enough, my lady. How may I serve you this day?"

She searched his face for God alone knew what, for God alone knew for how long. At last, she removed a tiny object from the pouch attached to her belt.

It was a loop of gold wire, curved and strung with three pearls of different colors: white, silver, and black.

She reached behind his head to pull his ear close to her lips. "I need you, Lord Accolon, to retrieve this bauble's mate."

He straightened. "Please permit me to remind you, Chieftainess, that groveling about on hands and knees is what slaves are for."

Her laugh tinkled like a delicate bell as she smoothed her hair where it had been pulled into its braid. "It isn't lost." She laid that warm, fragrant hand against his cheek. Of a sudden, groveling in the dirt at her feet was the only thing he wanted to do. Sheer force of will kept him upright, gazing into her violet eyes. "Find the crofter who lives near the place where you and I . . . danced last year, and bring him and his household to me." She rolled the pearls between the other hand's thumb and forefinger. "This will prove that you act as my agent."

He felt a tingle as her fingertips brushed his palm upon depositing the earring. A lower part of him stirred. He let his ire quell the randy beast. "You must be mad if you think they can stay here. My lady."

"Of course they shan't." She sidled closer, and her hip brushed the bulge. Damn her, he couldn't stop its twitches. A slow smile parted her lips. It took his last shred of self-discipline to resist the temptation of sampling them. "That is why you shall escort all of us to Maun."

It galled him to retreat, but he needed distance to keep from acting upon either of his suicidal impulses—to kill her, or to plow her. He dipped his head and backed toward the door. "You needn't trouble yourself. I can arrange everything." *And I can complete my mission to kill the Pendragon's brat. I could report that I had found him and his guardians dead of the pox.*

"Of that I'm sure." Her tone implied how far she trusted him, and it made him wonder when she had started reading minds. "But everything is arranged. The family is expecting you. I am visiting Maun to better acquaint myself with our people living there, and my husband agrees it's a fine idea for his best warrior and most trusted friend to escort me. The fact that I insisted upon traveling via a merchant's vessel, rather than diverting one of our warships from its patrol route, demonstrates my willingness to be wise with Clan Moray's resources."

"And clan matters pin Urien here. How convenient."

"So many, in fact, and of such a mundane nature that he shan't miss your presence for days." She nodded at the door, and he was thankful to oblige her. "But, Lord Accolon—" He faced her, a warning tingle crawling up his spine. "The next time you call me mad or use any other disrespectful term or tone, I shall lop off your pleasure pole and feed it to you."

He couldn't help but recall the gruesome demonstration in Laird Cuchullain's hall, and he couldn't help but wonder if in fact Morghe could read minds.

Masking a repeat of his risky but exhilarating response to Lady Dierda by sweeping a deep bow to his equally dangerous and alluring chieftainess, he couldn't help but grin.

Today is Eileann's bonding day.

Angusel stared at the rack of swords in First Ala's section of the armory, rubbing his forehead. It didn't help him recall where he had paused the inspection.

Truth be told, nary a day had passed since their meeting in the Caledonach ward of the Manx field hospital, seven moons earlier, when Eileann's sweet face hadn't shimmered into his mind's eye. Seventy times seven moons would pass before he could forget that heavenly voice. In fact he dwelled upon Eileann almost as often as he dwelled upon . . . another woman.

He glanced at Gawain, who pointed with his stylus. "That sword next."

"Aye." Angusel lifted it from its pegs, ran a gloved fingertip down its blade, and replaced it on the rack. "Two nicks, but it's serviceable."

Gawain made a tick in the appropriate column on his clay tablet. "What's ailing you? This task is taking far longer than the spears did yesterday."

The tolling of the bell at the Criòsdail temple, muted by distance and stone but undiminished in meaning, proved Gawain's observation correct. The other optios had departed.

"Go worship your god. I'll get Drustanus to help me finish here." The newest member of First Ala couldn't read a Ròmanach military treatise, but it wouldn't take long for Angusel to teach him how to tally arms and armor.

Gawain uttered a low whistle. "Today's the day everyone has been excused to attend Beltain festivities, remember?"

Aye, since Gawain had mentioned it. Belteine—which the Breatanaich called Beltain, and it meant "passion fire" in their tongue as well as in Caledonaiche—was the last rite in which Angusel ever wished to participate, especially this day, when the kindest lady in two realms would forever become lost to him. He gave his head a short shake. "I'll finish the inspection by myself, then." He reached for the tablet.

His assistant raised it overhead. "No, you won't. Sir."

Curiosity prevented Angusel from ordering Gawain to relinquish it. His upraised eyebrow invited an explanation.

"You might not be welcome to celebrate among your people, but nobody said you can't join me." Gawain deployed the thin wooden slab to preserve the tablet's marks, stowed it and the stylus in his knapsack, and crossed his arms through the straps. "Come. I've arranged for a pair of lusty lasses to wait for us."

Angusel surrendered with a tight grin, praying that the Breat-anach passion-fire activities would purge his mind of . . . the other women.

EILEANN AND the other virgins danced around the central Belteine fire. Her heart throbbed to the drumbeats, and her falcon-feathered ceremonial robe conspired with the flames to roast her from the in-side out. Each glimpse of her betrothed, his broad, oiled chest glim-mering in the firelight and his grin widening at her, ignited flames of an altogether different sort.

Throwing back her head, she leaped and spun harder.

For her final appearance in the Ruidhle na Righinnean, she would deliver a performance worthy of remembrance by the gods them-selves.

A priest's blast on the aurochs horn ended the dance. Eileann halted in front of Iomar of Clan Rioghail. Another year, this might have been considered a surprise; a virgin ready to alter that status at Belteine was free to choose her mate, who often received no advance notice.

No surprise registered in Iomar's gaze, of course, only intense de-sire.

He gathered her into his strong arms and fastened his lips to hers, stealing her breath and making her crave what he had to offer.

Gently she disengaged. "We must greet the mothers first, and partake of the blessing of new life."

"I know." He nipped at her neck, making her arch and gasp. "By this time next year, you shall be one of them." His confident prophecy sent a wave of heat sweeping through her body.

He slipped his arm around her waist and guided her toward the line of pregnant women that had formed nearby. Every woman, mother and virgin alike, was regarding Eileann, who as àrd-banoi-gin held the honor of being the first virgin to greet the mothers. She smiled at the man she had chosen to receive the gift of her virginity and become her life partner, who would help her fulfill her duty to ensure the continuity of Tarsuinnach leadership by begetting many heirs.

Iomar's lopsided grin reminded her of a young man whose outcast status made him forbidden to her as a mate.

Eileann stumbled and might have fallen against the first pregnant woman if Iomar hadn't lunged to steady her.

"Are you all right?" His concern throbbed in his tone and through his fingertips on her arms.

She apologized to the woman and slid Iomar a shy look. "Mayhap a wee bit nervous."

The woman giggled. "I'm thinking your husband has the remedy for that, my lady."

Eileann hoped that Iomar possessed the remedy for her thinking about Angusel too.

CHAPTER 12

$\mathcal{G}$ULL STRODE BESIDE Elian, trying to recall when the auld boar had walked so fast. It made him wish he'd dragged Elian to meet Lili's companions moons ago. Dockside shops, inns, taverns, gambling dens, and warehouses fell behind them in a blur of color, punctuated by the brisk step-*thock* of the centurion's tread on the cobblestones and his cheerful whistling of a ribald drinking tune about seven Sasunach sisters, each more lusty than the last.

Training recruits these past sennights had repaired Elian's self-confidence, and Gull was glad of his role in it. The grueling schedule helped Gull keep his mind off Angusel, and he was glad of that too, truth be told. A parent could worry only so much before it exacted a steep toll.

He was gladder that he and Elian were on their way to their favorite watering hole on this sennight's day of rest, though their primary reason for visiting the waterfront tavern—and earlier the whores— was to keep recruits from trouble that lurked in the off-duty hours.

Before their destination hove into view, Elian pulled up short.

Gull couldn't stop fast enough and jostled Elian's arm.

"Hey! Mind your course, dead Pict!"

Gull grinned, wondering when the epithet had become an endearment. "Then give a ghost a wee bit o' warning next time. Why did ye halt?"

Elian pointed at a trading vessel flying the Black Boar of Clan Móran—"Moray" in the Breatanach tongue. Crewmen leaped ashore, and shipmates tossed them ropes for winching the vessel into place. Watching the proceedings amidships stood a lovely lady, guarded by a glowering warrior. Both their cloaks—hers edged in gold and his almost as fine but plain—sported the Black Boar too.

"Ho, Lady Morghe!" Elian gave a grand wave, which the woman returned, and he abandoned Gull to greet her.

Curious, Gull followed.

The first passenger off the ship was a wee lad new on his legs, tugging on his father's hand and leaning forward like a hound straining at the leash, whilst his mother struggled to keep pace. Both parents lugged bulging knapsacks. The man bore a larger pack strapped to his back.

As his feet touched the dock, the lad surged and broke his father's grip. Whooping with triumph, he careened toward Gull, ignoring his parents' dismayed, "Eoghann, no! Come back!" They exchanged grimaces and rushed after him.

The lad shook his head, his little legs and arms pumping in furious rhythm. He missed spotting a loose board, tripped, and smacked headfirst onto the planking.

Gull dashed to his side and righted him. The tyke looked stunned, and his forehead already had sprouted a fair purpling knot. As his parents neared, he broke into a loud wail. Gull scooped him up. That set the howling boy to flailing and kicking. Gull held him at arm's length.

"So sorry, sir," said the father in gruff Breatanaiche, reaching for the lad. Gull felt thankful to deposit the squirming dervish into the man's arms.

"Nae harm done," Gull assured him as the mother joined them to coo over the struggling child, fingering his knot. Gull patted Eoghann's shock of carrot hair. "Ye be a brave one, mo laochan."

Movement of the lad's limbs and torso ceased. Between sniffles he gave Gull a puzzled stare.

"It means 'my little hero' in the tongue of my people," explained Gull to the trio, selecting "hero" rather than "champion" as a word he thought the lad might have heard.

Eoghann's high kick came with a squeal and a joyful grin.

A pair of tiny blue doves adorned the boy's bare heel. Gull knit his eyebrows.

Caledonaich gave children of the clan's àrd-banoigin such tattoos, but just one clan in Caledon laid claim to the pair of doves in flight.

Loholt, son of Chieftainess Gyanhumara and Arthur the Pendragon, alive? With Móranach guardians? Answering to the name Eoghann?

Before Gull could decide which question to voice first, the lady Elian had hailed and her companion jounced down the gangplank. Gull and Elian watched as the warrior steadied her while maintaining his balance. The pair traversed the distance and avoided mishap.

The woman appeared to look past Elian and Gull, a satisfied smile adorning her face.

Gull followed the line of her gaze in time to glimpse Loholt and his guardians disappearing into the crowd.

He could have flogged himself to fire-ravaged Ifrinn and back.

Elian would be hearing about his suspicions later; Gull knew not whom else he could trust and was thankful he hadn't blurted anything.

"Gull, I am honored to present Lady Morghe." The auld boar's cheeks flushed and he gave her a deep bow. "Please forgive me, *Chieftainess* Morghe."

Beaming, she pushed his shoulders until he straightened. "My dear Elian, it is so good to see you looking fit and fine. I'm sure Urien will be pleased to hear of it too."

Elian grunted, which seemed an odd response to Gull, who resolved to inquire about it later. He clapped Gull's shoulder. "My lady, I present Gull of Caledonia, my assistant for training recruits. And my closest friend."

Tucking a stray auburn lock behind her ear, she stepped closer to Gull and extended that hand. Gull grasped her fingers and kissed them. A wave of lust smote him. The wave receded when he let go, thanks be to all the gods. Being a tiller of another man's field was the fastest way to get oneself plowed under. He'd never conceived of such an act in his life—or death. Bowing, he gave his head a slight shake.

"I am right honored to meet ye, Chieftainess."

"The honor of meeting a man possessing such a fine way with children is mine, Gull of Caledon," she said in flawless Caledonaiche. Before Gull could quirk an eyebrow, she swept a graceful arm toward her escort. "And this is Lord A—"

The name ended in a loud "Ah!" as an arrow embedded in her chest. She staggered into the warrior. A dark red blot encircled the wound and grew at an ominous rate.

A second arrow tried to finish the work of the first, but Chieftainess Morghe's escort had lunged to shield her. The arrow deflected off his scale mail and shaved splinters from Elian's oaken leg.

"Find that archer!" the warrior roared.

Gull presumed the man had meant the command for him; Elian had pressed in close to the chieftainess, and Gull already had spun to start the hunt. A blur of movement on a nearby warehouse rooftop caught his eye. He ran after it.

SUPPORTING MORGHE'S head and shoulders on his lap, Accolon watched the old Pict sprint at ground level to pace the archer fleeing across the rooftop. The pair vanished beyond the end of the warehouse, and Accolon stared at Morghe. Her eyes were scrunched shut, her breath came in short pants, beads of sweat dotted her brow, and her face was whitening by the heartbeat.

Urien was going to flay him alive.

There didn't appear to be a second assassin. He and Elian shared a nod, and the centurion ordered the crowd to stand back. To the crippled man's credit, not one person dared to disobey.

"You," Elian said to a young man whose rigid bearing proclaimed him to be one of the off-duty recruits. "Bring medics!"

"Aye, Centurion!" The man thumped a quick salute and veered toward the fortress at a dead run.

Morghe groaned and swatted at the arrow. "Get it out!"

Accolon caught her hands, shaking his head. "You might bleed to death. I can't take that risk. The medics will—"

She gritted her teeth and damn near crushed his fingers. "You be the medic." Her grip and jaw relaxed, but her eyes remained tense. "Please."

Elian had sacrificed strips of his tunic. He shoved them at Accolon and knelt to pin Morghe's shoulders. Accolon stared at the centurion, panic clawing his gut. "This is no different than field dressing a wounded soldier." Elian glowered. "Do it, man!"

A soldier was the absolute last association he'd ever make with Morghe, but it did help a little. He drew his dagger. By no small miracle, his hand didn't shake as he lowered the point to her shoulder. "Chieftainess, I need to enlarge the wound to expose the arrowhead's barbs. Are you sure you don't want to wait for the medics?"

She inhaled a long, gasping breath. "Go ahead," she whispered.

Elian tightened his grip on Morghe. Accolon, grimacing, made the first cut.

HE'D PAY for this exertion later, of course, but running down the assassin proved easier than Gull had expected. Aye, the man had led him and a gaggle of soldiers on a fine chase through the alleys and twisted passageways of the port's seedier environs, having to abandon the rooftops when he outran his cover from the soldiers' spears and arrows.

What the assassin—or the soldiers, for that matter—didn't know was that Gull could be harder to shake than the killing pox, and just as deadly.

With a burst of speed and a powerful lunge, he collared the assassin and dragged him to the ground. Battle rage drove his fists and feet to pummel the man into oblivion.

"Halt, sir!" Gull stopped midswing, panting hard, and craned his neck at the decurion. "We need him alive for questioning." The officer's firm tone carried an apologetic note.

A glance at the captive revealed the bloody, bruised face, his eyes swelling shut. Gull shook his head and relaxed his aching fist. He shook it too. His reactions made no sense. As a master warrior, he should have subdued the assassin without resorting to crude, mindless violence.

Committing mindless violence upon the cù-puc who had damn near killed Chieftainess Morghe had been his sole urge.

Rubbing the sore fist, he shook his head again.

"Sir? Are you not well?" asked the decurion as his men secured the captive.

Gull grinned at the officer. "Nae thing that a stiff draught or three willna cure, lad."

He hoped.

"WHERE AM I?" came a faint voice from the bed.

Accolon had accompanied the medics who'd borne Morghe to the Port Dhoo-Glass infirmary. The physician had studied Accolon's handiwork, pronounced it good, gave him a sack of bandage rolls and salves, and suggested that she recuperate at the fort for a week. Accolon leaned in to swab her glistening brow. "The fortress. Prefect Conall's quarters. You're safe."

"The assassin?"

"Caught. Interrogated." Accolon allowed a brief smile to relieve his worry. "Dead."

"Who was he?"

"A Saxon who believed he had targeted Gyanhumara."

"God." Morghe struggled to rise but gave up, uttering a groan. "What is it with that woman and this damned spit of an island? The last time, she and I became caught up in an invasion that could have gotten us both killed."

Sighing, she closed her eyes. It made her look so fragile, so vulnerable . . . so desirable . . .

A sharp shake of the head arrested the thought. Yet it couldn't prevent him from saying, "I'm glad that didn't happen. Either time."

She cracked open one eye and gave him a sardonic look. "Are you, now? What does that mean, Accolon map Anwas, best friend of my husband?"

What, indeed?

Her lips parted. Her tongue flicked out, licking them.

He should resist the tacit, tempting invitation. But he was a dead man for letting her get injured. He may as well take a memory of heaven into hell.

Hovering his face a finger's width from hers, he whispered, "This day, Morghe ferch Uther, I am no man's best friend."

"Only this day?" She feigned a pretty pout, but an instant later the corners of her mouth quirked upward.

"This is the only day that matters to me."

The hand of her good arm grasped a fistful of his tunic and pulled him the rest of the distance. Her kiss was just as demanding. He matched its force. While staying clear of her injured shoulder, he slipped a hand beneath the coverlet to discover that she wore the bandage and nothing else. It covered one breast, but its twin he tweaked and teased until she gasped—and not from pain.

She tugged at the laces of his trews.

His hand stilled, and he pulled back.

Annoyance dominated her expression. "Urien and I laid together last night."

"Two nights ago."

"What? I've been asleep that long?" She probed the wound until the pressure made her wince. "That's why the pain isn't as sharp as I expected." Her grin reformed. Upon his thigh she began inching light spirals inward. "Two days or three, it matters naught. If I conceive, I won't know who the father is."

"Are you sure that's wise?"

"You and he are not so dissimilar in appearance. He aims to build a dynasty and will accept any son I bear as his." The grin faded, the spiraling stopped, and her gaze became unfocused. When she regarded him, the look was sharp and shrewd. "By the time more traits manifest, it will be too late."

"One of us will be dead?" His gut writhed. He knew damned well which of them it would be.

Her gaze softened. She combed the fingers of her good hand through her hair and used it to reel him closer. He couldn't resist. "My lord Accolon shall do well to remember that as chieftainess, I wield the power of life and death over those who look to me."

She guided his hand to fondle her nethers. He couldn't resist that command either. The way she arched and moaned excited him as no woman had done, and he quickened his sweet assault.

When she yanked his laces' knot the second time, he helped her strip off his trews and loin-binding linen. She opened to him, and—mindful of her wound, which she seemed to have forgotten—he buried himself to the hilt. In no time she had him bucking and gasping past the capacity for reason. He felt supremely pleased to make her buck and gasp a fair bit too.

He might doubt her ability to protect him from Urien's wrath, but this . . . ah! Ah, *this* would be one damned fine memory to cherish for an eternity in hell.

IN SPITE of the steel and leather that armored her from the neck down, Camilla felt naked as she strode beside her father, King Ælle, traversing the length of Wintaceaster Hall, flanked by King Cissa's royal guardsmen.

The West Saxon nobles' gazes seemed fixed upon her, brimming pity.

Not only had that demon-queen Guenevara killed the man she loved, but Camilla's attempt to exact revenge had failed in the most humiliating way imaginable: as a thwarted attack on the wrong woman. The Dragon King's sister, no less.

Her cheeks burned afresh from the memory of her father's wrath ignited by Ymyl's report. It was a miracle that Ælle hadn't removed her from command of the Cymensora garrison, and a bigger miracle that she'd convinced him to accompany her here, to request King Cissa's help.

She and Ælle reached the platform where Cissa sat upon his throne, and they dipped their heads. Cissa mirrored the gestures and bade Ælle to state his business.

"*Our* business," said her father with a pointed glance at her, "involves raising an army to attack the Dragon King and his consort, Guenevara of Caledonia. We invite our royal brother-in-arms to share in what shall surely prove to be a profitable venture."

"So." Cissa stroked his gray beard, a grin forming beneath his piercing gaze. "When subterfuge fails, a direct approach is sought."

Camilla wanted to crawl into the nearest hole.

"What we seek," said Ælle, "is to right a wrong—a wrong perpetrated against yourself, as well as against my daughter, in the murdering of your late brother's son."

Cissa regarded them for so long that Camilla believed she should look for a bolt hole. That marble tile looked promising. Perhaps she could pry it loose . . .

He rose and invited them to his private reception chamber. The guards that had conducted her and her father into Cissa's presence accompanied the party. At the doors, Cissa ordered his men to wait outside.

Cued by the king's entrance, thralls appeared through doorways to adjoining rooms. They bore food and drink, which they arranged upon the table before retreating. Meanwhile, Cissa stared at a deerhide map of Brædæn nailed to the timber ribs of one stone wall.

Ælle and Camilla helped themselves to wine goblets from the table and joined him. Camilla pressed the last goblet into the hand of her almost-uncle-by-marriage, and he thanked her.

Cissa tapped a scarlet X in the crook of a river forming a boundary of blue-marked Eingel territory. On Saxon maps, scarlet represented holdings controlled by or allied with the Bræde Dragon King. This particular X sat two score and five miles south and east of the Dragon King's largest fortress.

"The White Fort?" Camilla dared to ask. Ælle gave her an annoyed look. She kept her focus upon the map.

"Caer Gwenion in the tongue of the Brædeas," Cissa confirmed.

She asked, "What has that Brædan stronghold to do with our venture?"

"Perhaps nothing, my dear. Or everything." Cissa sipped his wine and gave her an indulgent smile. "It depends upon whether Caer Gwenion's chief, Melwas, a trading partner of mine, hates Arthur and Guenevara as much as we do."

Camilla shrugged. "He's a Bræde. Of course he's allied with Arthur."

"There are alliances . . . and alliances." This time when Cissa tipped his goblet to his lips, he took a long draught. "I shall make discreet inquiries regarding the firmness of Melwas's association with Arthur.

I expect an answer in a fortnight. You are both welcome to stay here until then if you wish. The news shall determine which course of action we shall take next."

Camilla noted the *we* and broke into the biggest grin she'd felt in weeks.

"Thank you!" She hoped the kiss she planted on Cissa's bewhiskered cheek conveyed the full depth of her appreciation.

A campaign into northern Brædæn would require months of planning and staging, perhaps even years. But she saw Cissa's participation as a sign that the gods favored her cause.

She couldn't lose.

CHAPTER 13

NGUSEL TROTTED STONN away from the straw target, flexing the soreness from his shoulder and letting the soldiers' whistles and lauds tell him that he'd scored a perfect hit.

"That's how it's done, lads." He rejoined them and halted Stonn. "Form a single line, and each of you have a go."

The men did as he bade them without so much as a curled lip, and one by one they sped off to fling their javelins at the target. In between casts, ala drudges removed the spent weapons from target or turf and ran them to the starting line while Angusel offered the soldiers suggestions for improving their approach, aim, and timing.

That the five turma decurions were practicing the drill made his chest swell, but when Centurion Cato stepped up to the line for a javelin, Angusel's jaw dropped. He clopped it shut.

The centurion grinned at him. "Can't have my men learning a tactic that I haven't mastered."

"Aye, sir." What to say to a man who'd spent more years in the legion than he had walked on this earth? Angusel drew a breath, praying for wisdom. "Be patient, gauge the distance, mind your mount's speed and course, heed your instincts, and throw it as hard as you can."

The centurion saluted Angusel with the javelin and pricked his horse's flanks to send him leaping toward the target.

To say that Angusel's unofficial training sessions with Drustanus and Gawain had been noticed would be like saying hot dung stank. Their commander sacrificed his evening free time to join them, offering suggestions, participating on rare occasions, but most often observing in silence from behind the fence. He'd demonstrated particular interest in the javelin drill, which the Caledonach alae practiced constantly since it was a fundamental battle tactic for them. The mainly Breatanach First Ala was trained to run the enemy through using leveled spears, a tactic Angusel was pleased to learn; he could see combining both in mounted combat. Breatanaich never used javelins.

Until today.

"A fine cast, sir!" he said as the centurion trotted his horse to the line. Though two hands wide of center, the strike's height was good. In battle it might mean missing the intended mark but felling an adjacent enemy. "Practice will improve your aim."

"Indeed, Cato," said a deep male voice behind him. "Well done."

Angusel knew that voice and fought his gut's churning as he guided Stonn to face the newcomer.

"Lord Pendragon!" He hated how shrill that must have sounded and cleared his throat as he thumped fist to chest. While Centurion Cato completed his salute, Angusel said, "I'm sorry, my lord, I didn't see you—"

The Pendragon raised a finger. "Cato, the Angli raids on Lothian and neighboring Caledonian lands are intensifying. I'm resuming the campaign."

Angusel recalled that the Pendragon's Angalaranach campaign had avoided a military disaster when it almost launched on an erroneous report. Then the pox hit headquarters, and the Sasunaich attacked Maun. It had taken the legion nigh on a year to rebuild.

"First Ala stays to defend headquarters, sir?" The centurion maintained a level tone, but Angusel detected disappointment and shared the sentiment. That aspect had been part of last year's plan.

Whatever answer Arthur would have given was forestalled by a courier approaching them at a full gallop. The optio reined his mount shy of plowing into them, dipped into a pouch slung across his chest, pulled out a wax-sealed parchment leaf, and thrust it toward the Pendragon.

Consternation wrinkled Arthur's brow as he took the message and read it. "Give this to Comitissa Gyan," he said to the courier, returning the parchment. Angusel tried to ignore the jealous twinge at the Pendragon's easy use of her name. "Tell her to prepare for leading all alae except the First and Sixth to the Senaudon staging area. The Comites Praetorii will of course accompany her. Sixth Ala and the remaining centuries shall guard headquarters under Merlin's command."

After the courier saluted and spurred his horse toward the praetorium, the Pendragon faced the ala. "I've been summoned to Caerglas for an emergency meeting of the Council of Chieftains. First Ala accompanies me. You shall escort Chieftainess Ygraine to Caerglas too. Pack your battle-gear and two days of rations. We leave within the hour."

THE COUNCIL of Chieftains, the northern Brytoni body that possessed no governing authority per se but which met during times of crisis, owned no set meeting place. When Ambrosius had held the office of Dux Britanniarum, and clan alliances were as complex and fragile as spiderwebs, the chieftains met at whichever military installation was most convenient for the man requesting the meeting, for the added protection a garrison of neutral soldiers provided. In the early days it could be any garrison, but over time the list of host sites dwindled to the largest installations along the Antonine and Hadrianic walls for convenience of lodging and of transportation via the centuries-old but well-built and maintained Roman roads.

Ever since Arthur's first meeting of the Council of Chieftains—the debacle four years ago that had nigh degenerated into civil war over who would succeed Uther as Dux Britanniarum—he hated attending them.

Oh, the meetings' reasons were valid: crop failures, plagues upon people or livestock, assassinations, raids—the latter two sometimes perpetrated by one member clan against another, for covetousness and greed were not confined to the non-Brytoni races competing for land across the Isle of Brydein.

Arthur gave a grateful grin to Bedwyr, who joined him and his three-man escort from an intersecting street as they strode toward the Caerglas praetorium's audience hall. "Did Bann call this emergency meeting?"

"My father is here," Bedwyr said, "but no. Lammor is quiet, thank the gods—or as quiet as it gets."

"Good," Arthur said.

This meant Chieftain Bann would officiate, rather than being the one presenting the problem. After the death of Cai's mother, Arthur and his foster brother, Cai, had finished growing to manhood in Bann's household, but they had been close friends with Bedwyr for as long as any of them could remember. Arthur admired Bann as a pensive leader whose devotion to a cause was absolute once he decided to join it. In fact Bann had exerted more influence regarding Arthur's election to the Pendragonship than any other man present.

Perhaps this meeting of the Council of Chieftains wouldn't prove to be the usual waste of his time.

"Does your mother know what's going on?" Bedwyr asked.

"No." He and Ygraine had discussed various possibilities during private moments while First Ala had escorted them here, but they had drawn no conclusions. If Clan Cwrnwyll had been presenting today's problem, they'd have been meeting at legion headquarters.

In addition, the Caerglas locale ruled out Loth—whom Arthur did not expect to see this day, as busy as he must be with Angli raids—and Melwas of Caer Gwenion. Melwas's youngest son had failed the legion's initiation test a few months ago, and although Arthur had tried to minimize the shame by extending an invitation for the lad to try again in a year, Melwas sent a scathing letter complaining about the "insult." Arthur had let Marcus craft the response; he owned neither the time nor patience for smoothing feathers ruffled by petty grievances.

The sobering fact remained that Melwas's territory could get overrun by an aggressive Angli expansion too. Arthur would not let that happen no matter who wore Clan Gwenion's mantle of chieftain-ship.

They reached the praetorium's double doors. Angusel and Gawain stepped ahead to open them for Arthur, Bedwyr, and Cato. Arthur expressed his thanks and preceded his men into the building.

There could be an issue with his brother-by-marriage, Alain, who was married to Arthur's older half sister Yglais. Alain stood to assume the chieftainship of Clan Cwrnwyll after Ygraine. In the meantime he governed Caer Alclyd, a modest but strategic fortress, and its shipping business and lands near Caerglas.

Arthur paused while Angusel and Gawain shoved open the audience hall's doors. Alain having a problem didn't make sense for two reasons: he didn't have a voting seat on the council and therefore was not empowered to call an emergency session, and Yglais was diligent about informing Arthur of important events at Caer Alclyd.

That left . . .

"Morghe!"

Every head in the hall swiveled toward Arthur.

His youngest sister was elegantly attired in her husband's Clan Moray gold-trimmed black, which lent stark contrast to the white bandage binding her shoulder and pinning her arm to her chest.

Protocol be damned!

He strode to the bench where she was seated, ignoring the angry stares garnered by his interruption. Urien and his adviser Accolon flanked her. Neither man looked pleased by Arthur's approach.

Arthur ignored them too and went to one knee at Morghe's feet, clasping the hand belonging to her uninjured arm.

"What happened? How much pain are you in?" He felt his concern slide toward anger. "Urien didn't—"

Morghe laughed, extricating her hand and waving it in a graceful if dismissive pattern. "Of course not. He prefers his ballocks where they are." She beamed up at her husband, cheerfully oblivious to the shocked murmurs skittering around the chamber. "Truth be told," she whispered, winking, "so do I."

Arthur stood while doing his best not to conjure the image of her and Urien in an intimate setting. "An accident, then?"

She tapped her chin. "That is one description."

"A Saxon assassin attacked my wife," Urien growled, "when he had been ordered to target yours."

"What!" This from Angusel near the back of the hall.

Arthur glared at the lad, who flushed. He said to Morghe's husband, "Details, please, Chieftain Urien."

Urien stepped into the center of the gathering. "This is in fact why I have called this meeting: to seek retribution for this grievous and wrongful injury upon my beloved wife. Camilla of the South Saxons— no doubt acting under the authority of her father, King Ælle—had set out to attack Chieftainess Gyanhumara on bad information regarding Gyanhumara's travel plans, and Morghe fell victim instead. She could have died!"

The noise from the other chieftains, which had been growing louder during Urien's speech, reached vehement proportions by the time he had finished.

No surprise there. Arthur would have joined them if he could have afforded to let his self-discipline slip any further.

Chieftain Bann rose from his bench to face Urien. He lifted his arms, and the crowd quieted.

"My lord Urien, we share your outrage, and we agree that this wrong must be redressed. But our troops are committed to the Angli campaign."

"Damn the Angli! They can wait! The Saxons need to be punished now!" Urien's coloring was rising toward a dangerous shade of red.

"Then I wish you good hunting, Urien," said Arthur. "I can fight but one war at a time. Most of the legion is at Senaudon. Upon my arrival there, after this council meeting is concluded, we march to Dunpeldyr. To pull them back a second time will doom Clan Lothian." *And my other sister and her children!*

He could have saved his breath.

Urien repeated his anti-Saxon sentiments louder and angrier. Once he had garnered agreement from a majority of the chieftains, he said to Bann, "I demand a vote! It is my right as a member of this council!"

Chieftain Bann, who had seemed prepared to grant Urien's request, stared toward the far doors, sympathy cascading over his countenance.

Arthur faced about.

And damned protocol for the second time to rush over to his sister Annamar and her two youngest children, Medraut and Cundre. All three looked bedraggled, weary, and fearful, and it wrenched Arthur's heart to its roots.

Annamar collapsed against him, sobbing, and he held her while the little ones and Ygraine and Gawain and the rest of the family, including Morghe and Urien, clustered around them. "Loth?" Arthur whispered to Annamar, hating the expected answer. "Is he—"

She dabbed her nose with a cloth. "He lives. And fights. Gareth too. As—as far as I know." Her chin trembled, but she set her jaw. "Loth sent us to Caer Lugubalion a week ago. You and Mama had departed for this meeting, so we came here straightaway." Ygraine, her own expression teetering on collapse, leaned in to stroke Annamar's arm. "I-I think—that is, I'm fairly sure that—that—"

Thrusting a fist to her mouth, Annamar jerked her head aside. Ygraine gathered her firstborn into her arms. Gawain hugged them both.

"Dunpeldyr may be under siege by now, Lord Pendragon," said one of the warriors who had accompanied Annamar and her children. "We need your help!"

"You shall have it." Council's permission or no, Arthur would find a way. He looked toward Chieftain Bann, who met his gaze. "My lord Bann, I suggest the council take that vote now."

CHAPTER 14

EILEANN CLUTCHED THE basket of smoked salmon as she angled across the compound toward the wise-women's isolated broch, making sure that no one paid her heed. And why should they, she assured herself. She often brought gifts to the clan's purveyors of womanly wisdom.

This salmon would represent not charity but payment.

Eileann reached the broch's outer door, tugged it open, and slipped inside, thankful that her mission hadn't been questioned. She did not wish to raise the clan's hopes just to dash them if the confirmation she sought proved to be naught but a vagary of nature.

Waiting to greet her, holding a taper to ward off the gloom, stood the trio's most recent inductee, a young woman known as "Spring Water."

"Ah, Fioruisge, well met." Eileann knew her birth name, of course, but out of respect for the wise-women's traditions, she kept it to herself.

The woman dipped her head. "We were expecting you, my lady."

She strode toward the inner chamber.

Expecting me?

Eileann swallowed and hurried after her.

The heart of the broch was a chamber well known to her, but its dizzying array of pelts, feathers, beads, herbs, dried meats, wax-sealed jars containing the gods alone knew what manner of salves, potions, and simples, and every cooking, cutting, pounding, serving, and stirring implement imaginable provided a constant source of wonder.

The biggest wonder: how the women could find anything in the clutter.

Fioruisge set the taper in a wall sconce and placed Eileann's offering on a sideboard.

Sgeir, whose alias meant "Rock in the Sea," the oldest of the three after the passing of Fioruisge's predecessor, Fairge, stood at a table near the hearth, kneading bread dough, her cane propped close. Sian, living up to her namesake "Wind Storm," bustled from shelf to shelf, examining jars and vials, and now and then removing one to join the growing collection on an adjacent table.

Sian's grouping—items that included pungent juniper and fragments of cones from the rare Ròmanach stone pine trees that grew outside an arena far in the south of Breatein—comprised what was needful for preparing a body for burial.

Sgeir was making a loaf to sustain the soul on its journey into the Otherworld.

Eileann felt her eyes stretch wide. "Who has died?"

A lump grew inside her that had naught to do with her primary reason for this visit. Her husband and father were leading the warband to investigate reports of an Angalaranach incursion onto Tarsuinnach lands. Her sister, eager to be blooded in combat, had gone too.

Sgeir laid a cloth on the dough and left it to rest, snatched her cane, and tottered to Eileann. "Time aplenty for that, my lady." She probed Eileann's belly and glanced at her companions. "The exalted heir-bearer indeed be with child." That the crone had divined the purpose of Eileann's visit came as no surprise, but her elation withered before Sgeir's stern but sad countenance. "Lady Eileann, we must talk."

Her bony fingers gripped Eileann's elbow to steer her to the nearest willow chair. Eileann sat. Sgeir pointed a look at Fioruisge and thence to the kettle steaming from the hearth pole. The young woman retrieved cups from a shelf and poured a round of the aromatic, pale green brew.

In serving Eileann, Fioruisge caught her foot against a stool and stumbled. Boiling tisane slopped onto Eileann's arm. She yelped and jumped to her feet, sucking the burn. Fioruisge stammered a mortified apology. Sian rushed over with a salve pot and pried Eileann's arm from her mouth.

Her clan-mark, the Tarsuinnach Falcon, signifying her status as àrd-banoigin, had flushed a livid shade of red.

Sian slathered on the salve and rubbed it in. The pain abated, but the redness worsened.

The three wise-women exchanged looks that were not encouraging.

"What does this mean?" Eileann tried not to sound as panicked as she felt but wasn't sure how well she succeeded. "Please—I know you view the tiniest broken twig as significant. Tell me, please!" A painful twinge flared in her belly but receded.

Sgeir heaved a sigh.

A stone-muffled commotion seeped into the chamber. Eileann took it to mean the clan was welcoming the war-band home. Of a sudden, she had never wanted to see her father and sister and husband so acutely.

Over the women's protests, Eileann dashed from the chamber. When Fioruisge gripped her wrist, she yanked free and surged out the door.

In the corridor, the shouts grew louder and transformed into lamentations.

Eileann burst out of the broch and into the worst hell she could imagine.

The war-band had returned, to the last man.

Not half were alive.

Horses bore their fallen riders lashed to their backs, led by the survivors.

Fist to mouth, Eileann hitched her skirts in her other hand and sprinted toward the wave of mothers and wives and sisters searching for their menfolk. Some reunions were punctuated by relieved whoops. Others ended in a flood of tears.

Eileann found her father in the midst of the bedraggled troop, sitting as tall in the saddle as his wounds would allow. They did not appear life-threatening, thanks be to Nemetona. Her sister, Rionnag, rode beside him, her armor bloody but not breached, as near as Eileann could tell.

Rionnach was leading Iomar's horse. Iomar's throat had been slashed.

Eileann's gut twisted.

Her father halted the band, and he ordered the warriors to dismount. Dynann raced over to throw herself into Rionnach's arms.

While Rionnag held the reins, Eileann dropped to her knees beside Iomar's horse, her face level with her husband's. Her fingers trembled as she reached for his face. She tried to summon thankfulness that the enemy had left her this mercy. Pain knifed her gut. Willing it gone, she forced herself to trace the eyelids that would never open, the lips that would never kiss hers ...

Pain ripped through her like the sword wielded by a ro h'uamhasach, that most terrible of battle-frenzied warriors who stabs and slashes and hacks at his foes until nothing remains but a mass of bloody flesh.

"Eileann!"

Who had spoken? Her mother? Her sister? One of the wise-women? Eileann couldn't tell through the merciless pain.

She threw back her head and uttered a great keening howl, powerless to stop it, even to inhale, until she collapsed, sobbing, in the dirt.

GULL AND a leather merchant were haggling the price of a new pair of plain but tough bracers—constant wear obliged Gull to replace them faster than a warrior ought—when stern shouts, gleeful squeals, and frightened yowls distracted him. Across the square, a woman chased her wee son, who had dashed after a cat.

The lad's hair was a familiar carrot hue.

While keeping the family in sight, Gull concluded his business, paying mayhap a bit more coin than he should have. He set off across the market square, buckling his new bracers in place as he walked, his pace and heading designed to appear purposeful without betraying his intentions.

The child's furry target raced between the wheels of a stationary handcart. The lad tried to dive after the cat but misjudged the cart's height and cracked his head on the sideboard. The cart shifted. Its rare glass vials and bottles tinkled as if trying to decide among themselves whether to fall and break.

Dazed, he reeled backward, palm to head and chin quivering.

The handcart's owner looked nigh as stunned as the child. The gods alone knew what that glassware housed, but in his travels Gull had seen perfumes and expensive salves come in such pretty containers.

The merchant kicked a pebble after the fleeing cat and then started fingering his handcart's contents. Gull stooped to examine the child. A knot had begun to form in about the same spot as before, if Gull's memory proved sound, but he seemed otherwise unhurt.

Loholt—*Eoghann*, Gull corrected himself; he dared not risk making a slip to alert anyone that he knew the truth—waited until his "mother" had arrived, panting and gasping and fuming, before throwing back his head and wailing as if tomorrow would never come.

"Hush, now," Gull crooned in Breatanaiche. "'Tis nae as bad as all that, mo laochan."

Eoghann, sniffling, wiped his face on his tunic sleeve and cocked his head toward Gull, who offered him an encouraging smile.

"Thank'ee, good sir," the woman said to Gull, looming over them both. "This one's a hellion, and no mistake." She gripped Eoghann's wrist and wrenched the lad away from him.

Gull stood and laid a hand on the woman's. "He's a good lad." He gave that hand, which was holding the boy's wrist, a strategic pinch, suppressing his satisfaction when her fingers loosened and Eoghann's lip stopped quivering. "He just needs a boatload of love, and two boatloads of patience."

The woman snorted. "And how many children have you raised, then?"

He couldn't help but smile. "One son." He nodded at the boy. "So verra like him in temperament."

She dipped her head in a parody of respect and stalked toward the street that angled through Port Dhoo-Glass's inland gates.

Eoghann twisted around to wave at Gull. "Good lad, good sir," the boy crooned as the widening distance made each word softer than the last.

As Gull gave an answering wave, he vowed to help this child however he could.

He directed his attention to the handcart, examining a few vials and asking the vendor about the perfumes' scents, while keeping the woman and the lad in his peripheral vision until he judged the time right to follow them.

FOR THE first time in a year and a half, Angusel was returning home.

To his birthplace, he corrected himself. "Home" had become a barracks chamber.

He marveled that Stonn seemed to remember the lands surrounding Senaudon, tugging at the bit and prancing higher by the league. It took Angusel's last mote of skill to keep his stallion from bolting down the path ahead of the Pendragon and Centurion Cato.

And why shouldn't Stonn be eager? He had the comforts of a familiar stable awaiting him, not scorn.

Angusel straightened in the saddle, submerging his resentment. Whatever might happen, he would comport himself as one of Arthur's soldiers, stoic and reserved.

That plan worked until the troop rode to within hailing distance of Senaudon's gate tower.

His mother chanced to be standing on the battlements, talking to Saigarmor, the guard captain. As Centurion Cato identified the troop, Alayna's face clouded. She had to resent the Breatanach occupation force—swelled tenfold for the second time in as many years by the soldiers being staged for Angalaranach action—but it seemed to Angusel that her scowl deepened when she made eye contact with him.

Angusel squared his shoulders and looked straight ahead as he'd been drilled countless times to do, thankful for the military protocol to mask the wound rending his heart.

Peripheral vision told him that Alayna had departed the battlements, leaving Saigarmor to act on her behalf in completing the welcome.

Arthur dispatched a soldier to find the Comitissa Britanniam and ordered First Ala to dismount and lead their horses to the staging area's picket lines while he wheeled Macsen about to join his family's litter.

The cavalry troop obeyed but hadn't advanced a score of paces when Alayna appeared, mounted, from through the gate and cantered straight up to the Pendragon.

"What is he doing here?" Angusel had never heard her sound so furious, and the pit in his gut confirmed that he was the *he* she had meant. He kept his gaze trained forward as he clenched Stonn's reins, mindful not to drag on them and hurt his horse's mouth. The heat in his cheeks and the sweat coursing down his back he did his best to ignore. "What gives you the right to violate Caledonach customs with such blatant disregard?" she demanded in Caledonaiche.

Arthur gave her a long, cool appraisal. "My soldiers are here upon my orders," he answered her, wielding an improved Caledonaiche accent. "All of them. If you have a quarrel, it is with me and no one else. Not even my wife. We can settle this quarrel, you and me, in the nearest combat ring and to the death, if that is your wish."

"My wish? You don't give a bloody damn about what I wish. I'll wager you can't guess what I wish!"

"That you had never underestimated me in the Battle of Abar-Gleann?"

Angusel heard the undercurrent of humor in the Pendragon's voice and pursed his lips to contain the smirk.

Alayna uttered a frustrated growl. As she reined her horse about, her frustration yielded to pity. Angusel risked a glance in that direction. Arthur's sister and her children were peering out from between the curtains of their litter, and the traveling had heightened the worry and sadness on their faces.

"Your kin?" Alayna asked Arthur.

He confirmed her guess. "Their home is under siege. They shall be staying in the encampment with Gyan and me until it's safe for them to return. We'll not trouble you any further than we must."

"Rubbish." That won her a surprised look from Arthur. Angusel's eyebrows raised too, but he flattened them before she could notice. "As you say, my quarrel is with you alone. If you take your kin to war, they will need a troop to guard them—soldiers who would be of greater use in stopping the Angalaranach threat." The pity dominating her face softened into compassion. "They look as if they could stand a spot of comfort, poor dears. They may shelter inside my fortress for as long as is needful."

Arthur regarded Angusel's mother long enough to have made her son squirm. Alayna stood resolute.

"Thank you, Chieftainess Alayna," said the Pendragon. "I shall not forget your kindness."

"I shall not permit you to, Artyr."

Angusel feared she might embarrass him by flirting harder than the coy grin she slid Arthur while uttering the Caledonach form of his name, but she took her leave and nudged her mount over to introduce herself to Lady Annamar and her children. After a brief exchange, which ended with Annamar expressing profuse thanks, Alayna instructed the litter's driver to follow her through the gates.

Alayna's son felt his chest swell because of her choices.

Before First Ala could resume course toward the picket lines, a figure emerged from the maze of tents and storage structures.

"Gyan? What has happened?" Arthur asked in Breatanaiche when she had walked close enough that he could keep his voice low.

Angusel studied Stonn's black mane, waving off the occasional fly, but he was too close to avoid hearing their conversation.

"Colgrim sent a force to attack a ferry port village belonging to Clan Tarsuinn," she said, also in Breatanaiche.

"A raid?" asked the Pendragon.

"Far bigger, though exact numbers are unknown. The clan"—she sucked in a long breath—"Chieftain Rionnach and his men repelled them, and most of the Angalaranach survivors escaped, but . . ."

Angusel dared to glance up. Her pursed lips couldn't conquer the quiver of her chin, and the Pendragon had leaned his face close to hers.

"Mo laochag," Arthur whispered, "let's finish this in private."

She blinked and touched her consort's cheek guard. "My headquarters tent, mo laochan."

Their innocent intimacy tore Angusel's heart. Keeping Stonn's reins slack, he clenched them till his fists cramped. The pain restored a dollop of reason. He forced his hands to relax, berating himself.

The Pendragon watched his wife's departure before redirecting his attention toward First Ala. He moved his head in a slow sweep. "Soldier Gawain," he said, "front and center."

Gawain led Arddwyn out of formation to approach his uncle and war-chieftain, whom he saluted.

"Change of plans, men," Arthur said primarily to Centurion Cato, though in a tone that carried to the ala. "I need a squad to scout ahead of the legion. Cato, select fifteen to twenty men from the First who are the most adept at fighting on foot. Your horses will not be crossing the Fiorth. Begin the mission by riding to Chieftain Rionnach's stronghold to learn what he knows about the Angli and to seek his assistance in moving the infantry cohorts across Clan Tarsuinn territory. I designate you as my emissary. Optio Ainchis Sàl can serve as your translator. I shall dispatch further orders depending upon your report of Rionnach's response. You depart at dawn." Arthur glanced at the men, appearing to make eye contact with several of them. "The rest of First Ala shall remain here with the Horse Cohort under the direct command of Prefect Peredur."

Angusel's disappointment surged as he noted that the Pendragon expected the scouts to leave their horses on the firth's north bank for the most perilous part of their mission—as well as Arthur's implication that he intended to leave the cavalry in reserve at Senaudon—but he knew better than to openly disagree with the army's war-chieftain.

And he knew better than to hope that Centurion Cato would select Drustanus as one of the advance scouts. He offered a swift, silent prayer that his friend would survive whatever the gods had in store for the First.

Centurion Cato saluted and made as if to reply, but the Pendragon raised a finger and shifted his gaze toward his sister's son. "Soldier Gawain, since of all men in First Ala you know Dunpeldyr's lands best, I promote you to the rank of optio and charge you with walking point to keep the scout squad clear of Angli patrols. Choose between one and three men to accompany you."

"Ainchis Sàl." Gawain grinned at Angusel. "He can be as annoying as that itch you can't ever reach, but his stout heart and clear eyes and strong arms are all the help I'll need."

"The unit's Caledonian translator?" Arthur knit his eyebrows. "It could put the mission at risk should he get injured or killed."

While Angusel mulled whether he could get away with speaking in his own defense, Gawain solved that problem for him. "When does an itch ever go away at the first scratch?" Gawain's grin yielded to absolute seriousness. "Ainchis Sàl can handle himself, sir, and his parade gear displays the phalera to prove it." He saluted Angusel. "Same as mine."

Angusel couldn't decide what astonished him more: Gawain's declaration, or the fact that it had made Arthur smile.

CHAPTER 15

ARTHUR WAS PLEASED that Gyan's tactic to force Gawain and Angusel to make amends had borne fruit, but the apparent mental state of the plan's author made his smile dim.

"Cato, arrange for the First to get remounts." Arthur saw the protests forming on Gawain's and Angusel's faces and added, "For those who want them. And see to the care of our mounts, then form the remainder of your scouting team. Optios, with me."

The three left their horses with soldiers, and they followed the path Gyan had taken, the widest avenue that had been established between tent rows in the staging area.

As the headquarters tent loomed into sight, Arthur pondered Gyan's demeanor. He hoped his brief smile had conveyed his silent promise that he would comfort her later.

He needed answers first.

Having witnesses they could both trust—witnesses who might well need whatever information she could impart—ought to help. He hoped.

Two features distinguished the headquarters tent from the rest of its mud-drab counterparts: its massive size and the dual dragon banners of the legion and the Comites Praetorii providing blazes of color at its entrance. A contingent of legionnaires commanded by a blue-cloaked Comites Praetorii centurion, Bohort, ringed the tent. Six, counting Centurion Bohort, guarded the entrance. Bohort and his men snapped salutes.

"No disturbances," Arthur told the centurion.

"Understood, Lord Pendragon."

Arthur beckoned Gawain and Angusel to follow him into the tent.

Gyan had rigged a curtain inside, presumably to cordon the sleeping chamber from the work area, for he saw only a large camp table, several rough stools, and apparatus for storing her armor. Her helmet sat straight on its pike; she had not been wearing it when she had walked out to meet Arthur and the ala. Her breastplate sprawled over its support frame at a haphazard angle as if she had yanked it off and thrown it there.

"Gyan?" Arthur called, not loudly.

She emerged from behind the curtain's slit, wearing her leather battle-leggings and padded, sweat-darkened undertunic, scrubbing a cloth across her face. After making eye contact with Arthur, she parted the curtain and tossed the cloth into the sleeping chamber.

Her eyes were puffy and red.

Arthur crossed the distance in three strides to circle his arms around her. She sagged against his chest. "What's wrong, my love?"

She sucked in a long, uneven breath. "My cousin Iomar fell to Angalaranach treachery."

"No!"

That outburst came from Angusel, and Arthur glared at him. The lad grimaced and glanced away. Gyan stared at her fingers tracing the embossed dragon on his breastplate, circling and circling and circling like they didn't know when to stop. He gently entrapped them. She struggled a bit before surrendering with a sigh.

As he asked her what happened, he heard Gawain behind him ask, "Angalaranach?"

"Angli," said Arthur and Angusel together.

"Sorry, sir," Angusel murmured.

Arthur let it pass and repeated his query to Gyan.

She sighed. "Iomar was such a good man. I might have made him my consort, if it hadn't been for . . ." She sighed again. "For you, Artyr."

It was so very unlike Gyan not to answer a direct question that Arthur curbed his swelling impatience by trying a different approach. "What was the nature of the Angalaranach treachery? Infiltration? Night raid? Poisoning the water supply? Ambush?"

His last suggestion made her straighten and look at him.

"They raided a Tarsuinnach village on the south bank of the Fiorth and torched a few buildings. But instead of leaving with their plunder, the michaoduin hid amongst the corpses. When Iomar and Chieftain Rionnach and the rest of the war-band arrived to investigate, based on the report of one of their ferry captains who had chanced to see the smoke, the Angalaranaich sprang their trap. The Tarsuinnaich drove them off, but the cost . . ." She shivered and chafed her arms.

Mother of God. He hated to press Gyan in her state, but he had to know: "How many, besides Iomar?"

"Half the war-band, dead or too maimed to fight."

Arthur grimaced. The next attack would obliterate that clan.

She hissed in a breath through gritted teeth, puffed her cheeks, and blew it out. "And Eileann lost her bairn. A girl-child . . ."

Her sobs erupted into his chest. He held her close, stroking her hair. Part of him felt bloody useless; another part knew better, and he hugged her tighter as her tears ran their course. Behind him he could hear rustling canvas and hurried footsteps. His young officers had departed without permission, but he could not have cared less.

"I DON'T understand," Gawain said as Angusel bent double and gulped air to fight the rising nausea. "Women lose babies, and life goes on. Who is this Eileann to you, anyway?"

"You are not Caledonian." The nausea abated, and Angusel trusted himself to straighten. He leveled a glare at Gawain. "I do not expect you to understand."

Gawain had pulled the tent flaps shut, but the muffled sounds of the Comitissa's grief filtered through, and it wrenched Angusel's heart. His powerlessness to comfort her wrenched it worse. He ground his knuckles into his chest. The scale armor blocked relief.

He needed air and distance to rein in his emotions, but since they had left without the Pendragon's permission, they'd be wise to stay close. He elected to walk the tent's perimeter. His choice drew a curious stare from Centurion Bohort, but whatever the officer saw in Angusel's expression made him keep his questions to himself.

The same could not be said about Gawain.

"Then explain it to me. Sir."

"Don't call me sir. You're an optio now, same as me."

As they strode wide of the tent's pegs and ropes, Gawain tapped his bone dragon badge. "Won't look right until I get an iron one of these. Sir."

Angusel stopped and turned so abruptly that Gawain almost stumbled into him. "You're going to annoy me into telling you, is that your plan?"

"Yes, sir. Whatever it takes. Sir."

"Whatever it takes"—Angusel mimicked Gawain in a girlish pitch, then lowered his tone and eyebrows—"to shut your damned gob. Eileann nic Dynann is her clan's àrd-banoigin." He summoned the Breatanach words to explain the concept: "That is, their line of succession proceeds from her. Caledonians prize their girl-children, and for the àrd-banoigin's firstborn to be a daughter is considered the greatest of divine boons."

Gawain's dawning comprehension became eclipsed by a grimace. "So, for her to lose the baby girl is a curse?"

Angusel knuckled his gut.

"I wish it was that simple," he whispered.

GULL CAST his gaze about the barracks chamber, but the lone item of value he possessed, besides his battle-sword and armor, which were stowed in the armory, was pinned to his cloak: Angusel's gold lion brooch.

Soon, if the gods felt inclined to be kind, he'd be giving it back to his brogach, and the lad could again wear it with the pride he deserved.

The familiar step-*thock*, step-*thock* alerted him that his plan for slipping away undetected was about to be thwarted.

"Where in hell are you going, dead Pict?"

Gull slung his knapsack, which he'd stuffed with his spare tunics and undergarments, over one shoulder and faced his best friend. Elian stood upon the threshold, the setting sun glinting off his metal-clad shoulders, his fists planted upon his hips.

"I've business at headquarters." He tried to shoulder past Elian, but he may as well have tried to shoulder past a sacred stone. He barked a shin on that thrice-damned wooden leg. The pain's jolt forced him back a pace. "Let me pass, if ye please."

"I do not please. And you do not need your every earthly possession for a jaunt to cohort headquarters, so I presume you intend to sail to Caer Lugubalion."

Gull scratched his jaw. He'd need to retrieve his armor and sword before boarding the trading vessel upon which he'd paid for passage to the larger isle.

"And what if I am? As ye are so fond of saying, 'tis none of your cac-lickin' business." His second surge for the doorway got denied too.

"Of course it's my business. You are my assistant." Elian's severity thawed. "And my friend. I would like to know what's making you bolt." He cracked a grin. "If you please."

Gull sighed out his frustration, placed his knapsack on the floor, and asked Elian to shut the door. The centurion complied. Gull made sure he was standing as far away from walls and windows as possible, and beckoned Elian to within whispering distance.

"I have found an important boy-child. One who is most dear to . . ."

Elian's eyes narrowed. Gull tapped the man's copper dragon legion badge. Those eyes widened. "Are you certain, man?"

"As certain as I am of how much hurt ye can do to a body with that great treenail ye walk upon."

Gull toed the "treenail" in question but got no response from the mild tease other than:

"Where is he?"

"A crofter's hut near the fort. His guardians visit on market days and bring him along. I followed them home a few days ago."

"Hmph." Elian stumped to his cot, eased onto his good knee while bracing a hand on the frame, and dragged his knapsack from beneath the bed. As Gull watched in stunned disbelief, he rose and made his way to the shelves they shared. He began stuffing the knapsack much as Gull had done with his own spare clothing.

"I donna need your help, auld boar," Gull insisted.

"Like hell you don't, dead Pict. How else do you think you'll get past the guards at headquarters? That devilish silver tongue of yours?"

"There willna be guards at Angusel's barracks."

Elian stopped in the middle of folding a tunic. "So you plan to tell him and not the real parents, to give him the chance to redeem himself to them. Fine idea. But you need someone to vouch for you at the fort's gate."

That aspect, in fact, he had not worked out, and he thanked Elian for the solution. The centurion's company, however, posed a different problem. "How will ye disengage from your duties here?"

"With the truth, of course." Elian held up his hands and uttered a short laugh. "A version of it that won't cause the quarry to bolt if the wrong thing gets overheard by the wrong person. I shall tell Prefect Conall that my assistant—and best friend—needs my help to resolve a personal matter that is no one's cac-licking business but ours."

Gull stooped to retrieve his knapsack, grinning for the first time since conceiving this plan.

EILEANN LAY bundled in the furs piled on the dirt floor of the wise-women's broch, where she had remained night and day with the brief exception of attending the rite to send Iomar and the other war-band members to their new lives in the Otherworld.

She had stopped feeling the floor's hardness or the cold. The pain in her womb—though she still bled from time to time—had disappeared. She had gone numb since that awful day when she had lost husband and bairn in one terrible, divine stroke.

Nothing mattered, not even the passage of time. In the window-less broch, Eileann knew it was night only by the soft snores of its other occupants.

The wise-women insisted that she was staying with them so they could attend to her healing, but she knew the truth in her throbbing gut.

An àrd-banoigin who lost her firstborn daughter could not be trusted to ensure the clan's line of succession.

The elders, priests, Sgeir as leader of the wise-women, and her parents had been debating her fate for days; no one had said as much to Eileann, but she could sense it in Sgeir's tension. While there existed no formal declaration in Caledonach law stating that an àrd-banoigin so cursed must undergo a sacrificial death, it was not a rare occurrence either.

Eileann could not understand why it was taking this long. The solution seemed obvious: she could renounce the position of àrd-banoigin in favor of her sister, Rionnag.

Mayhap they had decided that bit and were debating whether Eileann should die for the good of the clan.

She freed her arms from the furs. With the fingertips of her left hand, she traced the tisane-reddened Tarsuinnach Falcon. The skin felt tender.

A thought smote her. She sat up.

If the others couldn't reach a unanimous decision about her fate, she would make it for them.

Cold sweat trickled down her spine.

She sucked in a long breath, held it, and puffed it out. By this time her eyes had adjusted to the gloom, and a quick glance around the broch affirmed that all three wise-women were asleep. She pushed aside the furs, shrugged into her overdress, slipped on her shoes, and rose.

After groping through the clutter, suffering a rush of panic each time she bumped into a chair or scuffed her foot on the gods knew what, she found the door and eased herself out. In the long passageway leading to the outer door, she wished she could have lit a torch but had to make do with trailing a hand along the stone wall.

The predawn chill, once she had won free of the broch, reminded her that she had forgotten her cloak.

No matter; she could do without the hindrance.

She set her course by the glow emanating from the Sacred Flame housed inside the clan's open-air temple across the compound.

"My lady?" murmured the priest on duty. "Why are you abroad at this hour?"

Eileann glanced toward the graying eastern skies, wondering the same thing herself. "I—" The flames snapped and danced in a mesmerizing, menacing pattern as if daring her to proceed. She rubbed her arms, less from the air's coolness than from her chilling will. "Priest Giuthas, I need your help." She brandished her tattoo. "With this."

His hesitation spoke volumes. A sacrifice had to remain in perfect condition to be accepted by the gods.

If her death was right for the clan, why did the idea feel so dreadfully wrong?

She lunged past the priest and thrust her arm into the Sacred Flame.

Giuthas yanked her away, but her arm was already a lurid shade of red and blistering. The tattoo had been reduced to a collection of disconnected lines.

The excruciating pain made her head reel.

She gritted her teeth, wrenched from the priest's grasp, and fled the temple, the compound, and the only home she had known. Blood roared in her ears and her lungs screamed for air, and onward she ran, past startled gate sentries and down to the river, where she found a small boat.

The dock was flanked by a pair of spears stuck into the ground. Each spear was surmounted by a ram's skull—a prohibition against continuing in that direction, whether by water or by land—and the boat was not unattended.

"Fioruisge! You—I thought you were asleep!"

The youngest of the three Tarsuinnach wise-women shook her head with a grim smile. "None of us were." The smile disappeared. "The gods have dispatched me to help you attain your destiny." She extended her hand.

Eileann didn't take it. "Is it my destiny, then, to die by drowning rather than by a priest's knife? Or will you impale me on one of those spears?"

"Don't be daft." Fioruisge dipped her head in apology. "My lady. The gods have decreed a more important role for you than being Tarsuinn's exalted heir-bearer."

More important than . . .? "What of the clan? Is not my blood required to expunge this curse?"

"The clan shall manage. But hurry, or the gods' plan may be thwarted by those who do not understand it."

Distant shouts emanated from Dùn Fàradhlann. The gods alone knew whether the spears would prove an effective deterrent. She let Fioruisge help her into the boat. Together they cast off its moorings, and as her injured arm raged its protest, she grabbed an oar to shove free of the dock. With Fioruisge at the tiller, the current took hold of the craft to commence its journey toward the roiling Ab Fhorchu.

Eileann's knees buckled from the immense wave of guilt: in spite of Fioruisge's claim to the contrary, denying the clan her sacrificial death might bring divine doom upon everyone she loved. She could not fathom a destiny greater than that of being her clan's àrd-banoigin, and Fioruisge's statement seemed ludicrous at best.

If she was fated to die for her inability to birth a girl-child, the gods could do as they pleased to this boat.

The oar slipped from her fingers and clattered onto the deck.

Surrendering to divine will, she collapsed senseless into the boat's stern.

SOMETHING WAS wrong.

Dùn Lùth Lhugh, "Fort of Lugh's Power"—called Caer Lugubalion in the Breatanach tongue and the Pendragon's home fortress—should have been bristling with soldiers who should have been admitting visitors through the opened double gates at a reasonable if cautious pace. And at an hour past dawn, a queue of carts and wagons should have already begun to form.

The main gates were shut tight as a granite coffin, traffic was light, the wagon drivers and carters who were not expected were being denied entry without appeal, including the kind wagoner who had given him and Elian a ride from the docks, and those not on foot were ordered to dismount before being searched and interrogated by but a token guard unit stationed at the one-horse-wide side gate.

Gull's battle sense sent its warning prickle down his spine.

When it became their turn, the auld boar produced from his leather satchel the writ he had obtained from Prefect Conall. The lead guard perused the sheepskin scrap with detached boredom. Of a sudden he squinted at it, looked up, and scowled at Elian and Gull.

"Says here to let you in to see the Pendragon."

"That's right, Soldier," snapped the centurion. "Do it."

"Pendragon's not here." The guard fingered his sword's pommel, and the two men behind him did likewise. A glance at the auld boar showed him bristling. The man released his weapon. He and his companions adopted respectful expressions. "Please come back after the war, sir."

"War?" Gull asked, suspecting the answer but hoping to diffuse the situation. "What—"

Elian glared at him before directing that withering look upon the guards. "I am Centurion Elian, Manx Cohort, and my companion is the man who captured a Saxon assassin dispatched to kill the Comitissa Britanniam. We have urgent news that cannot wait for the end of the war, news of a most sensitive nature. Conduct us to the ranking officer. Now."

The soldiers saluted so fast, Gull might have laughed if he didn't think Elian would have flogged him for the discipline breach. The auld boar answered their salutes with a brisk nod. The lead guard assumed escort duty after commanding his companions to remain at their posts.

The march across the fort's grounds was uneventful, save for an odd instance when a lad of mayhap a dozen summers stopped the horse he was lunging in a training ring to give Elian a hearty greeting. The centurion and the lad conversed at the corral's rail while Gull and the gate guard remained at a respectful distance. No doubt the auld boar appreciated the rest too.

"Who was that?" Gull asked after Elian had joined them and they resumed their journey. He harbored a suspicion that made him grin at his friend.

Eyes forward, Elian quickened his pace toward their destination, the impressive front of which was no longer obscured by lesser structures. "None of your—"

"Cac-licking business," Gull finished for him, grinning wider.

"Damned right, dead Pict."

He resolved to interrogate the auld boar in private.

They walked in silence past lush trimmed hedges, more flowering plants than Gull could count, and an odd, square pool being filled by a stone maiden whose jug never seemed to run dry. Odder yet, the pool did not overflow. He might have stopped for a closer look, but Elian and their escort paid the weird wee pool and its keeper no mind as they continued toward the wide steps leading to the ornate and well-guarded doors.

The soldier presented the writ Elian had given him, and the door guards approved entry. He passed the writ to Elian, who stuffed it into his satchel.

Inside the headquarters building, which looked as opulent within as without, Gull was astounded to recognize the officer the Pendragon had left in command, who chanced to be approaching the doors. There could be no mistaking his air of authority even if Elian and the younger soldier had not given him the smartest Ròmanach salutes Gull had ever seen. The man's hair had become a casualty of the relentless march of years, and his midsection had thickened a mite, but those shrewd, dark eyes hadn't dimmed; he could be none other than the same auld—

"Emrys. Well met, honored adversary." Gull inclined his head. Elian gaped at him.

"General Merlin, you know my companion?"

The officer Elian called Merlin stepped closer, stroking his clean-shaven chin. "I don't believe . . ." Comprehension banished his confusion. "Gwalchafed, as I live and breathe. You seem to be doing both, I see. Though I haven't gone by the name Emrys since Arthur was a baby."

"'Twas your name when last we met. In battle. Arthur had to be a lad of ten summers or so then."

"Indeed. That battle changed me for the better, I hope. Now I am called Dubric in our temples, and Merlin everywhere else. But tell me: What miracle has brought the most fearsome of Caledonian chieftains back from the dead to visit those who believed they had sent him there?"

"A miracle, sir," Elian said, glancing at the guard, "that must be discussed in private."

Emrys—Merlin—addressed the guard. "Return to your post. I shall conduct Elian and Gwalchafed to my workroom."

The guard saluted, spun, and left.

As they trod the corridor, Merlin asked Gull, "Does Alayna know?"

"Nay. And folk call me Gull."

He canted an eyebrow. "Angusel?"

Gull smiled at Merlin's use of the lad's birth name rather than the duty roster's version. "Aye; 'tis himself I'm hoping to see. With your leave, of course."

Merlin gave Gull a look he couldn't decipher. His long-ago enemy stopped in front of a guard-flanked door, and one of them opened it. He ushered Elian and Gull inside.

"That poses a problem, Gull." Merlin bolted the door, walked to his worktable, and thumped a leather-bound, fist-thick stack of sheepskin sheets. "Ainchis Sàl a Dubh Loch has gone with Arthur to war."

CHAPTER 16

ANGUSEL KNELT UPON the rush-strewn floor of Dùn Fàradhlann's feast hall, wondering whether Chieftain Rionnach would welcome him as an emissary of the Pendragon or dismiss him as a Caledonach outcast. The rushes' tough stems pressed into the leather of his leggings beneath his knees, and he fought the urge to squirm under the older man's scrutiny.

Kneeling beside him, Centurion Cato—whom Angusel had introduced in Caledonaiche as "Cato, son of Majora, leader of one hundred men in the army of the High-Chief Great Fire-Beast" despite the fact that not one man in five had made this journey—seemed as composed as ever. Angusel marveled at that, since the Caledonach rite of welcome required that he and his commander make a show of disarming themselves. Gawain and the rest of the scouts waited, under guard and disarmed, at the rear of the hall.

"If you have come to help us defend against the Angalaranaich," the chieftain said, "you are too late. And too few in number to make a difference."

Rather than trying everyone's patience by having Angusel act as interpreter, Cato had decided prior to this meeting's commencement to give Angusel leave to speak on his behalf.

Buoyed by that faith and bridling the instinct to show offense at the chieftain's defiant choice of words, he drew a deep breath. "Artyr the High-Chief Great Fire-Beast does wish to help—"

"By providing men?" Hope bled through the chieftain's tone.

Angusel hated to disappoint the Pendragon's ally, but he had no choice other than the truth: "By taking the battle to the Angalara-naich."

"He must need our help," said Chieftainess Dynann, "else he would not have sent his emissaries to us." On her lips, the word *emissaries* teetered on the edge of insult. "Perhaps he does not know what we have suffered from Angalaranach treachery."

"He knows, my lady, and he grieves for those losses." This won him a hard stare from Dynann, a disbelieving snort from Rionnach, and mutters from other Tarsuinnaich. Cato's eyebrows lowered. Angusel reached a tough but necessary decision. "Chieftainess Gyanhumara"—he surprised himself that he didn't stutter the name he had not uttered for nigh on a year—"of Clan Argyll grieves too, especially for the loss of Clan Tarsuinn's exalted heir-begetter and ill-born exalted lady-heir. I witnessed her tears. They were genuine."

"Were they?" Chieftainess Dynann rose from her tall-backed chair and descended the dais's steps to within a sword's length of Angusel. Had her glare been a weapon, she'd have impaled him. "Did Chieftainess Gyanhumara grieve for our clan's exalted heir-bearer too?"

The raw emotion in her tone killed the response Angusel had been tempted to make.

Rionnach circled his arm around her, and she sagged into his embrace.

Angusel's eyes widened. "Lady Eileann is . . . dead?" He whispered the last word.

Dynann's eyebrows twitched, and she gave Angusel a curious, measuring look.

"Lady Eileann," Rionnach said in a flat tone, "is with the gods."

Mayhap not dead, then, but—

Rustling fabric in the third chair on the dais caught Angusel's attention. Ink adorned the sword-side forearm of their youngest daughter: the Tarsuinnach Falcon upon reddened flesh.

Bile seared his throat. He swallowed it and grimaced. Rionnag had replaced her sister as Clan Tarsuinn's àrd-banoigin. Eileann's whereabouts he dared not ask.

"Optio, report." Centurion Cato's crisp whisper wrenched his focus back to the mission. "Do we have leave to present the Pendragon's proposal?"

Angusel repeated the question in Caledonaiche to Chieftain Rionnach, adding that the proposal would include material benefits for the Tarsuinnaich too.

"Material benefits—meaning coin?" Rionnach asked.

"Aye, my lord," Angusel replied, "in exchange for provisions and the hire of as many ships as Clan Tarsuinn can spare to ferry troops to the south bank of the Ab Fhorchu."

"That is well, then, for the accursed Angalaranaich have caused us to ground our ships along its north bank at our busiest time of year." Chieftain Rionnach's countenance thawed as he extended his sword arm to the centurion. "Cato, son of Majora, you and your men are well come to Dùn Fàradhlann, seat of Clan Tarsuinn." The men gripped forearms. Cato retrieved his sword and rose. As the chieftain assisted Angusel to his feet, he said, "Tell Cato's men that they may share the clan's morning bread and ale while the four of us"—he nodded to his wife, Cato, and Angusel—"repair to my private chambers to discuss the Pendragon's proposal."

Angusel had never felt more relieved to obey.

MERLIN COULDN'T believe what his former—and formerly dead—enemy was telling him.

He strove to keep his voice low. "If this is a ruse, I will personally send you to hell for it. And I will do whatever is necessary to make sure you stay there."

Elian almost spewed the uisge Merlin had offered both of them. The centurion thrust a fist to his lips and coughed.

The man now calling himself Gull chuckled. "Same auld Emrys.

Ye always did have a blustery mouth. Mayhap our last dance didna change ye much a'tall." He made a show of draining his cup in a single pull and thunking it on the nearby table.

Merlin's face heated, but he finished his uisge and poured another round. "My apologies, Gull. That was uncharitable of me, and I ask your forgiveness. But please understand that the people most affected by this news are dearer to me than anyone else on earth." True enough, considering the potential impact on Niniane too, but he'd banish himself to purgatory before spilling that secret. "How can you be so certain of the child's identity?"

"He be the only person alive to bear the marking I saw."

"It could be an accident of birth, or fabricated"—he couldn't help blurting what the shade of Emrys lurking in the back of his mind suggested—"to create an impostor, perhaps."

Gull growled, but Elian shot him a look, and the Pict desisted.

Clearing his throat, Elian straightened in his chair. "General Merlin, I have lived and worked beside Gull for the past year and have known him nigh twice that long. He might on occasion choose to keep the truth to himself—"

"His death, for example."

"Yes, sir, but I have never heard him utter false information."

Gull nodded at Elian. "I have nae reason to lie to ye, Merlin, and the most important reason in the world—helping my son—to be giving ye the truth of this matter. I canna mistake what I saw." His lips quirked a wry smile as he raised both hands, palms out and fingers splayed. "Trust a man having this many years' experience in being dead to recognize another in likewise state."

As Gull lowered his hands, Merlin returned the smile. A host of sobering reasons, however, killed it.

"If this child is who you claim, then we must act now. We don't know who arranged his abduction and fosterage"—though Merlin had formed a compelling, if unprovable and therefore unshareable, suspicion—"and we could lose him. But since he's living in territory controlled by a man who may be but a paper ally . . ."

"You mean my kinsman who left me to rot on Maun without so much as a single copper mite in my begging cup because he knows how loyal I am to the Pendragon?" Elian snorted and retrieved his uisge for another swig. "That ally, sir?"

Taking a swallow himself, Merlin buried his gratitude that Elian had not raised his voice or mentioned Urien by name. Believing that one could not be overheard was never a wise assumption. He put down the cup. "I can't send men to extract the child. Killing that ally's clansfolk would give him the excuse he's been itching for to sever diplomatic ties with Arthur. That territory remains a critical strategic position for the legion. Losing the ability to station troops there is a risk we must avoid." A risk that nauseated him to the pit of his gut, given that Niniane refused to accept a transfer to a priory on the main island, as he had suggested countless times.

Gull stared out the window. "I ken why Angusel canna lead the rescue," he said in a subdued tone, "and it pains me to wonder if he shall e'er earn his redemption. But if I were the father of that dear wee lad, I'd be wanting him plucked from that vipers' nest as fast as the gods could will it." He snapped his head around, a lopsided grin much like his son's banishing the worry. "I can help ye plan the snatch, Merlin, if ye can find it in yourself to trust your auld enemy."

Merlin shifted forward in his seat. "Plan—what, exactly?"

"That depends upon whether ye believe that I can make men besides myself appear to be aught than what they seem." His expression became shrewd. "And if ye be the same auld Emrys who killed me the first time."

"Meaning?" The man who had striven to drown Emrys's violent, carnal past in a vat of holy water was beginning to fear that those long-ago sins might never die.

"One can do much with a wagonload of prisoners slated for execution, providing said prisoners form a goodly mix of Scáthinach warriors and Breatanach traitors."

Merlin had conversed with Chieftainess Gyanhumara and her countrymen often enough to recognize the Picti terms for the Scotti and Brytoni people. And he had concocted intrigue often enough, as Emrys, to recognize Gull's implied suggestion to use condemned men of both races to stage a fake Scotti raid—complete with bodies sporting the correct armor and weapons—to mask Loholt's extraction while making Cuchullain appear to be responsible.

He fingered his chin. "A dead man devising the rescue of a dead child using dead men. There's something one doesn't hear every day."

Elian's cheeks bulged to keep from spewing his uisge a second time. He swallowed it hard and coughed harder. Gull slapped his back until the centurion swatted him.

The hell of it: the more Merlin pondered Gull's idea, the more he liked it, since it could yield the bonus of setting Urien and his Scotti ally at odds.

The greater hell: Emrys would have proposed and executed this idea with cheerful abandon.

"What do you think, Centurion Elian?" He hoped his subordinate could offer a reprieve from this madness. "Will prisoners cooperate to make a staged raid look real enough to shift the blame and direct attention away from the target?"

Elian's gaze seemed to grow unfocused, then it sharpened. "You could make the guards' jobs easier, sir, by telling the prisoners that they are going to be released into the custody of Scotti emissaries. Said emissaries could be our men dressed to look the part." The eighteen-year combat veteran who had begun his career serving Arthur's father gave Arthur's cousin an earnest look. "That would be a plausible reason for 'raiders' to land on Maun's western coast. Under cover of darkness, of course—or as much of it as can be had at this time of year."

"Aye. And as for the auld boar's kin learning the truth, with luck that could take weeks," Gull said, "if ever."

None of that allayed Merlin's qualms. "You're asking me to promise men their freedom and then betray them to reunite one child with his parents."

"One important child," Elian said.

"And parents ye claim to care for above all other souls," Gull added.

All souls save one, and how would she react to this scheme? A pain in Merlin's head throbbed its answer. He rubbed the spot, praying for wisdom but hearing an echo of Emrys's cackling.

The greatest hell: he couldn't think of a plan bearing better odds of success.

"I'll approve that wagonload of prisoners, Gull. Tell me what else is required."

Gull's smile widened. Elian's eyebrows hitched up but lowered as he gave Merlin a nod.

CHIEFTAIN RIONNACH had ordered servants to bring extra chairs into his workroom, as well as bread and ale, but only his wife had chosen to avail herself of the comfort. The men remained standing.

"What else does the Pendragon require?" asked Rionnach.

"Any wisdom you wish to offer regarding the Angalaranaich at Dùn Éideann—"

"Wisdom?" Rionnach planted fists on hips. "That cannot be all Artyr wants of us."

Angusel squared his shoulders and tightened his jaw. "The Pendragon believes that the greatest chance of moving his army unseen lies in marching across Tarsuinnach lands to the ferry port at Caledàitan, thence by boats to the south bank of the Ab Fhorchu near Dùn Pildìrach."

In the translation for Cato, he substituted "Dun Eidyn" for Dùn Éideann, "River Fiorth" for Ab Fhorchu, and "Dunpeldyr" for Dùn Pildìrach. The Caledonach port town of Caledàitan had no Breatanach name, having never suffered Breatanach military occupation. For the same reason, neither did Dùn Fàradhlann.

Rionnach's shield-side fist curled around his sword's hilt. "You make it sound as if he seeks my permission to have my people's lands trampled by his men. How do I know he's not doing this selfsame thing as we speak?"

Angusel wanted to quip that the chieftain ought to confer with his own scouts but couldn't think of a tactful way to phrase it. "A moment, please, my lord." Swallowing panic, he relayed the question to his commander.

"Tell our honored ally that the Pendragon remains at Senaudon, awaiting my report of these proceedings, and he is prepared to accept Chieftain Rionnach's refusal." Cato gave Angusel time to translate that bit before adding, "However, the closer to Angli territory the legion is forced to sail, the greater the risk of Clan Tarsuinn suffering another attack."

Dynann stifled a gasp. Rionnach, arms crossed, held the pose long after Angusel had finished. "How many men?" he asked.

This Cato had discussed with Angusel while they had waited for the chieftain to grant their audience. "Three thousand, in groups of five hundred plus their retainers, two such groups departing Senaudon each day at dawn." Rionnach cocked an eyebrow. Angusel forged on, "The Pendragon plans to march with the first unit. All units shall keep to roads and cart tracks to avoid Tarsuinnach livestock and croplands. He proposes establishing a temporary encampment north of Dùn Fàradhlann at a site of your choosing, my lord Rionnach, so your men may monitor the troops' activities. This plan will allow each unit to reach the ferry port in two days."

"The Pendragon expects us to feed his three thousand men at this encampment, no doubt," muttered Chieftainess Dynann.

"Oh, no, my lady," Angusel said. "We travel with three days of provisions." Neither the chieftainess nor her husband looked ready to agree to Arthur's proposal. "If the legion can resupply at Caledàitan, the Pendragon intends to pay a fair price." He prayed that the briskness of his tone masked his growing despair that he might have failed.

Again.

Rionnach stroked his beard and cocked his head toward Centurion Cato. "What says your leader of one hundred men? Is all of this indeed the truth?"

Angusel translated the questions and their context for Cato, who gave the chieftain a sharp nod.

"What happens should the Angalaranaich attack us while the Pendragon is on the march through our lands?" asked Dynann.

"Or worse," said Rionnach, "what if we are attacked after the last of the Pendragon's men have left these shores? It's two hours from the north bank to the south using his proposed route, but the winds will be against him on the way back. That will double and mayhap treble the return crossing."

After hearing the Breatanach version, Cato instructed Angusel to say, "The Pendragon stands committed to protect all of his allies to the best of his ability. Should the worst come to pass, he shall send available troops to your aid as fast as possible."

Seeing hesitation written across these allies' faces, Angusel added, "This may sound like a vague promise, my lord Rionnach and my lady Dynann, but Artyr the Pendragon makes it a practice to do the honorable thing. This I know from personal experience. He could have believed his subordinate's claim that I had murdered a Breatanach herdsman without just cause, but he heard me out and chose to believe my account of the herdsman's traitorous dealings with the Scáthinach invasion commander."

"And he has chosen for you to remain in his service, even though your actions last year—actions resulting in the loss of his son—caused your banishment from service to the people of Caledon." Rionnach's tone was far from unkind, but his remark heated Angusel's face to the scorching point, and he looked down.

One day he might outlive that shame.

Centurion Cato asked him for the translation. The best he could bring himself to mutter was, "I recounted an incident from my past, sir, that I hoped would help our cause."

A light hand rested upon his shoulder. He snapped up his head. Chieftainess Dynann had risen to stand beside him. "Artyr chose wisely when he placed his trust in you." Her soft smile was so much like Eileann's that his heart gave an odd little lurch. "Angusel mac Alayna."

"Aye, lad," said Rionnach. "Tell Cato to advise Artyr that Tarsuinnach lands stand open to him and his men. I shall order our ships to be loaded with travel rations and other supplies, and muster at Caledàitan. Even if not all the vessels can unload that cargo right away, there should be enough available to transport a thousand soldiers and workmen in two crossings the first night. I recommend setting sail at one hour before midnight. With these short summer nights, the second crossing cannot complete before dawn, but it should stay dark long enough for the ships to avoid detection by Angalaranaich watching the firth from Dùn Éideann."

As Angusel rendered the chieftain's statement in Breatanaiche for Cato, he treasured Chieftainess Dynann's precious gifts to him: her affirmation, her smile, and her choice to address him by his birth name.

CHAPTER 17

ELIAN STARED AT the courser being held for him by Wart. The dead Pict sat astride his mount, damn him, as easy as if he'd been born there. Behind Gull ranged the half-dozen mounted soldiers General Merlin had assigned as their escort for the three-day journey to Senaudon. Wart's grin held no trace of mockery, but Elian couldn't resist mocking himself.

Horses were a hell of a lot taller than he remembered.

"Get on, auld boar." Gull kept his tone low, but his horse's pawing reflected its rider's simmering frustration. Elian glared at the couple of soldiers struggling not to smirk.

"I told you," he growled at Gull, "I'd rather ride in a wagon."

"I would rather get to Senaudon afore the war is done."

The dead Pict had a valid point. Damn him.

Wart stroked the mare's cheek. She nuzzled his palm and gave an appreciative snort. "Melys really is as sweet as her name. She's fast but she won't give you a lick of trouble." He glanced toward the mounting block. "You can do this, sir. You're the best horseman I know!"

Knew. "If any of you laughs at me"—he glared at Gull first and longest—"I will flay you alive."

Wart's expression became a study in deadpan seriousness. The smirks on the soldiers' faces died stillborn. The dead Pict bared his teeth to rival a skull's grin.

Right, then.

Elian sucked in a breath and stepped onto the mounting block. The hollow *thock* echoed across the stableyard and reverberated in his gut. Wart, standing at the mare's head on her right side, played the reins out and shifted closer to the saddle.

As if a lad of twelve summers could catch the likes of him, with his peg leg and the wooden brains to match, but he appreciated the consideration.

He gripped the pommel horn closest to him. Wart grasped the horn on the opposite side as a counterbalancing measure. The horns that worried Elian most, however, were the two flanking the saddle's cantle that kept a rider from pitching backward. He flexed his left knee, hoping—praying—that he had enough agility in his crippled leg to swing it clear without hurting himself or the horse.

Gull glanced sunward. The sun hadn't crested the fort's walls. "Are we leaving or nay? I can change my mind if ye prefer."

Melys swung her head to regard Elian, blowing a sigh and blinking at him.

"Don't rush me," he muttered. "Either of you."

He berated himself for the hesitation. What was the worst that could happen?

A thousand possibilities leaped to mind, none good and all ending with a mangled ego in addition to any number of physical injuries. To say nothing of their severity.

He shook his head to bridle his imagination, shifted his weight onto his left leg, crouched, and prayed for a miracle.

As he executed the modified vault, the underside of his right leg, where flesh met leather-capped wood, caught the top of the farthest cantle horn. It made him land harder in the saddle than he should have. Pain lanced his groin. His peg thumped the mare's side. Belling a startled neigh, Melys bolted. Wart dropped the reins and leaped aside. Elian grabbed them, mindful of the mare's mouth as he adjusted his seating and brought her under control.

"Not bad, auld boar," Gull said. "How do ye feel to be astride after, what? A year?"

Not good either, Elian thought, but better than he'd expected. "More like two."

He guided the mare to walk a circuit of the stableyard, making sure to ride past the soldiers so they could get a good look at his form. When that maneuver posed no problems, he tried a trot . . . and regretted it as his peg kept smacking the horse's barrel no matter how hard he squeezed his thighs. He slowed her to a walk and halted her at the mounting block.

"Ye're not quitting, are ye? Ye just need a wee bit of practice."

"I don't know what you saw, dead Pict, but I damn near beat this poor horse to death." Elian leaned down to stroke her neck. "I am so sorry, girl."

He flipped the reins over her head toward Wart. He didn't dare look at their escort; pity was the last emotion he wanted to see.

The lad caught them, holding Melys steady as he gazed toward the stables. At length he regarded Elian. "I think I can help you, sir." He cast a nervous glance at Gull, who had dismounted. "That is, if you sirs don't mind delaying your journey."

"If it means getting this auld boar to move faster than my dead grandmother, I'll wait," Gull said, handing his horse's reins to Wart to add to Melys's.

Elian eased out of the saddle and onto the mounting block. "A wagon moves faster than your dead grandmother," he reminded his friend.

"Ye never knew my grandmother." Gull clapped Wart on the shoulder. "I for one look forward to your solution, lad."

Elian's curiosity bested his cynicism and he voiced his agreement. In spite of his less than stellar performance, it had felt good to be astride. Liberating. He said to the men, "Don't go farther than the barracks or mess hall. I will send for you when we are ready to depart. You can find Gull and me at the visiting officers' mansio." He hoped for Gull's sake that they wouldn't need to spend the night there too.

"Aye, Centurion!" their escorts replied in concert, saluted, and dismounted. Each soldier led his own mount toward the stables.

Elian tightened his jaw; they made those basic actions look so damned easy.

As a beaming Wart followed them, leading Melys and the horse Gull had been given for this journey, the dead Pict stepped over to Elian and offered his shoulder.

While not happy to accept assistance, Elian had to admit that his friend's support made it easier to lever himself onto solid footing. He hoped that whatever Wart had in mind would prevent further bruising to his horse—and to his pride.

ARTHUR KNELT behind Gyan, tightening the straps that secured her greaves to her shins. Not for the first time did he feel thankful that she had chosen to adopt his officers' habit of wearing greaves as an extra measure of protection over her boots, along with the hundreds of feather-shaped bronze scales stitched in overlapping layers onto her leather jerkin, a modification she had commissioned after assuming the duties of Comitissa Britanniam.

If she would let him encase her in metal from crown to sole, perhaps then he might stop worrying about her safety.

And perhaps then the sun might rise in the west.

"That's good. Thank you," she murmured.

Pivoting, she thrust her hands toward him. He gripped them and rose. She let go to throw her arms around his neck, pulling him close. Their mouths met with desperate abandon, tongues twining. He and Gyan were operating on stolen time, a fact verified by each shouted infantry order and thunderous response that slashed through the canvas tent's sides. Too soon, they finished the kiss. Her beloved face reflected desire and regret, tempered by frankness; emotions he understood well, for they tormented him too.

"Now to get you ready, mo laochan."

My little champion. Her favorite endearment for him never failed to make him smile.

It dimmed as she strode to the apparatus storing his armor and hefted his dragon-embossed, muscled bronze breastplate. The set of her jaw and hiss of her breath betrayed how heavy it was for her, but she wrestled it off its stand and brought it to him.

Any of the soldiers—hell, probably most of them—would have been honored to arm the legion's highest-ranking officers. But they had resolved to assist each other on this, the day he would lead the first infantry cohort on its two-day march to Caledàitan while Gyan stayed to oversee the other cohorts' departures. She would remain in reserve at Senaudon with the Comites Praetorii and the Horse Cohort.

After attaching his own greaves, he grabbed his linen stole while she unbuckled the breastplate's straps. As he finished wrapping his neck, he stooped a bit so she could lift his breastplate over his shoulders and tug it into place, delighting in the little furrow of concentration that developed between her eyebrows and the soft smile adorning her lips that deepened as she got each of its buckles threaded and cinched. Thanks to her expertise, the breastplate fit perfectly, and he told her so.

The flush of her cheeks acknowledged his praise.

His studded, fringed battle-kilt came next. When he would have donned it himself, she insisted on helping with that too. She made quick work of those buckles. A breath later, he understood why: her right hand reached past the fringes to leave a tantalizing trail of tingles along his inner thigh.

He had never felt closer to her, heartbeats before this damned war would wedge them apart.

From outside came the trumpet's report that the troop stood ready.

"I wish we had time"—Arthur couldn't suppress the sigh—"mo laochag." When she'd taught him the phrase's female form, *my little lady champion* replaced the heartfelt but less descriptive *my love* as his favorite endearment for her. God knew she'd earned it a thousandfold.

He prayed to God, Iesu, Mari, and every saint and angel he could name that he wouldn't need to make her earn it again by calling the cavalry to action.

"I know, Artyr." Failing to suppress her sigh too, she stopped branding his flesh and straightened. "I pray we will have time to spend together after this thrice-cursed business is done."

He captured her hands and brought them to his lips. "After we are done fighting, I'll give you all the time you could wish for."

His heart meant the promise to its core. His head asserted that their lives might not ever be that simple. Yearning and resignation warred in her eyes; he interpreted the expression as her believing his heart *and* his head. He gave her hands an extra squeeze before releasing them, as much to assure himself as to assure her that his head must be wrong.

Their last kiss—before buckling on their sword belts, pinning their cloaks in place, grabbing their gloves, and snatching their helmets from the pikes—silenced their fears . . . for the present.

THE SUN had dropped well past its zenith, and Elian had lost track of how often Gull had circled the mansio's dining chamber where they had eaten their midday meal, when Wart arrived, breathless from his dash, to report that he was ready to demonstrate his idea.

As Elian leaned for his bedroll and saddlebags, Gull pushed him straight. "We may be wise to leave those things here." The dead Pict gave Wart an apologetic smile, which the latter returned. "I meant no insult to you, my lad."

Elian sighed and spoke to the innkeeper about reserving a bedchamber. If they used it tonight, they might never get on the road.

They followed Wart to the stables. The lad beelined for the storage room, bade them wait outside, and emerged lugging the funniest contraption ever to contemplate gracing a horse's back.

Wart had picked apart the stitches in the leather covering the cantle's oaken horns to saw them down to half their usual height. The excess leather he had folded over each horn and sewn in place as extra padding. That wasn't the funny part.

The saddle blanket was crafted of the undyed, quilted fabric used for the tunic worn under armor. It extended longer than the typical saddle blanket on both sides, and similar modifications in length and thickness had been made to the saddle's padded thigh flaps; those weren't the funny parts either.

What made Elian slap his hand over his mouth was the boot that had been cut away in back and lashed, using the saddle's forward baggage stays and the boot's laces, to the saddle's right side.

All he could manage was, "What—what the hell?"

He regretted it the instant Wart's proud smile faded and his posture deflated.

"In the spring when we were training the older foals," he whispered, "I helped a soldier get to the infirmary. He'd been kicked real hard and trampled, and his leg broke. The physician cut his boot to set the leg. I asked for the ruined boot because, well, sir, even then I was thinking about you." The saddle drooped, as did his gaze.

Thought of laughter fled. Elian lifted the saddle off Wart's arms. "Lad, I am honored to try your creation."

Wart's stance and expression rebounded. "Thank you, sir!"

"How did ye e'en hear tell of Centurion Elian's injury?" Gull asked. "He was living on Maun till we sailed here."

Wart nodded at Gull but addressed Elian. "One day as I was preparing their horses for drills, I heard the Pendragon and Comitissa Gyan talking about ways they could help you. I asked what they meant, and she told me how you lost your leg in battle. Ever since then, I've been thinking about how I might help too, but I didn't know what to do until this morning when I saw you trying to mount."

Grinning to mask his awe, Elian ruffled the lad's tawny hair. "Let's give this a go, then, shall we?"

"Yes, sir!"

The shorter cantle horns were the key to helping him mount easier once Melys was made ready, her reins in Gull's hands; no bolting horse or pinched ballocks this time, thank God.

It felt odd to have Wart guide his peg into the boot, however. He tried to lift it out himself, either by flexing the remains of his right leg or by leaning to use his hand to move the peg, to no avail. The upper part of the boot's heel, creating a lip to keep the peg from slipping free, proved too tall an obstacle for Elian's liking.

"Sir, what are you doing? The peg needs to stay in the boot if you don't want to hurt the horse," Wart said.

"I know, but I need to be able to move the peg in and out myself," Elian replied. "It could get tangled if I fall, and Melys could drag me."

"Don't fall, ye daft auld boar," Gull suggested.

Elian shot him a glare that went cheerfully ignored.

"Right, sir." Wart rubbed his chin, staring at his handiwork. "I could cut down the ridge, but then we'd have to replace the boot if you don't like the lower height. Oh, I know!" He eased Elian's peg out of the boot, adjusted the straps and laces, and gave the boot a firm downward tug. "Try this, sir, without me helping."

Elian used his right hand to guide the peg into place. With the boot hanging a trifle lower, there remained enough of the ridge to keep the peg from bouncing free, but he found it easier to pull it out by himself. He moved it back into position, bade Gull to release the reins, and rode the mare through her paces around the stableyard. Even at a trot, the boot kept his peg stable.

It probably looked weird as hell, especially from the rear, but he couldn't have cared less.

He halted Melys in front of the pair and gave the younger of the two a wide grin. "Well done, Wart. But you know what this means, don't you?" Wart shook his head, looking worried. "I would like you to come along. Strike that; with heaven knows what might happen on the road, I need you, my lad."

The worry vanished as Wart mirrored Elian's grin. "Really, sir?"

"I'll speak to the chief groomsman. Pack three days' rations and personal items, and pick a horse that can keep pace with ours. We shall leave at dawn." Elian looked at Gull, shading his eyes from the sinking sun's glare. "Objections, dead Pict?"

"For you, auld boar, never."

"It's settled, then," Elian said to Wart. "Off with you!"

The lad rendered an excellent legion salute and sprinted for the barracks building nearest the stables.

The old boar couldn't remember when he'd felt this eager to start a journey himself.

CHAPTER 18

THE SITE THE scouts selected for the first marching camp lay across a series of fallow fields. Stakes marked an area that could contain tents for as many as two thousand soldiers and their support workers, should the Pendragon decide to speed up the march. A creek bordered one side of the fields, and the surrounding forests provided game and wood. The scouts also staked routes approaching and leading away from the marching camp to prevent the army from trampling crops or spooking pastured livestock.

Angusel couldn't quell his worry that the army might miss the markers. His gut churned faster as the noise made by five hundred soldiers and their attendants grew louder. When the Pendragon appeared in the expected location, glowering as he rode Macsen at the head of the infantry column, Angusel sighed the breath he hadn't realized he had been holding.

In the next breath he felt smitten by awe and, aye, truth be told, a touch of terror. This was no parade to impress folk. This was the army on its way to war, being led by the most terrifying commander Angusel had ever known, Caledonach, Scáthinach, and Sasunach leaders combined.

He had never felt gladder to be fighting for the Pendragon rather than against him.

Arthur raised his fist. The centurions marching behind him shouted the order to halt. Since Chieftain Rionnach and the scouts had remained mounted, Arthur did not dismount, and neither did his aide, Centurion Marcus. The Pendragon ordered Cato to give him and Marcus a quick tour of the camp's layout while Cato's men stayed with the infantry soldiers for a ration break. When Chieftain Rionnach joined the Pendragon, Angusel wondered if he would be summoned into service as interpreter before recalling that Arthur's command of Caledonaiche had become quite good.

He couldn't decide whether to be disappointed that his war-chieftain didn't need him, or relieved.

When the leaders returned from their circuit of the fields, the Pendragon praised the scouts' efforts. That felt more unnerving than a reprimand would have.

Arthur ordered his centurions to have their men commence building the camp and its perimeter defenses. After the centurions departed, the Pendragon, Chieftain Rionnach, and Centurion Marcus dismounted.

"I cannot thank you enough for helping my scout squad." Arthur gave the reins to Marcus and dismissed him to find a tethering spot for their horses until the guarded picket line could be established.

"You have good men under your command," the chieftain said.

"Indeed. I shall need the scouts to identify a second marching camp location near Caledàitan. Today, as soon as we are finished here." He had spoken Caledonaiche to Chieftain Rionnach, but he translated it in Breatanaiche to Centurion Cato, who had remained mounted. Cato saluted the Pendragon and ordered the scouts to mount. While they obeyed, Arthur addressed his ally, switching to Caledonaiche. "I have no wish to pull you from your duties, my lord Rionnach. Have you an adviser you can send to Caledàitan with my scouts?"

"Aye, Lord Pendragon. I have arranged for—"

The sound of hoofbeats made everyone look at a horse approaching them, whipped into a dead run by its rider. She slowed her mount into a tight circle around Rionnach, Arthur, and the others.

Chieftainess Dynann halted the horse, dismounted, and flung herself into her husband's arms. Raw anguish reddened her eyes and streaked her cheeks.

"My wife? What has happened?" The chieftain spoke with quiet gentleness, stroking her hair, but the underlying alarm rang clear.

"Eileann—she may b-be—" Her words dissolved into sobs muffled by Rionnach's chest. His arms tightened about her, but shutting his eyes didn't prevent her husband's tears from slipping free.

He sucked in a breath. "How do you know, Dyn?"

She scrubbed her face with both hands and took several breaths. "One of our fishermen saw a boat out on the firth, drifting seaward. It had but two women in it. One was working the sail and rudder. The other . . ." Her chin quivered. "Th-the other was laid out like—like a—"

Like a corpse, Angusel's brain finished. His heart ached.

"The man wasn't certain?" This from the Pendragon, who garnered several surprised looks, and for good reason. Most Breatanaich would not have deigned to involve themselves in a private Caledonach matter.

Chieftainess Dynann gave a slow shake of her head. "Oh, he was certain, Lord Pendragon. He sailed right up beside them and gave Fioruisge, one of our wise-women and Eileann's escort, a portion of his catch."

The death offering. Angusel shuddered. Stonn pawed the ground, blowing a soft snort. Angusel stroked his horse's neck, seeking comfort. The familiar warmth didn't help.

Pressing fist to chest, Arthur bowed his head longer than Angusel expected. "I am so sorry, Chieftainess Dynann, Chieftain Rionnach." His gaze, when he redirected it at Eileann's parents, appeared resolute. "If I may do anything for you, please name it."

Chieftainess Dynann glanced first at her husband, who dipped a nod, and then at Arthur. "I would like your permission to crave a boon of one of your officers."

"Of course, my lady." He beckoned to Centurion Marcus, who was returning from his horse-tethering errand. As the army's most senior centurion quickened his pace, the chieftainess pulled a fabric-wrapped bundle from her saddle pack. Arthur said, "My aide, Marcus, shall perform whatever task you require."

"That is most generous of you, Lord Artyr," Chieftainess Dynann murmured, stepping beyond Centurion Marcus, "but the officer best suited to this task—if he consents—is him."

She pointed at . . .

Me?

I am outcast. Clanless.

Unworthy.

Angusel tossed a panicked glance at Arthur. "Lord Pendragon?"

"You have my leave to do Chieftainess Dynann's bidding, whatever it might be," he said. "Rejoin the scouts after you have finished."

"Fioruisge has kin in Caledàitan, including the town apothecary." The chieftainess hefted the bundle and faced Angusel. "This is Eileann's traveling harp. Because she ran from her . . . obligations, we are not allowed—that is, I would l-like her to have it . . ." The renewed trembling of Dynann's chin stopped her, and Rionnach sidled closer so she could lean upon him. She hugged the harp to her chest.

Angusel's mind tripped on *obligations*. As he'd feared, the Tarsuinnach priests had planned to sacrifice Eileann.

Her death granted the michaoduin their accursed wish.

Her escape had robbed her parents of the opportunity to keen over her body.

Rionnach was saying, "—carry the harp to Caledàitan, lad, you may leave it with Neoinean, the apothecary." He caressed his wife's arms. "There is no need to search for . . . that is to say, we don't know Fioruisge's plans. We assume that she intends to buy burial spices from Neoinean, so you needn't wait for her. Them." The chieftain blinked thrice.

Like hell I won't wait.

"Of course, my lord and my lady." Angusel saluted them and bowed his head, much as his war-chieftain had done. "It will be my greatest honor."

While the chieftain took the harp and tied it to Stonn's saddle, Dynann reached for Angusel's nearest hand. "Go with the gods." She gave him another almost-Eileann smile. Her eyelids sagged under immeasurable sadness. "Both of you."

RIONNACH CALLED for volunteers to escort Dynann to Dùn Fàradh-lann. Every man in the chieftain's personal guard stepped forward. He chose two, gave his wife a kiss and a few whispered parting words, and watched the trio ride south until their forms disappeared past the tree line.

In the slope of the chieftain's shoulders, Arthur read the man's uncertainty. Having lost a child, he understood that hollowness too damned well. He had learned that getting back to the business at hand helped keep the despair at bay, but he bridled the urge to suggest the tactic.

Rionnach squared his shoulders, pivoted, and called to his side a warrior who, by his silver-trimmed ebony leather armor, Arthur judged to be captain of Rionnach's guard.

"This is my chief adviser, Piosan," said the chieftain to Arthur, though his gaze appeared to include the scout squad. "He shall oversee site selection for your second marching camp and assist in buying rations for your army. Angusel mentioned that your men carry a three-day supply, and I for one would not want to head into enemy territory with but a day's food in my pack."

Arthur gave a half smile in recognition that the chieftain had used Angusel's birth name; his ally could interpret the expression as he would. A potential problem, however, killed it: "Each of the legion's cohorts travels with its own war-chest, so payment for that unit's supplies cannot be tendered until it arrives at the ferry port."

Piosan chuckled. "If the merchants acquire too much at once, they'll lose it at the betting tables that selfsame night." Expression sobering, he bowed to Arthur. "You may trust me, Lord Pendragon, to see that you are treated well and that your coin is distributed as it should be."

Rionnach raised a finger. "Piosan, tell the Pendragon your idea for communicating across the firth."

Arthur furrowed his eyebrows. "You don't have signal towers?"

"Aye," said Rionnach, "shining for friend and foe."

"That's a risk I have to take." Arthur addressed Piosan, "But you have a better way?"

"Aye, my lord," Piosan replied, "using fishing boats. By day they'll be about their business. Then, at a prearranged time after dark, they can line up across the firth to receive a signal that's shielded on three sides, relaying it from the south bank to the north and back."

"Directed light—brilliant!" Arthur barked a laugh at the unintended pun, and he didn't mind others sharing the mirth. In Brytonic he described the signal plan to Centurion Cato. "However, if you judge that the legion should abort the crossing, do not signal the first boat."

He did not state what anyone who could understand his modification had to be thinking: a massacre of the scouts would leave no one to send a signal.

"Yes, Lord Pendragon." If Cato felt discomfited by the implied consequences, he hid it behind decades of military bearing. "That ought to prevent misunderstandings."

"Exactly. No light—no crossing." Arthur translated the order for his allies.

"I'll arrange the details with the Caledàitan fishermen," Piosan said. "That lot can advise of a suitable south-bank landing site for your army too."

Arthur gave Cato that information before regarding the chieftain. He rendered a legion salute and held the pose. "My lord Rionnach, I stand in your debt a hundred times over. Paying you in thanks and in coin does not—"

"Nonsense, Artyr." Rionnach pried Arthur's forearm from his chest and gripped it like a brother warrior. "If you can drive the Angalaranaich from these lands and restore to my people their livelihoods, I shall consider this debt well repaid."

Arthur could not have been more pleased to agree.

BEING DEAD had its advantages.

Being dead meant that Eileann didn't have to work on the boat. Being dead meant that the kind, brave souls they encountered offered food, ale, flowers, tools for home and hearth, and respectful expressions of sympathy. Being dead meant that cowards who might prey on two traveling women stayed away.

Being dead meant that no one dared to follow them.

It also meant having to make extra sure that no one could see Eileann sit up to eat, drink, or just to stretch. To say nothing of having to scratch an itch or relieve herself in the bucket that had housed seven of the gifted fish. She was grateful for the wise-woman's eyesight and vigilance.

That they sailed only by day made her extra grateful. Better had the nights been darker and longer, but being dead meant that Eileann was forced to accept what lay beyond her control.

Being dead meant that what she couldn't control amounted to nigh on everything.

The scrape of the hull on rocks and the slowing of movement alerted her that Fioruisge had selected a spot to land. The setting sun's glare had softened to dusk.

The boat rocked a little as Fioruisge eased out. Eileann shifted on her bier but not to the point that she felt in danger of sliding off. After Fioruisge's first near-disastrous attempt at the commencement of the voyage, both of them had learned to be careful.

Eileann's stomach had begun reminding her that it wasn't dead, and she could do with a few minutes behind a bush, but she held her pose, awaiting Fioruisge's confirmation that it was safe to move.

The click of flint striking steel, followed by a low whoosh, suggested that Fioruisge had lit one of their torches. They would have preferred setting up camp without light, but the moon hadn't risen. Eileann heard the prolonged crunch hinting that Fioruisge was trying to plant the torch in the sand. Muttered oaths and quicker crunching attested to her lack of success.

"Here, good woman. Let me help you."

Eileann knew that voice. What she didn't know was whether to be panicked or relieved.

Her heart, having decided on the former, began thrashing about in her chest.

The crunching changed in quality, perhaps made by a tool, and a series of stomps followed.

"Thank'ee, young sir, but please come no closer," said Fioruisge. "This is a death barge."

"I know," came the soft response. Continued footsteps across the rocky beach confirmed his disregard of the wise-woman's warning. Eileann felt the boat jerk forward. Sounds of the rope slapping wood told her that the boat had been tied to a tree trunk. "That ought to hold it for the night, good woman."

Lighter tread suggested that Fioruisge had walked toward him. "What business brings you to this place? If I may be so bold to ask."

"A special offering." The heavy sorrow of his tone made Eileann wish she could banish it.

The rustling of fabric, followed by Fioruisge's gasp, confused her. What could he be holding that would surprise a wise-woman?

A soft thrumming almost made Eileann choke.

My harp!

"Please permit me to place it for you." Fioruisge could have tried to sound insistent.

"I promised her parents that I'd deliver it to your kinswoman in Caledàitan. My squad's route from Dùn Fàradhlann took us along yon bluff." Into the pause drifted a brief scrape, softer than the beaching boat, as if the speaker had pivoted. "When we noticed a lone wee boat heading to this inlet, I took a chance that it might be bearing . . . her."

"The dead do not suffer disturbances by the living."

This dead one might . . .

"Please, good woman, I must do this. Her fingers upon this harp helped me in ways I cannot begin to describe. I had hoped—" He sucked in a breath and expelled it as a groan. "I never thanked her."

Those footfalls, closer now, knelled disregard. Fioruisge didn't seem to be trying to stop him. Eileann fought to keep her eyelids relaxed and her breathing shallow, steady, slow, and undetectable.

The boat tipped a bit.

"Gods. So beautiful . . . when did she p-pass? Yestermorn?"

Eileann presumed Fioruisge must have nodded.

The crack of wood on wood told her that he had placed the harp in the boat, either harder than he had intended or else it might have fallen. Its strings jangled a discordant hum. He uttered a strangled moan. The boat tipped farther.

"Sir, no! Stop!"

Eileann rolled. She tucked, crossing her arms over her face, an instant before crashing onto the deck. Metallic pain smacked her head;

she'd collided with a pair of armored shins.

They both yelped. She sat up and he leaped back.

"My lady! You're—"

Fioruisge rapped the boat's rail with her staff. "Shush. Both of you." Her soft tone brooked no argument.

He extended his hand. Eileann grasped it and stood, gaze locked to his. His warmth felt wonderful. She guided his hand to her back and closed in. He obliged, encircling his strong arms about her. She laid her head upon his chest. The cool metal scales tugged her hair a bit. That felt wonderful too.

Being dead could never compete with this.

Renewed knocking on the boat forced them apart. Fioruisge said to Angusel, "Help her down. While she sees to her needs, you and I must talk."

He passed her harp to Fioruisge and instructed Eileann to grasp the rail. Using his right arm as the plant, he vaulted out of the boat. Fioruisge helped him tip it, easing Eileann's disembarking.

Bending to throw first one leg over the rail, then the other, reminded her that she did need to find the nearest bush. She jumped onto the sand and dashed for the trees.

What Fioruisge discussed with their visitor, she couldn't hear. An admonishment about preserving her secret, most likely. She finished, adjusted her skirts, and emerged from cover to find both of them regarding her. Fioruisge's countenance, her arms wrapped around the harp as she clutched it to her chest, displayed an unreadable expression. By contrast, a parade of emotions cavorted across his face: joy, affection, pride, and . . . fear?

She blinked, and his fear yielded to determination and hope.

CHAPTER 19

ELIAN SQUINTED AT the cloud-streaked azure sky, wondering what in hell he'd been thinking when he had volunteered to accompany Gull. He closed his eyes with a sigh, waiting for the gales of laughter to begin. His aches already had.

"Sir!" Worry ratcheted Wart's tone several steps higher than usual. Elian felt the waft as the lad knelt beside him. "Are you hurt? What can I do to help?"

"Here's a stick." The dead Pict sounded nigh as close as Wart. "Poke the auld boar with it."

Uttering a frustrated growl, Elian opened his eyes and pushed himself into a sitting position. When his would-be benefactors pressed closer, he waved them back. His bellyful of self-pity was about to make him retch. He didn't need anyone else's.

Surprise surged when he inventoried the expressions, including those of the soldiers, who also had dismounted. While a few stayed back, holding the horses, the rest had clustered around him. He saw naught but genuine concern.

Wart stood. "I am so, so sorry, sir." His voice quavered.

Elian reached toward the lad. "For what? You had no way of knowing how slick that rock would be." He gave the hand a slight shake, and Wart grasped it to begin the process of helping Elian regain his footing. He surprised himself to realize he didn't mind when Gull stepped behind him to assist by levering his torso. He thanked them both.

"I should have seen the moss." The lad frowned at what had proven to be a less-than-ideal mounting block.

"Nonsense." Elian swatted straight his battle-kilt's fringes, hoping his tone's briskness would erase the frown. "It was a tiny tuft. You would have needed an eagle's eyes to spot it."

Wart's chin quivered. "Still, sir, you . . . you could have . . ."

Died? Oh, yes. If he hadn't pushed himself clear, he might well be dithering with the devil. Looking at Wart, he realized what a shame that would have been. He was damned lucky to have escaped with a scrape on his left arm, just below the shoulder fringes, and a wrenched muscle or two. The officers' bathhouse in Caerglas, where they would spend the night on this, the second of their three-day journey to Senaudon, ought to employ attendants possessing the skills to address muscle pulls. He touched the scrape. It stung, but his fingers came away clean.

Elian drew Wart into an embrace, surveying the gathered soldiers' faces. Relief met his gaze, not mockery, not even when he fastened his scrutiny upon Gull. After a moment, he felt the young arms tighten, and he got his third surprise of the hour with how gratifying that felt. "By God's grace, I didn't." Pushing the lad to arm's length but keeping hold of his shoulders, Elian grinned. "You do know this means He has more planned for me. For us. Right?"

"Right, sir!" The warmth radiating from Wart's repaired countenance felt surprisingly good too.

WALKING POINT beside Gawain in full daylight was a hell of a lot harder than when Angusel had been deployed on horseback in the dark to find the Sasunach army that had invaded Maun. Beyond the added exertion of walking instead of riding, he missed the comfort of Stonn's presence.

The firth crossing, the night before, had completed without incident. While it was as dark as it ever got at this time of year, the fisherman had deposited the squad near a rocky bluff where the scouts could hide and rest in split shifts such that half stood watch while their companions slept. Four men remained to guard their camp and build a three-sided rock structure for focusing the signal beacon across the firth; the other scouts spent the morning combing the vicinity for evidence of the enemy's presence. Finding none, they regrouped at the beach for the midday meal and then set about the task of defining the marching camp's perimeter and staking the likeliest places for the legion to pitch tents for sleeping, working, and storing supplies. The south bank's sandy terrain heightened the challenge, but they managed.

Past nightfall, Centurion Cato sent the all clear. An answering flash confirmed the signal's receipt.

Angusel hadn't been serving guard duty when the first cohort arrived, but the scraping of vessels onto the sand had woken him, and he had joined his brother scouts in helping to secure the boats. He was thankful that Arthur had ordered the scouts back to sleep while a detachment of the cohort stood watch, or today they'd be sleepwalking inland toward the trading village of Hafonydd.

He didn't envy the scouts who had been tasked to fan out from the main column. While he and Gawain, as the point men, maintained a slow, steady pace forward at about a quarter of an hour ahead of the column, the flankers ran out and back in rotating pairs to expand knowledge of the surrounding area. Several flankers had observed evidence of Angalaranach patrols in the form of fresh, multiple hoof-tracks and manure, and in the kicked-about remnants of campfires. This information was reported to the other scouts each hour, after everyone regrouped for rest or rations.

Thus far, they hadn't discovered anything about the Angalaranach army's deployment that the Pendragon hadn't anticipated. Centurion Cato kept his squad on task to investigate Hafonydd and then report to the beachhead for new orders.

In wartime, reality had no use for plans.

Gawain and Angusel reached the ridge separating them from the village and commenced their cautious assent. They crested the summit and descended far enough to hide their silhouettes while maintaining a safe distance.

His partner uttered a low whistle.

"What is it?" Angusel squinted toward the collection of huts, cottages, pens, and sheds clustered between the river and the rock face but couldn't discern details. "Angli?"

Gawain shook his head. "Nobody. It's deserted."

Angusel squinted harder. Every living thing had departed, down to the last hog and dog. He couldn't help but draw a comparison with the other empty village belonging to Gawain's Lùthean clansfolk that he'd seen, and he shivered.

This time, there would be no snow to disguise the bodies.

"Dead?" he hated to ask.

Gawain stared toward the village. "I don't think so. I'm hoping the villagers got wind of Angli troop movements and fled to the safety of Dunpeldyr." He shrugged at Angusel. "I say we wait for Centurion Cato. He should decide what we need to do next."

Angusel agreed. They found a boulder big enough to hide both of them and sat in its shadow. He uncapped his wine skin for a swig, as did his partner.

"So." Gawain stowed his wine skin and gave Angusel a frank look. "You've been mum about the side journey you took two days ago. You didn't have the harp when you regrouped with us. Were you able to leave it with . . . her?"

It was no one's damned business; he'd sooner die than betray Eileann. The hair on his arms prickled, and he chafed them.

But he couldn't fault his friend's concern.

"I gave the harp to her escort," was as much of the truth as Gawain needed to know.

Gawain shook his head, and his gaze appeared unfocused. "I can't imagine what I'd do."

Angusel grasped Gawain's forearm. "Your father and brother and the rest of your clan will be all right." He lifted the hand and grinned. "We've been sent to make sure of it."

Gawain's nod looked sad but thankful.

When Centurion Cato found them, he surveyed the village for a few minutes before ordering most of the men, including Gawain and Angusel, down the hill to investigate the buildings while keeping the rest on the ridge to serve as lookouts. They deployed in pairs and fanned out.

As THE sun slid closer to the horizon, Eileann's worry rose. Fioruisge was long overdue.

Eileann's reunion with Angusel had gifted her more doubts than assurances. As far as the Caledonach people were concerned, her parents and kin included, they were outcasts. While it might make sense for them to be together, what future could she and Angusel forge? What would become of their children—if any?

Thought of her wee lost baby girl twisted her gut, and she hugged herself till the pain passed. The physical pain, anyway.

What of this vaunted destiny Fioruisge insisted that the gods had in store for her? What should she, Eileann, be doing? Was it safe to seek shelter with Fioruisge's kinswoman in Caledàitan?

At midday, as Eileann and Fioruisge had shared a meal of bread, fish, and cheese out of the fishermen's death offerings, Eileann voiced her questions.

"I shall need to seek divine guidance, my lady. Can you please mind our fire? I must forage for the needful herbs."

Eileann had agreed and busied herself with gathering wood and tinder. The secluded inlet Fioruisge had selected for their camp met their needs, but Eileann deemed it prudent to stay away from the water's edge. Smoke rising from the fire they had built behind their boat ought to discourage opportunists from believing they could pilfer an abandoned craft.

With water for tea simmering in the pot Fioruisge had bartered for a few of the death-offering fish, supported by its iron tripod and dangling over the fire by the tripod's central hook, and with the sacks containing the foodstuffs hoisted in a nearby tree, life didn't seem quite so uncertain.

That had been at least two hours ago.

Eileann had long since finished her tea and dismantled the pot and tripod. Now she sat near the fire, shielded from view offshore by the boat's hull. She prodded the smoldering wood with a stout stick she'd reserved for the task and prayed to any gods who might be listening that Fioruisge had not befallen harm.

A crackle of footsteps shattered her reverie. Eileann gripped the poker—its hot, charred point would give an attacker a painful surprise—and stood.

"Of course I'm all right, my lady."

Eileann exhaled her relief and relaxed her grip; she couldn't recall when she had stopped wondering how Fioruisge could read her mind. Rather than bother her with a barrage of questions, which would have gone ignored since wise-women never imparted their lore to the uninitiated, she laid the poker near the firepit and settled onto one of the bough beds to watch.

Fioruisge fished the griddle from her pack and placed it on the coals. While the iron heated, she stripped leaves from twigs she had gathered and dropped them onto the griddle. She wielded her knife to shave strips of a mushroom over the browning, curling pile, now and again stirring it with the knife's point. After the pile had dried to her satisfaction, she grasped the griddle by its wooden handle and removed it to a flat rock. With the uncharred end of the poker, she ground and mixed the bits. In time, the griddle cooled enough that Fioruisge could use her hand, padded by a fold of her skirts, to sweep the herbs into the pot, which Eileann had filled with fresh water. Rather than reassembling the tripod, she nestled the pot among the coals long enough for bubbles to form and break.

After pouring a measure of the brew into a cup, Fioruisge offered it to her.

Scrunching her face, Eileann peered into its murky depths. "I thought you were the one who needed guidance."

"Surely you don't believe it took me that long to find a handful of mushrooms and herbs." Fioruisge pressed the cup into Eileann's hand. Its warmth was welcome, but her instincts blared caution. "I have received my guidance; now, my lady, 'tis time for you to seek yours."

Eileann lifted the steaming cup to her lips and took a tentative sip. The liquid had a faint earthy taste that wasn't as unpleasant as it looked. A hint of mint lured her for another sip, and another, and another. Soon the cup was empty.

And the ground was spinning.

GAWAIN AND Angusel were searching their third empty building—everything that hadn't been taken by the villagers likely had been plundered by Angalaranach patrols—when the rumbling began.

Gawain cracked open the door and peered out. "Mother of Christ," he whispered, easing the door closed. He leaned on it and shut his eyes. "A mounted Angli patrol."

"How many? A dozen?" The horses' noises supported the guess.

"At least."

Angusel wished the shed had a knothole on the street side. The hoofbeats seemed to be diminishing, but he deemed it yet too risky to open the door. He prayed as hard as he knew how that their companions hadn't been discovered.

"Mother of Christ! This close to Dunpeldyr . . . this impossibly, damnably close—" Gawain's words formed as low, harsh rasps, and he was breathing so hard Angusel feared he would lose consciousness.

He dug his fingers into Gawain's forearm where the skin lay exposed above the bracer. "Steady, lad." In one of life's little perversities, he recalled a moment when he had experienced similar trouble. Angusel repeated the advice he'd been given while trying not to think about its giver, the man who had just become her consort, or what that man had done to her to earn the honor: "Breathe."

Gawain gasped a breath, held it, and released it in a trembling sigh. His second and third breaths were deep but controlled, and Angusel withdrew.

"Dunpeldyr must be under siege," Gawain said.

"We don't know that. They could be an advance unit."

Gawain had opened his mouth when a series of shouts rang out, followed by the clash of arms. They exchanged a glance and drew their swords. Gawain yanked open the door, and Angusel followed him into the hell that had erupted in the road.

Battle frenzy consumed him, but not soon enough to prevent the blood already gushing toward the street's sewage ditch. Howling, he unleashed raw rage upon his sword-brothers' killers, banishing the michaoduin from this hell into the next.

THE YOUNG woman bearing the recent burn scars approaches the hut's rough-hewn door. She pays no notice to the wheezing of her lungs or the hammering of her heart. Such bodily responses have become commonplace.

One prayer consumes her:

Dear gods, I'm tired of running!

She wills her leaden legs to shuffle her closer to the door. Her arm is slow to rise; her fist shakes a trifle before it strikes the wood.

A long howl pierces the gloom, muffled by the door but nonetheless eerie.

She shrinks back, fatigue forgotten as she wonders where next she might run.

One word seeps through the hut's walls:

"Dead."

Shock roots her in place.

"Dead, dead, dead, dead, dead, dead."

The door creaks open. On the threshold, backlit by wavering candlelight, stands a man—a warrior, to judge by his slashed leather-and-scale armor and the bloodstained sword clenched in his right fist. Shadows obscure his face.

Odd; she senses no menace in him.

He raises his free hand level with the ground. The balled fist drips blood.

Her heart stutters. This man is no mere warrior. He is a ro h'ua-mhasach, a champion ordained by the gods to fight so deeply in the throes of battle frenzy that his foes' corpses pile in his terrible wake like cordwood.

She should be screaming her throat raw.

Curiosity kills the unborn screams.

"Dead." A drop falls from his fist to spatter the ground. "Dead, dead, dead." Three drops join their brother. "Dead, dead, dead, dead, dead, dead, dead." He crashes his fist into his chest.

This display should horrify her. She feels naught but overwhelming compassion for him.

She strides forward to catch the bloody fist. He breaks her grasp without harming her. His hand closes around hers with infinite gentleness. He peers into her face.

Uttering an alarmed groan, he releases her, whirls, and dashes deeper into the hut.

Her hand tingles where his fingers had touched it. She steps through the bloody traces to follow him.

CHAPTER 20

ANGUSEL THRUST THE pitchfork into the dried, trampled, hay-bound muck, braced on the handle, and coughed. He pulled his blood-spattered neck stole over his nose to block the cac dust he'd kicked up, wondering why Eileann popped into his mind now, of all damned times.

It did lift his spirits to imagine her sweet face and lovely singing and soft warmth.

Dunaidan, whose grimy face took a miracle to recognize, staggered through the propped-open barn door, shoving a handcart piled with Angalaranach corpses.

"Last of the buggers," he gasped. "Lend a hand, sir?"

Angusel's exhaustion almost made him miss hearing the respectful tone bestowed by one of his former tormentors in First Ala.

"Of course."

Leaving the pitchfork stuck in the floor, he wedged his shoulder under one cart handle while Dunaidan did likewise with the other. Grunting and straining, together they levered up the cart to empty its contents into the mass grave Angusel had hollowed out of the barn's floor, which had been compacted by the gods alone knew how many decades of livestock occupation. The bodies rolled and hit with the dull, final, sickening sound Angusel had heard too often this evening.

Once would have been too often.

"I'm sorry you got stuck with this backbreaking duty, Dunaidan. I'd rather see you work one of your pranks on me."

Dunaidan gave a stiff shrug and a stiffer grin and righted the cart. "I can piss in your mouth while you sleep if you think that'll help, sir."

The disgusting, sennights-old memory bent him double, clinging to the tines-down pitchfork and howling with laughter. His rational self wondered why. "That—" He gasped in a breath, chuckled it out, cleared his throat, and spat. "That was you too?"

"I can't say nay and I won't say yea." Dunaidan gazed toward the shallow grave, grin gone. "How many now?"

Angusel's sigh banished his last trace of mirth. "Eighteen men. And the four horses we buried where they fell."

Given a choice between working sums and reliving torture, he'd take whatever promised to keep the grief and guilt at bay the longest.

They planned to torch the barn later; the scouts couldn't risk an unexpected bonfire summoning a second Angalaranach patrol. But being buried in cow dung was a damned horrific way to start one's afterlife sojourn, even for a despised enemy.

"Plus our three. That would be, uh, twen . . . teen . . ."

"Twenty-one men."

Including Centurion Cato.

Dead.

Dead, dead, dead.

And four too badly hurt to continue our mission.

And Loholt.

Dead.

Because of me.

Because I wasn't fast enough or strong enough or skilled enough to save them.

His sword hand balled into a fist and crashed into his chest.

Dunaidan stepped from around the cart and grasped Angusel's shoulder. Angusel stared at the bodies, that shoulder flinching. Dunaidan withdrew and reached for the shovel.

Since there wasn't enough time to dig a proper pit, it had been decided to conceal the bodies under hay, first slaking them with powdered lime from a barrel Angusel had found in the barn. With Dunaidan shoveling the lime onto the grave's latest additions and Angusel using the pitchfork to push rather than toss, they completed the work quicker than Angusel would have preferred.

Dunaidan replaced the barrel's lid, threw his tool aside, and walked toward the barn's door. Angusel knew where his subordinate was bound, for he should be going there too: the village's temple, where other scout squad survivors had dug individual graves for their fallen brethren.

"Coming, sir?" called Dunaidan from beyond the door.

Angusel wished he didn't have to but dropped the pitchfork and complied. Dunaidan removed the wedges, shut the barn's door, and slid the latch to secure it from scavengers.

If only the guilt could be locked away.

The shades of three sword-brothers would be far harder to face than those of eighteen times eighteen enemies.

THE SUN had sunk well below the horizon. Fioruisge lit the torches, fighting to stem her worry. Lady Eileann should have awoken hours ago.

She drew a mote of comfort from the fact that her charge looked peaceful, resting upon the bed of thick pine boughs, her eyelids twitching and her expression shifting in subtle changes wrought by the visions.

The warrior had been right: she was so beautiful, even in the guise of death.

Had she, Fioruisge, given her the wrong dose? She didn't believe so; she and Lady Eileann were of a size, and they'd imbibed equal measures of the vision-inducing concoction.

Mayhap the gods weren't ready to release her from their realm.

A chill raced up Fioruisge's spine.

Mayhap they intended to keep Lady Eileann for themselves, and there wasn't a blessed thing that one humble wise-woman could do to change such a decision.

Mayhap this wasn't about Lady Eileann but was part of a test they had devised for Fioruisge, to expand her knowledge or hone her skills. Such events had been known to happen.

She prayed for a speedy resolution. The pit in her stomach warned her not to raise her hopes.

As the campfire blazed and the torches snapped around the perimeter, Fioruisge grabbed a wine skin and a fistful of dried fish and settled close beside Lady Eileann for the longest, most frightening wait of her life.

No ONE questioned Gawain's offer to take command of the scouts. Up until that debacle at Morghe's wedding, he had been a decurion in the Comites Praetorii.

Nothing, however, had prepared him for the tasks that awaited a unit's commander after a battle: evaluating the surviving men and seeing to the needs of the wounded, rounding up and corralling the spooked horses, ordering the dead horses buried and their riders' bodies hidden, detailing a hunt for escaped foes to prevent them from alerting their king, setting a defensive perimeter, sending out parties to scout for patrols, assessing Angli troop strength from the number of campfires that had begun flaring to life in the distance, foraging for game and supplies . . . the list seemed endless.

The tasks of burying and memorializing their own dead made those jobs seem like a Beltain romp.

They had chosen an area guarded by the village's chapel, away from the river, that had been fenced and no doubt consecrated, for the site contained several grassy, cross-topped mounds. With the three soldiers' graves arrayed between Gawain and the rest of the unit, he drew a breath, exhaled, and swallowed the lump threatening to clog his throat.

"We thank each of you for your sacrifice. We hate like hell that you're gone, but we are thankful that you fought with us when we needed you most." It seemed easiest to address the dead on behalf of their surviving companions. After what the squad had endured, they could use a heaping scoop of easy.

"Centurion Gawain?"

Gawain turned.

So much for easy.

Corwyn, one of the men he'd sent after the horses and the last to arrive, was leading a horse by its reins. Across its back was slung a body. Three arrows protruded from it.

In the first minutes after the skirmish ended, Gawain had learned from a witness that Cato had dispatched Driw to warn Arthur; therefore, Gawain had deemed it unnecessary to send another messenger.

The Angli arrows delivered the message that Arthur remained ignorant of what had happened.

Two men set to work digging the fourth grave. Corwyn steadied the horse while two other men yanked out the arrows and eased Driw down.

Judging the grave deep enough, the diggers climbed out, assisted by those assigned to lower Driw into place. The four men uncoiled ropes, positioned the body with utmost care, and repeated the terrible task they had performed thrice before. Everyone, including Gawain, attacked the dirt piles to cover their fourth fallen brother-in-arms. Their motions were sharp and swift, as if blaming the soil for Driw's fate.

Grimy, sweating, and winded, they stared at the freshest mound in morose silence.

The crimson officer's cloak, brush-crested helmet, and red-ringed copper legion badge of a sudden felt as if they'd been crafted of solid lead. Gawain wished he had buried those objects with Centurion Cato; he, Gawain, was the last person in the legion who deserved to wear them. He yanked off the helmet and placed it upon Cato's grave, and then started on the brooch.

A hand closed over his. He looked up.

"Don't," Angusel said. Like the rest of them, he was smeared with blood and grime. Unlike them, he reeked of the duty for which he had volunteered. "Your kin need you. We need you." He let go and stooped to pick up the helmet. Cato's helmet.

Gawain refused to take it. "I'm not him."

"None of us is." Angusel shoved the helmet into Gawain's gut, hard. Gasping, Gawain had no choice but to grab it; there was no way in hell that he'd dishonor its owner by letting it fall. Angusel stepped back a pace. "You know these lands. It's why you took command." A mischievous glint lit his eyes. "Right, sir?"

He had a point, damn him.

Hugging the helmet, Gawain pitched his voice for the assembly. "Arthur may not agree to let me keep this self-appointed promotion. I can never replace Centurion Cato, but I will stand in his stead for you." It felt damned wrong to settle Cato's helmet over his own head, but in doing so he noticed the men's faces begin to look expectant, hopeful even. He used the act of making a final adjustment to form a mental plea for the loan of Cato's wisdom.

His dead commander didn't disappoint him. "Priority goes to our four wounded men, who must get to the medics at the beachhead. I want eight volunteers as escorts. That makes one horse for each man. The two remounts stay in case I need to dispatch couriers." The first eight men to step forward, including Corwyn, he called aside. "Gather your gear, assist anyone who cannot pack or mount under his own power, and meet up here. You depart as soon as possible. Corwyn, I place you in command of this detail and charge you with telling Arthur what has happened here. Whether you eight return or are given different duty assignments, I leave to the Pendragon's discretion."

"Aye, Centurion," Corwyn said, saluting. The other volunteers followed his example.

Some centurion. One who failed to summon the confidence to verbalize the promotion that Corwyn deserved for leading this dangerous but vital mission.

Gawain swallowed his unease; Cato's men—his men—deserved better. To the company, he said, "The rest of us shall hold here to await Arthur's orders."

The flurry of activity lasted for several minutes. Departing men circulated among the graves to offer final words and salutes. The gestures ended with the sign of the cross or with fingers swiping wet cheeks, smearing the filth. A few men did both.

Gawain couldn't think of anything else to say over the graves except, "Rest well, all of you, and know that we shall finish this fight for you."

That bit won a round of muted affirmation from the other men, including the wounded, and it heartened him.

He raised his hand and brought it forward in a gesture he'd obeyed from Centurion Cato a thousand times. The column surged toward the beachhead and disappeared in the deepening twilight.

THE YOUNG woman steadies her breath. The escalating thrum of her heart, she ignores as she stands rooted upon the threshold.

The hut is unremarkable save for a golden brooch lying on the stump serving as a table, a lion's head. The ro h'uamhasach warrior snatches it up, groaning, and flings it into a corner. It clatters into the wall and bounces to the floor. "Dead! Dead, dead, dead!" He leans on the stump, his shoulders heaving in time with his sobs.

She steps past her fear to glide up behind him and lays a hand upon his back. The heaving slows, stops. His fists remain clenched to the stump. Her other hand joins its sister, and together they trace a light trail across the warrior's shoulders and down his arms until they reach the harpstring-taut hands. Under her touch, the fingers uncurl.

He inhales a long, shuddering breath and blows it out in a heavy sigh as he straightens and faces her.

Candlelight reveals his face.

Her face heats. Her heartbeat quickens. Her chest starts to heave. This time, she notices.

DO NOT fail me.

Prince Badulf Colgrimsson sat behind the camp table in his headquarters tent, hidden deep in the Brædan forest his men had named Bárweald for its abundance of wild swine. A part-eaten slab of that roasted meat, grown cold overnight, lay on the wooden trencher before him. Across the table, beside the trencher, lay his sheathed sword. He fingered its hilt, hating that his mind kept forcing him to relive that parting with his father and liege, and hating his powerlessness to change the audience's outcome.

Last year's loss of cattle, resulting in the loss of many Eingel souls, in battle as well as through starvation, had enraged Colgrim far more than Badulf had ever witnessed.

Do not fail my people again.

The prince traced the scar on his neck, his father's most recent reminder of the price of failure. The thin slash stung in its implications, if not in actual fact.

Greater stung the embarrassment of being sent into Brædan territory with but five hundred men under his command, men Colgrim expected Badulf to send scurrying thither and yon across this open, alien landscape like a pack of starving rats in the hopes of luring the Dragon King's army away from Colgrim's target.

They'd been focused upon this mission for a week, and thus far all they had managed to accomplish was penning the local Brædan king and kin inside his near-impregnable fortress, dubbed the Fort of the Spear for its position atop a steep, conical hill. Terrorizing these Brædeas carried its advantages, to be sure, but it fell far short of the glory required for Badulf to win his father's favor.

"My prince?"

Badulf looked up to regard Ornest, his second-in-command, who looked more grim than usual. "What news?"

"We may have lost a patrol."

Woden's ballocks. "Which one?"

"Wihtred's. They were slated to ride through the abandoned village and complete their circuit by dawn."

"This isn't the first time a patrol has been delayed. One of the horses could have thrown a shoe, or a soldier might have gotten sick, or they could have encountered wolves."

The veteran soldier's posture stiffened. "Indeed, sir."

"But?"

"The Dragon King's army has begun crossing. Our scouts estimate a thousand men so far. The latest report puts them at their beachhead, but Wihtred and his patrol could have clashed with an advance unit last night."

Badulf stroked his short-cropped beard; in spite of the potential loss of eighteen good men, his mission to lure the Dragon King's army away from Colgrim's objective was succeeding. Imagining the king's reaction to said success, the king's son resisted the temptation to grin.

"Order the units to implement phase two."

"We're not going to avenge our kin?" Ornest kept his tone polite, but Badulf heard the note of frustration and appreciated the sentiment.

He stood. "We do not know whether they need avenging. I will lead out a party to follow their assigned route. If they have been killed and the opportunity presents itself, then of course we will take action. But this mission stands at a critical juncture, and we cannot lose sight of it."

Ornest pressed his fist to his heart and bowed his head. "Quite right, my prince. Please forgive me."

Badulf stepped from behind the table to clap the hauberk-clad shoulder. "Woden's speed to you, my friend, and to the men. May his holy eye watch over you."

As Ornest departed, Badulf Colgrimsson couldn't help but recall King Colgrim's admonition:

Do not fail me.

That day, Badulf had been shocked speechless by the king's implied lack of faith.

Today his mind supplied the response that he should have made:

I won't fail you this time, Father. I swear.

CHAPTER 21

"LORD PENDRAGON? SORRY to disturb you, but—"

Habit made Arthur cross himself; the Hafonydd chapel had been stripped of everything that hadn't been nailed to the floorboards. The carved oaken altar remained the building's sole distinguishing feature aside from its steep-pitched, belfry-crowned roof. Its bell was missing. He hoped the priest had either hidden the precious items or had ordered them carried to the safety of Dunpeldyr.

"Let me guess, Marcus. A wagonload of issues requires my immediate attention." He stood and faced his aide.

"As always, sir." The centurion proffered a brimming leather mug in one fist and dried beef strips in the other. "But first you need to eat."

As always. Arthur had ordered the cohort to go on ration break when they reached the village, but he had made straight for the chapel to pray for the scouts who had fallen here last night.

He motioned for Marcus to precede him through the chapel's

door. The Hebrew David of old, in his warring days before becoming king, might have gotten away with consuming food and drink inside God's temple, but on campaign Arthur wasn't about to take such a chance, not with the legion having lost one veteran officer already.

He stepped into a world where tents and perimeter defenses rose as far as he could see. The forge lent its warmth but obliged every passerby to wave aside the smoke billowing from its newly lit charcoal. Half-dug latrines etched into the mud, deepening by the moment, while headquarters and workshops buzzed with men lugging supplies or wielding tools. Even in the overcast murk, Arthur made out fresh supports on the rotting wood of abandoned buildings. The men's progress surprised him. Not Marcus's efficiency in directing the work, but that Arthur could hear the rumble of the second cohort's imminent arrival too. He didn't think he had tarried inside the chapel that long.

Of any wagonload of decisions, Merlin had taught him that personnel issues should be resolved as soon as possible.

"Find Gawain and have him report to me." He took the mug and meat, and Marcus saluted him.

Chewing on one of the beef strips, Arthur watched his aide stride off. That first piece convinced him he was hungrier than he realized, and he finished the rest. But as he lifted the mug to his lips, an idea gave him pause.

The act of finding one man in a thousand ought to buy him a few minutes.

Careful not to spill the ale, he veered into the cemetery and stopped at the fresh graves. A head-size rock carved with an initial crouched atop each dirt mound. Three of those initials he knew from the scout's report.

The fourth . . .

Arthur's eyes felt too wet. He blinked, and the angular *C* on the fourth rock sharpened. Cato had despised sentimentality. With his rod and whip, the centurion had forged ironclad self-discipline, far beyond what his father and foster father had accomplished.

He had never shared a pint with his first mentor in the art of mounted combat. Regret stung his eyes and wrung his heart.

"Thank you, sir." He tipped the mug. The ale dug a little crater in the soft dirt. Foamy mud spattered the rock. "For all of it. The drills, the discipline, the advice, the falls, the encouragement to get back up and try again . . ." He swiped at his eyes, again beseeching God to welcome Cato and the other fallen scouts.

"Optio Gawain reporting as ordered, sir."

Bloody hell.

Arthur blinked a final time, finished the ale, stooped to leave the mug inverted on Cato's grave and wipe the rock, and rose to regard the newcomer.

Newcomers.

Gawain, his armor marred by the unmistakable mud-and-blood filth of combat, was standing at rigid attention. Across his palms lay Cato's crimson cloak, stiffened with bloody streaks and topped by the centurion's red-ringed copper dragon badge. Behind Gawain stood Angusel, just as spear-straight but filthier and reeking of dung, bearing Cato's helmet as if it were a gilded cup upon a salver.

Corwyn, the scout who had reported to Arthur last night, had described Gawain's post-skirmish orders, after taking command of the unit's survivors, in words laden with respect bordering on reverence. The report had convinced Arthur to allow Gawain to retain the centurion rank.

However, his nephew's choice to revert to the noncommand—and therefore safer—rank of optio put an altogether different face on the situation.

Arthur crossed his arms. "Report."

Gawain's posture tensed, and his fists trembled as they clenched the cloak. He began with an estimate of the number of Angli troops, five hundred, arrayed between Hafonydd and Dunpeldyr. If the Angli had encircled Loth's fortress with similar numbers, it would amount to a far smaller army than Arthur was expecting. Confirmation became top priority.

As Gawain transitioned to relating the facts of the skirmish and its aftermath, giving many of the same details as Corwyn had reported but delivering them with the simplicity of unvarnished truth, Arthur reached a decision.

"You are out of uniform, Centurion."

Angusel chewed his lower lip but couldn't stunt the grin.

Gawain gave a slight shake of his head. "Sir?"

Because the lad was kin, Arthur chose to forego the usual reprimand for questioning orders. He sensed that Gawain needed this nudge, much as Cato must have come to the same conclusion when Arthur had been a young legion optio, before Uther had ...

He quelled that memory before it could butcher his focus. Losing focus had been one of the flaws Cato had beaten out of him.

"That gear is yours, Centurion Gawain," he said. "Select replacement soldiers from among the cohorts here. Increase the scout squad's size if you deem it necessary. You and your men are excused from camp duties; your next mission will commence at sundown. I need an accurate estimate of the enemy force's size and deployment around Dunpeldyr."

Gawain's companion was bursting with promise too. Gyan had been wise to pair them, and Arthur decided upon the best way to continue that pairing. He said, "You are to serve as Gawain's second-in-command, *Decurion* Ainchis Sàl. Visit the quartermaster and trade this for a red-ringed one before heading out." He tapped Angusel's plain iron dragon badge. "I'll tell him to expect you."

Arthur held the centurion's rank badge and cloak so Gawain could remove the brown one that he hadn't the time to replace before leaving Senaudon. No military duty compared with the pleasure of pinning upon a soldier a badge that represented a higher rank; today, in spite of the loss of Cato and the other three scouts, that pleasure surged tenfold greater.

With a crisp move, Angusel passed the helmet to Gawain, who removed his legion standard helmet to don the brush-crested one. The look they shared, which seemed to run deeper than the brotherhood of combat, reinforced the rightness of Arthur's decision to promote them.

As his youngest centurion and decurion saluted and left him standing among the fresh graves, from somewhere came the notion that Cato would have approved.

WATCHING ELIAN mount after the party had finished their midmorning ration break, Gull had to admit that in two and a half days, the auld boar had improved a fair bit. He would always need a block or a stump, and mayhap a body or two to lend a hand in case he lost his footing or the horse decided to move. But Elian's confidence showed in his mastery of the mare after he got settled in the saddle and its boot, and Gull was glad to see it.

Elian guided Melys in a tight circle to face Gull while Wart and the soldiers Merlin had sent as escort mounted.

Gull was stuffing implements and uneaten rations into his horse's saddle packs.

"Move your arse, dead Pict. We can reach Senaudon by noon."

"Right." And then he'd learn of his status in Clan Alban . . . half a blink before Alayna ordered him tossed over Senaudon's steepest cliff.

He slung the packs and his bedroll across the horse's back, tied them down, mounted, and kicked him into a trot. With each jolting step, Gull's dread grew.

The sound of a dozen sets of hoofbeats and the rising dust cloud told him that Elian, Wart, and the escorts were following. Elian kneed his mount abreast of Gull's.

"What ails you?" Elian shifted the reins to his sword hand so he could twist far enough to regard Gull without pulling the mare off course. "You've not said a dozen words at a stretch today."

Gull checked his sword. Its scabbard was secured by his saddle's front thongs, and he tugged on it to make sure it wouldn't bounce against the horse's foreleg. "I've naething to say."

"Nothing to say to your wife, I warrant," Elian muttered.

From behind them, Gull heard their escorts snicker. He wheeled his mount about and borrowed a phrase he hoped they would re-spond to: "Mind your cac-licking business."

The men possessed sense enough to shut their gobs. So did Wart, but Gull saw the quiver of his lips before the lad glanced away. Gull relented and nudged his horse closer to murmur an apology. Wart's expression brightened, and Gull resumed his place at the head of the line.

"Does your directive apply to me too?" If Elian was trying to look innocent, that damned grin was causing the auld boar to make a poor go of it.

"Would it help if I said it did?" Elian's grin widened. Gull sighed.

"I didna think so."

A double handful of miles—and increasingly familiar scenery—passed before Gull said to the auld boar, "I'll not be going to Senaudon."

"You must be joking!" Elian gave Gull a long look but did not halt the company. "Tell me you did not come this far to give up."

"I came this far for Angusel. Nae one else."

"I thought you wanted to be at the staging area when your son returns." Gull saw the *if* in the sympathetic cant of Elian's eyebrows. "I think it's a good idea."

Gull couldn't disagree.

Neither could he face the woman and folk he had chosen to abandon.

A few miles later, he arrived at a decision.

"The wee hut I used for a time after I 'died' lies in a hidden hollow nearby, and with luck it should be empty." Gull regarded his friend. "I'll show ye how to find it so ye can send for me if ye must." One side of his mouth tugged upward. "There be your dozen words and aught to spare, auld boar. Does that satisfy ye?"

Elian grunted. At the next fork, Gull guided his horse onto the southernmost track. The auld boar, the boarling, and their escort followed him.

THE SUN'S rays coloring the insides of her eyelids like a flame made her shut her eyes tighter. The hand jostling her shoulder convinced her to open them.

"My lady! Clota be praised!" Fioruisge was looming so close to her face, Eileann smelled tea herbs on the woman's breath. The idea of licking Fioruisge's nose was tempting.

"I'm fine. Truly." The sun was at just past zenith and well past the time to be up and about. She pushed herself into a sitting position. Fioruisge stepped back. A breath later, Eileann wished she hadn't moved. Her temples felt caught in a vise. She pressed the heels of both hands to her head. The hammering intensified.

"Drink this." Fioruisge grasped one of her hands and pressed a cup into it. Eileann's expression must have caused her to add, "'Tis naught but watered wine."

The sip confirmed the claim. Its tart essence refreshed her. Eileann finished the measure and lifted the cup. Fioruisge obliged her from the wine skin she was clutching, and Eileann downed that in a straight pull too. "Why am I so parched?"

Fioruisge looked apologetic. "You slept far longer than I expected, my lady, and I never intended for that to happen." Apology yielded to determination. "What did you dream?"

"I—" She tried to recall the images, but their details danced out of reach. "There was a warrior," she said at length. "A hut. Oh, and a brooch, a golden lion's head."

"A warrior, you say? Was there blood?"

Dead. Dead, dea—

Nodding, she shivered in spite of the heat and rubbed her arms. "What does it mean?"

"I'm not certain. My vision was confusing too." Fioruisge slipped her hand under Eileann's elbow, helped her stand, and hustled her to the boat, leaving Eileann no time to marvel at the wise-woman's admission. "My cousin must look at you. She would know if the potion affected you in ways I cannot ken."

Eileann climbed into the boat and lay upon the bier. Fioruisge pushed it into the shallows, hoisted herself over the side, took up the paddle, and shoved the boat free.

NOT IN all the cattle raids he'd ridden combined had Gawain seen as many flies as campfires marring the fields surrounding Dunpeldyr, and he and Corwyn were viewing the northern side of the hill fort. The scout pairs that had been dispatched to the south and east hadn't reported back, but he presumed they were observing similar numbers.

Those campfires meant three to five times the soldiers they had reported to Arthur, six to ten thousand in total. The legion would need a miracle; his clan, a bigger one.

A hand gripped his shoulder. "We can do this, Centurion," said

Corwyn, his partner in this endeavor.

Oh, yes. We can die. Gawain shrugged Corwyn off, fighting to shrug the fear too.

Gawain's unit, deployed across the land to glean the maximum amount of information, was half the strength of a typical century, and that many because Arthur had brought the eight uninjured skirmish survivors to Hafonydd and had given Gawain leave to accept enlisted volunteers—men of Lothian, every one. Men worried about their kin, straining like leashed hounds to destroy the ravening Angli evil. He had harbored doubts regarding whether those hounds could keep steady heads for this leg of the mission, but he'd have been a beast to have denied anyone.

He felt beastly enough for ordering them to observe but not engage.

Corwyn looked expectant. Gawain didn't owe him a response, but the prospect of staying mum felt beastly too.

"Right. We should—" Gawain broke off to watch light flare in the distance, southwest of their position, as if one of the campfires had been stoked with the driest tinder imaginable. Another flared close to the first, and two more, and yet more, and more, and more.

"Cac," Corwyn muttered. "Do you think our lads have been discovered, sir?"

He'd be a fool to think otherwise. "Go. Alert Arthur. I'm moving in closer."

His uncle might deem that decision foolish, especially for a unit commander; so be it. Dunpeldyr was his birthplace, not Arthur's, and he'd rather be thrice damned for eternity than fail to come to its defense.

Corwyn saluted him and dashed off.

Gawain glanced eastward at the lightening skies, praying that Corwyn would avoid Driw's fate. He kept his sword at the ready and surged toward the spreading rash of signal fires. Smoke was impeding visibility, but he followed the shouts and the clash of steel on steel that grew louder by the step. He lengthened his stride and changed his prayer.

Please, God, let Arthur get here fast!

By the time he could see scouts battling enemies whose numbers were swelling by the second, he was in a dead sprint.

CHAPTER 22

ARTHUR REGARDED THE soldier standing before him, who was breathless and smelled of the smoke that lent credence to his report. Fatigue was asserting its grip upon his posture.

Gawain's revised estimate of eight thousand Angli soldiers surpassed Arthur's expectation of the size of Colgrim's army. The cavalry would close the disparity, but getting the horses across the firth looked impossible.

So be it.

"Thank you, Soldier Corwyn." The lad straightened a bit. Arthur should have dismissed him to take the rest he had earned, but, "I've an urgent mission to entrust to you, if you're fit to ride one of the Angli horses you helped capture."

"Name it, my lord!"

Arthur nodded at Corwyn's salute. Lacking the time to write a message, he retrieved his bronze seal from the box containing his writing supplies and passed it to the soldier. "Ride to the beachhead.

Give this to General Cai as proof that your words are mine. He is to march all but one of the cohorts to Dunpeldyr. The cohort that landed earlier this morning shall remain to secure our beachhead. If Cai doesn't need you for another mission, you may rest there and then stand guard or whatever task the cohort commander requires of you."

Corwyn repeated the message verbatim. Clutching the seal of the Dux Britanniarum in his right fist, he saluted, spun, and departed. Arthur wished upon the lad a silent Godspeed and then set about the business of preparing a thousand men for imminent battle.

GARETH MAP Loth, heir to the chieftainship of Clan Lothian, stood beside his father in Dunpeldyr's inner courtyard. In the gloom of predawn, the traitor Llygaidda's futile kicks and convulsions slowed and, finally, mercifully, stopped.

The bodies of the apothecary's wife and son—a lad of Gareth's age, though Gareth had not known him well—lay cooling in the executioner's wagon. Heaven alone knew what had driven Llygaidda to poison Dunpeldyr's well. The bulging sack of Angli gold found behind a false wall in his shop had damned the family.

Loth dropped his hand to Gareth's shoulder, and Gareth signaled the executioner to cut down Llygaidda's body.

It was a far easier command to give than the one to open the trapdoor.

Most days, the things his father put him through to prepare him for leading the clan weren't so bad. To say that today was not one of those days would be the grandsire of understatements. The pleas, the sobs, the ear-splitting screech and thud of the door, the awful sounds of strangulation . . .

"Son. With me."

Gareth looked around. Loth had made him inventory the emergency water stores—the hill fort had enough to last its villager-swelled population three days, maybe a week under merciless rationing—and Gareth couldn't imagine what else needed the immediate attention of the clan's chieftain and his heir.

While the executioner drove the wagon toward the archway leading to the lower courtyard—thence, Gareth presumed, to dump the bodies down the hillside since the Angli siege was blocking access to the clan's burial grounds—Loth was making determined strides beside a soldier. They were heading toward the staircase that ascended to the battlements. Gareth ran to catch them.

"See there, my lord?"

That was the soldier addressing Loth; no one ever used that title with Gareth. Not that he was itching to hear it.

Gareth hopped onto one of the dressed stones archers used for improving their view over the palisade and followed the line implied by the soldier's pointing finger.

A huge cloud obscured the southern portion of the camp, drifting westward toward Hafonydd. Gareth squinted hard. Through thinning patches, he could make out the vague forms of—

"Soldiers fighting?" he asked.

"Aye, young sir."

"Hrmph." Loth crossed his arms. "About damned time Arthur got his arse here."

"My lord," said a second sentry, "those may be the Pendragon's men, but it's mayhap half a century."

The man was right, Gareth realized. Why in heaven's name had Uncle Arthur sent such a tiny unit? Didn't he know how many Angli vermin swarmed out there?

Didn't he care?

His thoughts flashed to his mother, younger brother, and baby sister. The smoke tendrils drifted toward the western horizon in the direction they had taken a fortnight earlier.

"Father, look!" Gareth shifted to the far side of the stone to let Loth step up beside him. A second, brownish cloud emanating from the village had collided with the smoke. To his eyes there could be but one interpretation, and it set him to bouncing on the balls of his feet. "Uncle Arthur has sent a far bigger unit!"

That Loth didn't scold Gareth for failing to comport himself with dignified calmness put another notch in his tally of today's abnormal events.

For several minutes they surveyed the scene. Gareth tired of bouncing and switched to slapping the stone; the distance and lack of visibility made it impossible to tell what was happening. What his eyes couldn't supply, however, his heart did in gut-wrenching abundance.

"We should help them, Father. From our position, we can create a second front." Loth regarded Gareth with mild interest. "Our two units can be like a hound's jaws, trapping the Angli between us. After all, Gawain—" His father's look sharpened into a warning, but Gareth was too worried to care. "We don't know if Mama, Medraut, and Cundre made it to safety. I won't watch my brother die!"

Clenching his fists, he jumped down and stalked toward the staircase. Son or no, heir or no, departing without the chieftain's leave was gross insubordination—in fact, such a departure had opened the rift between Gawain and their father several years earlier—but Gareth couldn't have cared less about that either.

A hand clenched his shoulder, halting him. He knew that hand. What he didn't expect was the compassion radiating from its touch.

"You think he's out there, fighting for us?"

Gareth eyed his father. "You think he's not?" He gave a disgusted snort and resumed his course.

"Son, wait. Please."

He rounded on his father, fists on hips. "What, Father? You're going to order me to stay here and do nothing?"

As he spoke, Loth was closing the distance, but slowly, as if he were trying not to spook a deer. "Yes." As Gareth readied his protest, Loth raised his hands. "I like your military suggestion. It was sound thinking. But I shall lead the men. Clan Lothian's heir must stay clear of danger."

By this time, his father had drawn close enough to circle his arms around him. Gareth didn't resist. After his rational self accepted the wisdom of Loth's reasoning, he completed the embrace.

"Does this mean"—Gareth sucked in a breath—"that you'll greet Gawain like this too?"

Loth's laughter rumbled like a sudden summer storm and was just as unexpected. "I knew I should have sent you with your mother. You sound more like her by the day." He clapped Gareth's shoulders, his countenance sobering. "Gareth, my beloved son, I mean that in the absolute best of ways."

After a brief squeeze, Loth released his hold, called his high-est-ranking officers to his side, descended the steps, and was gone.

THE NUMBERS did not tally.

Angusel, gripping his point-down sword and bracing his shield hand on the corresponding knee, took time to catch his breath and assess his surroundings. The smoke made it impossible to see his men. But he should have been able to hear them. If—gods forbid—they were dead, then their killers should have been hunting down the rest of the Pendragon's men, himself included.

He couldn't hear a thing over the wheezing of his lungs. When that quit, he hooted the recall signal and hoped for the best.

It made no sense. They should have been killed to the last man within minutes, given the odds they were facing.

Given the odds they thought they were facing.

Not that he was complaining to be alive, he hastened to remind any gods who could see him through the damned smoke.

"This area is clear, Decurion." Angusel straightened to face Dunaidan, newly arrived and struggling to breathe. The soldier coughed and cleared his throat. "Leastways, I think so. I've run out of men to fight."

Scouts in Angusel's vicinity converged upon his position with varying degrees of swagger—or stagger. Their commander sighed his relief.

"Same with me," Angusel said. Centurion Cato might have given Dunaidan a dressing-down for being uncertain; he wasn't about to follow that example, given the way this mission had unfolded, and he suspected their work was nowhere close to being done.

"What now, sir?" asked Dunaidan while the men coughed and spat and gasped to clear their lungs and steady their breathing.

"Eat and drink."

That order won Angusel a round of grateful murmurs.

After he had followed his own advice, he closed his eyes to focus on the distant sounds of combat. Upon opening them, he pivoted and pointed with his sword. The fortress, called Dùn Pildìrach in Caledonaiche and Dunpeldyr by Gawain and others of the Breatanach race, lay beyond the blade's tip, rearing like an island in a swirling sea of smoke and dust.

"We go that way, men," he said.

The enemy's numbers might not be adding up, but it did not negate the fact that Gawain's kin and clansfolk needed help.

BADULF AND his patrol had traversed the landscape until well into the darkest hours, looking for the lost men with no success, when the signal fires confirmed the enemy's presence. He knew those of his men who could see the fires would follow their standing orders to converge upon the light. The fires' timing likely meant that the lost patrol had been bested by the Dragon King's men. He hated having to give up on them, but his focus by necessity shifted to contacting the men stationed at positions where the signals couldn't be seen, east and north of the hill fort.

He prayed for the strength to avenge the patrol members' deaths a hundred times over.

By daybreak he had succeeded in leading the men he could find into the fray. Their new orders: fight a little and then melt away, repeating the cycle to maintain the illusion of superior numbers and to keep drawing the enemy in. The smoke was an annoyance, to be sure, but one they had created by design, and they had prepared by tying wet cloths around their faces and their horses' muzzles. As predicted, the smoke worked in their favor to maintain the enemy's confusion.

An hour later, with the first wave of the Dragon King's men confirmed to be bearing down upon the region and twice as many Brædeas on the march from their beachhead, Badulf issued the order to keep the enemy engaged but with emphasis on slipping away.

That changed when he saw the company of mounted men issuing from behind the gates of the Fort of the Spear, thundering down its steep hill as if Skoll, Hati, and Fenrir snapped and slavered at their heels. One of the Brædan riders carried what had to be the king's

KIM IVERSON HEADLEE

banner.

Badulf ordered his aide to sound the blast that would direct all Eingel eyes upon him. He raised his spear above his head.

"My brave sword-brethren, we have been blessed with a singular chance to earn high favor from King Colgrim! Those who wish to complete our original mission may do so with no shame or stain." His spear pumped the air. "Who is with me?"

One in four shouted, repeating his gesture. Badulf would have preferred a higher number; so be it. He placed Ornest in command of the rest. Ornest saluted and rallied those men to him.

Badulf couched his spear, ordered his recruits to do the same, and led them in pursuit of their newest and most valuable target.

CHAPTER 23

WITH HALF HIS men off God knew where, and half the men who'd joined him at the skirmish's onset lost to injury or death, the chances of mounting another attack looked slim. Gawain dreaded the idea of facing his uncle if he survived this debacle. His was going to go down as the worst command in history.

Movement in the near distance arrested that thought. The smoke was clearing, but not fast enough to abandon caution. Gawain and his men readied their weapons.

Swords drawn, Angusel and a dozen others lurched into view. Forgoing the friend-or-foe protocol, Gawain gave the order to stand down. The scouts rushed to greet the one another.

Gripping Angusel's shoulders, Gawain squinted past him into the smoky swirls. He released his second-in-command. "These are the men who survived with you?"

"With me, aye," Angusel said. "There may be others scattered about."

"Not bloody likely. Cut off with no chance to regroup with either of us"—Gawain clenched his jaw against the mounting grief—"they have to be dead."

Angusel disagreed. "How many did you and your men fight?"

"I don't know. A score, maybe two score? It was damned hard to see through the smoke."

"Aye. And how surprised are you that all of us didn't get killed? I don't think the enemy force is near the size we estimated."

Gawain rubbed his chin. "Fair point. But why would they—cac." He spun Angusel about and pointed past his shoulder. "Do you see what I think I see?"

A huge gray blur had formed near Dunpeldyr's summit and was descending.

"Gods! I don't care how big their troop is or how much speed they can build up. There have to be far more Angli deployed near the fort than we engaged out here on the fringes. They are going to get slaughtered."

Gawain's barked laugh masked the fear stabbing his stomach. "That's my father. Always thinking he can do damn near anything." A growing rumble caused him to look westward.

"The Pendragon?" Angusel asked. "Marching from Hafonydd, it would make sense."

"If that's not him, we are dead." He called for the fastest runner and charged him to find the legion and implore Arthur to hurry.

"The gods do favor the brave," Angusel said after the soldier had sprinted off.

"Right." Gawain commanded the attention of the scout unit's survivors. "Pray that your gods have favors enough for us all."

ARTHUR DIDN'T like it, but he held the captured Angli warhorse to the pace of his cohort's double-quick march. This close to Dunpeldyr, he could hear the battle, and the itch to engage the enemy worsened by the stride.

However, he ordered his centurions to give their men a few minutes' rest after they reached the top of the ridge. He had not planned to enter the fray this soon after a hard march, but the message from Gawain had revealed time as an enemy.

He prayed that Cai and the remaining cohorts would catch up soon.

From this distance, it was impossible to tell what was happening on the battlefield beneath the smoky haze, but Arthur could see what appeared to be a sizable breach in the Angli's rear defenses. This seemed strange to him, since the scouts had been ordered to spread out around Dunpeldyr and not engage. But whatever had transpired, he wasn't about to question this piece of good fortune. He ordered his centurions to ready their men. Three breaths later, the cohort charged down the ridge, aiming straight for the breach to make the most of the opportunity God had given them.

RUNNING AT the phalanx's point position, Angusel gripped his sword, gauging the shortening distance to the enemy's line. Beside and behind him to either side streamed a half dozen of the unit's fastest and best swordsmen. Gawain, Corwyn, Dunaidan, and the remaining score of soldiers comprised the formation's core. Their objective was as simple as their course was straight: rip through the Angalaranach defenses and keep ripping all the way to Chieftain Loth.

With a whoop, reveling in his flaring battle frenzy, Angusel increased his speed and crashed into the line. The fighting intensified as his sword-brothers engaged. The Angalaranaich wavered. After a few heartbeats, the wavering became running.

In war, nothing was simple.

Those retreating Angalaranach soldiers curved around to engulf the phalanx from the sides. Angusel heard the renewed clash of arms and prayed that Gawain and the rest were holding their own. He kept on task and pressed forward.

He let the gods tally his fallen foes.

GAWAIN PUSHED past the pain and exhaustion to wield his sword with desperate determination. On foot, he could see his father's Amber Bear standard, rising high and proud over the seething sea of Angli foes. He didn't know how many scouts had survived this far into the siege's ranks but couldn't let ignorance-spawned guilt slow him.

He had to get to Loth before the Angli could get to either of them.

Two Angli soldiers tried a coordinated attack on him. He sent the first sprawling with a body block. The man scrambled to his feet and dashed off. His companion wasn't as lucky. As Gawain yanked his sword from that soldier's gut, he saw dark streaks arc across the sky. A flight of spears had been launched toward him, though from their trajectory he judged they would land beyond his position.

A shout went up from both sides: one triumphant, the other alarmed. The Angli redoubled their efforts. The Amber Bear rocked violently. As Gawain stared in growing horror while scouts defended him, the standard toppled.

"To me!" he shouted, plying his sword with renewed vigor.

"SCOUTS, TO me!"

Angusel ignored Gawain's command. He'd fought his way closer to Chieftain Loth than his firstborn son had.

Even Angusel had been too late.

His battle frenzy ignited with fresh fervor, and he joined Chieftain Loth's men to prevent the tragedy from becoming worse.

Three Angalaranach warriors rushed him. The first he kicked in the groin. While that man rolled on the ground, Angusel struck with his sword at the second's unprotected neck. The third tried to stab him from behind, but Angusel whirled and landed a blow that sent the Anghalar sword—and hand—flying. By this time, the first soldier had recovered enough to rejoin the fight, screamed at seeing his companions' fates, and tried to retreat. Angusel stopped those screams with the same deadly efficiency he'd applied to countless foes.

It hadn't been enough.

Again.

GAWAIN BURST through the perimeter formed by Dunpeldyr soldiers and legion scouts holding the Angli at bay.

"God, please, no! Father!"

Heedless of the melee, Gawain rushed to his father's body. A spear protruded from his chest. It hadn't stopped quivering.

Dropping his sword, Gawain sank to his knees and grasped the limp hand. "I'm sorry! I'm sorry! I'm sorry!" A remote part of him wished he could say something meaningful, but his brain wouldn't cooperate. His gut twisted. Sobs welled. He choked them down to whisper, "Father, I am so, so sorry."

The hand twitched. Gawain's eyes widened. He gripped that hand in both of his and kissed it. Tears streamed down his cheeks.

"Not your fault, son." Loth's rasp was so low, Gawain wasn't sure he'd heard it aright. "Mine."

"Father!" Hope swept through him like wildfire. Blinking, he whipped his head around. "Help me! Help Chieftain Loth! We must get him to safety!"

The Angli onslaught pressed harder. Not one man could disengage.

"Gawain."

His father hadn't addressed him by name since he had joined the legion. He had never been addressed by Loth with such deep affection.

Flailing his free hand, Loth drew a shuddering breath. "Help . . ."

Gawain caught that hand. "Save your strength, Father. Of course I'm going to get you help." *Somehow, please, God!*

Loth's helmeted head thrashed from side to side. Gawain caressed the exposed portion of his face, and the thrashing calmed. Loth winced long and hard. "Not me. Gareth. He will need—" He gritted his teeth, groaning. His fists clenched, his back arched, and his face creased into fathomless agony.

Gawain threw himself atop Loth's body as best he could while avoiding the spear, which he dared not remove. The convulsions worsened. Despair spawned of utter powerlessness darkened Gawain's vision.

THROUGH A lull in the fighting, Angusel glanced around. Gawain slumped over the chieftain's body, his shoulders shaking.

The Angalaranach numbers were dwindling—mayhap because of the legion's arrival—but not fast enough. A warrior garbed in the richest armor he had seen this day was closing upon Gawain and his father, sword cocked to kill, triumphant glee and malevolence twisting his face. Angusel had no time to decide whether the Angalar wanted the chieftain's fine sword or his head, or both. He surged and stretched to block the blow that would have ended his grieving friend's life. The Anghalar weapon slid down his blade and grazed his thigh, but he fought past the pain to keep the warrior at bay. Then scouts rushed in, and the rich Angalaranach soldier was gone. Dead, Angusel hoped.

After the worst of his panting abated, he plucked Gawain's sword from the bloody mire.

"Centurion."

Gawain didn't raise his head. "Don't call me that."

Angusel rammed Gawain's sword into the ground, gripped his breastplate's neckline, and hauled him up. "It is your rank until the Pendragon says nay." He freed the sword and shoved it into Gawain's hand. "Help me and the rest of your men, Centurion, or you'll have naught but cac to bury."

Gawain's glare seethed with malice, but he rejoined the fight.

Angusel could live with that.

CHAPTER 24

LIAN WATCHED TWO officers duck past the drawn flaps of the headquarters tent, and he did his best to catch them. He ignored the damned thump-scrape of his peg and the curious stares he drew from soldiers who must not have witnessed his arrival at the staging area, with Wart in tow, the previous afternoon. The Comitissa's personal guards remembered him; they approved his entry into her presence with sharp salutes and countenances devoid of judgment.

Of the reason for her summons he hadn't the first guess, and he clenched his jaw.

It didn't help one jot that the men he was trailing wore the expensive silvered armor and bronze dragon badges of officers who outranked him. When he could see their faces, recognition set in: Peredur of Caledonia, the Comitissa's half brother and prefect of the Horse Cohort, and Gereint map Erbin, a man Elian knew by his badge alone, which identified him as commander of the Senaudon occupation cohort.

He willed his aching jaw to relax. It refused to obey.

"At ease, Centurion Elian," said the Comitissa in that lilting voice he enjoyed. Its tone on a different day might have proffered an invitation to join her for tea. Her being fully armed save helmet and gloves belied that notion. "Please. This is not a disciplinary hearing." She gestured toward the arc of stools in front of her camp table.

Since the three other men—the third being her aide, Centurion Rhys, whom Elian had seen assisting her during her days on Maun—claimed seats, so did he.

Comitissa Gyan elected to remain standing. "I have received an urgent dispatch from Chieftain Rionnach of Clan Tarsuinn. The Angli have crossed from Dun Eidyn to the north bank of the Fiorth and are marching on Dùn Fàradhlann."

Prefect Peredur jumped up, hand to hilt, toppling his stool. "We must buy time for Artyr to return with the infantry! The Angalaranaich aren't mounted. We can beat them there and set up a defensive perimeter. When do we leave, Gyan?"

She gave him an arch look mitigated by a faint smile. He righted the stool and sat.

"Prefect Peredur's supposition is correct," she said to the group. "We cannot wait for Artyr's approval. The Horse Cohort and the Comites Praetorii shall prepare to move out as soon as we're finished here. I have already dispatched a request for my father, Chieftain Ogryvan, to meet us at Dùn Fàradhlann with Clan Argyll's war-band. Prefect Gereint, how many of your men can ride? I don't intend for them to fight mounted; they shall reinforce Chieftain Rionnach's stationary defenses while the rest of us harry the enemy's flanks. For this plan to work, I need soldiers who won't slow the column."

Gereint rubbed the stubble on his upper lip. "Maybe half, if that, Comitissa. I'm sorry."

"Don't be," their commander said. "It's a higher number than I expected."

"Too high," said Prefect Peredur. "Mounting three hundred extra men will put a serious strain on the cavalry's remounts."

"Those horses will be your remounts after they carry my men to the fort," Prefect Gereint pointed out.

Peredur gave his peer a conciliatory nod. "I'd prefer to procure more horses, but I don't know where we can find a tenth that many in so little time."

"I do," said an authoritative female voice behind them in the language Elian had learned in the course of working with the dead Pict. His back felt the freshened breeze and warmth through the opened tent flaps, but he resisted the urge to look at the intruder. His fellow officers glanced at each other, shifting on their stools.

"Please forgive the interruption, Comitissa Gyan," said one of her guards in Brytonic. "The chieftainess insisted."

Expression neutral, the Comitissa raised an open-palmed hand. "Chieftainess Alayna is well come to this gathering." Her gaze sharpened as she continued in the Picti tongue, "I wonder, my lady, how you learned of it."

As Elian heard the guard's departure, confirmed by the tent's lower light level after the flaps fell shut, he stood to yield his stool to the woman who didn't yet know she remained married to his best friend. Peredur, Gereint, and Rhys stood too.

The instant she brushed past the officers, Gull's reluctance to reveal himself to her made sense. She was rattling a parchment leaf as if the Comitissa were to blame for its contents. Elian could well imagine a whirlwind withering to the barest puff at this woman's feet.

"I don't trouble myself to keep spies in your camp, Chieftainess Gyanhumara, if that's what you're thinking. I suspected that you must have received a similar message to this one: a plea for help from Chieftain Rionnach."

The Comitissa Britanniam refused to wither. "And you intend to help him? A rival Caledonach clan no longer bound to yours by marriage?" She folded her arms, eyebrows knitting. "By providing horses to the army led by the two people you most despise on this side of an Domhaneil?" Elian pondered the phrase that sounded like "an DOH-ah-neel;" from its context, he guessed that the Comitissa must have referred to the Picti afterlife. "Why would you do such a thing?"

The woman still marriage-bound to Clan Tarsuinn—though it was the dead Pict's job to thus enlighten her—tossed her head. "Oh, my horses won't come free, Gyanhumara. Nor will my two hundred mounted Albanach warriors."

"Right," muttered Prefect Gereint to Elian, in Brytonic. "The Pendragon's gold spends just as well as anyone else's."

Comitissa Gyan glared at Gereint. He gave a sheepish bob of his head.

"Gold is of course welcome," said Chieftainess Alayna, switching to Brytonic but not deigning to regard anyone except the Comitissa. "What I want, however, is the chance to prove to the Pendragon that Clan Alban is no longer a threat to the people he is sworn to protect."

"By fighting alongside the Pendragon's men?" Surprise colored Comitissa Gyan's words. Elian heard disbelief too.

Chieftainess Alayna jutted her chin. "Fighting, aye, and dying if need be. Myself included."

Comitissa Gyan stalked closer to her, flexing her left hand as it hovered at her sword's hilt. "Providing horses I can understand. Why risk half the men Arthur's treaty limits you to keeping for Senaudon's defense? Why risk your own life?"

"Those two hundred will be defending Senaudon. If Dùn Fàradh-lann falls, Senaudon is the next logical Angli target." The upward cant of the Comitissa's eyebrow acknowledged the claim's truth. Peredur, Gereint, and Rhys murmured agreement. Chieftainess Alayna drew a slow breath. "I want to rewrite that accursed treaty. Sheltering Arthur's sister and her children was a start." Her tone softened but remained not one whit less assured. "If I must, I shall ink it with my own blood."

Elian spared a glance for his brother officers. They appeared as impressed as he felt.

"Yours is no mean offer, Chieftainess Alayna, and I thank you for it. This will add half again as many to the force I lead to Tarsuinn's relief, though I daresay you knew that," the Comitissa said. "I cannot make promises on behalf of my consort; nevertheless, depending upon the battle's outcome, your actions may well convince Arthur of your commitment to join our ranks as an ally who need not be bound by mistrust-forged limitations."

"Then it's settled," said the chieftainess, nodding in turn to Comitissa Gyan and Gereint. "I'll inform the man I shall be leaving in command of the remaining Albanach warriors to confer with Prefect Gereint about a modified defensive strategy for Senaudon."

"I need Prefect Gereint in the field." The Comitissa looked not at Gereint but at Elian. "Centurion Elian shall command Senaudon's defenders, Brytoni and Caledonian alike."

If Elian hadn't relieved himself before this meeting, he'd have been watering the ground. Eighteen years of legion training lent him the strength to resist the temptation of questioning her order. He gave a crisp salute and a crisper, "Yes, Comitissa."

Fists on hips, Chieftainess Alayna gave Elian a nigh endless appraisal. Her gaze seemed to sweep from the top of his head to the top of his boot, lingering upon his damned peg. "What, *him*?"

She may as well have said, "What, a cripple?" To judge by the pity upon the men's faces, they could have been thinking it too.

No pity marred the Comitissa's expression. "Centurion Elian led a combined unit of foot and horse troops on Maun." She glared at the dead Pict's wife. "You need not fear for Senaudon's safety."

The pleasure Elian derived from his commander's confidence died when Chieftainess Alayna said, in the tongue of her people, "How can a man who does not know Caledonaiche—to say naught of being ignorant about the people themselves—hold any hope of protecting them?"

Comitissa Gyan seemed ready to reply, but Elian gave a subtle shake of his head. Pressing her lips together, she inclined her head toward him.

Elian raised his right fist to his chest and held it there. "My lady," he began in the Picti language, "I learned Caledonaiche from a master of blade-cunning whom I am honored to call my best friend. In addition, he taught me a fair bit about Caledonach swordsmanship, pride, and honor. I vow to defend your home and your people as if they were my own." He bowed his head over the salute.

"Well said, Centurion . . . Elian, is it?"

"Aye, my lady." He raised his head and lowered his fist.

"So like my name; how appropriate. You have my blessing to move your effects to the fortress for the establishment of your command."

"That is most gracious of you, Chieftainess Alayna," said the Comitissa. "The Pendragon and I appreciate it greatly."

"I look forward to *seeing* how much you and your consort appreciate what I'm doing for you." With a swirl of her cloak, Chieftainess Alayna spun and strode toward the tent's opening. Before she stepped outside, she glanced over her shoulder. "Come, Prefect Gereint, and help my horse master select mounts for your men." Upon receiving approval from the Comitissa, Gereint saluted her and followed the chieftainess from the tent.

Elian waited while Comitissa Gyan instructed Prefect Peredur and Centurion Rhys regarding the troops' departure. At last she dismissed them.

"Have you questions about your new command, Elian?" Flashing an apologetic smile, she invited him past the inner curtain and bade him speak while she packed.

A lifetime's worth, but the question relating to the issue requiring her approval was, "May I invite a civilian to assist me?"

"Do you mean Wart? Of course." No, but he didn't gainsay his commander. She was rummaging through a chest, withdrawing tunics and gloves and such to lay upon her cot, when of a sudden she stopped, straightened, and faced him. "Please forgive my bluntness, and if this is none of my concern, do please tell me so, but Arthur and I have wondered about his absent father. Is he your son?"

It was nobody's cac-licking concern, as he had informed Gull when the dead Pict had asked the same question—after sending Wart to scrounge firewood where the nearest grove lay a quarter mile from the campsite—during the first night of their journey from Caer Lugubalion. But Elian wasn't about to say that to his commander and the wife of the man who had given him the will to live.

He implored her to resume packing while he crafted his answer.

"I was—intimate—with Wart's mother before he was born. But I shipped to Maun not long afterward, and Venna never breathed a word about the chance of my being his father, either when he was born or later, whenever I visited Caer Lugubalion on legion business and we renewed our companionship.

"When I got promoted to command the Tanroc garrison, they both understood that my visits had to stop. And then the Scots attacked, and, well, you know that part, Comitissa." She gave him a sympathetic murmur as she stuffed her saddlebags. "I'd hoped to see Venna at headquarters earlier this week, but Wart told me she had died not long after my promotion. I'm thankful that the Pendragon let him earn his bed and board by helping in the stables, my lady. Wart might not be the son of my flesh, but I cannot deny that he is the son of my heart."

She patted his hand. "I appreciate the tale, Elian. There have been times when I swear Wart must think Arthur is his father, the way he trails him like a puppy. It's a wonder the lad didn't stow himself in my consort's baggage for the march here."

Elian chuckled. "He's my pup now. I'll make sure he doesn't soil the rug."

Her smile faded when a trumpet call, close and shrill, rendered the tent's sides useless: the call to assembly. It killed Elian's intention of asking permission to let Gull assist him; so be it. If the dead Pict accepted Elian's invitation—no sure wager, that—Elian felt certain he could obtain forgiveness from his commander after the fact.

While Comitissa Gyan threaded the straps into the saddlebags' buckles, Elian rolled her bedding and tied it tight with its attached leather thongs. "Thank you for helping me, Centurion," she said, "and for your willingness to accept the joint command."

Willingness? He didn't for one heartbeat believe he'd had a choice. *Dereliction of duty* was not a phrase he had ever put into practice. "And I thank you, Comitissa, for having faith in me."

"You nurtured that faith by distinguishing yourself at Tanroc and after, with Angusel and the Manx recruits." She grinned. "And by climbing back into the saddle in such a creative manner."

"That was as much Wart's doing as mine, Comitissa."

Her helmet, as she donned it, eclipsed the grin. He lifted the bedroll and saddlebags for her. She accepted them with a nod and strode from the tent.

As he followed her, fighting to ignore the damned thump-scrape of his peg, he prayed hard that he, Elian, would not prove to be the puppy that soiled the rug.

CHAPTER 25

ALAYNA NIC AGARRA stood at the shield-size, polished copper mirror in her chamber and tugged at her jerkin. The image rippled in a few places where the smith had failed to roll the metal perfectly flat.

Brownish and distorted: just like her life had become.

The recent memory of her treatment of Angusel—born of her anger at Arthur—lanced her heart. She pressed a palm to the spot, ignoring the bronze studs' chill and willing the ache to ease. Had she carried the day at Abar-Gleann, none of these events would have come to pass. In retrospect, she had never felt prouder of her son than when she'd seen him riding near the forefront of the Pendragon's escort, approaching Senaudon.

With this accursed war about to swallow everyone whole, she prayed to all the gods for the chance to make amends with Angusel. She wouldn't blame him if he refused.

Sighing, she swept her hair behind her ears and settled her helmet into place. Guilbach had never missed an opportunity to tease her for not pinning her hair as every other warrior who kept long locks did. Her choice had its roots in a childhood sparring match with her sister, Airde. Alayna had unbound her hair so observers could tell the identically sized and armored lasses apart. Alayna's superior martial skills had denied Airde the hope of using Alayna's hair to gain an advantage.

Years later, she'd resumed the practice to prove her prowess to Guilbach. The tactic worked, and his teasing became a cherished part of their precombat routine.

She caressed the woad Tarsuinnach Falcon screeching across her shield-side forearm, and her heart's vise tightened. The fact that, a decade later, she still yearned for her beloved consort no longer surprised her.

A rap on the door made her turn her back on the mirror. "Enter."

Saigarmor, Alayna's second-in-command—an excellent warrior Guilbach had trained, though the man's skills would never surpass those of the blade-cunning master—marched into the chamber. She requested his report.

"The Pendragon's horse-warriors have begun to depart, my lady. His wife and her brother lead the column. Gereint moves out his troops next."

Alayna had expected Gereint's wings to be following Alban's to enforce Alayna's promise. Gyanhumara's demonstration of faith gave Alban's chieftainess a brief smile.

"Thank you, Saigarmor. Order both Albanach wings to mount. I shall be down presently."

He saluted, spun, and left. Alayna grabbed her gloves from a side table and tucked them into her belt. From the same table, she retrieved her cloak pin, a gold lion's head with a sparkling, pale blue stone for an eye, Guilbach's bonding-day gift to her. As she settled her cloak across her shoulders and pinned the brooch over her heart, she prayed that she would not have to search the Otherworld to reconcile with Angusel too.

No SOUND on earth compared with a mounted war-band. Thunder

might boom awhile and then fade, like hoofbeats did, but it lacked the jingling of bridles, the creaking of saddles, the neighing of horses, and the conversations of their riders.

Gull, chopping firewood near his hut, stood too far away to hear the gear or riders, but the horses' banter sliced through their hooves' thunder. After he had split eight more logs and realized the end of the column had yet to pass his position, he lodged his axe in the stump, pulled his plain-spun tunic over his sweaty chest, and set off for a closer look.

Careful to make no more noise than a deer would, he moved from bush to rock to tree across the hollow to the far ridge, which bordered the road that connected Senaudon with other settlements along the Ab Fhorchu. If he had guessed aright, he needn't fear discovery by outriders this close to Senaudon, but the exercise of caution cost him naught save a wee bit of time. All the while, rank upon rank of horsemen trotted past.

The former chieftain of Clan Alban inched up the ridge as close as he dared, and the riders kept appearing. The entire horse troop of the Pendragon's army, to judge by the number of dragon banners and by the fact that these warriors rode in grim silence. Gull marveled at that; Caledonach war-bands did not bother to exercise stealth unless they had an unaware enemy in their sights, and the Caledonaich appeared to outnumber the Breatanach riders by ten to one. Mayhap the Pendragon had imposed silence to keep clan rivalries to a minimum.

Or mayhap, he realized when the Albanach lion banner hove into view, with herself armed and riding tall in the midst of her similarly armed men, they were riding to war.

Gods! She looked glorious in her ebony leather battle-gear. The tops of her Albanach and Tarsuinnach tattoos peeked above her bracers; and her hair flowed dark and lush from beneath her helmet, across her shoulders, and down her back as if it were protecting her too. He recalled the many times he had admonished her—lovingly, of course—for tempting enemies into thinking they might gain a handhold upon those gorgeous locks. Her reply had never varied: "If they try, they shall die."

And die they did, though in those days most often by his sword.

Gull studied the men riding closest to her. Saigarmor and that lot could strive to protect her as he once had done, but how many would sacrifice their lives for her without hesitation as he once had vowed? Who among them did she trust as much as she once had trusted him?

His heart formed an answer that was disappointing, for her sake, but not surprising.

A crow flapped, scolding, past him to perch on a branch overhead as Alayna's mount neared his location. She stared at the bird, mayhap trying to decide how bad an omen it represented, until the twist of her neck became too uncomfortable. As she dropped her gaze, it seemed that she was looking straight through the brush at Gull.

He couldn't help but bend his lips into the lopsided grin their son had inherited from him.

Was her flicker of surprise real, or had he imagined it?

An instant later, all he could glimpse was the back of her helmet, her hair and cloak, and her horse's hindquarters.

In the next breath, his brain reported the huge disparity in the sizes of Alayna's and the Pendragon's troops. A sharp truth smote the grin from his face. If he had not abandoned her, this massive column of horsemen might have become hers to command, with the Pendragon a conquered ally struggling for every scrap of dignity she might choose to lob at his feet.

Gull resolved to help her bear that burden.

At his hut a few minutes later, an unexpected visitor threatened his resolution.

"Let me guess. The auld boar misses me already?"

Wart kicked at a rock buried in the dirt. "I don't know about that, sir, but he did ask me to tell you that he needs your help." Upon dislodging the rock, he met Gull's gaze. "At the fortress. Centurion Elian commands its defenders."

"Does he now?" Gull grinned. "Then he's a daft auld boar. With my wife gone—"

"You know about that?"

"Aye, that wee parade of hers and the Pendragon's was hard to miss, but I know not where they're bound. Do you?"

Wart scrunched his face. "Doon Far—Fair—?" He gave an apologetic shrug.

Gull's grin collapsed.

"Dùn Fàradhlann?" He prayed to all the gods he could name that he had guessed wrong.

"Aye, sir, that's the place. If a man could sit a horse, he got sent, save the few hundred defenders staying here."

His reasons for following the horsemen multiplied. Not only would he be striving to protect his wife but the place of his birth and his kin.

He dashed into the hut, headed to the corner where he kept his armor and weapons, and began arming himself.

Wart followed but stopped on the threshold. "You're coming with me, sir?" A thread of hope wove through his tone.

Gull's first impulse was to call the lad a daft boarling, but he decided that might sound cruel, given that Elian refused to acknowledge Wart as his son. Tightening the bracer over the Albanach Lion, he said, "Centurion Elian knows I canna reveal myself to Clan Alban before doing so to their chieftainess. Besides, he has you and several hundred other good men to help him keep order." Wart's young chest swelled, and Gull gave him a brief smile. "Please saddle my horse, Wart. Ye may tell the auld boar that the dead Pict is off to defend his home and resurrect himself to his wife."

WART FOUND Elian as he was getting acquainted with Prefect Gereint's workroom, after having completed an initial tour of Senaudon's grounds and defenses. In addition to its spaciousness, the workroom had the virtue of a large window overlooking the River Fiorth where the watercourse remained narrow enough to span by bridge before splaying into its much wider form. This workroom contained shelves and trunks and baskets stuffed to bursting with supply lists, disciplinary reports, duty rosters, and the like. Not that Elian would have stood a prayer of deciphering any of it, but Gereint had assigned one of his optios to handle that aspect of the command and to familiarize Elian with the duties and procedures.

Elian would have felt less awkward working in any other chamber, but the prefect had insisted, and of course that had ended the matter.

"I'm sorry, sir," said Wart, wringing his cap. "But that's what he told me to say to you."

Elian pivoted on his peg and step-thumped away from the window to grip the lad's shoulder. The wringing stilled. "I suspected I might be sending you on a fool's errand, and I thank you for being so prompt about it."

"Of course, sir." Wart's brow wrinkled. "What else would I have done?"

"Most lads your age might not have been so willing to report a failure." Elian smiled. "Then again, most lads wouldn't have been clever enough to invent that saddle modification for me either."

Wart's answering smile was brief. "Shall I go to work in the stables?"

The vast Alban complex of stables, paddocks, and pastures stood nigh empty, since most of the horses had borne their riders—old or new—to war. Elian said, "I have a different undertaking in mind for you." He made his way to the door to summon Optio Cyntaf from the outer workroom. "How many lads of this one's age live at the fortress?"

The young officer shrugged. "A score, perhaps, sir. I expect most are children of Chieftainess Alayna's warriors who haven't undergone their trial-of-blood rite for acceptance into Clan Alban's warband. Lasses too, as is the Caledonian way."

The very thing that had gone horribly wrong for the son of Elian's best friend.

"Do the warrior candidates have a trainer now that half the warband is gone?"

"I'd have to inquire, sir, but I doubt it," Cyntaf said. "From what I hear, Chieftainess Alayna handpicked her best men."

"Please do inquire. Inform these lads—and lasses—that if their trainer is gone, you and I shall fill that gap." Commanding the well-established defenses of a nigh-impregnable clifftop fortress didn't require a boatload of work, and Elian was glad for another useful way to occupy his time. He nudged Wart toward Cyntaf. "Equip him with practice gear, and then introduce him to his peers."

"I'm to start weapons training, sir? With you?" By Wart's wondering smile, one might have deduced that Elian had invited him to pitch a tent in God's throne room.

Elian returned the smile as confirmation.

Cyntaf saluted Elian and asked Wart his name.

"Ma gave me the name Wat, Optio Cyntaf."

Elian couldn't provide God's throne room, but the thrill shivering in his soul proved his readiness to tender the most precious thing that did lie within his power to bestow.

Pursing his lips to contain the flood of emotions, he laid his hands on Wart's shoulders. "For your faithful service to me, thinking of my needs even when I could not be with you, I name you Wastad." He drew a breath, blinked, and exchanged a brief nod with his officer. "Today, with God and Optio Cyntaf as my witnesses, I give you my name: Wastad map Elian."

Wart's eyes widened and his jaw dropped. "D-da? You're my—oh, sir! Do you mean it?"

"Of course, son, with my whole heart."

Wart lunged into Elian's arms, forcing him back a step. The peg skidded on the slate but held.

If it hadn't, he'd have been glad of that too.

FIORUISGE'S COUSIN Neoinean was kind and gentle as she poked and prodded and put Eileann through questions and paces in the storeroom of her apothecary shop. No one would accuse her of not being thorough.

"Will I be all right?" Eileann asked. The apothecary had finished the examination and helped Eileann don her overdress. "What did you find?"

"You appear healthy, my lady, if . . ."

"What?"

The woman, who appeared close in age to Eileann's mother, gave her a sad smile. "You have endured much in mind and in body. I sense your dolor."

"Dolor?" She couldn't argue with Neoinean's assessment. The frequency was slowing, but at times she felt overwhelming sadness manifest for reasons she didn't know how to explain. "Is that why

Fioruisge's brew had a stronger effect upon me?"

"Mayhap." After wrapping herself in her shawl, which she had shed prior to the examination, Neoinean sat beside Eileann on an adjacent crate. "As for your emotions, my dear, give yourself time—"

Escalating crowd noise seeped through the shop's walls. Memories of that awful day when Eileann had lost her bairn as well as her husband pummeled her. She gasped, hugging herself and staring into her soul's void.

Neoinean bade her wait in the storeroom while she investigated. The panicked shouts surged louder the instant she opened the door. Eileann's heart clenched.

A few breaths later, Fioruisge and Neoinean rushed into the storeroom. Fioruisge thrust a cloak and pin toward her. Eileann accepted the garment.

"Riders bear news that the Angalaranaich have crossed to the north bank and are marching on Dùn Fàradhlann as well as ferry ports along the north bank." Neoinean's eyes flickered, and she drew a deep breath. "Folk fear that Caledàitan will be next."

How dare they . . . Eileann gripped the cloak.

"My lady, we must leave too," Fioruisge said. "Now!"

They took my husband. My dear baby girl . . . Her knuckles whitened. *My life. From me, Àrd-Banoigin of Clan Tarsuinn. Because of them, I am outcast. Dead. How dare they?*

"Aye, the storeroom has a door opening into the alley." Her cousin pointed the way. "Come. You needn't be jostled by the crowd in the street."

Now they threaten my kin and my home? How dare they!

When Neoinean tried to grasp her arm, Eileann shrugged her off and rose. She flung the cloak about her shoulders and fastened it with the pin.

"I am through with the Angalaranaich and their treachery!"

She headed for the door, but Fioruisge scurried to block her way. "You are no warrior. You have no men to protect you. These diseased excuses for human beings will use you for their sport, kill you, and then piss on your corpse."

"Don't you think I know that? Don't you think our running has taught me how to be careful?"

"All the care in the world will avail you naught if you don't have a plan," said Neoinean. "Be reasonable, my lady. I know of a place we can go that should be safe. Breatanach servants of the One God have an enclave outside town. They trade ale they brew for my herbs and medicines, and I know them as good, decent men. Their god must be strong. I've seen storms take roofs here in town but leave their buildings untouched by wind or hail."

A tempting idea, but, "What of my parents and sister? Have they such a refuge? Would they go there and forsake our people?"

"Nay," Fioruisge murmured. "They would stay and fight. To the death."

"And I am going to help them."

Fioruisge folded her arms. "Even with the knowledge that they wanted you dead?"

Eileann felt ire surge through her tightening eyebrows. "It was my duty to die that day—a duty I might have returned to fulfill if you hadn't been at the dock, spouting nonsense about a different destiny."

"It wasn't nonsense," Fioruisge insisted. "It still isn't."

"Neither is my intention to help the clan however I may."

The wise-woman gave a conciliatory nod.

"How can one woman—" Neoinean thinned her lips in a grim smile. "How can one angry and determined woman hope to thwart Angalaranach treachery?"

"I shall unleash the fury of a ro h'uamhasach upon their heads." Both women looked doubtful. "I have dreamed of such a one. And I have seen him in the flesh. He fights for the Pendragon."

"The warrior who found you a few days ago?" asked Fioruisge. "He does not bear god-marks."

Fioruisge had a fair point; Eileann had not seen any tattoos on Angusel, sacred or otherwise. "Perhaps not yet," she allowed.

"You mean to perform an tùs for this man. Anoint him as a champion." Neoinean's eyes widened at Eileann's confirmation. "My lady, are you sure that's wise?"

Fioruisge's look became ashen, and she gripped Eileann's hands. "The anointing rite can be fatal for both parties if the gods reject the candidate. Those who would become priests must accept the risk of death during ordination as a condition of their calling. There never has been such an obligation for warriors, who must face the risk of death every day."

"Thank you for your concern, but I am aware of the risks." Eileann pressed Fioruisge's hands before releasing them. "And the potential consequences. I believe this is how the gods would have me interpret the vision they gave me." To Neoinean she said, "Do you have the needful herbs, dyes, and implements for the rite?"

"Of course," replied the apothecary.

"This is madness, my lady," Fioruisge insisted. "You have no idea where this warrior is, to say naught of where you might meet him."

"We could meet in a place the Angalaranaich ought not be interested in if their focus is Dùn Fàradhlann. The Pendragon should find my suggestion worthwhile if he's looking to save time transporting his men. As for where Angusel is now, he must be with Artyr somewhere on the south bank of the Ab Fhorchu."

"Somewhere." Fioruisge snorted. "He might meet you if the Pendragon chooses to order his army to Tarsuinn's defense. If there's been fighting, he could be dead."

Eileann chewed her lip; resolve made her stop. "Please take a portion of the coin we have received in trade for death offerings and find those couriers. Ask them to wait dockside for an urgent commission bound for the same destination. Bribe them if you must. Meantime I shall visit the religious enclave. After I pay Neoinean for her wares and services"—the apothecary smiled her thanks—"I should have funds to hire a servant of the One God to craft me a message."

CHAPTER 26

ELP...

Gawain stood apart from the throng—those who had survived the siege of Dunpeldyr—outside the great hall's double doors. As he watched, the guards uncrossed their spears and tugged on the doors' rearing, snarling bears to admit a visitor swathed in the gold-trimmed, dark-blue-streaked, forest green Clan Lothian mantle of chieftainship that upon this wearer looked two sizes too big.

Not me.

Gareth.

By custom, only immediate family members were permitted to view the chieftain's body before the funeral.

Given the final state of his relationship with Loth, Gawain wasn't sure he fit the description.

He had failed everyone.

Gawain. Help ...

His mother, his brothers, his sister, his centurion, his men who had died following him, his clansfolk, and their beloved dead . . .

I'm going to get you help.

Clutching the fold of his scarlet legion officer's cloak—Cato's cloak—which dragged across his heart, he blinked hard and bowed his head.

A hand clamped to his forearm and yanked it down.

"Go to him."

Gawain met the stern gaze of Terwyn, the warrior who had overseen his arms training from childhood up till the day he had joined the legion. The day he had abandoned his clan, his home, his family, his duty.

His father.

Of course I'm going to get you help.

Grimacing, Gawain turned to leave.

Terwyn tightened his grip.

"I can't!" Gawain wrenched free. "I failed him. I couldn't—"

Compassion softened the veteran's look. "A terrible thing, that wound. There was nothing anyone could have done."

"I should have reached him sooner. Gotten him out of there. I should have saved him. Somehow."

Somehow, please, God!

Gawain shut his wet, stinging eyes. The unanswered prayer's agony lanced his soul.

"The fighting was too intense, Lord Gawain. No one could have saved him."

Lord.

Centurion.

Gawain shook his head.

"I have to see to my men."

"Your men can wait." That wasn't Terwyn.

Gawain faced about. Arthur had arrived, escorted by Angusel and the scout squad survivors. Their wounds bore fresh bandages, but in the aftermath of yesterday's battle, while Lothian servants had toiled to make their chieftain fit for his final public appearance, not one man in the lot had taken time to clean blood and grime from anywhere else on their persons, Arthur included. It made Gawain realize he hadn't bathed since God alone knew when either.

If a soldier could walk without falling over, he'd been dispatched to ascertain how many Angli troops remained in the vicinity. Gawain had begged Arthur not to exempt him. Hell, if he had been falling over, he still would have volunteered.

As far as anyone could tell, the enemy, to the last bastard, had vanished.

Arthur gave Angusel a pointed look. Gawain's friend and second saluted and ordered the scouts to stand fast.

"Come, nephew." Arthur strode for the doors.

Not me.

His uncle looked back, wrinkles furrowing his forehead. "Must I make it an order, Centurion?"

Centurion?

Not me.

Gawain willed his feet to obey.

Trancelike, he kept pace beside his uncle as they approached the crowd. People noticed them, and an avenue opened. Subdued murmurs of welcome and sympathy wrapped him, tighter and tighter, like bandages on a spurting wound. He knew the people meant well, and he appreciated their support, but he could find no words for them. No words except:

I'm sorry! I'm sorry! I am so, so sorry.

THE BIER stood on a platform between the two firepits in the center of the hall. The fires had been doused so that the man who had governed Clan Lothian for three decades could be viewed for a few days longer. The tall windows had been shrouded for the same reason. The hall's light came from the twelve pine-scented candles surrounding the bier.

Loth lay supine, his great sword, Llafnyrarth, "Blade of the Bear," clutched in his right hand, its amber-inlaid scabbard strapped to his left hip, and his shield covering his chest. In the candles' fitful light, it looked as if he might awaken, pluck the coins from his eyelids, and pocket them, stretch a bit, perhaps scratch an itch, and begin his usual bellowing.

Gareth had hated that bellowing, for it always boded ill for someone, and most often that someone was him. Today he'd trade his soul to hear those blustery notes just once. They were getting harder by the hour to remember.

The hall's only sounds came from his battle to control his grief.

The doors creaked open. A shaft of sunlight sliced the gloom and fell across the body. The candles' flames jerked like chained prisoners.

Gareth whirled.

Two silhouettes stood framed in noon's light. One was the tallest man Gareth had ever seen, and the stockier one he knew better than the back of his own hand.

He grabbed fistfuls of mantle, pushed aside the memory of Loth's lectures about acting dignified, and dashed into his brother's arms.

"Gawain! Oh, Gawain, I—I—" He clung to his brother so he wouldn't rush out to throw himself off the battlements. But it had to be said. Then maybe Gawain would do the throwing. Gareth drew a breath. "This—the battle, Father's death, all of it—this is my fault!"

Clutching his shoulders, Gawain pushed him to arm's length, his mouth opening and closing like a fish that doesn't understand why it cannot breathe.

"Loth was killed by your spear, then?" asked their uncle, arms folded.

"What? No! But I—that is . . ." Gareth, pinned in Gawain's grasp, sighed and looked down. "He may as well have been."

Gawain let him go. "Explain, brother."

Gareth related the events of yestermorn. "Father wouldn't have been out there but for my foolish insistence on taking action. I am so sorry!"

"It wasn't foolish," said Arthur.

"Your insistence saved my life, and the lives of many of my men." Gawain looked away. When Gareth could see his eyes, they were wet. "I'm the one who should apologize." Gawain skimmed his fingertips over a fold of the clan mantle. "For doing this to you."

Gareth unclasped the amber-and-gold bear brooch that should have remained their father's for years to come. "Take it, Gawain. Please."

Gawain swatted Gareth aside, stepping closer to the bier and on into the candles' circle.

"I defied him in life." He laid a hand atop their father's, the hand that was clasping the sword. "I will be thrice damned before I defy him in death."

Gareth pulled off the mantle, bunched it in his other fist, and held it and the brooch toward his brother. "Then as your chieftain, I command you to rule the clan."

Gawain refused to take the accursed cloth, but Arthur did. "Loth chose you, Gareth. Trained you." He unfurled the mantle with a snap and draped it across Gareth's shoulders. "Yes, he left us too soon. He was a good chieftain, ally, husband, father, and friend. And you're, what, now? Fourteen?"

"Almost," Gareth said.

Arthur gave a slow nod. "No one in your position would feel ready for this. You would trade your soul for more of Loth's training, wouldn't you? I'll wager you don't believe you will ever be good enough for the clan. Or for him."

"Damned right." Gareth despised the mantle dragging at him, the weight he seemed powerless to shed. In his fist, he clutched the bear brooch so hard the pin stabbed his palm. "On all counts."

"Chieftains don't have to make decisions alone." Arthur took the brooch from Gareth and pinned it in place.

"He's right, Gareth. Let me help you with your first decision as chieftain." Gawain emerged from the candles' perimeter, holding across both upturned palms their father's sword, sheathed within its priceless scabbard. "Don't—that is, I strongly suggest that you don't bury this with him."

Merciful God above, the last time Gareth had tried to heft Llafnyrarth, not so long ago, he couldn't keep its point from gouging the floor. His father had ordered Gareth to pay for the repairs out of his personal stipend and oversee the work. The yelling had lasted a week longer.

However, after the floor was fixed and the blade honed to perfection, Loth had given Gareth a wooden practice sword weighted with a lead core and had guided Gareth in training with it every day. Until the siege.

"I'm not ready." Gareth saw the protests forming on the faces of his kin and held up a hand. "I need more strength and training before I can wield Father's sword. Until that day, I shall depend on Terwyn and others to help me finish becoming the chieftain—and the man— our people deserve."

Arthur gave Gareth a sharp legion salute. Gawain's astonishment bordered on the comical. A grin tugged at one corner of Gareth's mouth.

"For today, my brother, I shall depend on you to carry our father's sword to its place in the council chamber." He completed the grin. "Without dropping it."

That won a choked-off laugh from their uncle.

"Of course. It is my honor." Gawain tightened his grip on the weapon and set course for the hall's double doors. Before the guards could open them, he glanced at Gareth and winked. "My lord."

Gareth gasped.

Gawain grinned.

"Get used to it," Arthur advised, "but don't stop appreciating it."

He was less certain he could perform the first directive than the second.

One of the doors opened to admit Terwyn and a legion soldier who couldn't have been much older than Gareth. Bandaged wounds and bloodstained armor proclaimed the young man's role in the recent action. While the soldier saluted, Terwyn went to one knee at Gareth's feet.

"Please forgive the intrusion, my lord, but this officer has received news too important to wait."

Gareth bade his father's—*his* adviser to rise.

"Decurion Ainchis Sàl," said Arthur to the soldier, "report."

"Lord Pendragon, Chieftain Rionnach advises that a second Angli force has departed Dun Eidyn. His scouts put their numbers at five thousand. They crossed the Fiorth at its narrowest neck and are marching north."

"Straight for Dùn Fàradhlann. Bloody hell." Arthur clenched his fists and gritted his teeth. "Dunpeldyr was a diversion."

"Sir, if you intend to return," said the officer, "I may have an idea that will save the legion time. A second . . . dispatch mentions a large beach several miles upriver from Caledàitan that should be shielded from Angli attention, near the ferry port of Abar-Dùr—"

A flick of Arthur's finger halted the report, and it halted Gareth's speculation about the softening of the young man's tone.

"I would move heaven and earth to help such a staunch ally," Arthur said. "But if the Angli have targeted Rionnach, his fleet cannot transport us."

Gawain shoved their father's sword into Gareth's hands. After Gareth shed his surprise, he realized Llafnyrarth didn't seem as heavy as he remembered.

"I'm sorry," Gawain said to Arthur, hands spread in supplication. "I should have advised Centurion Cato to have us scout westward from the beachhead, closer to Dun Eidyn."

Their uncle's fist landed on Gawain's shoulder and tapped thrice. "I don't have time to assign blame, and you, Centurion, do not have time to wallow in it." Arthur gestured, palm up, at Gareth. "How many Lothian ships are available to transport the legion?"

Gareth balanced the sword flat on his left shoulder and gave a helpless shrug with the right. "It's possible that a few fishermen and traders have returned for the day. Terwyn?"

The adviser agreed. "I shall see what I can arrange, my lord."

"Thank you," Gareth said. "Please assure the captains they shall be compensated. Meet me later outside the treasure vault so I can give you get what you need." The dead apothecary's Angli gold would make a fine start.

Terwyn bowed and departed.

"And I thank you." Affection tinted Arthur's slight smile. "Chieftain Gareth."

"I'm sorry that Lothian can't spare you men, Uncle Arthur." He rubbed his lip, trying to recall what Terwyn had told him that morning. "We have graves to dig, enemy pyres to build, weapons and armor to recover, and a well shaft that must be plugged, drained, cleansed, and refilled. Plus the evaluation of structures in the villages and making any needful repairs before letting the people go home."

The soldier Ainchis Sàl requested permission—of Gareth—to speak. Gareth cocked an eyebrow at Arthur, who inclined his head. Intrigued, Gareth bade the officer to continue.

"Chieftain Gareth, there is a barn near Hafonydd hiding the bodies of eighteen Angli soldiers that it may be best to torch and rebuild." Ainchis Sàl gave a long blink, drew a breath, puffed it out, and tightened his jaw. "I'm sorry, sir, but our scout squad had no time to give them a decent burial."

"I shall add it to my list. Thank you, Decurion." Something in the young man's demeanor made Gareth wish he could speak with him at greater length. God willing, he'd get a chance later. He redirected his attention at Arthur. "Food, drink, weapons, and anything else the legion needs that's within my power to provide is yours, Uncle."

His offer included gold, but he'd have been surprised if Arthur asked for it, and not for reasons of politeness. The extra weight would hamper the legion's speed and divert soldiers to guard the chests. Gareth had disagreed with Loth about not compensating Arthur and his men in coin for recovering the cattle stolen by Angli raiders last year, and Loth's second son resolved that the debt would stay at the top of his list until he repaid it.

Arthur smiled as they gripped forearms. "I'm glad to see Clan Lothian in such capable hands." The smile died. "With your permission, Gareth, I would like time with your father." He said to Gawain and the decurion, "Alone."

"Of course; take as long as you need." Gareth swept his free hand toward Gawain and Ainchis Sàl. As the trio strode toward the doors, the guards dragged them open. By tacit agreement, Gareth exited first. He felt as self-conscious—and doomed—as an ice floe in hell.

He emerged, blinking and squinting, into the sunlight. After his eyes adjusted, he stood surveying the people. *His* people. With each cheer and shout of his name, the mantle didn't feel quite as heavy. He squared his shoulders and gave the crowd a grateful smile. Praying with all his soul that Arthur was right, he unsheathed his father's sword—*his* sword—and with quivering muscles, he raised it overhead.

"HEAR THAT, old friend?" Arthur hoped that Loth had considered him a friend despite their prickly relationship. "Your people are cheering for your son."

The sound muted as the doors closed, plunging the hall into gloom.

Guilt dragged at his heels as he passed the candles' perimeter to within half a stride of the bier. "I'm sorry I couldn't get my men to Dunpeldyr fast enough. I'm sorry I couldn't prevent"—he reached for the hand that had wielded Llafnyrarth more often than he would ever know, the hand forever empty now that Gareth, as was his right and duty, had claimed the magnificent blade—"this."

He sank to his knees on the cold slate, bent his head over that hand, and shut his eyes. The sting worsened. "I'm sorry," he forced himself to whisper, "that I took your firstborn from you."

It was the raw truth. Regardless of what he had told Loth—and himself—he never would have accepted Gawain into the legion if Loth had supported Arthur's ascension to the office of Dux Britanniarum. The idea to enlist had been Gawain's, and it had represented dereliction of duty to kin and clan, but Arthur had applauded it. Hell, he had reveled in the knowledge that his nephew had chosen a soldier's life with him rather than a ruler's life with his father.

With Gareth committed to assuming the chieftainship and Gawain refusing to buck what he perceived as Loth's final wishes, Arthur saw no way to undo their choices.

He raised his head, blinking, and stood to stare at the unforgiving face.

"I failed you in so many ways, Loth, and I'm sorry for all of it. As God is my witness, I vow to protect your wife, your children, and your clan to the absolute best of my ability. To that end, I shall destroy the Angli threat and deliver King Colgrim to you so that you may deal with him in your own way." It had to be Arthur's imagination, of course, but he'd have sworn Loth's face seemed less stern. "And if one day I must convince Gawain to take up Lothian's mantle of chieftainship, then by God I shall do it to my last breath."

The flames of the bier's candles lurched, goaded by Arthur's movements as he departed. He sensed the odd—and oddly comforting—notion that Loth had gifted him a parting "Hrmph."

CHAPTER 27

INGELCYNN HAD A saying:

"Men plan, and the gods laugh."

Badulf had planned to impress his father with news of the Brædan ruler's death, but lacking proof—regardless of how close he'd come to obtaining it—King Colgrim's response, on the ferry docks where Badulf and his men had regrouped with the last units of the main Eingel army, had been a skeptical snort.

That snort had come less from his father and king than from the gods themselves, damn them.

As a result, he and his men drew the thankless duty of watching a barren strip of sand, miles away, for signs of enemy troop movements rather than helping friends and kin secure their king's primary objective.

Shifting on the stump so that his numb arse cheek might revive, he wondered whether serving the Dragon King's head on a gilded plate would be enough to redeem himself in his father's eyes.

However, this duty carried the advantage of allowing his men time to heal.

A pair of figures emerged into view on the beach, close to the water's edge. Both wore cloaks and long garments that whipped about their ankles in the wind as they stood face-to-face. Both were shouting and making exaggerated arm gestures.

Badulf's men nocked arrows to their bows. He signaled them to desist. Two women could not be a threat to the Eingel army, but they did pique his curiosity. From this distance, he didn't stand a prayer of discerning the women's words even if he could understand their language.

A bit of sport was a fitting reward too. He'd keep the prettier of the two for himself, of course, until he tired of her.

It was good to be a prince.

Grinning, he motioned for two of his soldiers to join him in shifting closer to the intruders.

"FEIGNING DEATH has killed your wits!" Fioruisge flailed her arms like a gale-stricken hemlock. "My lady, please come back to the chambers we hired in town. If your chosen champion arrives, 'twill be with an army at his back, and we shall learn of it."

If.

The wise-woman was right. Eileann didn't know whether Angusel had received her message, to say naught of his ability—or willingness—to heed her suggestion.

But it seemed a betrayal not to be here, waiting for his boat and watching it glide to a halt on the sand, opening her arms to him as he vaulted over its side and pelted toward her . . .

"My lady, are you listening?"

She shook off her reverie with a toss of her braids before she could drown in its depths, pleasant though those depths might be.

"Of course, Fioruisge. You go on ahead. I'll be along in a few minutes. When you see Neoinean, please tell her to—" Three dark shapes reared against the flaming orb of the setting sun and lurched toward them, oozing menace. "Run! Run now! Go!"

Fioruisge shrieked and set off, bunching her skirts in her fists and lengthening her stride. Eileann tried to follow her.

She did not get far.

Rough hands clamped onto her arms and yanked her around. She screamed, long and loud, until one of the men slapped her silent and latched his mouth onto hers. Her cheek ached, but she kept screaming into that rancid mouth, bucking and twisting and kicking.

A swift rip and her breasts burst through the ruined dress. While his companions pinned her arms, the man who'd slapped her clutched her waist and bent to suckle them, pinching the nipples between his teeth. His vile hands groped between her thighs.

She gulped in a breath, tipped her stinging face toward the heavens, and shrieked her desperate prayer.

THE LÙTHEAN merchant's ship, the first of four procured by Chieftain Gareth, which had wallowed at the winds' mercy for the last several hours, burdened with the Pendragon, scouts, and as many soldiers and retainers as could cram aboard and not hamper the crew, had finally reached the sandy inlet Eileann had mentioned. From his spot near the prow, Angusel squinted through the setting sun's glare for the tiniest sign that she might be waiting for him.

The scrape of the vessel hitting the sand was pierced by a woman's scream.

He slung his shield across his back, hoisted himself atop the rail, and jumped overboard, landing on the wet sand in a crouch. He drew his sword as he straightened and broke into a sprint. Not far from the water's edge, a woman was struggling in the clutches of three armed men. The crunch of feet on sand suggested that a number of the Pendragon's men had followed him. Not that he needed help. The three cù-puic, however, would need help to keep Angusel from dicing them into fish bait.

The men saw him, threw the woman to the sand, and ran toward the tree line. One seemed familiar to Angusel, but he couldn't decide why. As they neared the trees, the familiar man shouted an order.

Arrows darkened the sky.

And, dear gods, the woman was Eileann.

"Stay down!" he yelled to her. "Cover your head!"

She did both, and she drew in her knees.

Behind him, he heard outcries of the fallen, followed close on by Arthur's Ròmanach command to make the turtle formation, where stooped-over men interlocked their shields for projectile protection while moving forward. The sharp thuds of steel-barbed arrows hitting metal, but no pained shouts, proved the formation's effectiveness.

Even if Angusel hadn't been too far out in front to join them, he'd have been thrice damned before he'd abandon Eileann. He bent double to let his shield transform him into a turtle and hurried over to her. She was sobbing, and her dress was ripped, but she seemed unhurt. On all fours, he covered as much of her as he could.

"You came! Oh, thank the gods, you came!"

He stroked her mottled, tear-streaked face and shushed her. Arrows still whizzed past them. Those with different flight sounds had to be coming from the ships. Enemy yelps proved the validity of that guess. A few Angalaranach barbs glanced off his shield. One grazed his shield-side knee before embedding in the sand beside him. The pain burned. He bit his lip, fighting the groan.

She shifted onto her side and hugged her knees under her chin.

"May I lower myself a bit?"

Her squeak didn't sound like a refusal. He brought himself down and around her, bracing his forearms on the sand, letting his helmet guard her face, and cradling the top of her head with his gloved hands.

Gods, she fit as if they had fashioned her for him, and he thanked them to the core of his soul.

ARTHUR SCUTTLED along with the rest of his men in the midst of the turtle formation while the arrow flights slowed, then stopped. His archers in the boats that had beached after his might have convinced the Angli to abandon their ambush, or they might be conserving ammunition, preparing for a direct attack.

He halted the turtle. A slow, mental count to one hundred yielded no answers.

Ordering Angusel to be the bait was tempting, but Arthur couldn't see how far ahead the decurion had run. Regardless, he should be protecting the woman.

As the perimeter soldiers continued holding their shields vertical and facing outward, Arthur ordered the optios to slip off their helmets and raise them on the points of their swords above the shield roof.

The ploy, he was thankful to note, did not draw Angli fire.

Arthur commanded the unit to break formation and dash for the tree line to search for the enemy. The soldiers obeyed and no enemy arrows launched. He waved the rest of the cohort ashore. Some he detailed to unload the baggage and supplies to free the ships for retrieving the next wave of troops, some to set a perimeter on the beach, care for the wounded, and bury the dead, and the bulk of the remainder he sent to join their brethren in the hunt for Angli foes in preparation for securing the campsite, farther away from the beach, in the fork where two tributaries converged to form the much wider watercourse that gouged the sand to feed the firth.

That left the matter of his insubordinate young officer. Arthur put Marcus in command of the work details and stalked across the sand, trailed by guards. Angusel and the woman had risen, and he finished draping his cloak about her. She stood shivering as she held closed the remains of her dress with a hand attached to a forearm bearing red scorch marks. The lad snapped into a rigid stance in spite of a glistening arrow wound on the outside of his left knee.

"Ainchis Sàl a Dubh Loch. Did you hear me command you to stay aboard?" He elected to conduct the conversation in Caledonaiche to prevent a misunderstanding.

"What! You—?" His eyes grew round as shield bosses. "Nay, sir."

Arthur believed him. Deficient hearing did not excuse insubordination, but he couldn't deny the lad's selfless, if reckless, heroism. "Give me one good reason why I shouldn't flog you."

Angusel had the ballocks to jut his chin. "In my position, sir, you'd have done the same."

Bloody hell, the whelp was right.

"Very well, what would you do to an officer who dashed off, without permission or assistance, to rescue one woman on enemy-held ground, endangering not just himself and her, but his war-chieftain and hundreds of his sword-brothers, plunging the fate of the campaign into peril?"

"Twenty stripes." The woman gasped; twice that number was the death sentence. Angusel's gaze didn't waver. "And demotion to enlisted rank, sir."

The whelp was right about that too. Today, however, Arthur needed every soldier who could march and wield a sword, and every leader. "Be thankful that I am not you. Decurion."

Angusel blew out a breath. "I am, sir."

"Lord Pendragon, I am so sorry," said the woman. "I never meant to draw you and your men into a trap."

"Why were you here?" Arthur knit his eyebrows.

"She is the source of the second message, sir."

"The private message you let me assume had come from Rionnach." Grinding his teeth, he dug his right fist into his thigh to keep it from colliding with his officer's jaw. "Deliberate deception is worth twenty stripes in itself."

"As you will, sir." Sighing, the lad grimaced as if he expected Arthur to produce a whip from thin air.

"No, my lord!"

Clutching Angusel's cloak and her torn dress in her left fist, the woman reached out her other hand and shifted toward Arthur. His guards lunged to close the gap, but he halted them.

"Please do not punish him for upholding his vow to protect my identity." She pressed her palm to Angusel's chest, her forearm scar looking angrier in the harsh sunset. "With the Pendragon as my witness, I release you from that vow, Angusel mac Alayna." Sucking in a breath, she faced Arthur. That scar and its location, her utterance of Angusel's birth name and easy use of Arthur's title, and the fact that she'd possessed the wit and means to craft such a message as well as knowing where to send it, had suggested her identity to Arthur.

He elected to keep the speculation to himself.

"I implore you to forgive Angusel, Lord Pendragon," she said. "I ask this boon on behalf of the man I had hoped that my ill-conceived choices might have helped: my father, Chieftain Rionnach."

Arthur noted that she had revealed herself without speaking her given name. "Perhaps not so ill conceived, my lady. Your presence disrupted the Angalaranach ambush. My troops' landing could have been far bloodier."

First blood would have been shed by the scouts, including one of whom she seemed quite fond. Angusel might have reached the conclusion on his own, if his eye's twitch was a clue.

"Although you hadn't the experience to presume that this beach was going to be watched," Arthur continued, "it is the best site for us to land by virtue of shaving a day off our travel, which would have been spent marching." He took her free hand into his. "I thank you for the suggestion, and I am glad that my impetuous officer could effect your"—he couldn't resist uttering the first word that leaped to mind—"resurrection."

Chuckling, she withdrew her hand. "I believe your officer is not so impetuous as to ask this next question. Does Angusel have your permission to escort me to the rooms I have hired in town, and to stay with me for as long as I require?"

Arthur couldn't decide which amused him better, Eileann's implication or Angusel's flame-cheeked, gape-mouthed reaction to it. "He does, my lady, upon two conditions." He glared at the lad. "First, that you understand this is a continuation of your duty to protect and assist the daughter of an ally, and it is in no way to be viewed as a reward."

"Of course, sir!"

"Second, report to camp by sunup, ready to march." Arthur pointed toward the site where soldiers had begun erecting tents and fortifications.

"Trìbruachan," Angusel said. Sorting through his Caledonian vocabulary, Arthur realized that the lad had invented a name based on the camp's proximity to three river banks, which Arthur found he preferred to the standard marching camp numerical designation. They shared a nod. "Noted, sir."

"I shall order Centurion Gawain to report your arrival to me regardless of the hour. If your—duties—this evening render you unfit to fight, the twenty stripes and demotion shall be waiting for you. Is that clear?"

While Angusel barked his affirmation, Eileann said, "Lord Pendragon, I promise that Angusel shall return to you on time and more fit to fight than any other man under your command."

Arthur would have dismissed her statement as but a foolish boast if not for her earnest seriousness.

CHAPTER 28

PEREDUR NIC HYMAR had dismissed his ala centurions and was reaching for his gloves on the field table of his headquarters tent when the flaps parted, admitting harsh light from the setting sun, and his sister. Gyan lacked only her gloves to resume the fight. His stomach twisted.

If she died, the first head her consort would have the right to demand would be his.

If she died, Per would invent a way to behead himself.

"Please tell me you've heard from Artyr," he said. "Is the legion close?"

From her grim expression he inferred a lack of knowledge. "Have faith in him, Per. He will get his men here as soon as he can." Her expression softened. "How bad are your casualties?"

"Half the men and mounts injured in last night's supply-line raids are fit to fight tonight. The wings attacking the head of the Angalaranach column today have fared worse, but we should have the numbers to make a good go at slowing them come dawn. The lame and dead horses have been replaced by remounts, and the horses that lost their riders to injury or death have been recovered to become remounts themselves." Fingering his chin stubble, he performed a fast calculation. "In total, the cohort is down mayhap one pair in twenty."

"That is welcome news. Father's and Alayna's estimates were much the same." She pursed her lips. "But?"

He tugged on his sword-side glove, then opened and closed the fist several times to work the leather into place while collecting his thoughts. "Last night we had the advantage of surprise. That diminished in today's attacks on the enemy's forward units, but our riders halted the advance. Tonight the Angalaranaich will be expecting us." With his ungloved shield hand, he reached toward his sister's face, realized her helmet's cheek guards would be in his way, and lowered the hand. "Gyan, please consider remaining here."

She gave that hand a squeeze.

"What? And gut First Ala by withdrawing my guards from its ranks? I'd rather not test Artyr's claim that he will execute any man he perceives to have abandoned his duty to me."

She had a point. Several, in fact. The Pendragon's legendary protectiveness of Gyan ran straight to the core of her guard unit's formation, men chosen for their superior fighting skills and for their oath to die for her. As her brother, he had applauded that decision. The Comites Praetorii had combined with First Ala, since one in five of that unit's members had been serving as Arthur's scouts for the past sennight. Despite Gyan's participation, Per had applauded that move too. Her elite guards bolstered the First's numbers above full strength, and they recorded the highest kill count of all wings last night, Chieftainess Alayna's vaunted horsemen included, thanks in no small part to the javelin training the men of the First had received from Alayna's son.

Being prefect gave him the right to order First Ala to stand down from tonight's raids. It would provide Gyan and their encampment extra protection but at the cost of putting the other alae, along with Alayna's two units and Ogryvan's four, at greater risk.

His rank gave him no right to order his commanding officer to stand down, and it galled his soul.

It did, however, give him latitude to implement the second-best course of action. "If you insist on fighting with the First, then so shall

I." Per pulled the glove onto his shield hand and knit his fingers with forceful thrusts. "May the gods have mercy upon the Angalaranach soldier stupid enough to target you."

He held the tent flap for Gyan to precede him outside.

"I think I can help with that." She stepped between two of her guards, who had been flanking the tent's opening. Her slim smile, when she faced about, reminded him of her consort's. "What say you, Prefect Peredur, to arming your troops with flaming arrows?"

The Caledonach salute he gave his sister—upraised fist clenched, splayed open, and clenched again—conveyed equal measures of fierceness and pride. "I say, Comitissa Gyan, let the burning begin!"

ANGUSEL FELT silly, standing in the outer chamber of the rooms Eileann had hired at the riverfront inn of Abar-Dùr while she knelt beside him, fussing over a scratch from a damned Angalaranach arrow that hadn't gotten stuck in his leg.

To say naught of the embarrassment of her having sponged him clean of the blood and grime, but the water's warmth had felt wonderful, and her fingers' warmth . . .

He gave his head a sharp shake. "I should go. You've seen me survive far worse wounds than this."

"Any wound, no matter how slight, will heal faster if it's covered."

Her being right didn't make him feel less silly.

It did, however, remind him of an unpaid debt. He stooped to grasp her hands and help her rise. "Thank you." Upon lifting those delicate hands to his lips, he gave them a lingering kiss. "And thank you for your harping in the field hospital that day. It helped me"—beyond his power to describe—"a lot."

"I'm glad," she murmured.

Into the pause drifted the sound of chanting muted by the door to the inner chamber.

"What are your ladies doing?"

She gripped his sword hand with both of hers. "Sanctifying the chamber."

An enticing idea, and dawn was hours off. However, "Eileann, I appreciate what you've done for me, but I need to report to camp." He couldn't risk losing his war-chieftain's trust.

When he would have pulled away, she held him with surprising strength. "I promised Artyr the Pendragon that you would become a better warrior, and that's what this ritual shall do."

An tùs?

The anointing had not been performed upon a warrior of Clan Alban for generations, and for excellent reason. The last Albanach to try had died. He had proven himself as the clan's champion in combat countless times, so the story went, but the gods had deemed him unworthy. Clan Alban was fortunate not to have been destroyed after losing him.

Angusel expected the gods to scoff at the idea of anointing as champion the warrior who couldn't prevent Chieftain Loth's death. Or Loholt's.

The woman who'd been introduced to him as Neoinean the apothecary opened the door. Out wafted a burst of scent so intense it set his nose to itching. He scrubbed it, but Neoinean stopped him and guided the fist to his side.

"Breathe, lad," she said, "and all shall be well."

Well? How could he, a Caledonach outcast with but a few skirmishes to his credit and a growing list of failures to his eternal shame hope to receive the gods' favor?

But the dutiful soldier followed the order and inhaled. So did the beautiful lady who had refused to release his hand. They shared a glance. She smiled at him, deep and genuine, and his thrashing heart slowed. When Eileann glided toward the inner chamber, pulling him farther into the aromatic cloud, he did not resist.

FROM HIS position in the trees crowning the ridge west of the beach, Badulf looked down upon the Dragon King's marching camp, feeling his frown straighten. Most of his men had escaped the blown ambush and subsequent Brædan patrols, and he had already chosen the soldiers who would be accompanying him. The cloud cover was deepening night's gloom. The next hour would be the darkest. Activity in the camp was dwindling; the perimeter sentries remained alert, but their fellows had begun banking fires to retire to tents, including the Dragon King himself. That tent lay in the heart of the camp.

Getting to it would pose a great challenge, to be sure, but the reward for killing the enemy army's leader would far outweigh the risks.

Imagining the gratitude he'd earn from his father and king, Badulf grinned.

Misty rain began spinning out of the sky. Its strengthening sent the remaining off-duty Brædan soldiers to their tents. The visible sentries had pulled up their cloaks' hoods, but Badulf knew from experience how difficult it could be to stay alert under the persistent patter.

A glance at his own men, hooded but canted like leashed hounds on the scent, assured him that they would not succumb. The promise of receiving extra treasure from King Colgrim, and the lust to avenge their fallen brethren here and at the Fort of the Spear, had led them to forgive Badulf for the unfortunate timing that had diminished the ambush's effectiveness.

He raised his fist to signal them to creep down the hillside, a few men at a time to minimize the sounds of their passage.

The Brædeas did not stand a chance.

ANGUSEL STOOD in the center of the bedchamber, naked save for the linen binding his loins and wounds. Eileann couldn't take her eyes from his muscular form, but her gut writhed in reminder of the sheer magnitude of what she wished to accomplish for him. His acceptance of the rite's requirements helped to calm her. As Fioruisge continued the soft chant, pleading for the gods' blessings, Neoinean lifted a flagon first to Eileann's lips, then Angusel's.

"This shall help you be receptive to divine guidance," Neoinean assured them.

The warm wine bore a spiciness that tasted sharper than the mulled drink Eileann favored. Its heat, in taste as well as temperature, honed her senses to razor clarity. She felt aware of colors and patterns she had never recognized: the myriad hues of a candle's flame, the outraged textures of her scorched clan-mark, the weeping wounds gouging her soul . . .

Neoinean filled a terra-cotta cup with gray-blue woad dye. Eileann noticed a hairline crack running from rim to base. Neoinean placed the cup into Eileann's hands. When they trembled, threatening to spill the dye, the apothecary stilled them.

"Where is the brush?" Eileann asked, as much to forestall the inevitable as to seek an answer.

A heartbeat later, she chided her fear. Outcast or not, Clan Tarsuinn needed him.

Them.

"No brush. The anointing is as much about the connection between the anointer and the anointed as it is about the connection between the anointed and the gods. Use your finger, like this."

Neoinean dipped Eileann's index finger into the dye, tapped the excess on the rim, and guided it to sketch the shape of a salmon on Angusel's forehead, near the hairline. Eileann felt a wee tingle as she completed the fish. His surprised expression told her he had felt it too.

"Now state to the anointed the god-mark you have drawn and its purpose." Neoinean stepped away and regarded Eileann, cocking an eyebrow as the silence stretched.

Eileann cleared her throat and gazed at Angusel. "The salmon of Clota. For wisdom." She wasn't sure how a warrior fighting in the throes of battle frenzy could exercise wisdom, but she was not going to cast doubt upon her teacher's example or the purpose the goddess had revealed.

Angusel bobbed his head, his curly black hair obscuring the fish.

Palms angled upward, Fioruisge changed the chant to echo Eileann's words and embellish them, begging for the goddess's gift to be bestowed upon the anointed.

"Use what you know of the gods and their abilities, my lady," said Neoinean, "to draw their marks upon the anointed where you believe those divine gifts will benefit him the most."

"Please draw the god-marks so that my armor hides them." Angusel glanced at Neoinean, uncertainty creasing the salmon. "Does the anointing permit this?"

"It does," stated the apothecary.

"They are meant to be seen!" Eileann itched to shake sense into him, but touching the anointed was forbidden save to craft the god-marks. "How will the gods find you if you hide the marks?"

"The anointed does not wish to offend those who have rejected him, and that is a worthy consideration." Her teacher, apparently exempt from the touching stricture, patted Eileann's shoulder. To her surprise, Fioruisge wove Neoinean's words into the chant. "Fear not, child. The gods will see the marks as you draw them, and they shall not forget. Priests and warriors may choose to make their god-marks permanent, but the rite does not require it."

Eileann inclined her head at Angusel. "As you will, then."

Behind shuttered eyelids, she cast about for an image to draw and received a double blessing. Upon opening her eyes, she asked Angusel to lift his arms so she could anoint his biceps. The sketches looked crude, childish, and incomplete. She prayed for them to work; she hoped that the longer and stronger tingling was a sign that they would. "The bull of Lugh on your sword arm for strength, and the stag of Cernunnos on your shield arm for cunning."

Fioruisge added Eileann's pronouncements, raising her arms higher with each new verse.

Whatever concoction Neoinean had given Eileann must have taken full effect. In swift succession she drew the spear and rod of Nemetona on Angusel's right thigh for fierceness, the mare of Epona on his left thigh for speed, and the sun of Lord Annaomh over his heart.

"For hope," she told him about the sun, and wondered at the word choice the god had inspired. The sun of Annaomh represented justice, leadership, and truth. Lord Annaomh was revered for those traits, as were the warriors who honored him. And yet hope was appropriate, since the strengthening sun delivered salvation from winter's grip, and the Lord of Light embodied salvation from the eternal ravages of his twin brother, Annàm, and the evil Samhraidhean.

Angusel beamed without touching her, as was proper for this phase of an tùs. The time for their touching would come, but not soon enough for Eileann's liking.

The final image burned into her brain and killed her swelling excitement.

She gasped, fist to mouth.

"What is it, child?" asked Neoinean.

"A mark I dare not draw upon the anointed," Eileann whispered. That the image was unlike any she had seen for this god represented the least of her worries. "I fear what it may do to him—to us both."

The apothecary rapped her finger thrice on the tabletop. "Draw it here."

Hand shaking so hard that she spattered more dye than she placed, Eileann forced herself to complete the request. When no mishap befell her or the table, Neoinean commanded her to proceed. Dreamlike, Eileann watched as if her hand belonged to a different woman. It did not shake as it shaped the god-mark upon Angusel's back. The jolt sparked by the mark made her cry out. Her hand stung as if it had been pierced by a flaming arrow. She dropped the empty cup to chafe her throbbing palm. The cup broke along the crack.

Angusel groaned through clenched teeth and jerked his shoulders, gasping.

Her pain subsided. Angusel's breathing steadied, and his muscles relaxed. Eileann dared to regard her work.

This sketch had emerged as the best drawn of the lot. The red whip scars that had torn her heart as she had washed him lent vivid detail.

"The—the crossed bloody cudgels of Lord Annàm, embellished with an ox s-skull." She swallowed hard, suffering the heart-freezing effects of the fallen god's gift before Fioruisge could chant about it. "For terror."

A strange look formed on Angusel's face. He cocked his head from side to side and snapped a demand for silence. The rite was not finished, but all three women complied; his tone brooked no disobedience.

Strain as she might, Eileann could not hear anything unusual. Angusel rushed to the window, swept aside the leather covering, and peered out.

A tendril of smoke wafted in. Far from being the pleasant smell of a cooking fire, this scent was acrid and conveyed the stench of fear.

He released the leather and faced her.

"Angusel, what—?" The sight of him killed Eileann's words.

His chest was rising and falling rapidly, the sun of hope with it. As his fists clenched and biceps flexed, the bull and stag appeared ready to leap off his arms. The mare, the salmon, and the spear and rod quivered to share in that readiness. She quailed at the idea of taking another look at the ox skull and cudgels.

That design might be oozing his blood.

In the restless candlelight, his eyes seemed to glow bright and feral. The intensity of his gaze frightened her.

"Help me arm. Please," he rasped. "Trìbruachan is under attack."

CHAPTER 29

MERLIN INTONED THE matins service's final amen and relaxed his arms. During the benediction, the group of worshippers—servants and soldiers offering extra prayers for Arthur, Gyanhumara, their men, and their allies—had grown by one. The newcomer remained standing beside one of the torchlit columns flanking the entrance to this tiny side chapel inside St. John's as the flock filed out. Merlin halted before him. The man's posture was as rigid as those columns, despite the mud-spattered implication that he had traveled hard through the long summer twilight to arrive at Caer Lugubalion by midnight.

The courier snapped a salute.

"Not here, Optio." Though Merlin strove to keep his voice low, he heard in the echoes invading the nave a remnant of Emrys's mocking laughter. He banished the specter with the barest shake of his head and led the courier from the church to the praetorium.

Rather than make the man march the longer distance to his own workroom, Merlin chose to receive the report in Arthur's. He summoned a pair of guards to the outer doors before he and the courier occupied the inner chamber.

Merlin found the flint and steel in the niche beside the door where Arthur kept it and lit the nearest lamp. The optio secured the door at Merlin's command, pivoted, and saluted him.

This salute Merlin returned. "Have you word from Arthur?" Decades of asking that question, beginning with his father, Ambrosius, had trained him to keep his tone brisk and prevent anxiety from bleeding into it.

"No, sir." He dug into the pouch slung across his chest and removed an unsealed parchment leaf. "Your weather report."

Merlin's heart rate accelerated. Willing it to slow and not succeeding, he accepted the document but took a long, prayerful blink before reading its contents.

Hot, two thunderstorms, and a flash flood.

Prioress Niniane was on her way here with Loholt, escorted by Merlin's men, but both the boy's guardians had been killed.

Emrys's silent cackles suggested how angry she must be.

BRACED ON the stone sill, Eileann watched Angusel sprint toward the sliver of fiery haze, her heart hammering in time with his feet hitting the street's paving stones. In his left fist, he clutched a spear. His drawn sword flashed in his right. The scabbard bounced at his left leg. His shield rode his back.

It could not erase the memory of the design beneath.

Back against the wall, she slid to the floor, heedless of the stones snagging her gown. She hid her face in her hands and sobbed.

Two pairs of arms encircled her, but she felt as broken as that dye cup.

"This is wrong! Wrong," she wailed to anyone who might care to listen, god or mortal. "Why did he not complete the rite?" She had a guess that she couldn't bear to voice.

"The anointing was complete." Neoinean's tone sounded firm but not unkind.

"And it would appear, my lady, that you have done your work well," Fioruisge said. "You cannot deny that the gods have called him to do their bidding."

"Their bidding," Eileann muttered. "The gods care not one whit for what I want. They wouldn't let him stay for the bonding."

While Fioruisge released her embrace and rose, Neoinean grasped Eileann's hands so hard she yelped. The woman eased her grip but would not let go. "You and Angusel mac Alayna already share a bond that no man—or woman—can break. There will be those who try. You yourself will try to break it one day, and you might deceive yourself into believing you have succeeded. Do not be deceived. The act of love is just that, an act. Do we watch two beasts engaged in the act and then conclude that they must be in love? Of course not. We get so distracted by our emotions for our beloved that we forget the act itself carries no power to bind two souls together. The binding occurs, strand by strand, in the choices performed before, during, and after the act that demonstrate kindness, compassion, consideration, and sacrifice toward one's beloved.

"This night, Eileann nic Dynann, you demonstrated those facets," Neoinean stated, "and so did he."

Eileann wrenched free to hug herself. "I don't see how abandoning me to go do what he was trained for can be called an act of sacrifice." She pressed her face to her updrawn knees. "To say naught of kindness or the rest of it."

Neoinean snorted, grabbed the halves of the broken cup, and stood.

"When you are ready to see, my lady," Fioruisge said, "you will."

Eileann hoped she would not be too old to appreciate that day when it dawned.

Sighing, she berated herself. She might not comprehend the gods' plans for Angusel, and what little she understood she might not like, but she couldn't deny the sense that she needed to continue helping him.

But how could she, a barren, outcast woman, be of use to one touched by the gods?

Shutting her eyes did not stem the tears. She hugged her knees harder and rocked, keening the grief and pain and doubt and fear that had harried her since that awful day she'd lost her husband and bairn. What Fioruisge and Neoinean were doing, Eileann did not know and did not care. Nothing existed outside the soulless void of her merciless, unblinking mind's eye.

Slowly the mental grayness coalesced into the shape of one of the god-marks. She couldn't follow Angusel into battle; the Angalaranach brutes on the beach had revealed that path's madness. The goddess Epona, however, showed her how to help the young man to whom she was bonded.

Eileann released her knees, dried her face and nose on her tunic's sleeve, straightened her legs, and raised her hands. The women helped her gain her footing. They regarded her with questions painted across their faces. She answered the most obvious:

"Ladies, we must hie to Caledàitan." When that didn't draw immediate protests—the gods alone knew what state the town might be in following the people's panicked rush to leave it—she felt emboldened to add, "To look after a horse."

WIND WHIPPING his short hair forward, a welcome sign it was still blowing favorably, Caius Marcellus Ectorius—called Cai by his friends and intimates, and General Cai by the men—stood at the lead ferry ship's prow. Swift action on the part of the Picti chieftain Rionnach had caused the available Clan Tarsuinn vessels to be dispatched to the legion's beachhead before Angli forces could capture them. The remaining cohorts were crossing twice as fast as Arthur had calculated based on using Clan Lothian vessels. The uncommon wind shift helped the legion by another factor of two.

Most days Cai kept God at arm's length. This night, he offered an earnest petition for the winds to stay favorable till the crossings completed.

That prayer changed when the designated north-bank beachhead hove into view, and he realized his foster brother and best friend was in deep trouble.

Fires raged through the camp, the clamor of arms and screams of men ripped the night, and across the beach raced dozens to escape the fires—and the fighting.

Disgust rankled Cai's soul.

He commanded his ship's captain to aim it at the largest batch of cowards and run it aground, and he dispatched an optio to hoist the flag to convey the order to the rest of the ships. At the first scrape of the hull on sand, he ordered his men to disembark and contain the deserters. He donned his helmet, vaulted over the side, and stalked into the first knot.

"General Cai! Thank God you've come," the closest dared to snivel at him. This one had lost his helmet, and his hair hadn't grown past his nape since leaving Senaudon. So much the better. "Save us! Save—"

Using a move Arthur's barbaric wife would have applauded, Cai silenced the annoying noise in one swing. The body fell. The head flew a ways, hit the beach with a gritty thud, and rolled, spraying blood, its mouth forever contorted into the word *us*. Sand sticking to the lips glistened in the moonlight.

Deserters and Cai's charges alike scrambled back and riveted their gazes, reflecting varying degrees of dread, upon Cai. Movement ceased in visible ripples as deserters learned what the general had done to one of their fellows. Behind them, the battle at the camp raged on. Cai knew Arthur's time had to be short, but he deemed these moments would serve the greater good.

He cleaned his double-headed axe in the sand and swung it to the ready. "Who else wants saving?" Dead silence. "No one? Good. Get your sorry arses back to camp. Fight with honor, and I shall forget that I found you here. Any man caught on the beach, in the woods, or anywhere else that doesn't help the Pendragon will join that one in hell." He spat on the headless corpse.

Brandishing the axe, he took an abrupt, lunging step. The ex-deserters sprinted toward the fray.

Of the cohort Cai had accompanied to the beach, he split the unit into three columns and sent the first two units of a hundred men apiece to shepherd at double time the ex-deserters, as well as to kill Angli they might encounter on the way to what remained of the legion's encampment. He ran amid the central column, praying that he and his men would arrive soon enough to do Arthur any good.

ANGUSEL HAD no idea what was happening, or why. His feet pound-ed unerring across terrain he'd never seen, not even when he had escorted Eileann to Abar-Dùr. His fists, one clenching his spear and the other his sword, did not cramp. Head, arms, legs, heart, lungs: his entire body felt engulfed in flame, but the fire was . . . sustaining him?

Gods, what had Eileann done?

Harper called us. For you. Run.

Not one voice but a chorus, blended and yet distinct; comforting and yet commanding.

Terrifying.

His thousand questions vanished.

He ran.

CLOSE ENOUGH to count the burnt tents—counting the intact ones would have been faster—Cai saw a warrior dashing across the bor-dering stream, stone to stone without pause, as if he ran that route twice a day.

The fighting appeared to be about done. Cai's flanking units had flushed out and killed, captured, or driven off the Angli archers. Camp activity was shifting to recovery and assessment. Haze-veiled silhouettes worked to douse the flames, lug supplies, help wounded companions, and move the dead. Those silent silhouettes looked less like men than wraiths.

That warrior should see it too, but he sprinted toward the en-campment as if on the most urgent mission imaginable.

The general halted the column.

"Shall I kill him, sir?" asked the soldier beside Cai, sliding a finger under the string of the bow slung across his chest.

Cai squinted at the figure, who seemed oblivious to the arrival of three hundred soldiers. To judge by the helmet's brush, the warrior was armed in standard legion gear, but not as a centurion.

"No. He's one of ours." Cai hoped.

He restarted the column on a course and speed to intercept the soldier; no easy feat, as it transpired. He had never seen a man move so fast in full battle-gear. Truth be told, it was disconcerting. And exhausting, but he'd flog himself before admitting it, not even to Arthur.

My God—Arthur! Is he dead?

"He isn't, sir."

Cai had looked back, preparing to order a detachment to conduct a quiet search for Arthur. He pivoted to meet the gaze of that disconcerting soldier, who had planted his spear, sheathed his sword, and snapped to attention. His self-discipline was marred by the understandable effort to rein in his breathing. Recognition flickered across Cai's brain: Angusel, the cast-off puppy of Arthur's wife, who went by the name Aonar . . . no, Ainchis—Ainchis-something. Decurion Ainchis-something, to judge by his rank badge. He could spare no patience for recalling the duty roster. Whatever Angusel chose to call himself, the officer standing before Cai, chest heaving and nostrils flaring and breath hissing through clenched, bared teeth, was no puppy.

This was a hellhound.

"WHAT?" GENERAL Cai bellowed.

Angusel gripped the spear's shaft tighter to fight the urge to flinch.

Nay, *bellow* wasn't the word, but it seemed that way compared with having heard . . . the general's thoughts?

How? Why? What is happening?

We help you as we see fit.

Really?

He used the excuse of taking and expelling a slow, deep breath to try sensing more thoughts; not just the general's but anyone's. Nothing coherent pierced the din of his breathing. Once that quit, he began hearing in his head a soft, steady, high-pitched hiss.

Gods.

Pressing his fingertips to his helmet at the spot under which the salmon lay hidden seemed to calm the madness. In the next heartbeat came his mental apology for insulting the gift.

A feeling rippled through him that his brain labeled a divine chuckle.

RECOVERING HIS breath lightened Angusel's countenance several degrees from that of hellhound. "I—know—where the Pendragon is, sir." With that odd vocal catch appeared an odd expression, as if Angusel couldn't believe his own claim.

Cai had no time for this foolery. He dismissed his unit to assist the surviving soldiers wherever needed and then ushered Angusel aside. He whispered, "Can you take me to him?"

"Aye, sir." No uncertainty marred this response, either in timing, tone, or visage.

The decurion snatched his spear and darted unchallenged past the camp's reestablished perimeter, leaving Cai to keep pace as best he might.

CHAPTER 30

ARTHUR LAY FACEDOWN upon a salvaged cot inside a structure thrown together from a few of the smaller tents that had escaped the fire, champing on a bandage roll while a medic dug out charred leather fringes and bronze rivets that had fused with his left shoulder. Sitting wasn't an option; a broken, flaming tent pole had impaled his hip through the battle-kilt to create the next wound to be cleaned and dressed. The medic's valerian had dulled as much pain as it could, and what remained wasn't bad enough to make Arthur faint, so of course he was going to punish himself by reviewing what had happened.

Again.

Part of that penance entailed marching his memories back to his father's death, at the hands of these same Angli bastards, before he could recall a worse military disaster.

Another part included the reminder that he damn well should be looking to the men's needs before his own but for the fact that their seeing the untreated injuries on him would have damaged morale far worse than this alternative. He could not afford to lose consciousness in front of them.

"Sir," said one of the soldiers on duty outside Arthur's private makeshift hospital ward. "The Pendragon cannot be—"

Arthur discerned no clue whom the guard might be addressing, but a name popped into his mind that made no sense. Through a gap in the tents, he could tell that dawn's advent remained a rumor. It was impossible for Cai to have gotten his cohort here so fast, given the limitations in vessels and winds, but he had to admit the idea gave him a flicker of hope.

He dared not indulge in it.

The heavy rustle of fabric confirmed that someone had invaded his corner of hell as the medic finished applying salve and bandages to Arthur's shoulder.

"Mother of Christ, Arthur."

The concerned tone yielded to a low chuckle. The hell invader didn't state what they both must be thinking: this had to look like a scene from when they were boys growing up in Ector's household, an incident involving a little too much rough play a little too close to a lot of live coals in the kitchen's hearth.

Picturing Cai's old butt scars made Arthur chuckle into the bandage gag.

He spit it out to say, before Cai could, "A tempting target."

They said it together and shared a bigger laugh.

"You need balance." Cai went to one knee on Arthur's uninjured side, wiggling the Dux Britanniarum seal—which in his haste to leave Dunpeldyr, Arthur had forgotten to retrieve—before his face.

The cold bronze on his bare ass almost made the seal's owner wet himself. He couldn't prevent relieved tears from leaking out.

Although by a miracle the medic kept working through the foolery, cutting and cleaning and blotting and all, either the hip wound wasn't as bad as Arthur had believed, or the laughter was a better painkiller than its herbal counterpart.

To say that Angusel felt self-conscious, as the Pendragon and General Cai each informed the other about what had transpired in a style of banter forged by years of shared experiences and trust, would be like saying Arthur was wounded.

Out of that banter emerged a bleak picture: the boldest Angalaranach raiders had killed sentries and disguised themselves in the looted legion armor to infiltrate and wreak fury upon the sleeping camp, setting fires where they could and melting into the forest to let their companions' arrows augment the fire's work. Their primary target had been the headquarters tent. If not for the arrival of General Cai's troops and the fact that Arthur had fallen asleep at his camp table, there might not have been much of a cohort left—or a Pendragon to lead the legion.

And here Angusel stood on the intimate side of the veil, having followed the general into the sanctum without thinking. To leave would be to admit that he'd had no right to be present.

You do. You're Pendragon's blade.

A poor blade, he thought as his fingers flexed and curled around his spear, getting to the battlefield after the michaoduin were scattered, captured, or dead. Not that he was blaming the gods for the unfortunate timing, he hastened to add.

Blades don't always have to cut.

What good's a blade that won't cut?

Sometimes blades are meant to heal.

Angusel once had watched Prioress Niniane use a red-hot dagger to cauterize a soldier's gash, but he couldn't imagine how that dollop of divine wisdom might apply to him. Soon the Pendragon would roll over, sit up, and discover who had intruded upon the private reunion. He shut his eyes and did his best to stand very still.

The cot's ropes creaked. Angusel held his breath, willing himself to not be noticed.

"Decurion Ainchis Sàl."

He opened his eyes, released the breath through puffed cheeks, faced the war-chieftain, and raised his fist to his chest. Arthur had turned onto his uninjured side. The medic finished tying the hip's bandage.

Hissing through clenched teeth, the Pendragon pushed himself up. Before either General Cai or the medic could react, Angusel propped his spear on a stack of crates and rushed forward to grasp Arthur's hand, the one not attached to the burnt shoulder. When that failed to provide sufficient leverage, Angusel stepped in and stooped to wedge his shoulder under Arthur's sword arm.

Together, slowly, they stood.

ARTHUR APPRECIATED the unsolicited assistance, but his first instinct was to accept as little of it as possible. Taking a tentative step away from Angusel and having pain bolt from hip to brain, however, cured him of that folly.

"More valerian, sir?" asked the medic.

Arthur gave a tight nod. The medic fished a muslin packet from his sack, grabbed the cup he'd given Arthur for the earlier dose, and excused himself from the tent.

While Arthur leaned on Angusel, Cai replaced the ruined battle-kilt with the spare and then moved around to Arthur's left side to prod the injuries. Fresh pain made Arthur flinch hard. Bridling the urge to scream proved harder. He glowered at his in-danger-of-becoming-ex-friend.

"You are in no shape to fight," Cai whispered.

The pain receded enough that Arthur could trust his volume control. "I have to be. The men need me. Gyan—"

He appreciated her initiative, but God alone knew what was happening to her and the Horse Cohort, having to face the lopsided numbers Arthur suspected, and his best option was to move as much of the legion as he could, as fast as he could. Those damned Angli raiders had plunged both of those aspects into greater risk.

"I had planned to push through the Coilltichean Chaledon to Dùn Fàradhlann today." Cai's blank stare prompted Arthur to say, "The Forest of Caledonia, where we are now."

"Ah. But nothing is stopping us from reaching Rionnach's fortress today," Cai insisted.

Arthur disagreed. "We're going to have to raze every bush and sapling and leave a trail of guards in our wake."

"My men did a thorough job of clearing out the bastards in the camp's vicinity. In spite of how it may look—or feel," Cai said with a grim chuckle, "we can call this engagement a win. It's a safe wager that the Angli survivors are halfway to regrouping with their column."

Arthur snorted.

Years ago, Uther had begun drilling out of him the habit of considering any risk a "safe wager," and Merlin had finished the job. He wished that Cai had paid attention to those lessons, but he couldn't fault the optimism.

As for chalking this night's outcome on the "win" slate, he would reserve that judgment until the campaign was done.

HORSES ARE *victory's key.*

If Angusel felt self-conscious before, that was nothing compared with being stuck underneath his war-chieftain's armpit. But the awkwardness of this position—to say naught of its stench—could not quell the idea lancing his brain.

The return of the medic, however, prevented him from voicing it. Arthur lifted his uninjured arm from Angusel's shoulders to accept the tisane and took a long draught, swaying a bit. Angusel readied his shield-side arm to catch his war-chieftain, but Arthur had the sense to finish the dose. He surrendered the cup to the medic and dismissed him with thanks and a request to prepare valerian-laced wine skins.

As the medic saluted and departed, and Arthur resumed using Angusel to support himself, Angusel realized that a better opportunity might not occur.

"Lord Pendragon," he began in Breatanaiche, keeping his eyes trained forward, "may I offer a suggestion?"

General Cai stepped into his field of view, arms crossed and gaze stern. Angusel clenched his jaw.

"You may, Decurion," Arthur said.

"If marching is going to be a problem for you, sir, and leading from a litter is not the best solution either—"

"Damned right about that," Cai muttered.

"I suggest you send for Macsen." When that didn't draw rejection, Angusel soldiered on. "And perhaps all the horses we stabled at Caledàitan. Then the centurions can be seen better in battle, your couriers can travel faster, and we scouts can range farther from the column and report more often."

Respect thawed the severity of General Cai's countenance. "The decurion is correct, Arthur, on all counts. I'll tell Marcus to arrange it."

The general's approval buoyed his spirits, but Angusel felt the Pendragon's disagreement course through the fingers clutching his shoulder. "No. Have him arrange a litter for me. We depart as soon as Culhwch's cohort arrives. It will take too much of the day to get those horses here, time Gyan and her men can ill afford."

Given Angusel's mounting worry for the Comitissa, he couldn't disagree.

But as her consort hobbled with Angusel toward the tent's opening, spouting a stream of orders to General Cai about fortifying the camp and leaving a unit to watch the beach and direct the later-returning cohorts, Pendragon's blade prayed for a way to make the divine inspiration come to pass.

WITH NO wish to try the Ab Fhorchu's current at night in the craft they'd used to travel upriver, and with no wish to stumble across Angalaranach brutes who might be patrolling the riverbank road to Caledàitan, Eileann and her ladies had chosen to buck the branches and brush and brambles of Coilltichean Chaledon. To say that their course had been slowed to a near crawl would be like saying . . .

Arthur was wounded?

Eileann paused, one hand braced against the boulder they were groping their way past and the other pressed to her throbbing head. At the Abar-Dùr inn, after she had learned whence the gods had called Angusel and why, she had offered prayers for the Pendragon and his men. She hoped that none of them had been hurt or killed by Angalaranach treachery, Angusel and Arthur most especially, but she had experienced too much of that treachery to raise her expectations too far.

However, she couldn't deny the weird fact that she *knew* Arthur had been wounded in the fire. Badly wounded but alive. Angusel was unhurt and helping him.

Where in heaven's name had that knowledge come from?

Her heart formed the answer, and her head confirmed it.

"Get those horses here."

The headache intensified. She tried quelling it with a long swig of watered wine from one of the skins they'd purchased from the innkeeper.

The mental command wouldn't abate.

"My lady?" Fioruisge, walking third in line, had caught up and touched Eileann's shoulder. Eileann winced and clapped hand to mouth. A squeak escaped. "I am so sorry I startled you. Are you not well?"

"I needed time to catch my breath."

She capped the wine skin, draped its cord across her chest, and resumed her pace, offering a mental apology for lying about the gods' gift.

"—time Gyan and her men can ill afford."

"What?" Eileann regretted the slip as Neoinean rushed to her and Fioruisge.

The predawn gloom showed worry in the cant of their silhouettes.

Neoinean's palm felt warm on Eileann's forehead, cheek, and neck. When the apothecary grasped her hands, it felt as if the woman had soaked them in an icy stream. Tingling erupted at the point of contact to course throughout Eileann's body, prickly and terrifying.

"What is happening to me?" In straining to hold her voice to a whisper, its tone came out harsh and feral.

Neoinean wrapped her in an embrace. "Fear not, child. It seems the gods have acknowledged your worthiness too."

"What does that mean? Will she be all right?" Fioruisge asked. "Do we need to stop and seek shelter?"

"No!" Crows roosting in a nearby tree took flight, squawking. Much quieter, Eileann continued, "We must press onward as fast as we can. I believe the gods are trying to tell me that the Pendragon needs the horses he couldn't take across the Ab Fhorchu."

Neoinean stepped back a pace, arms crossed. "Right. Valuable warhorses guarded by scores of soldiers. Such men would never believe three bedraggled women who bear no proof of the Pendragon's plight, even if we could find a Caledonach in the lot we could appeal to before he or his companions spear us on sight."

Puffing a sigh, Eileann closed her eyes and slumped against the closest tree large enough to bear the weight of her despair. Neoinean was quite right, of course. The language barrier wasn't the first fraction of the problem. What chance did they have of surviving such an encounter?

The mental command repeated, intense and urgent. Her plea for the gods to give her a solution, however, went unanswered.

"Ladies, we have come too far to quit here." She opened her eyes, pushed away from the tree, and resumed the march, which was growing easier as dawn approached. "Let us abide by our original plan and visit the men who had helped me craft that message for Angusel. I can retrieve my harp from them and play as payment for whatever food and drink they may spare us." A bed would be lovely too, but she dared not hope for that much kindness.

Fioruisge and Neoinean murmured varying levels of agreement. Both women followed her. Each trudged in the silence of her own thoughts.

All Eileann could think about, step after stumbling step, was the Pendragon's horses and what magnitude of miracle would get them to him. She knew, with the same certainty as she had known about Arthur's injuries, that the gods expected it of her. But her plans shipwrecked on the shoals of doubt, driven by her acceptance of Arthur's pronouncement that she was inexperienced in military matters.

Burdened by the increasing effort to breathe and lumber onward, she stopped struggling to shape a plan. If the gods wanted her to accomplish the impossible, then they were going to have to provide a way.

In her wearied determination to reach Caledàitan, she lost track of how long they had been walking. Forever, it seemed.

The sun breasted the horizon. Eileann, Fioruisge, and Neoinean each lifted a hand to shade their eyes. They emerged, blinking and panting, from the Coilltichean Chaledon as light beams bathed the world in a golden glow, including the walls of Caledàitan, which stood abristle with the Pendragon's soldiers, and the compound where the One God's servants toiled. Peaceful servants who were acquainted with Eileann and who spoke Caledonaiche in addition to Breatanaiche. Spiritual men whom she hoped would understand her claim of divine inspiration and who might be just as eager to help the Pendragon as his soldiers were.

Men who would be easier for those soldiers to believe than three daft women who had tramped across half this Angalaranach-infested land.

For the first time in the gods alone knew how long, Eileann felt a genuine smile spread across her face. She squared her shoulders, freshened her step, and strode toward the One God's sanctuary.

CHAPTER 31

WITH SUNUP CAME increased caution. The legion's first three cohorts would soon emerge from beneath the vast, leafy canopy of the Coilltichean Chaledon onto open terrain. Gawain's half of the scout squad, patrolling the column's westward flank and therefore closer to the enemy, was exposed to the greater risk.

Greater chance for glory, Angusel couldn't help thinking as he and Dunaidan, along with three additional scout pairs, crept inside the tree line to avoid detection while scanning for movement across the plain. The remaining pairs were ranging ahead of and behind his position along the legion's path toward Dùn Fàradhlann, reporting to him at regular intervals before rotating to the column, much as they had done on the approach to Dunpeldyr.

He couldn't speak for how Gawain's men were faring, and the gods stayed mum on the subject, but his men's reports had not varied by as much as one syllable: no one had seen any creatures—man or beast—larger than a fawn.

Their decurion was tempted to strip down, break cover, and dash howling across the plain.

"Get that great gray brute under control."

"Sorry, sir. I don't know why he's decided to—easy, now. That's better, my lad."

Angusel ducked behind a massive oak, bracing on its trunk and shaking his head.

"Aught wrong, sir?"

Dunaidan had whispered the question, not a random voice in his head. Angusel stepped away from the tree to continue the mission.

He'd be thrice damned before he would tell a subordinate that tramping through this gods-forsaken territory at the eastern edge of the Coilltichean Chaledon rather than riding it, as he and his brother scouts should be doing, was causing him to lose—

"We should be damn close. No sign of them yet?"

Angusel gripped Dunaidan's arm and pulled him into a crouch behind a thicket. "Please tell me you heard that voice."

The look on his subordinate's face told him what he didn't want to know. "Mayhap 'tis time for you to go back to the column, sir. You've been out here longer than the rest of us."

He couldn't admit to this Breatanach soldier of unknown religious bent that Caledonach gods were preventing him from getting tired and driving him mad in the bargain.

"I'm in command. Of course I have to—"

The drumming of hoofbeats made them swivel their heads toward the plain. The approaching dust cloud had to be visible to most scouts in Angusel's half of the squad. He whistled the daylight recall signal, in case this was an Angalaranach ruse. With luck, scouts who couldn't hear the signal but saw the cloud would decide to regroup.

With better luck, they would arrive in time.

Unsheathing his sword, he chose brush he could peer through while being dense enough to conceal his location. Dunaidan and the dozen scouts who'd responded to the recall did likewise.

The mounted unit slowed at the tree line. The men, their faces obscured by legion standard helmets, were unknown to Angusel. The horses were a different matter. The decurion rode Arthur's white stallion, Macsen. An enlisted man was seated astride Gawain's Arddwyn. Angusel's soaring elation eclipsed the other horses' names.

The "great gray brute," bit in teeth and trying to wrench the reins from his rider's grasp, was Stonn.

As the horsemen set course parallel to the trees toward Dùn Fàradhlann, Angusel waved his men to stay hidden.

He stepped out of cover. "Ainm!" he yelled in Caledonaiche, appreciating that the Pendragon had adopted for the whole legion the friend-or-foe identification scheme the Comitissa had devised while commanding the Manx Cohort. The Angalaranaich had attacked Trìbruachan in stolen legion armor; the michaoduin could have done that to steal the legion's horses from Caledàitan.

The lead rider ordered his men to halt and nudged Macsen toward Angusel. The soldier kept a wary distance. He transferred the reins to his shield-side hand and flexed his sword hand.

"Decurio Alun, Quartus Centurium, Primae Cohortis," came the proper Ròmanach reply: *Decurion Alun, Fourth Century, First Cohort.* Men of this unit, Angusel recalled with rising excitement, had been assigned to guard the horses and perimeter defenses at Caledàitan. In Caledonaiche, Decurion Alun requested Angusel's name.

Angusel could not fault the extra caution weighting the man's tone.

"Decurio Ainchis Sàl, Prima Ala, Equitum Cohorte." *Decurion Ainchis Sàl, First Wing, Horse Cohort.* He had never felt so pleased to spew Ròmanaiche in his life.

And he never dreamed he'd be pleased to see Alun, a soldier who'd come within spitting distance of witnessing Angusel's execution when he'd been Arthur's hostage on Maun. They exchanged nods.

Both officers signaled to summon their men. Riders greeted their favorite mounts in joyful if muted reunions; no less so with Angusel and Stonn, who nosed about him for treats that of course didn't exist. He was too happy to see his horse to let the animal make him feel guilty. As he scratched the jawline, Stonn leaned into his palm and blew a forgiving snort.

Satisfaction surged through Angusel, as if he was channeling the feelings of those around him.

Not so, Blade. Only Harper's.

A BLOODY bandage lost its stench in the heat of full-on battle frenzy.

A bloody bandage also was a bloody nuisance in a full-on fight.

Gull had appropriated the discarded linen to disguise his face, but he needn't have worried. On this, the third day of a harrowing cycle of attack, retreat, regroup, rearm, drink, eat, rest, and repeat, everyone was too exhausted and hurting to pay heed to anyone's needs save his own. The exception, of course, was the horses. They were examined, treated, rubbed down, watered, and fed with precise care and highest priority.

Without the horses, Dùn Fàradhlann would have begun flying the Angalaranach Crimson Eagle banner two days ago while this company glutted ravens for a score of miles in every direction.

He stroked the sweat-soaked neck of his current mount, a nimble chestnut gelding. The brave lad gave a halfhearted head toss, as if wanting this day's business to be done. Gull could sympathize.

His stomach rumbled. He dug in his bian-sporan for an oat bannock and made short work of it. After retrieving the skin from his saddle pack, he chased the hard, flat cake with a long swig of watered wine and stowed the skin.

Around them, his fellow Albanach riders were eating, drinking, or performing their little rituals to prepare for making another run at the enemy, as were Chieftainess Gyanhumara and her men. Ogryvan's Argaillanach warriors were asleep and would attack after sundown. Gull couldn't see the bulk of the Pendragon's horse-warriors, who'd been hitting the Angalaranach column at points farther south. By his reckoning, the allied cavalry had halted the enemy's advance about a mile from Dùn Fàradhlann, but at the rate they were losing men and mounts to Angalaranach arrows, they would be forced into permanent retreat by the morrow. Mayhap sooner.

"My heroes!" Gyanhumara called. Her next words became lost as she rode toward the opposite end of the line. But he could see the effect of her attention. Even Alayna's men straightened in the saddle and responded with a hearty "Aye, Commander Gyan!"

Alayna didn't shout, but Gull gaped when she waved a javelin at the Pendragon's wife.

When Gyanhumara got to his position, spouting exhortations to fight for the Tarsuinnaich with conviction and honor, he found that he wasn't immune. He squared his shoulders under her brief but intense scrutiny, reminding himself that his foremost mission was to protect not this woman but Alayna.

Given Gyanhumara's fierce beauty, irrefutable skills, and genuine caring for the warriors under her command, including those whose allegiances lay with a rival clan, Gull could ken why his son was so smitten by her.

He prayed that she would not further shatter Angusel's heart.

Brandishing a javelin in each fist—one of the few warriors Gull had ever seen who chose to control her mount with knees alone so she could wreak death twice as fast—the Pendragon's wife resumed her place at the line's center and ordered the charge to commence. Riders set heels to flanks to send their mounts leaping to follow her.

Even Gull.

GAWAIN WAS grateful beyond measure to be astride Arddwyn, but the challenge to stay hidden as he and Corwyn and the other scouts of his half of the unit kept watch along the column's westward flank was growing by the minute. The hilly, wooded terrain—Angusel had called it a Picti name, Coil-something, that meant "Forest of Caledonia"—had yielded to gentler, greener land that would make ideal pastures once the armies stopped killing every living thing in their paths.

The complexities of riding and scouting kept him from dwelling upon his father's death and the thirst for vengeance too much.

Gawain.

Abruptly he straightened in the saddle. Arddwyn slowed, and he kneed his mount to keep pace with Corwyn's.

This close to the barren crest of a rise, the risk of exposure to enemy troops had to be affecting his mind; he must have imagined Loth's voice. The sense of affection blanketing his brain couldn't have been real. It had to have been a memory of the last minutes he and his father had shared.

Draw your sword.

Gawain did halt Arddwyn at that, shaking his head. Corwyn reined in his mount beside him. A few more strides and they would reach the top.

"Sir? What's wrong?" Corwyn whispered.

Gawain opened his mouth but got no chance to reply. Shouts, clangs, and neighs spilled over the hill, as if the forward scouts had come under attack. His gut churned.

He drew his sword. So did Corwyn. They nudged their horses to inch to the top of the ridge. And damn near bumped into an Angli foot patrol.

The bastards looked nigh as startled as Gawain felt.

Arddwyn needed little prodding to leap into their midst. Between Gawain's sword and his horse's hooves, the first three fell before they could utter a squawk. Their companions yelled plenty—none of it recognizable—but their charge proved no match for two mounted men lusting to avenge their chieftain, father, and brothers-in-arms.

The survivors spun and ran straight for a far larger line that had to be the main column. A squad was racing toward Gawain's position, another toward that skirmish he'd heard between his forward scouts and a second Angli patrol.

Eagerness surged through Gawain like a winter gale. Determination iced his soul.

I shall avenge you, Father, upon all of them!

He tightened his grip upon his sword and upon Arddwyn's barrel.

Corwyn drove his horse to block the way. "Centurion, no! We must warn the Pendragon!"

"Stand down, Soldier. I must—"

He is right. Heed him.

Gawain tugged off his right glove, stuck two fingers into his mouth, and blew recall. The surviving forward scouts heard and disengaged. If he could get them and enough of his remaining men formed up to charge the Angli flank—

Do not make your mother mourn twice in the same week.

Gawain jerked his head as if he'd been slapped. An image of her kneeling, weeping, between two biers while Gareth stood nearby, powerless to comfort her, flooded his brain.

Dear God, no! Mother!

"Centurion!"

Corwyn's desperate tone broke his reverie, and he glanced about. The forward scouts had arrived, as had those who'd been scouting to the rear. Dozens of Angli foot soldiers were swarming up the rise.

Gawain wheeled Arddwyn about and signaled retreat. On horseback, gaining distance over their running enemies was easy. But as a precaution, he set a course that angled away from the legion until the Angli could no longer see them.

With luck, the scouts' actions would be perceived as a raid, even though the Horse Cohort had been attacking elsewhere for the past three days.

However, Gawain knew better than to trust to luck when ravens circled the skies.

BADULF BRANDISHED his rank to storm past the guards—and his fears—to enter his father's headquarters tent.

King Colgrim stood behind his camp table, flanked by a half dozen of his generals. They huddled around a deerhide map of the region that had been marked with the location of the Eingel army and the enemy's attacks upon the column. Badulf swallowed a gasp; half a bottle of red ink had to have been spent painting the clashes. The generals were arguing strategies for countering those attacks so they could resume the march upon the target fortress. Badulf's father remained silent, stroking his beard.

That beard looked far grayer than Badulf remembered. He almost felt sorry for the man.

Colgrim gave Badulf a terse nod. The generals fell silent to regard the prince. "News?" snapped the king.

"Aye, sire." He couldn't count the number of times he had witnessed lesser men be whipped, imprisoned, banished, or executed for delivering a report his father didn't want to hear. Badulf sucked in a breath, exhaled a silent prayer, and hoped for the best. "Moving the Eingel army forward is no longer the issue. My men have confirmed that the Dragon King's foot troops are fast approaching our right flank."

CHAPTER 32

THE COHORT WAS nearing a pond notable by the aligned
dung piles and scores of fresh hoof- and footprints leading to and away from it. Its most recent visitors had had
a good idea. Arthur halted his unit for a ration break but declined to
dismount. Hurting while astride Macsen—here among Second Cohort, since he had accepted Cai's offer to lead the column—was pref-
erable to hurting anywhere else he could imagine, including a litter.

Especially a damned litter.

He kneed Macsen out of formation and ordered his mounted officers to join him at the pond's bank. God alone knew when they would
get another chance to water their horses before charging into the hell
of war.

They stood at hell's gates, if he read aright the absence of insect,
bird, and animal sounds, as if every creature was hunkered down and
holding its breath in sheer dread of the coming conflict.

Thirsty Macsen strained at the bit. Arthur held him steady to let
the other riders water their horses first. A soldier toting oats pacified

his mount while Arthur watched the undulating horizon.

Satisfied that no enemy army was going to appear within the next brace of minutes, he twisted to reach for the wine skin he had tucked into the right-hand saddle pack. The action stretched his damaged left hip. He hid the wince behind his gloved fist while feigning a cough.

"You all right, sir?" asked the soldier feeding his horse.

"Of course." It wasn't a total lie; Arthur expected to feel better after he took a generous swig of the watered, medicated wine and the valerian took effect. "Carry on."

In response, the soldier disengaged the feed bag—Macsen had finished its contents and used the man's inattention to shake the bag—and refilled it for the next horse from the sack he'd been lugging. Arthur nudged his horse into the shallows. Macsen busied himself with slurping the water.

Arthur followed his horse's example and took a long pull from the skin.

The pounding of hoofbeats made him twist the opposite way. Macsen jerked up his head and belled a challenge at the newcomers.

"Easy, lad," Arthur murmured, patting his warhorse's neck. "Those are our scouts."

At that pace, he mused as Gawain and his men thundered close enough to recognize after having passed the perimeter sentries' friend-or-foe challenge, their news couldn't be good.

"Lord Pendragon, the Angli army lies past that rise, less than a mile due west." Gawain glanced over his shoulder in the direction Arthur's cohort was headed. "We've just come from informing General Cai. He has halted First Cohort and awaits your orders."

Arthur rubbed his chin stubble. The cohorts would have to close ranks. That meant getting his on the move after conferring with the scouts. "Angli numbers?" he asked.

"By the combined estimates of my men"—his nephew drew a deep breath—"four thousand."

That estimate, allowing for losses from cavalry raids and desertion, jived with Rionnach's report. "How fast are they moving?"

"They're not, sir," said Corwyn, the scout who had reported to Arthur at Hafonydd.

"Not toward Chieftain Rionnach's fortress," Gawain clarified. "Around half a century's worth of Angli foot troops tried following us, but we took a route to our column that should have confused them."

While he commended Gawain's quick thinking, his mind reeled. The estimate put the odds at two to one, since the infantry's last three cohorts would be arriving much later in the day, perhaps in time for the mop-up work. The cavalry must be improving those odds—that the Angli army was stopped was a sure sign of their success—but at what cost?

He knew one way to find out.

"Centurion Gawain, dispatch two men to find Decurion Ainchis Sàl and give him new orders: half his men are to continue watching our east flank, and he and the other half are to ride in search of Comitissa Gyan and the Horse Cohort. The cavalry must hit the Angli from the north and west while General Cai and I move the infantry in to attack from the east." Arthur squinted sunward, calculating. Optimal timing would hinge upon Angusel's ability to find Gyan fast. He inhaled, sent up a mental prayer on the exhale, and trusted his gut. "Tell them to commence their attack at the sun's zenith. The men you send on this mission and those of Ainchis Sàl's squad may rejoin First Ala, or wherever Comitissa Gyan needs them to fight."

"You heard the Pendragon," Gawain said to Corwyn. "Pick one of the lads and go!" After Corwyn saluted them, bade another soldier to join him, and they spurred their horses eastward, Gawain asked Arthur, "What of me and the rest of my men?"

What, indeed?

Gawain had to be aching to avenge Loth—hell, Arthur was too, Loth and Uther both, but if this operation didn't succeed, there would be no one left for the avenging.

"Send two of your men south to intercept Prefect Culhwch of Third Cohort. He is to have his unit in position to attack by sun's zenith. Then your men are to continue to the Trìbruachan beachhead with word of the attack plan and that the remaining cohorts are to make best speed for Dùn Fàradhlann. The rest of the scouts shall continue patrolling our west flank. Should any segment of the Angli column turn toward us before we commence the attack, inform the closest cohort commander and me immediately."

"Aye, my lord."

As Gawain snapped orders like a veteran and his men obeyed him, Arthur heard the strand of disappointment buried beneath his nephew's military protocol.

He reached a decision that Uther never would have approved. So be it; his father could haunt him later.

"Centurion, where are you going?" he called as Gawain kneed his mount after the scouts trotting toward the rise that separated the legion from their foes.

Gawain wheeled Arddwyn about. His puzzlement would have been amusing if the situation hadn't been so serious. "To ride with my men, of course, sir."

Arthur ordered the scouts to halt and spurred Macsen to catch them.

Before leaving Trìbruachan, he had sent Marcus to accompany Cai because his well-meaning aide had aggravated Arthur with his mother-hen fussing over his damned burns. That personnel change had left Arthur one aide short.

He said, "Centurion Gawain rides with me. Look for my banner to deliver your reports to him."

The decision yielded the bonus that Arthur would be informed faster.

After Gawain designated one of his men to take command and dismissed them to their patrolling, the look he gave Arthur was one of profound appreciation.

ANGUSEL SAW legion horse-warriors clashing with Angalaranach troops and dug his heels into Stonn's flanks. He didn't have to order his men to keep up.

The riders were hurting and spent. Fewer javelins were being loosed than in a typical volley, and of those, fewer were reaching their marks. The horses were in little better condition, lathered and snorting hard and lumbering with sluggish gaits.

Leveling his spear, he commanded his men to do the same and increase to attack speed. He leaned over Stonn's neck and gave him his head, as did the riders of his unit. Charging the Angalaranach flank bought him and his men enough surprise to plow through their ranks, disrupting the Angalaranach archers' attack and allowing the cavalry wing to disengage.

Angusel shouted the order for his men to guard their retreat. This was the first ala they had encountered. Since Stonn was better rested than the horses who'd been performing this grueling work for three days, he set him on a pace and course that wove toward the head of the unit.

He'd expected to have to explain his mission to countless underlings before finding the Comitissa. It had never occurred to him that she and her brother would be leading this wing.

And he never would have imagined that his mother and scores of Albanach horse-warriors had joined forces with them. Alayna was leading her troops toward the Angalaranach line. As she made eye contact with Angusel, her mouth rounded in an *O*. She shouted orders to abort the charge and bring the Albanach riders around to follow the Comitissa's unit.

They had ridden to within a bow shot of Dùn Fàradhlann's walls, where a camp with a forge had been established for weapons, horseshoes, armor, and tools, when the Comitissa lifted her fist to signal a halt. The Comitissa's warriors dismounted and pulled cloths from their saddlebags to rub their horses' quivering muscles.

One of the riders, a Comites Praetorii decurion, finished cooling his mount and caught Angusel's gaze. To his surprise, the rider was Tavyn nic Dynann, Eileann's brother and the man who had ordered Angusel expelled from the Caledonach ward of the Port Dhoo-Glass field hospital last year. Tavyn appeared to be fighting in spite of bloodstained bandages that wrapped both upper arms and his sword-side leg. Out of respect for the warrior's tenacity, Angusel gave him a legion salute.

Tavyn responded with a Caledonach one. Angusel's astonishment almost prevented him from hearing Tavyn's weary murmur of thanks. He clapped Angusel's leg as he led his horse past. Angusel clopped his teeth together.

The Comitissa dismounted, gave Macmuir a rubdown, and led him to where Angusel had halted Stonn. Whether or not she had observed the brief exchange, he had no idea, but he hoped so.

Alayna and Prefect Peredur, leading their mounts, accompanied her. Angusel slid from Stonn's back. Reins in his shield hand, he pressed his sword-side fist over his heart and bowed his head.

"The arrival of you and your squad was most welcome." It grieved him to note how exhausted the Comitissa sounded. "Thank you, Decurion."

Lowering the fist, he raised his head and was rewarded with a glimpse of her fading smile. Of a sudden he yearned to coax it back. And he needed no god to tell him how. "Comitissa, your consort reports that half his foot troops stand ready to engage. And"—this was not part of the Pendragon's message, but it was no lie—"he sends you his love."

The lifting of her mouth's corners lightened her fatigue and his spirits. "Is that all to Artyr's message?"

"Nay, my lady. At sun's zenith, the Pendragon needs the Horse Cohort and their allies"—Angusel gave a sharp nod to his mother, which she returned—"to attack the enemy along their western and northern flanks." Recalling the conditions of the riders and mounts gave him pause. "That is, if they are able."

"They are." Prefect Peredur said to his sister, "I shall relieve Gereint and take command of the western flank. With your leave, of course, Comitissa."

She gave it. "Before you go, apprise Father of the attack plan."

"Of course." Peredur embraced her, mounted, and trotted toward the collection of tents whose banners displayed the Argaillanach Doves.

That Chieftain Ogryvan had brought Argyll's war-band made sense when Angusel recalled that Arbroch lay but a score of miles due north of Dùn Fàradhlann, and it helped him feel better about the allied cavalry's chances.

The Comitissa watched her brother awhile before facing Angusel's mother. "Chieftainess, what say you to combining your men with mine and my father's for the charge?"

"I say it's a sound plan. A sounder one would be to let my wings lead." Alayna glanced sunward. "Your men and mounts do have a wee bit of time to eat, drink, and rest."

"Agreed; thank you, Alayna. We shall meet you at the formation area."

Before leading her horse away, Alayna favored Angusel with a lingering gaze. "It is good to see you." Her free hand rubbed his shoulder. "Son."

Angusel gaped at his mother. After his interactions with the Comitissa and Eileann's brother, though, he supposed that he shouldn't have been surprised. Alayna smiled and headed to the Albanach warriors, giving the dismount signal.

"Decurion." The Comitissa's voice startled him, and he whirled to face her. "Arrange to deliver confirmation to Artyr that I have received his orders." After Angusel sent the two closest scouts on that mission, she asked him, "Are you here to join the Comites Praetorii or to rejoin First Ala?"

"I'm to rejoin the First," came his automatic reply. Her posture stiffened and her smile vanished. His gut clenched. "Or wherever you need me to fight." He prayed that the suggestion wouldn't sound as lame to her as it did to him.

"The First it shall be, then, for you and your remaining men. Get food and drink for yourselves and your horses, and collect rations of javelins from the forge."

With a swirl of her gold-trimmed dark blue cloak and a tug on Macmuir's reins, she strode off to prepare her men for the final attack.

Her men.

GULL, IN the rear rank of the first Albanach wing, obeyed Alayna's order to dismount. She dismissed her riders with an injunction to return ready to fight before the sun reached its zenith, but he dared not lead his warhorse close enough to overhear what his son might be saying to the Pendragon's wife. That the conversation had angered the woman became obvious in its abrupt conclusion.

Watching Angusel shuffle off, Stonn in tow, in the direction opposite to that which his superior had taken, Gull couldn't stand idle. He led his horse on an angle to intercept them.

"You are new to this camp," he said in Caledonaiche when he'd drawn close enough for Angusel to hear his conversational tone. "The watering troughs stand over there."

Angusel followed the line suggested by Gull's finger without appearing to notice who was doing the pointing. "Many thanks, friend," he muttered and corrected his course. After a few paces, he halted and faced about. "Wait. You sound a lot like—"

Finger to lips, Gull hastened to close the gap. He let Angusel push aside the fake bandage, and he winked when his son sucked in a breath. "Keep it to yourself, if ye please," he said in Breatanaiche for a dollop of privacy in the mostly Caledonach camp. "I'm guarding your mother, though she doesna know it." He tugged the bandage into place.

In silence they walked their mounts to the troughs. While both horses slurped the water, Angusel crossed his arms and speared Gull with a disgust-riddled gaze. A breath later, the spear seemed to deflect inward. "That is what you and I do best."

CAI SPRINTED among his men, using the downward slope to help them build momentum and using whoops and shouts to build their confidence.

Without either of those elements, given the unfavorable odds, this cohort would be obliterated in minutes.

Cai, however, made it a point to never tell his men the odds. Those who noticed for themselves would either fight harder to survive, or they wouldn't. And those who didn't notice were fighting hard enough. Or they weren't.

When the shock of the initial collision passed, it felt good to be venting his rage on enemy flesh after the past week of stomping and paddling about, chasing mists and shadows.

The foes who felt his axe were no shadows, and their blood sprayed far thicker than mist.

He was losing men too. He heard it in the screams and sensed it in the thinning around him. But he couldn't let that stop him from wading deeper into the Angli ranks, mowing down anyone within his reach. Arthur was counting upon him, and he would sooner let the Angli gut him than fail his best friend.

Cai commanded his men to increase the speed of the attack.

FIGHTING AT the head of the main Eingel column was not the assignment Badulf had expected to receive after having spent so much of this campaign away from it, but he welcomed the challenge and its implication.

After this day was done, he'd have earned the privilege to fight at Colgrim's side.

For eternity.

"Orders, sir?"

Badulf blinked. He was still standing atop the knoll amid his unit commanders and personal guardsmen, which surprised him. For an instant he'd felt the weft of his wyrd. He gave his head a slight shake. The rumbling of the approaching cavalry wing sounded a great deal louder, and he could almost smell the horses inside the churning dust cloud.

"Form the spear line and dig in hard! Let no man or beast through! Those who fail to hold shall answer to me!"

The commanders shouted acknowledgment as one and sprinted down to their units. Men rushed to obey, forming a vast thicket of spears that winked bright and deadly in the noon sun. Beyond them stood rank upon rank of Eingel foot soldiers, swords drawn and shields at the ready.

Badulf called the archers into position around him and ordered them to nock the first flight.

The enemy cavalry was almost upon them, charging from the north and west. Badulf sent his fastest guard to order a spear line to form along the western flank and prayed that the man would make it in time. This was no raid. The Dragon King had to have ordered his last man and mount into this attack.

He hoped.

If a cavalry unit of that size was waiting in reserve, the Eingel army would be doomed.

He ordered the archers to let fly. After the first, unified flight, the archers followed standing orders to empty their quivers. Not enough horses dropped to abort the charge. The first ranks of riders loosed their short, slim, swift spears. Countless brave Eingel soldiers fell. The line weakened. The enemy riders spurred their mounts into the wavering spears.

The north spear line shattered. The one to the west never formed.

Badulf drew his sword, summoned his guardsmen, and ran, screaming his rage, into the bloody chaos.

CHAPTER 33

THE DIN WAS nigh unbearable.

Morghe stood, composed, at the rear of Dunadd's hall, watching her husband and his ally bellow accusations at each other while men of both factions shouted their reactions and opinions. The tension flooding the hall could have breached a dam. Quite understandable; the report Urien had received from Maun had implicated the Scots in a raid that had claimed a score of Brytoni lives.

Word from Morghe's Manx agents had been specific as to which lives had been lost.

Losing control of a pawn was unfortunate, but having that information come to light would doubtless reignite Urien's obsession for exacting revenge upon Gyanhumara, which had lain dormant while he adjusted to his roles as chieftain and husband. A revenge-bent chieftain could make Clan Moray suffer; Morghe shuddered to contemplate what it might do to her leadership position or their marriage. Thus she had taken particular care to destroy the report.

The noise escalated to deafening proportions. When Urien and

Fergus stripped off their tunics and yelled for weapons, she decided that enough was bloody well enough. Flanked by Accolon and two of her personal guards, the Chieftainess of Clan Moray glided forward.

"My lords, please!" Urien and Fergus halted, fists raised, to regard her. "If you continue, the only man to benefit will be my brother. I daresay neither of you wants that."

She glanced toward the tunic Urien had discarded. One of her men stooped to retrieve it, shook off the clinging floor rushes and mystery bits, and presented it to his chieftain. Urien relaxed his stance and accepted the garment, thanking the man.

Fergus found his tunic and gave it a perfunctory shake. After making himself properly attired, he swept Morghe a deep bow. "Me lady Morghe be most wise. The Scáthaichean people have no cause to attack our hosts in such a manner."

"Really?" Urien finished donning his tunic with pulls so hard Morghe wouldn't have been surprised to hear the fabric rip. "In what manner do you have cause to attack us?"

With a light chuckle, Morghe cupped her husband's cheek. After he inhaled and his jaw relaxed, she trailed the hand down to his chest, where he grasped it.

"My lord husband jests, of course," she said to Fergus. "What he means to say is that we intend to investigate the raid and learn the truth behind it."

Urien removed Morghe's hand and surged closer to his ally. "If a rogue faction of your people proves responsible, I expect you to find and execute them to the last man."

"The existence of such a group isna likely, Chieftain Urien, but I agree to your terms," Fergus said. "To that end, I request that a detachment of my men accompany yours."

"A worthy suggestion, my lord Fergus," Morghe said. "I suggest that Lord Accolon be appointed to lead the investigation."

Urien's surprise was not unexpected. He was relying upon Morghe's skills more often by the day, and she reveled in his growing trust and her growing power. "I wish for you to head this delegation, my lady wife. I need Accolon to remain here for—"

"Alas, my lord husband, as much as I might like to comply, I should not." She needed to distance herself from the raid's site to avoid implication. The reason she could give him, however, was, "I carry Clan

Moray's heir."

In the space between Urien catching her up into his arms and lowering his beaming lips to hers, she saw Accolon's dismay. Those reactions were not unexpected either.

GULL REMOVED his helmet so he could shed the fake bandage in favor of unobstructed vision. He didn't care who noticed. Most riders were too busy with their preparations to make comment upon Gull's. Those who might realize that he was using a disguise stood too low in rank, here at the rear of Alayna's unit, to do aught about it.

He knew from sad experience that mayhap one in ten would not survive to utter such a report, and not by his doing.

Clutching the bloody linen, his fist trembled. He should have revealed himself to Alayna when he joined her war-band, or during one of the times their paths had chanced to cross at camp. Now he wasn't sure whether he could.

He hadn't even seen his friend Ogryvan, since their units had been assigned different schedules, one fighting while the other slept. Not so with this unified attack.

Having a sword-brother recognize and report him would be a relief.

He glanced at the riders flanking him, but their attention was directed forward. Alayna, facing the unit, had raised her javelin overhead.

"My brave champions, the time for our glory has come! There shall be no retreat until our final foes lie trampled beneath our horses' hooves! Fight with such fierceness and honor and courage that the gods themselves stand up to take notice!"

One of those three Gull could provide. He stuffed the linen wad under his breastplate, snugged his helmet into place, set heels to his mount's flanks, and obeyed his wife's command to commence the charge.

PER PLUNGED Rukh into the Angalaranach ranks. The michaoduin disengaged and ran away. They did not throw down their weapons or dash off screaming in random directions; the vast majority had put the descending sun at their backs.

They had to be going after Arthur's foot troops.

Per drew rein, sheathed his sword, and called riders to him. Of the nine who responded, he dispatched seven to order the wings fighting on this flank to maintain pursuit of the eastward retreating Angalaranaich even should they became unhorsed. By his reckoning, the cavalry had improved the legion's odds from two to one to perhaps one and one half to one, but Arthur still stood in sore need of every man fit to wield a weapon.

This also meant that Per could not spare troops to hunt Angalaranach deserters slipping away to the west. He did, however, send the remaining pair of riders to warn Centurion Elian.

He drew his sword and urged Rukh into the action.

If Arthur was going to need the extra help, Gyan would too.

ELIAN STOOD at the workroom's window, gripping the sill and willing a courier's boat—hell, a raft if it could carry passengers—to glide up the River Fiorth. As a beggar, with his every moment being like its predecessor and harboring no expectations of change except as dictated by the whims of nature and bodily needs, he had forgotten how much torture it could be to await news from a faraway battlefield.

As commander of Senaudon's defenses, he'd mitigated that torture by conducting drills, overseeing the collection and distribution of food rations and supplies, conferring with Optio Cyntaf regarding the patrols' reports, and the like. However, the military routine's monotony was asserting itself.

And he was groping his way as a father. He'd already learned enough from Wart, on the practice field and off, to predict that no moment in either of their lives would be its predecessor's twin. Being the sole parent of a smart and active lad astride the cusp of adulthood was anything but monotonous. But even that couldn't stem Elian's yearning for word of how the legion was faring.

A sharp rap rattled the door. Elian pivoted to face it and bade Cyntaf to enter.

The optio wasn't alone.

Cyntaf held the door open for two other optios to step into the workroom. Their armor bore damage and blood traces from recent combat, and their visible flesh sported cuts and bruises aplenty, but they seemed alert. They saluted Elian in the Caledonian manner and identified themselves in the Brytoni tongue as Horse Cohort soldiers. Elian gave them a legion salute and requested their report.

The men shared a look, and the darker-haired one spoke in a lilting but passable Brytoni accent: "Prefect Peredur sends word that the Pendragon's forces are fully engaged near Dùn Fàradhlann. Angalaranach—sorry, sir, Angli deserters may be headed this way."

"Have you a message for us to take back, Centurion?" asked the second optio.

The people Elian had in mind would be far too busy to welcome such a mundane report as his, though one of them might appreciate hearing that all was as well as could be expected in wartime for the folks she had entrusted to his care. But the couriers would serve the greater good by remaining at Senaudon until—God forbid—a crisis dictated the need to dispatch them.

"No. Get yourselves cleaned up and fed. Visit the forge to repair your armor and weapons. I presume you have stabled your horses?" While both made vigorous nods, he made eye contact with his aide. "Good. Optio Cyntaf here will assign you beds in the barracks after we add you to the patrolling schedule."

As Elian returned the young men's salutes and they departed the workroom, he dug his knuckles into his chest to ease his heart's wistful pang. He wouldn't be riding out on patrol, of course. Physical limitations aside, he'd have to prepare for housing and interrogating a potential influx of captives; increasing the guards around Lady Annamar and her children; ensuring that all the fort's children, including Wart and the lad's warrior-candidate peers, stayed safe; and implementing whatever other measures he could devise to counter the escalated risk.

Tingling erupted beneath his knuckles and enveloped his body, even his phantom leg, and he smiled.

CUT OFF the head, and the body dies.

The same could be said of enemy forces.

Badulf had felled a fair number of men and mounts, but there seemed to be an endless supply. That could change—should change—*must* change if he could kill the Brædan cavalry leaders. He'd have preferred attacking the Dragon King again, of course, but he was thankful for whatever opportunity Woden chose to bestow. From atop the knoll he had observed two cavalry wings attack the section of the Eingel column under his command. Surrounded by his personal guardsmen, he fought his way toward the closer wing leader, a sumptuously armed warrior with long dark hair, wielding sword and horse with lethal precision and shouting like . . .

A woman?

Such a thing was unheard of among the Eingelcynn. As the breeders of heirs, women were cherished and protected. Even the barren Eingel women were valuable in other ways, and not to fill out the army's ranks as fodder for enemy weapons. To place one in command was unthinkable to the point of obscene.

And yet this woman was a master at killing women's sons. Five had gone to meet the gods in the time Badulf had paused to observe her. If she chose to risk her life and the future of her people in this manner, then so be it.

Admonishing his men to stay extra vigilant around him, he yanked a spear from the throat of the closest Brædan corpse, set his stance, and took careful aim.

"MOTHER, NO!"

The tighter Eileann shut her eyes, the sharper the battlefield came into focus. Horses rearing and flailing their hooves to strike men senseless; warriors clashing, falling, bleeding, dying . . . all of it absent the sensations of sound or smell or touch, only the relentless parade of terrifying images she lay powerless to stop.

"No, no, no, no, no, no, *no!*"

Eileann opened her eyes in time to see Neoinean and Fioruisge rush into the tiny hut the One God's monks had offered her, abject worry dominating their expressions. Pushing herself up from the cot with one hand, she lifted the other to wave her ladies off.

"I'm fine, truly. I didn't intend—"

Pain raked her back. She arched, dimly aware of hands grasping her shoulders, her face tilted skyward and mouth taut in an *O* that cramped her jaw.

The howl that emerged was guttural, deafening, and fierce with rage.

BADULF'S SATISFACTION lasted until riders closed ranks around his target, repelling all attackers. Furious horsemen bore down upon his position, eliminating the chance to finish the work his spear had begun.

Worse, his men were falling into disarray; the lines were gone, and as many Eingel corpses clogged the field as enemy ones. If that was happening here, it was a fair assumption that his father's troops needed reinforcements. Better to give ground than to hold as ordered and be slaughtered to the last man.

Badulf unhooked the horn from his belt and blew retreat. When he judged that enough Eingel soldiers were looking his way, he stowed the horn and brandished his sword.

"To me!" he cried. "All good Eingel men who would help King Colgrim, rally to me!"

Scores responded, whooping and shouting. With those on the flanks holding off enemy cavalry troops, Badulf led his men south toward the bulk of the Eingel column.

SCRAPING PAIN shattered the spell of watching his mother, fighting in the wee valley below his position, be swept from her horse by a damned spear. Howling in fury, Angusel spun toward his attacker. His chest armor shifted; the enemy's blow must have severed its laces.

That problem he'd solve before trying to reach Alayna. First he had an Angalaranach cù-puc to kill.

He checked his swing. The cù-puc was bleeding to death at his feet from a gaping neck wound. An unhorsed First Ala soldier panted over the convulsing body, his sword dripping red. The battle had flowed down the grassy knoll toward Alayna and her guards, leaving Angusel and his benefactor alone among the dying and dead.

"Ainchis Sàl! Are you hurt? Shall I find a medic?" The voice and the fact that the soldier hadn't addressed him as sir or by rank spurred a memory.

"Drustanus, well met." He wondered if his voice sounded as harsh to his friend as it did to him. "Help me get this off." Feeling the resurgence of his battle frenzy, Angusel pulled his scale mail with savage yanks. "Now!"

Drustanus drew his dagger and cut the remaining laces. The mail slid, chattering, to the ground. Angusel stepped clear, flexing his arms, but the padded undertunic felt clammy, chafing, and restrictive. Drustanus helped him strip it off too.

The chill smiting his torso felt delicious. He flexed his back muscles to the brink of pain, as if he was unfurling wings. Given the other unbelievable things the gods had done, wings would not have surprised him. He took a lunging step toward Alayna, but a sharp gasp made him stop and whirl.

"What?" It came out less a word than a growl.

"You do need a medic." Palms raised, Drustanus inched a retreat toward the legion's lines. "Your back is bleeding."

Angusel read his friend's meaning in his eyes' whites as he felt the cold lines along his spine, and he rasped a laugh. "Good."

Sword at the ready and not caring whether Drustanus followed him or not, he charged down the hillock and on into the fray, hacking and shoving and kicking and thrusting at anyone in his path. Men fell screaming around him and countless ran screaming away, but his gaze remained fixed upon the dear form lying beyond his reach.

Two warriors, swords drawn, closed upon her.

Angusel drew upon the gods' gifts to redouble the force and speed of his blows, reliving Chieftain Loth's fall and praying that he would not fail his mother too.

CHAPTER 34

N OTHING LOOKED MORE forlorn than an unlit prayer candle.
As the nones prayer-service worshippers exited the
side chapel, Merlin continued the habit he had begun
when Arthur had taken the army on campaign, lighting the remaining candles. Good thing St. John's was built of marble, or it would
have burned to the ground a week ago.

Most days the candles burned in honor of Arthur, Gyanhumara,
Cai, Peredur, Gereint, and the officers and soldiers under their command. He had commemorated Elian, Gull, Wart, and their escorts the
day they had departed. This time, he remembered the Scotti and Brytoni prisoners who had died to help one very important little boy,
and his erstwhile guardians.

Overwhelming guilt forced him onto his knees, and he bowed his
head—not in prayer but in surrender to the truth. He could light candles to hell and back, and he would feel no better for having ordered
those people's deaths.

"Bishop Dubricius?"

Ah, that beloved voice. Merlin didn't deserve to hear it. He shut his eyes tighter and clenched his hands. They began to tremble.

Bless me, Prioress, for I have sinned!

The rustling of robes told him that she had knelt. A soft hand grasped his. The shaking stilled. He summoned the courage to open his eyes and found himself looking not at one face but two.

The first face he had counted the days since last beholding it; the second, until a week ago, he had lost hope of ever seeing.

Niniane had corralled Loholt with one arm. The boy bucked, and she lifted her hand from atop Merlin's to keep Loholt from pitching forward and perhaps hurting his head on the stone floor. While she maintained a firm grip on the child, Merlin stood and helped her rise.

"Prioress Niniane, what a fine young friend you have." Merlin's lips stretched in a direction they hadn't tried since the legion's departure. Loholt giggled, kicked a bit, and buried his face in Niniane's shoulder.

The coy giggles dissolved into wails when they exited the church and came face-to-face with the soldiers who had rescued the boy. Niniane, rubbing his back, murmured soothing words. The cries continued unabated, and she switched to swaying him. Merlin, thankful that his bishop's robes had eased his introduction, ordered the men to await him in the antechamber of his workroom in the praetorium. Loholt's crying didn't stop until after the last soldier had marched out of sight.

Niniane headed for the religious women's cottage she stayed at whenever she visited Caer Lugubalion. Normally an unassailable choice for reasons of propriety and its proximity to St. John's, Loholt's care dictated the need for secrecy and security, commodities unavailable in a house full of well-intentioned women. Merlin slipped a hand under her elbow and pulled her the opposite way.

She halted to regard him. He watched a battle erupt in the cant of her posture between dismay and the need to avoid upsetting the boy. "Your Grace? Surely you do not intend for us to stay in the praetorium? That would not be proper."

"Agreed, Prioress." By *us* he presumed that she meant herself; she had to know that Loholt would live in the praetorium with Arthur and Gyanhumara after the war. "I have arranged chambers in the mansio for you and the boy. You'll be the only guests residing there.

The innkeeper, Iawn, and his wife shall meet your needs. Food, drink, clothing, medicines, swaddling—whatever you require."

She sighed but allowed him to set a course for the dignitaries' inn. "What of the payment?"

Experience had taught him that she would refuse to let him cover the costs. He had hoped to suggest that she work in the infirmary in exchange for bed and board. However, Loholt's visceral fear of soldiers would make the task of guarding him while Niniane worked elsewhere untenable. Thinning his lips, he cast about for a different solution when of a sudden Loholt gave an expansive yawn, sighed, and fell asleep on her shoulder. Smiling, she adjusted him for her comfort without waking him or breaking her stride.

So natural, so endearing . . .

Merlin killed that thought before it could stray into impropriety.

"This," he whispered, nodding at the sleeping child. "Your caring for him until his parents return is payment aplenty."

By this time they had reached the mansio's front entrance, where they stopped. The guards flanking the door saluted the trio with their spears and then resumed their alert stances. Loholt slept through the military greeting, and Merlin made a mental note to modify the soldiers' post locations to be discreet without sacrificing too much potential response time.

The worry that the lad might develop a fear of his warrior-parents he buried for a later day.

He did not need to escort Niniane and Loholt inside; the innkeeper was expecting them, and he told her so.

"My lord bishop is most kind."

Merlin forced a smile as he focused upon the moral strictures belonging to the title she insisted upon using for him. Emrys the soldier had never denied the pleasures of the flesh, and Merlin harbored no intention of uncaging that wild beast. Ever.

"Please don't hesitate to tell me, Prioress, if I may do anything else to make your task easier."

She might have dipped a curtsey if she hadn't been holding the boy; she smiled and dipped her head instead. The way her lips formed a perfect little kissable bow was not helping to control the beast. Merlin gripped the ring and dragged the door open, concentrating on the coldness of the iron rather than the alluring way she glided inside, holding her sleeping charge.

He held his sigh until after he had shut the door behind them.

Maker of all things, You we pray . . . keep us from Satan's tyranny; defend us from unchastity.

If Merlin could make these words from the compline hymn composed by his sainted ancestor, Ambrose of Mediolanum, his mantra, perhaps the prioress might not drive her lord bishop stark mad.

"STAY WITH me, Alayna!"

Gull, having fought his way close to her as he'd done during the earlier attacks, had been the first to reach her when she fell. He ordered her men to form a perimeter. While deciding how best to handle the spear, he felt thankful that he could use the bandage linen for its noble intended purpose rather than a cowardly one. He pulled it from beneath his breastplate and crumpled it into a wad.

The spear had pierced her chest close to the heart. He couldn't take off her torso armor without removing the spear, and she might bleed to death if he tried. Leaving the armor in place, he yanked the spear free and jammed the wad into the bleeding hole. Her eyes rolled back.

"Alayna! No! Don't leave me, my eternal love!"

Mo sìorransachd, the endearment he once had spoken to her every day.

She woke, blinking. "I must be dead if you're here, Guilbach, but why"—she gave a great, groaning gasp—"gods, why does it hurt so damned much?"

"You're not dead." Her wound kept oozing, and he bore down harder. "Neither am I."

"N-no! No, that's impos—"

She swooned.

"Alayna!" He tried to shake her awake. She didn't.

"Leave my mother alone, you filthy son of the unmanned."

Angusel?

The voice was wrong: deep and hoarse and menacing. Gull supposed that it was possible for Alayna to have a son he didn't know about. Possible, but given her temperament, not likely. Regardless, he had to find out.

He noted the position of where he'd stuck his sword, raised his empty hands, stood, and turned.

CLUTCHING LOHOLT, though not hard enough to wake him, Niniane closed her eyes, propped the opposite shoulder against the shut mansio door, and sighed.

The intense longing in Merl—Bishop Dubricius's gaze had almost made her weep. Heaven alone knew where those tears might have led.

At the sound of approaching footsteps, she snapped her eyes open. An older man and woman were regarding her; the innkeeper and his wife, she presumed. The man—Niniane couldn't recall the name the bishop had mentioned—wasn't quite scowling, but the woman was stretching out her arms and making sympathetic little clucking noises.

"Ah, lass—forgive me, Prioress, but ye seem weary to the bone. Here, please allow me." The woman stepped closer, wiggling her callused fingers. Niniane lifted Loholt and passed him to her. He woke, squeaking, but the innkeeper's wife soothed him to sleep with practiced ease. "Me name's Mavis," she whispered, "and I'll be pleased to watch the tyke whene'er ye like."

"As your duties permit, wife," rumbled the innkeeper, ominous as a thunderhead.

His warning went unheeded; Mavis was striding for the stairs. Grunting, he waved Niniane to follow her, and he trooped up behind them.

The room Mavis entered was cave dark. Niniane found herself squinting but couldn't make out much in the gloom. She expected Mavis or her husband to light a lamp, but the woman didn't stop marching until she had reached the chamber's far wall, grasped a fistful of fabric, and pulled.

Thick, brocaded curtains swept aside. A wealth of afternoon sunlight spilled through tall windows to reveal a spacious chamber furnished with a large bed, a sideboard provisioned with silver eating and drinking implements, several trunks for storing personal effects, a table and pair of chairs, and a fireplace. The cold hearth was laid with fresh tinder and split wood ready to light. The reds and golds of fine rugs, linens, and cushions lent their warmth to the room.

"Iawn, ye forgot the lad's cradle." With Loholt balanced on one hip and dozing, Mavis placed her fist upon the other. As Iawn shuffled for the door, Mavis's countenance softened. "Please forgive us, Prioress. Me dear husband will be but a few minutes."

"Thank you for your kindness, good Iawn," Niniane murmured. The answering grunt didn't sound quite so gruff.

Mavis lowered Loholt to the center of the bed and bolstered him with cushions enough to build a fortlet. Apparently satisfied that he wasn't going to roll off, Mavis showed Niniane the trunks and shelves and drawers, maintaining a nonstop if whispered monologue about features of the chamber, the mansio, and its outbuildings, including the private stables and bathhouse.

Odd; this chamber seemed familiar. Niniane sought the reason amid its embarrassingly expensive details: the cheerful colors, the plush fabrics, the carved furniture, the shiny silver, the coolness of the room despite the light blazing through the glazed windows . . .

Dear, holy God!

It was the chamber she had Seen in her prophetic vision with— she sucked in a swift, soft breath, surrendering to the truth—Merlin.

THE WARRIOR was his son, but not as Gull had ever seen him. Angusel was naked to the waist. Smeared god-marks and blood had painted grotesque swirls of blue and red across his body. Whatever blood was his, its loss did not appear to be weakening him. Helmetless, biceps bulging, and breath rasping, the rage blazing in his eyes was nigh unbearable. Gull fought the instinct to look down.

Gone was the fragile boy forged by Gull's damned choices, devoured by the ro h'uamhasach looming over him.

Gull spared a glance for the Albanach warriors and was thankful to note that they had recognized Angusel—and the ravening creature he had become—and had refused to engage him. Else the ro h'uamhasach would have killed them to the last man. The swath of Angalaranach corpses strewn beyond the perimeter testified to the truth of that speculation.

"Angusel, it's me. Your father."

The Albanaich exchanged glances, murmuring in astonished confusion; they must not have overheard his conversation with Alayna. Angusel's expression remained furious and intractable.

"Liar. My father is dead. Unless you want to meet him, get away from my mother. Now."

Gull believed him. And he believed that Alayna was going to die unless she received help soon.

While he racked his battle-spent brains for a way to break the gods' grip upon his son, a second figure entered the spiritual fray. A score of the Pendragon's blue-cloaked soldiers joined the Albanach perimeter guards. Angusel, sword leveled, lunged toward the newest threat, who yelled at the Pendragon's men to stand fast.

Their swords crossed in a ferocious shower of sparks. They traded thrusts, blocks, kicks, and staggering blows. When the challenger risked closing in, the swords rasped against each other until the combatants stood gasping, hilt to hilt and eye to eye.

"Decurion! Halt at once!"

Think of your fealty oath.

Angusel's head jerked.

What? No! I must kill all threats!

He disengaged his sword and cocked it.

"Do you hear me? Stand down. Now!"

The Dove is not yours to kill.

His jaw dropped. He clopped his mouth shut, blinking. The red haze that had tinted his vision during this latest, weirdest bout of battle frenzy yielded to normal colors that resolved into recognizable shapes: his kills, his clansmen, his injured mother, his father, his . . .

"C-comitissa? Gods, no!" Gripping his sword, he used the opposite hand to dash sweat from his forehead. If she had asked him when he'd lost his helmet or how, he couldn't have answered. He plunged the sword into the ground and crashed that fist into his chest, head bowed and eyes closed. Tears stung. A groan escaped. "I'm sorry! Please forgive me."

Her bare fingers pushed aside his forelock, traced the salmon, and caressed his cheek. A current of soothing warmth coursed to his soles. "Of course I do, Angusel." When he dared to meet her gaze, she said, "For this and for . . . everything." She yanked up his sword. As she offered it to him, her lips parted as if she wanted to say more. She glanced at Alayna, puffed her cheeks, and blew a soft breath. "Angusel mac Alayna," she said with battlefield pitch, "I reinstate your fealty oath to me. If you wish it to be."

A thousand thank-yous could not express the gratitude welling from his soul. With his mother hurt and the fighting not done, there was no time. But his mouth got a better idea. As he took possession of his sword and used it to salute her, he cracked the lopsided grin he knew she loved.

GULL WAS thankful for Gyanhumara's public pronouncement on his son's behalf, but he had a wife to save. He stooped to bind her wound as best he could and then gathered her into his arms, shouting to no one in particular, "Find a horse for me and Chieftainess Alayna! And I need volunteers to guard our retreat to Dùn Fàradhlann."

She woke as he was speaking and glanced about before gazing up at him. Between surges of pain glimmered the teasing glint he had missed so gods-damned much. "Well. My men scrambling to do your bidding. One might think you had never stopped being their chieftain." Her grin, set against the alarming pallor of her face, surprised him. "Mayhap you haven't."

Gods. As if he was worthy to have ever assumed that role. "Save your strength. Please. We can speak of such matters later."

"Father! I'm sorry I almost attacked you." The apology came with Gull's sword, which Angusel must have retrieved while Gull was helping Alayna.

"Don't be," Gull insisted, grasping the hilt. "You weren't yourself." Future battles would reveal whether the lad would become a ro h'ua-mhasach as a matter of course; his father tried not to dwell upon that horrific possibility. Such warriors were not renowned for their longevity.

Angusel took Alayna from Gull and helped her stand. Gull sheathed his sword, untied the scabbard from his belt, and retied it to the saddle of the horse a warrior had brought over. After mounting, he guided the horse to a stump. Alayna stepped upon it but yelped when she flexed the muscles of her injured shoulder. Between Angusel, standing on the stump and lifting her from below, and Gull trying to be as careful as possible handling her torso, they got her settled astride the horse in front of Gull.

"Do you need me to escort you?" Angusel's tone revealed a war between worry for his mother and duty to his sword-brothers . . . and restored sword-sister.

Gull opened his mouth to reply, but Alayna beat him to it. "I'll be fine, son. Your father and I have much to discuss." Her head shifted a mite. Gyanhumara, the lone warrior of note in Alayna's apparent field of view, aside from their son, had donned her glove and drawn her sword. "Go be your commander's blade."

Angusel's eyebrows quirked, and he glanced at Gyanhumara. He pressed Alayna's nearest hand between both of his. "May the gods keep you, Mother." He kissed the hand before releasing it.

She smiled. "I'm sure they will, Angusel." The smile faded. "Find yourself a helmet and chest armor."

Gull chastised himself for not offering his breastplate earlier. Mounted and holding his wounded wife, he'd have a damned impossible time taking it off, time Alayna could not spare. He removed his helmet and thrust it toward his son.

Angusel touched the fish, sun, stag, and bull god-marks. "Here's all the armor I need."

Oh, to possess that youthful, ironclad, and thoroughly stupid certainty. Gull grinned in spite of his doubts.

Settling the helmet into place, he watched his half-naked son dash, sword in hand and back flashing the bloody ox skull and crossed cud-gels, beside his war-chieftain's wife toward the combat din while the Pendragon's men broke away from Alayna's perimeter and reformed around them. As he kicked his mount north toward Dùn Fàradhlann, flanked by his volunteer Albanach escorts, he prayed hard that Angu-sel's prediction would prove true.

CHAPTER 35

THE FIRST THING Eileann noticed when she woke was that she couldn't roll over. Her limbs had been restrained. Not painfully so; her arms remained at her sides, her legs were not drawn apart, and soft linen bound her ankles and wrists, not scratchy rope or tough leather.

Linen muffled her calls.

She heard the scrape of chairs. Fioruisge and Neoinean bustled into view, waving calming motions with their hands and making shushing noises with their lips.

"Thank the gods, your seizures and howling have stopped," Fioruisge whispered, pulling the linen from Eileann's mouth. "If our good hosts had seen you in that state, they might have insisted on applying their idea of care." The fearfulness of Fioruisge's tone gave Eileann no wish to experience firsthand what she'd meant.

"How do you feel, my lady? What did you see?" asked Neoinean.

As the memories flooded her brain, Eileann understood why her ladies had taken precautions. It wasn't so much a matter of what she'd seen—fighting and killing, over and over, in a blur of bodies and blood—as how she'd seen it. She felt as if she had been trapped inside Angusel's body, fighting and killing with every blow he must have dealt. Upon further personal inventory, she realized that her limbs felt as leaden as if she'd been the one wielding a sword. And she became aware of smaller, sharper, scattered pains, as if the weapons that had damaged his flesh had cut hers too.

"A battle," she told them, "and death. Oh, gods, so much death."

Fioruisge reached toward Eileann's ankle bonds. "Is it over?"

Eileann directed her mental focus inward. Up sprang images of running, with occasional slashing and stabbing, but mainly running in a group of countless allied warriors. Colors seemed pale but normal, not veiled in the vivid red haze that had permeated her . . . what? Dreams? Visions? Nightmares?

The images shifted to reveal a massive array of soldiers bristling with swords and spears from horizon to horizon.

"No!" Sheer willpower bridled the outburst to a harsh whisper as her muscles jerked and the gory crimson began its creep past the edges of her mind's eye.

Neoinean pinned Eileann's shoulders to the cot. Fioruisge, appearing sad but determined, tightened the bonds and slipped the gag into place.

HALF THE legion would have killed to fight at Arthur's side, Gawain included, but guarding the wounded Pendragon was a different matter altogether, mounted and visible to friend and foe alike. While a thick line of foot soldiers under Gawain's command maintained the perimeter, felling those who sought the legion's top target, Gawain had lost track of the number of times he'd had to change Arddwyn's course to block a spear thrown at his uncle.

Each deflection reminded him of the spear he had failed to stop. Each reminder honed his resolve for revenge.

The Angli attackers grew harder to kill as Arthur pressed the advance toward the Crimson Eagle guarded by scores of the best-armed and most-skilled soldiers in their army. That banner belonged to the enemy's king and the man responsible for Loth's death.

As Gawain and his men lurched closer and the fighting intensified, killing that bloody bird became the only goal that mattered.

His soldiers weakened the Angli line and he saw his chance. Rage
lent him renewed strength. Hacking and slashing with his sword, he
drove Arddwyn through to create a breach. Legion men poured into
the gap after him. Whether Arthur numbered among them, he didn't
know; his focus remained fixed upon the object of his wrath, an old
man in gold-studded steel armor astride a black horse.

The act of leaving his supreme commander's side might be viewed
as dereliction of duty, but Gawain could not have cared less. As he
felled the last royal guard and closed in with his men, he watched the
Angli king's expression collapse into abject terror.

ANGER OVER the blatant disobedience warred with pride and satisfaction as Arthur watched Gawain, surrounded by his men, sweep
Colgrim from the saddle, dismount, and subdue the Angli king with
a sword-weighted backhand to the jaw that sent the king's helmet
flying. Gawain leveled his sword at Colgrim's throat. Shouting Angli
soldiers surged toward them. Gawain pricked Colgrim's neck, drawing blood and a wince. The king snapped an order, and his soldiers
stayed their weapons.

Arthur, in too much pain to risk dismounting, nudged Macsen toward Gawain and Colgrim.

Gawain cocked his sword.

Colgrim spouted incomprehensible but pathetic-sounding words.

"You want mercy, you vicious old bastard?" Gawain yelled. "Did
you show mercy to my father or Cato or anyone else you murdered
in your greed to snatch Brytoni and Caledonian lands for yourself?"

"Gawain—"

Movement in the corner of Arthur's eye distracted him, and he
twisted as fighting erupted near their position. Gripping Caleberyllus
and grimacing through the pain, he faced the latest threat.

BADULF FOUGHT past the enemy's line and into a son's worst fears: his father was kneeling at the mercy of a Brædan soldier's sword. Horrified, he watched the man hitch it back as Colgrim pleaded to be spared.

He knew with dreadful certainty what that sword was going to do next. Attack was not an option. His father would die before the first order left his lips.

"Stop!" Badulf screamed. "I implore you, please!"

AN ANGLI shout rang out, commanding and yet pleading. Arthur couldn't understand the words but could guess the intent.

"Centurion, hold!" To Gawain's credit, he obeyed Arthur but kept his sword trained on Colgrim. "Do not harm the prisoner unless I order it, understood?"

"Yes, sir."

Reprimanding Gawain's borderline sullen response took lower priority than learning who had uttered that shout. Arthur found his answer in a man in expensive if bloody armor trying to claw his way clear of the legion line to reach the Angli king. The soldier bore a striking resemblance to Colgrim. His sheer desperation spoke volumes for his relationship to Gawain's prisoner.

Behind the latest Angli arrival and that man's soldiers surged a welcome sight: Gyan, afoot and flanked by a helmetless and bare-chested Angusel and numerous Comites Praetorii and Horse Cohort warriors. She and her guards looked battered, bloody, and spent. But on her order, they assumed attack stances, as did Gyan.

Relief flooded his soul.

The younger Angli man renewed his pleas, drawing Arthur's gaze. The scene sparked his worst memory: himself, years ago, frozen in fear among reserve troops he could have ordered into action while

Uther was tortured and killed by the bastard Gawain was holding captive. Uther's execution, compounded by Arthur's mistakes, had forged the man he was today: disciplined, relentless, and unbeatable.

It stood to reason that killing Colgrim would make a worse enemy of Colgrim's son.

Killing Colgrim, as satisfying as that might feel, could never resurrect Uther. Or Loth.

Arthur maneuvered Macsen to within a stride of Gawain and leaned over as far as his wounds would permit. Pain forced a gasp, and he prayed that no one had noticed.

"Stand down, Gawain. Colgrim is of no use to me dead."

He didn't perceive his mistake until it was too late.

As THE Dragon King bent in the saddle to converse with his soldier, Badulf saw the man wince. His movements' stiffness confirmed Badulf's suspicions.

It wasn't much, but he thanked Woden for the boon.

"The Dragon King is injured! Eingel men, attack!"

Guarded by his invigorated men, Badulf rushed the Brædan leader. Colgrim used the diversion to wrench free and run from his captor, who left Arthur unguarded to pursue him. Praying that his father would reach the safety of the Eingel lines, Badulf lunged to drag the Dragon King from his horse.

"LORD PENDRAGON!"

Eileann heard the anguish of this shout as clearly as if she had been standing beside Angusel. The red haze dropped over the images in her mind's eye with the abruptness of a hammer stroke. Arthur's form was a dim blur as he struggled to regain his footing and pick up his sword.

A sound seeped into her consciousness: loud, rapid, wooden, and not battlefield noise.

"My lady, do you need help?" called one of the monks in Caledonaiche. The knocking resumed.

Had she cried out for the Pendragon too?

Neoinean hastened to the door but didn't open it. "A wee bit of a nightmare, kind sir. Fioruisge and I are attending her ladyship. If we need assistance, we shall summon you."

Eileann didn't hear the monk's answer; she had closed her eyes, and the battlefield lurched into view. A richly armored enemy warrior leaped into the vision's path, his sword cocked to kill. He seemed familiar in the most gut-wrenching of ways.

This man killed Pendragon's kin.

This man tried to hurt Harper.

This man wounded Blade's mother.

Her limbs, straining at the bonds, cramped in agonizing waves.

She screamed into the gag.

"My lady! Please open at once!" The monk again, thumping to wake the dead.

"Pray!" Fioruisge this time. Eileann had never heard her sound so fierce. "All of you, pray to your god—our lives depend upon it!"

Of that Eileann was certain. If Angusel didn't prevail, they would die on Angalaranach swords.

She added her fervent prayers.

Killed Loth? Injured my mother?

A burst of strength felt like divine affirmation. An Angalaranach body dropped with each swing of his sword, and his vision's haze grew redder by the splash. But he resisted completing the transformation to ro h'uamhasach long enough to ask:

He menaced Eileann—where?

The beach near Trìbruachan.

Of course. He had battled the warrior near Loth's fortress too, saving Gawain's life as he had lain grieving over his father's body.

Had Angusel killed that Angalaranach machaoduin then . . .

The Angalaranach warrior kicked Arthur's feet from under him, tore off his helmet, and stood poised to stab him through the neck. Gawain, having recaptured his exalted prisoner, scratched the old man's throat. The Angalaranach chieftain yelped. The thrice-cursed cùtorc holding Arthur captive glared at Gawain.

Angusel used these distractions to creep up unseen behind the would-be Angalaranach champion. Silence enveloped the battlefield, thick as autumn fog.

The bloody rage haze darkened.

The sword sheared through flesh and bone.

The headless body toppled.

Pendragon's blade gave a roar.

THE DOOR burst open, but Eileann barely heard the bang over the feral noise she was making. Her brain registered words like "devilry" and "possessed," which made no sense. Through Angusel she was bonded with the holy gods, not devils.

Neoinean and Fioruisge seemed to be making similar protests, to no avail. Two monks bustled them, struggling and yelling, from Eileann's chamber.

The monk who remained did not untie Eileann or remove the gag. He bent over her, flicking water droplets from a palm-size silver vial and chanting in a strange tongue. The droplets smote her flesh like icy needles. He uncovered a pot, and perfumed smoke billowed into the room.

She felt a shift in her awareness, as if she were slipping away from Angusel.

Nay, not slipping. She was being dragged.

Help me, Angusel! Help me!

GAWAIN HAD been so focused on running his fleeing captive to ground that he hadn't seen Arthur's peril. Too far away to help, he cursed his wrath-fired stupidity. Arthur was going to flay his back to the bone. If they survived.

Stealthy movement behind the Angli prince, however, gave him a shred of hope. Gawain scratched his captive in a bid to buy time. As Gawain and the Angli prince traded glares, he prayed for Angusel's success as hard as he knew how.

Angusel took his swing. The Angli king and his men stood in shocked silence. Body and head hit the earth. The old man sank onto his knees amid the carnage, keening and sobbing. His grief needed no translation.

The remains of his army broke with him, throwing down their weapons and surrendering to legion and Caledonian survivors who had begun scrambling to contain the captives.

Angusel too had collapsed onto his knees, wheezing like a bellows. That calmed as Gawain watched, and he didn't appear to be suffering major injuries or blood loss, but he seemed dazed, his face a blank slate, devoid of emotion and awareness. His shoulders' slump testified to his exhaustion. A breeze could have felled him.

Gawain needed to devise a way to tether his prisoner. He found an officer's dropped whip, lashed the handle to the man's unresisting hands, and played out the rest of its length, holding the tail as a leash. It wasn't long enough, and Gawain had no wish to drag close a captive who might disturb his friend.

By this time, Uncle Arthur had finished a reunion with Aunt Gyan and limped to Angusel with her assistance. They took turns talking to him, checking him for wounds, patting his shoulders, and chafing his arms. Clutching it by a patch of bloody blond hair, Gyan tried offering Angusel the severed head.

The slate remained blank, its body unmoving.

Colgrim surged toward the trio, pointing at the head and spouting anguished gibberish. Gawain yanked the prisoner's lead and cuffed him into submission. As he tightened his grip, his worry grew apace with the whitening of his knuckles.

If the legion's leaders couldn't rescue Angusel from the prison of his mind, then no one could.

SOMEBODY WAS speaking words.

Two somebodies, he realized.

"Angusel, come back to me!"

Help me, Angusel! Help me!

Which one do I assist first?

Hear the Dove but heed Harper.

Angusel blinked, shook his head, and glanced around. He couldn't recall kneeling. Nearby, a captive of Gawain's wailed over Angusel's last kill. General Cai and Centurion Marcus, shouting worried streams of invectives at Arthur amid scores of their men, converged upon his position. Beyond them, Caledonach and legion warriors worked to subdue Angalaranach survivors, assisted by a cohort just now running onto the battlefield.

"Thank you, Decurion Ainchis Sàl."

Angusel jerked his head toward the Pendragon's voice and winced, hand to neck. His war-chieftain was looming over him, assisted by the Comitissa, who was acting as his crutch, as Angusel had done . . . when? This morning?

Gods, it had seemed an eon.

His head felt trapped in a vise. He flexed aching muscles to press the heels of his hands to his eyes. The fractured images would not disappear. He didn't think the aches could.

"It will never be enough to clear my debt to you, but you have earned your choice of postings." Using his wife as a counterweight, the Pendragon offered his hand. "And a promotion."

Sighing, Angusel gripped Arthur's forearm to haul himself up. His legs ached too. "My lord Pendragon is most kind, but—"

Harper is in dire trouble.

The sun of hope cured his pain.

"I'm sorry, my lord and my lady. I must attend an urgent matter. Have I your leave?" That last bit was for courtesy; he'd help Eileann with or without the Pendragon's blessing.

"What could be so damned—?"

"Of course, Angusel," said the Comitissa.

"Gyan—" the Pendragon growled.

"Let him go, Artyr. I believe the gods need him elsewhere."

"Thank you, my lady."

Angusel broke into a run without bothering to salute either of them. They could flog him for that discipline breach later.

Across the battlefield, he made out several shapes lumbering toward him, led by a riderless gray. He adjusted his angle to intercept his warhorse and the riders chasing him.

"Angus! What happened to calling me"—the words grew fainter by the stride—"Gyan?"

Angusel smiled.

He answered to different goddesses now but would consider this one's implied request.

By this time, Chieftain Ogryvan and Prefect Peredur, escorted by scores of mounted Argaillanach and Horse Cohort warriors, had ridden close enough for Angusel to recognize them. Ogryvan must have heard the shout too, for he glanced toward her and grinned as Angusel caught Stonn. Her father's grin vanished. "Is Gyan all right, lad, do you know?"

Angusel snapped an "Aye, my lord," mounted, collected the reins, and spurred Stonn eastward.

WHATEVER THE monk was doing to Eileann with his magic chants and water and smoke seemed to be having the desired effect. She could no longer sense Angusel in the bond no matter how hard she tried, and she didn't know whether he had sensed her mental pleas.

Despair gripped her soul.

The grayness descended and darkened, driving out all images, the bad as well as the good, until nothing remained but vast loneliness. No friends, no husband, no bairn, no kin, no parents, no clan. No Angusel. Nobody. She had a word for that.

Aonar. Alone.

Keening into the gag, she prayed for the grayness to take her.

The steadily louder thud of hoofbeats spilling through her hut's tiny window was the single most hopeful sound under heaven.

SAME AS when he'd known how to lead General Cai to Arthur in fire-scorched Trìbruachan, Angusel didn't sense the gods telling him where to find Eileann, but he rode straight to Caledàitan. Stonn, may-hap with the gods' aid, made the hour-long journey in nigh half that time.

At the compound, he dismounted and flipped the reins over Stonn's head toward the first monk to rush over, who was gripping a hoe dangling weedy bits. The man, viewing Angusel with wide eyes and slack jaw, retained the sense not to brandish his garden tool like a weapon.

"Watch him. He can graze, but don't let him drink too much." The Breatanaiche rasped out, and it was not his intent to terrify these servants of the One God. Yet. "Please. I shall not be long."

He followed his instincts to one of the huts and tried the door. It was locked. The door splintered under the force of his shoulder's blow.

Eileann lay inside, gagged and strapped to a cot while a monk uttered a Ròmanach prayer chant and waved an incense pot around her. The man looked toward Angusel. The incense pot's chain slipped from his grasp. The pot shattered, releasing a noisome cloud. The monk gasped and sketched the symbol of his god at the points of his body.

The god-marks must have frightened him; Angusel had not wiped them off or covered them. That, or the head-to-toe gore. The portion of himself that he'd bothered to clean, as best as he could with the back of a bloody hand while pounding down the road atop Stonn, had been his face so he could see better. He'd probably done little better than smear it.

Eileann's plight enraged him.

Red haze began to descend.

Do not murder One's servant.

The haze cleared. He drew a breath.

"Release the lady. She is under my protection." This time he didn't care how gruff he sounded.

The monk's rapid compliance satisfied him. Angusel gathered Eileann into his arms, reveling in how right she felt there. She laid a cool palm against his cheek, not seeming to mind how grisly he must look. That felt right too. It felt more right to kiss her, deep and tender and long.

Holy love suffused his soul.

To judge by her radiant smile, she had enjoyed the kiss almost as much as he had.

Wringing his hands, the monk dipped his head. "Please forgive me, great lord. I had naught but her best interests at heart."

Angusel snorted, and not because he'd failed to recognize that the man believed he was trying to help her using the ways of his god, however misguided.

"I am not great or a lord."

You are wrong, Blade, on both counts.

He felt dubious about that. But the gods had never lied, and he chose not to debate them.

Cradling Eileann, he shouldered past the monk and the broken door and veered toward Stonn and the gardener-monk. Eileann's ladies waited with him. The younger woman was clutching Eileann's harp.

Eileann stretched out her hands, and the ladies clasped them. "Thank you," she murmured. "I owe you both a great debt."

"Nonsense. It was our honor to serve you," said the older woman—her name slid beyond Angusel's power to recall it—to Eileann. "Fioruisge is welcome to stay with me as long as she wishes. If you need us, my lady, send for us at my apothecary shop."

"Take care of your ro h'uamhasach," said Fioruisge. "He shall need it."

"I know." Eileann beamed up at him. "I can sense it through the bond."

Angusel had no idea what she meant but planned to ask her later. They had a lot to discuss; that much he could sense, bond or no bond. However, duty compelled him to return to whatever awaited him with his commanders, his parents, and his clan.

He mounted and offered his hand to help Eileann climb up behind him. The gardener-monk assisted her as Fioruisge tied the harp to Stonn's saddle using one of its pairs of baggage stays. Angusel felt

Eileann settle her arms around his waist and press her cheek to his back, apparently oblivious to the dried blood, as if embracing the terrible god she had invoked.

Harper embraces us all.

Upon touching his heels to Stonn's flanks, they cantered toward the westering sun.

Epilogue

THE EXALTED HEIR of Clan Alban of Caledon stood on the ferry dock on the north bank of the Ab Fhorchu amid his men. Swords at the ready, they were watching the latest wave of ferries being loaded with legion soldiers and their captives. Not much had transpired in the past three days of this process that their guards couldn't handle, but with this lot, even injured and dispirited, having Angusel's unit on hand, one of several extras, was a sound precaution.

Angusel studied the relentless slap of water on pilings. It wasn't helping.

At the feet of the headless Angalaranach prince, Arthur had offered him his choice of postings and repeated the promise in camp that night. Angusel had declined the promotion to centurion. Even if he had believed, as the Pendragon did, that the legion contained a hundred men willing to obey one who might be gods-blessed in strength and skills but half their age, he wanted no truck with that madness. The office had begun to forge Gawain—whom Arthur did not demote for dereliction of duty but flogged and banned for a year from competing for a Comites Praetorii slot—into a leader of whom Centurion Cato would have been proud. That was tribute aplenty.

Gyan had offered Angusel a place as a decurion in the battle-thinned ranks of the Comites Praetorii, but he had felt too wrung out to accept that posting and not make of mess of it either. She had claimed to understand. He hoped so. One of them should.

His refusals had resulted in this temporary assignment, overseeing the departure of Angalaranach soldiers from the north bank. The critical work, however, would commence for their keepers after the crossing: ensuring that the Angalaranaich, down to the last child and cow, withdrew from Dùn Éideann, called by the Breatanaiche name Dun Eidyn in the treaty Arthur had inked with the help of Breatanach slaves freed from the conquered Angalaranach chieftain's retinue.

Angusel had asked to be sent as far from Dùn Fàradhlann as possible. A kinder posting would have put him aboard the first southbound ferry.

"Lord Angusel."

His gold lion cloak-pin—presented to him by his father with word of his formal reinstatement as Àrd-Oighre h'Albainaich, and which the Pendragon had given him dispensation to wear until his unique, gem-eyed dragon rank badge could be fashioned—of a sudden felt as heavy as a millstone.

He sheathed his sword and faced the vaguely familiar voice. The title's use had to mean that the man hailed from Clan Alban. A Caledonach legion soldier would have addressed him as Decurion Angusel—Gyan had changed the master duty roster herself—or sir.

The speaker's deep bow had caused his cloak's hood to slip forward, obscuring his face. The fingers of his sword hand lay flat over his heart. In his shield-side fist, he clutched Stonn's reins as well as those of his own mount.

A hundred millstones dragged at Angusel's heart.

Since he'd been addressed in Caledonaiche, he responded in kind. "Please rise, good sir." He felt self-conscious for having to say such a thing to anyone, but he'd become resigned to the fact that he would have to grow accustomed to it. The young man straightened, and he pushed back his hood, revealing a shock of dark hair and chiseled cheekbones not unlike Angusel's own. Angusel sucked in a swift breath. "Coileach. Gods! You don't have to call me lord." The presence of the son of his mother's sister could have but one meaning. "My mother—is she . . .?"

"Aunt Alayna has asked for you." Coileach pressed Stonn's reins into Angusel's hand. "Uncle Guilbach secured the Pendragon's permission for you to come with me."

Angusel knew they ought to hurry, but he borrowed half a minute to switch to Breatanaiche and order Dunaidan to take charge of the squad.

"The gods alone know when I will return," he told his second.

He polled them, but they stayed mum.

"Right, sir," said Angusel's onetime tormentor, rendering a crisp legion salute. "You can count on me."

Angusel gave Dunaidan an appreciative shoulder slap, swung into the saddle, and joined Coileach, who had ridden his horse off the dock.

The trip from the ferry port to Dùn Fàradhlann was but half the distance of Dùn Fàradhlann to Caledàitan, but it felt eight times longer as they cantered past queues of soldier-encircled prisoners, mountains of armor and weapons being sorted for reuse or repurposing, endless rows fresh burial mounds, and mile upon mile of funeral pyres. The closer they rode, the grislier the vista became.

Most of the pyres had nigh burned out, the roasted-meat smell all but gone. Soldiers had begun shoveling dirt atop the pyres to smother smoldering cinders, but Angusel's gut roiled as if the stench had been fresh.

His kills' memories gagged him.

Gods, help me to forget this.

You can't. No one ever should.

He swallowed bile and rode on.

The Horse Cohort encampment outside Dùn Fàradhlann was bustling; likely the infantry camp north of the fortress was too. A grateful Chieftain Rionnach had given Arthur leave to take as much time as the men needed to rest and heal in preparation for a triumphal march to Caer Lugubalion by way of Senaudon. Angusel's assignment had made him miss Clan Tarsuinn's celebratory feasting, not that he cared beyond satisfying his body's basic needs. Camp rations did that job just as well.

Eileann's return to her parents had been anything but triumphal. Though they had assured her that the Tarsuinnaich no longer sought her sacrificial death, she had clung to Angusel during the tense reunion as if needing him to shield her. But when he had introduced her to his mother, who'd been given chambers in Dùn Fàradhlann rather than a cot in the field hospital, Eileann discovered a purpose in which she had felt comfortable enough to stay behind while Angusel commenced his captive-watching duty.

Eileann was the sole reason he hadn't bolted for a ferry on the first day.

He led Coileach to the picket lines, where they left their horses, since that was better than trying to wedge the animals into the full-to-bursting Dùn Fàradhlann stables. When the commanding officer would have refused, since Coileach was not a legion soldier, whatever he saw in Angusel's expression must have made him change his mind. Angusel thanked the man, and he and Coileach strode for the fortress.

The chambers Alayna had been given were large, luxurious, full of light—and not what the Chieftainess of Clan Alban would have selected for herself. She loved largeness and luxury, but Angusel knew she preferred a darker, richer, intimate atmosphere, not the pale yellows and blues of the fabrics that surrounded her in this room.

And there was not a single cat in attendance.

He stopped inside the threshold. That she would never see her own chambers, her beloved cats, or the rest of her clansfolk made his heart clench. He blinked hard.

"Son. I thank the gods you're here." Her voice sounded raspy and fragile. She cleared her throat. "And thank you, Coileach, for bringing him."

His cousin strode to her side, went onto one knee, grasped her nearest hand, and bowed his head. "It was my honor." He rose and kissed her cheek. "Walk with the gods, Aunt Alayna."

On his way toward the door, Coileach paused to give Angusel's shoulder a sympathetic clasp. He departed, easing the door shut behind him.

Gull and Eileann, who had been sitting near the bed so quietly that Angusel hadn't noticed them at first, rose too. Eileann set down her harp and reached for Angusel. That broke the spell, and he crossed the room to join her.

This close, he couldn't miss seeing his mother's sweat-beaded, waxy pallor. In contrast, her cheeks were flushed as crimson as those of a battle-frenzied warrior.

She was battling, he realized, and losing.

Her spear wound had developed a raging fever that was poisoning her body.

"Give me your hands, my children." As she raised her arms, Angusel grieved to note how much they trembled. He and Eileann each grasped one of her hands. Alayna brought their hands together and covered them between both of hers. "You have a fine, lovely bride, son."

He and Eileann had yet to consummate their relationship—there remained issues to resolve, beginning with the goddess who kept appearing to him during the act of love—but he wasn't about to argue the *bride* part of his mother's statement. That he would marry Eileann one day, he knew beyond doubt.

He couldn't think of anything to say except, "Thank you, Mother. I'm glad Eileann pleases you."

Alayna smiled, but the noise she made was more cough than laugh. Blood flecks spattered the coverlet. She let go of Eileann and Angusel to swipe at her mouth. "I'm glad she pleases *you*." She cleared her throat again. "I have drafted a petition to the Albanach elders—"

"Aye, to reinstate me as exalted heir." His ears buzzed as if to keep him from hearing her repeat that which she had already told him. The chieftainess he knew never deigned to tell her son anything twice. "Thank you for that kindness." He refrained from adding, "Again."

"Not that, son. I've suggested that Eileann become Clan Alban's exalted heir-bearer after me. Your father will be chieftain, of course, for as long as he remains fit to serve."

"What?" Gull and Angusel said together and shared a surprised glance.

"Didn't I mention that, mo sìorransachan?" she murmured.

The look Alayna gave her consort was so loving and intimate that Angusel entertained the notion of leaving the chamber and taking Eileann with him. Upon seeing Gull's tender response dawn across that battle-forged face, he abandoned the idea. Whatever conversations his parents had shared during the past three days—and many of those words had to have been fiery—in that moment, they appeared at perfect peace with one other. Angusel felt boundless gratitude to have witnessed it.

"The council ratified your chieftainship unanimously. I'm afraid that your status, my dear," Alayna said to Eileann, "may take time to approve."

Time that his mother didn't have, if Angusel read aright the sorrow weighting her tone.

"If the gods will it," Eileann murmured.

Amen, Angusel added without thinking. In the next breath he hoped they would not be offended by his use of a word taught to him by men who honored a different god.

It does not. We serve One too.

Angusel might have questioned that revelation but for his mother's long, gasping breath. Her muscles contorted, and she let out an agonized scream. While Eileann swabbed her brow, Gull and Angusel kneaded her arms and legs. The spasms eased, but she kept panting through clenched teeth.

Please give Mother's pain to me!

This time, they did not reply.

The Chieftainess of Clan Alban departed this world much as she had lived in it, fighting till her last breath. For years she had pursued causes of her own devising, but in the end she had chosen to sacrifice herself protecting folk outside the clan.

There was, her son knew, no greater path a person could walk.

We welcome our blest daughter.

The tears sliding down Angusel's cheeks felt leavened by godly pride.

He knelt and bowed his head until his face touched Alayna's forearm. The wave of his emotions crested, broke, and crashed. Twining his fingers with her limp ones, he sobbed that pride onto her lion tattoo.

After a few . . . what, minutes? Moments? Eons? A pair of gentle hands rubbed his shoulders. Eileann's touch gave him the strength to disengage his hand, rise, kiss his mother's brow, and soldier on with his destiny.

Their destiny.

Eileann cupped his cheek and wiped his tears. With that hand she pressed his scale-encased chest, over the sun of hope, whose eternal flame would always nourish his heart and fire his soul. He placed his hand atop hers and gave it a light squeeze.

While Alban's once and again chieftain closed Alayna's eyes, kissed her lips, and straightened her limbs, Alban's exalted heir vowed to become the embodiment of her finest example.

Explicit Liber Tertius

kih, MMXVIII
Isaiah 17:12 (NIV), Soli Deo Gloria

Author's Notes

IRST AND FOREMOST, I want to thank you for your patience while I worked on this book. Your faithfulness means a lot to me, and I appreciate it very much. I hope it has been worth the wait for you.

The creative mind is a fragile flower. Anything can disrupt its blooming: job, spouse, children, extended family, disaster, relocation, personal health, the death of a loved one. Those issues affect everyone, of course, and in seventeen years, I've had my share too.

The concept for *Raging Sea* was suggested to me at the turn of the millennium by my then literary agent. Job, health, and family issues, plus the development and New York publication of an unrelated novel, *Liberty*, relegated *Raging Sea* to the back burner. After my agent and I parted company in 2010, it never occurred to me to abandon Angusel's coming-of-age story, since by then it was entrenched in the series' structure, but I lost the impetus to write new material for three more years. Then followed a five-year period wherein I repeated the frustrating cycle of getting geared up to work on the book and make some headway . . . only to have a major life event derail my efforts.

If I could understand what happened in May 2018 that allowed me to jettison some forty years' worth of emotional baggage relating to my deceased parents, I would become a life coach, go on the speaking circuit, and make a mint. Maybe that's just as well, however, because I do prefer writing to public speaking. All I know is that two weeks later, I woke up in my hotel room on the Friday morning that Balticon 52 was scheduled to begin, a shaft of sunlight slicing through a gap in the curtains to hit my eyelids, and the idea for Angusel's interaction with the seven Caledonach gods, always in seven syllables whether in thought or in action, burning my brain.

A fellow creative mind will appreciate just how very wonderful that stroke of inspiration felt.

Angusel's divine interaction pays homage to the lyric from Lancelot's introductory song in the musical *Camelot*: "C'est moi, c'est moi, the angels have chose/To fight their battles below." Angusel's great physical strength in spite of his youth reflects another nod to the musical; after Lancelot defeats Arthur in an impromptu joust, Lancelot's squire informs the bemused king that "when [Lancelot] was sixteen, he could defeat any jouster in France."

Aficionados of Arthurian lore may also recognize echoes of Tennyson's *Idylls of the King* in Eileann's river journey. Although Eileann was feigning her death, the Guinevere-Lancelot-Elaine dynamic will reverberate in The Dragon's Dove Chronicles, volume 4, *Zenith Glory*.

A major plot point of *Zenith Glory* constitutes another reason I dragged my feet with *Raging Sea*; the event in question lies well beyond my comfort zone as a writer. However, I believe the direction I have taken with *Raging Sea* will help me push through my reluctance and deliver to you—in what I hope proves to be a far more timely fashion—the next epic installment in this series.

kih, 2 December 2018
Wytheville, VA

PEOPLE

ENTRY FORMAT:

Full Name (Pronunciation). Brief description, which may include rank, occupation, clan, country, nickname(s), name's origin and meaning, banner, and legendary name. Place-names and other affiliations are given in the person's native language.

Approximate pronunciation guidelines are supplied for the less obvious names, especially those of Scottish Gaelic and Brythonic origin. When in doubt, pronounce it however it makes sense to you.

Accolon map Anwas. Centurion in First Ala, Horse Cohort, Dragon Legion of Brydein; Urien's second-in-command and friend. Clan: Moray, Dalriada, Brydein. Legendary name: Sir Accolon.

Adim Al-Iskandar. Arms merchant, hails from Constantinopolis. Name origin: variant of "Adam Alexander."

Ælferd Wlencingsson. Late West Saxon prince. Son of Wlencing; nephew of Cissa; was betrothed to Camilla prior to his death in the

Second Battle of Port Dhoo-Glass at the hands of Gyanhumara. Banner: green griffin on gold.

Ælle (ALE-leh). King of the South Saxons. Father of Camilla. Banner: gold Woden's hammer and fist on black. Historically, he reigned in Sussex (the "South Saxons") from 477 until perhaps as late as 514, though no document officially recording his death exists.

Agarra. Late chieftainess and Àrd-Banoigin of Clan Alban of Caledon; Alayna's mother; Angusel's grandmother. Name origin: based on Scottish Gaelic verb *agair* ("to claim").

Airde (ahEER-day) nic Agarra. Daughter of Agarra; Alayna's younger sister; Coileach's mother; Angusel's aunt. Clan: Alban, Caledon. Name origin: Scottish Gaelic *àirde* ("height").

Alain. Heir to the chieftainship of Clan Cwrnwyll of Rheged, Brydein. Husband of Yglais; Arthur's brother-in-law. Legendary name: King Alain Le Gros.

Alayna (ah-lah-EE-nah) nic Agarra. Chieftainess and Àrd-Banoigin of Clan Alban, Caledon. Daughter of Agarra; sister of Airde; wife of Guilbach; mother of Angusel; aunt of Coileach mac Airde. Name origin: Scottish Gaelic *àlainn* ("beautiful, elegant, splendid").

Alisa. Brytoni female name, evocative of "Alice"—or "Alisande."

Alun. Brytoni officer in the Dragon Legion of Brydein.

Ambrose of Mediolanum. a.k.a. Aurelius Ambrosius, St. Ambrose of Milan. Fourth-century lawyer, governor (consular prefect), bishop of Mediolanum (Milan, Italy), and one of the original four doctors of the Church; credited with preventing British emperor Magnus Maximus (Macsen Wledig) from invading Italy in AD 384. In the Dragon's Dove Chronicles, St. Ambrose is an ancestor, through the influential Roman Aurelia family, of Merlin and Arthur.

Ambrosius Aurelius Constantinus. Late Dux Britanniarum. Elder brother of Uther; father of Merlin. Nickname: Emrys (EM-rees). Legendary names: Ambrosius Aurelianus, Emrys Wledig.

Angusel mac Alayna, a.k.a. Anguselus, a.k.a. Ainchis Sàl. Àrd-Oighre of Clan Alban, Caledon. Son of Alayna and Gwalchafed. Nickname: Angus. God-name: Blade (Caledonaiche *Lann*) Name origin: inspired by Scottish Gaelic *an càs* ("the trying situation"), *sàl* ("sea"). Legendary name: Sir Lancelot du Lac.

Annamar ferch Gorlas. Oldest daughter of Gorlas and Ygraine; Arthur's half sister; wife of Loth of Clan Lothian; mother of Gawain,

Gareth, Medraut, and Cundre. Clan: Cwrnwyll, Rheged, Brydein. Legendary names: Queen Margause, Margawse.

Anwas. Late high-ranking warrior of Clan Moray; father of Accolon. Clan: Moray, Dalriada, Brydein.

Aonar a Dubh Loch. A name Angusel gives himself, based on events in this story. Name origin: Scottish Gaelic *aonar a dubh loch* ("alone from the black lake").

Arthur map Uther, a.k.a. Arturus Aurelius Vetarus, a.k.a. Artyr mac Ygrayna. The Pendragon, Dux Britanniarum (succeeded Uther). Son of Uther and Ygraine. Clan: Cwrnwyll, Brydein. Nickname: Artyr. God-name: Pendragon. Banner: scarlet dragon rampant on gold. Legendary name: King Arthur Pendragon.

Artyr (ar-TEER) mac Ygrayna. See Arthur. Caledonaiche matronymic name format meaning "Arthur, son of Ygraine." Name origin: Scottish Gaelic *ar tir* ("our country").

Badulf Colgrimsson. Angli prince. Son of King Colgrim. Name origin: Old English bád ("pledge"), *wulf* ("he-wolf," "wolfish person," "devil").

Bann. Chieftain of Clan Lammor of Gododdin, Brydein. Father of Bedwyr. Staunch ally of Arthur. Legendary name: King Ban of Benwick (Lancelot's father; I made him Bedwyr's father in response to authors who conflate the characters of Lancelot and Bedivere).

Bedwyr (BAYD-veer) map Bann. Highest-ranking officer of the Brytoni fleet. Son of Chieftain Bann. Clan: Lammor, Gododdin, Brydein. Legendary name: Sir Bedivere.

Bohort. Centurion in the Brytoni army; standard-bearer of the Comites Praetorii. Legendary name: Sir Bors de Ganis.

Caitleen. Scáthaichean noblewoman. Wife of Fergus.

Caius Marcellus Ectorius. General (legate) in the Brytoni army, Camboglanna garrison commander. Son of Ectorius and Calpurnia; Arthur's foster brother. Nickname: Cai. Legendary name: Sir Kay the Seneschal.

Calpurnia. Wife of Ectorius; mother of Cai, foster mother of Arthur. Distantly descended from the ancient patrician Roman Calpurnii family.

Camilla Ællesdottr. South Saxon princess. Daughter of King Ælle; betrothed to Ælferd. Banner: green griffin, gorged with gold crown, on gold (in honor of her dead fiancé).

Cato. Commander (centurion) of First Ala, Horse Cohort, Dragon Legion of Brydein; son of Majora. Clan: Moray, Dalriada, Brydein.

Cissa (KEE-sah). King of the West Saxons. Ælferd's uncle. Banner: white horse crowned on purple. Historically, Cissa probably was King of the South Saxons, ruling jointly with Ælle until Ælle's death, though no reliable Saxon monarch genealogy exists, and titles and territories may have been more than a little bit fluid.

Cleopatra. Cleopatra VII Philopator, of Greek ancestry and the last pharaoh of Egypt; she ruled during the mid-1st century B.C.

Coileach (cohEEL-ay-ack) mac Airde. Alayna's nephew. Clan: Alban. Name origin: Scottish Gaelic *coileach* ("cockerel").

Colgrim. King of the Eingelcynn. Father of Badulf. Banner: crimson eagle on white. Name origin: Old English *cól* ("cold"), *grimm* ("fierce, savage").

Conall. Prefect of the Manx Cohort of the Dragon Legion of Brydein. Clan: Argyll, Caledon.

Corwyn. Brytoni soldier in First Ala, Horse Cohort. Name origin: Welsh *corryn* ("spider").

Cuchullain (koo-CULL-len) og Conchobar. Laird of the Scáthaichean of Eireann (succeeded Conchobar). Son of Conchobar; husband of Dierda. Nickname: Cucu. Banner: silver wolf running, on pine green. Legendary name: Cú Chulainn.

Culhwch (KEEL-hook). A cohort commander (prefect) of the Dragon Legion of Brydein.

Cundre ferch Loth. Daughter of Annamar and Loth; sister of Gawain, Gareth, and Medraut; Arthur's niece. Clan: Lothian, Gododdin, Brydein. Legendary name: Kundry.

Cyntaf (KEEN-tahv). Brytoni optio assigned to the Senaudon occupation cohort. Name origin: Welsh *cyntaf* ("first," "swiftest").

David. Ancient Hebrew warlord and later king of Israel.

Dierda (dee-ER-dah). Scáthaichean noblewoman. Wife of Cuchullain. Nickname: Dee. Name origin: variant of the name Deirdre.

Driw (DROO). Soldier in First Ala, Horse Cohort, Dragon Legion. Name origin: Welsh *driw* ("faithful").

Drustanus. Horse-warrior in First Ala, Dragon Legion, Brydein. Nephew of Marcus. Legendary names: Sir Tristram, Tristan.

Dumarec. Late chieftain of Clan Moray of Dalriada, Brydein. Wreigdda's husband; Urien's father. Banner: black boar's head on gold.

Dunaidan. Soldier in First Ala, Horse Cohort, Dragon Legion; Angusel's friend. Name origin: Brythonic *dun* ("hill fort"), *aidan* ("silver"). Legendary name: Sir Dinadan.

Dynann. Chieftainess of Clan Tarsuinn of Caledon; wife of Rionnach; mother of Tavyn, Eileann, and Rionnag. Nickname: Dyn. Name origin: Scottish Gaelic *dian* ("keen," adj.).

Ectorius Marcellus Antonius. One of Uther's officers and a staunch friend. Late husband of Calpurnia; father of Cai; foster father of Arthur. Nickname: Ector. Legendary names: Sir Ector, Antor, Anton.

Eileann (ee-LAY-ahn) nic Dynann. Second child of Dynann and Rionnach; sister of Tavyn and Rionnag. Àrd-Banoigin of Clan Tarsuinn. God-name: Harper (Caledonaiche *Banachrui*, inspired by Scottish Gaelic word for "female harper," *bana-chruiteir*). Name origin: Scottish Gaelic *eileann* ("island"). Legendary name: Lady Elaine.

Elian (EHL-ee-ahn). Centurion in the Dragon Legion of Brydein. Dumarec's cousin. Clan: Moray, Dalriada, Brydein. One ancient variant of Lancelot's story claims that he had three Elaines in his life, much as Arthur was supposed to have been married to three Gwenhwyfars. Religious implications aside (e.g., a Maiden/Mother/Crone analogy), the three "Elaines" in Angusel's life are his mother Alayna, his mentor Elian, and his wife Eileann.

Emrys (EM-rees). See Merlin. Brythonic variant of the name Ambrosius, a nickname Merlin had used until Arthur's birth.

Eoghann. See Loholt. Name origin: Brythonic variant of the name Egan.

Fairge. Late wise-woman of Clan Tarsuinn. "Fairge" is an alias; her birth name is unknown. She was replaced by Fioruisge. Name origin: Scottish Gaelic *fairge* ("sea" or "ocean").

Fergus og Róig. Scáthaichean warrior. Cuchullain's foster brother; husband of Caitleen. Nickname: Fergi. A composite of the "Fercos ap Roth/Fergus mac Roth" listed in the ancient Welsh list of Arthur's warriors and the "Fergus mac Róich" of Irish mythology who was one of Cú Chulainn's foster fathers.

Fioruisge. Wise-woman of Clan Tarsuinn. "Fioruisge" is an alias; her birth name is unknown. She replaced Fairge. Name origin: Scottish Gaelic *fioruisge* ("pure spring water").

Firduar. Scáthaichean warrior. Cuchullain's sword-brother and extremely close friend, based on Ferdia/Ferdiad/Fer Diad of Cú Chulainn mythology. Nickname: "the Ghost." Name origin: Scottish Gaelic *fir* ("person"), *dubhar* ("shade;" i.e., ghost).

Gareth map Loth. Heir to the chieftainship of Clan Lothian. Second son of Loth and Annamar; brother of Gawain, Medraut, and Cundre; Arthur's nephew. Clan: Lothian, Gododdin, Brydein. Legendary name: Sir Gareth.

Gawain map Loth. Officer in the Dragon Legion of Brydein. First-born son of Loth and Annamar; brother of Gareth, Medraut, and Cundre; Arthur's nephew. Clan: Lothian, Gododdin, Brydein. Legendary name: Sir Gawain.

Gereint map Erbin. Prefect of the Badger Cohort (*Praefectus Cohortis Meles*), Dragon Legion of Brydein; commander of the occupation force at Senaudon. Son of Erbin. Legendary name: Sir Geraint.

Giuthas. A priest of Clan Tarsuinn. Name origin: Scottish Gaelic *giuthas* ("pine" (tree)).

Guenevara. See Gyanhumara. Name origin: Eingel/Saxon variant of the name Gwenhwyfar.

Guilbach (GOOL-bahk) mac Leanag. Late Chieftain and Àrd-Ceoigin of Clan Alban, Caledon. Alayna's consort; Angusel's father; Elian's friend. Clan: Tarsuinn, Caledon. Nicknames: Gwalchafed, Gull. Name origin: Scottish Gaelic *guilbneach* ("curlew").

Gwalchafed (GWAHL-kah-vehd). See Guilbach. Nickname bestowed on Guilbach by troops of Uther the Pendragon honoring his battle prowess. Name origin: Brythonic *gwalchafed* ("summer falcon").

Gwelda. A prostitute on Maun. Clan: Moray, Dalriada. Name origin: Welsh *gweld* ("see").

Gyanhumara (ghee-ahn-huh-MAR-ah) nic Hymar, a.k.a. Gwenhwyfar ferch Gogfran, a.k.a. Guenevara of Caledonia. Chieftainess and Àrd-Banoigin of Clan Argyll of Caledon. Daughter of Hymar and Ogryvan. Nickname: Gyan (GHEE-ahn). God-name: The Dove (Caledonaiche *Calmag*, my invented feminine singular form of Scottish Gaelic male noun *calman*, "the dove"). Banner: two silver doves flying, on dark blue. Name origin: Scottish Gaelic *gainne amhran* ("rarest song"). Legendary names: Queen Guinevere, Guenevere, Guenever.

Hador (HAY-dore). Saxon warrior; Camilla's second-in-command. Name origin: Anglo-Saxon *hador* ("bright", "brightness").

Hymar (HEE-mar). Late Chieftainess and Àrd-Banoigin of Clan Argyll, Caledon. Ogryvan's wife; mother of Peredur and Gyanhumara. Name origin: Scottish Gaelic *amhran* ("song").

Iawn (YAN). Brytoni man; husband of Mavis; innkeeper of the mansio at Caer Lugubalion. Name origin: Welsh *iawn* ("correct").

Iesu (YAY-soo). Brytonic variant of Jesus.

Iomar mac Morra. Àrd-Oighre of Clan Rioghail, Caledon. Son of Morra; Ogryvan's cousin. Name origin: Scottish Gaelic *iomair* ("to row").

Lagan. Scáthaichean warrior; Cuchullain's charioteer, based on Laeg of Irish Cú Chulainn mythology—and physiologically akin to the moniker "Little John" of Robin Hood folklore. Name origin: Scottish Gaelic *lagan* ("little dell").

Lili. A prostitute on Maun. Clan: Moray, Dalriada. Name origin: Welsh *lili* ("lily").

Llygaidda (hlee-GAY-thah). Apothecary at Dunpeldyr. Clan: Lothian, Goddodin, Brydein. Name origin: Welsh *llygaid da* ("good eyes").

Loholt mac Artyr. Àrd-Oighre of Clan Argyll, Caledon. Firstborn son of Arthur and Gyanhumara. Name origin: Scottish Gaelic *lo h-oillt* ("for terror").

Loth (LOTE). Chieftain of Clan Lothian of Gododdin, Brydein. Arthur's brother-in-law; Annamar's husband; father of Gawain, Gareth, Medraut, and Cundre. Banner: amber bear on forest green. Legendary name: King Lot.

Lucius. Brytoni warrior. Accolon's second-in-command at Dunadd. Clan: Moray, Dalriada, Brydein.

Majora. Brytoni woman; mother of Cato. Clan: Moray, Dalriada, Brydein.

Marcia. Nun at Rushen Priory.

Marcus Cunomorus. Centurion in the Brytoni army; Arthur's aide-de-camp. Uncle of Drustanus. Legendary name: King Mark of Cornwall.

Mari (MAHR-ee). Brytonic variant of the name Mary; the Virgin Mary.

Mavis. Brytoni woman; wife of Iawn, the innkeeper of the mansio at Caer Lugubalion.

Medraut map Loth. Third son of Loth and Annamar; brother of Gawain, Gareth, and Cundre; Arthur's nephew. Clan: Lothian, Gododdin, Brydein. Legendary names: Sir Mordred, Modred.

Melwas. Midlands Brytoni chieftain headquartered at Caer Gwenion. Clan: Gwenion, Gododdin, Brydein. Legendary names: Maleagant, Meliagrance, Meliagraunce, and numerous variants; best known as the renegade king/chief/knight who abducts Guinevere.

Merlinus Aurelius Ambrosius Dubricius. Bishop; general (legate) in the Brytoni army, garrison commander of Caer Lugubalion. Son of Ambrosius; Arthur's cousin. Nickname: Merlin. Latin name is based on Roman format and means "Merlin of the Aurelii, son of Ambrose, called Dubric." Known in Welsh ecclesiastical history as St. Dubric (or St. Dyfrig, depending upon the source); feast day November 14. Legendary name: Merlin.

Morghe (MOR-gheh) ferch Uther. Chieftainess of Clan Moray of Dalriada, Brydein. Daughter of Uther and Ygraine; Arthur's younger sister; Urien's wife. Latin name: Morganna Aurelia Vetara. Legendary name: Queen Morgan Le Fay.

Morra. Chieftainess and Àrd-Banoigin of Clan Rioghail, Caledon. Ogryvan's second cousin; mother of Iomar. Name origin: derived from Scottish Gaelic *móire* ("bag" of *pioba-móire* ("bagpipe")).

Neoinean (nay-WEE-nayAhn). Caladonach woman and apothecary living in Caledàitan; an older cousin of Fioruisge. Clan: Tarsuinn, Caledon. Name origin: Scottish Gaelic *neòinean* ("common English daisy").

Niall. Late Scáthaichean general; Cuchullain's friend. Killed by Gyanhumara in the First Battle of Port Dhoo-Glass.

Niniane (nee-nee-AH-neh). Prioress of Rushen Priory. Legendary names: Niniane, Nimue, Lady of the Lake.

Octavia. An elderly nun at Rushen Priory.

Ogryvan (OH-gree-van) mac Glynnis, a.k.a. Gogfran. Chieftain of Clan Argyll, Caledon. Hymar's consort; Peredur's stepfather; Gyanhumara's father. Nickname: "the Ogre." Legendary name: King Leodegrance.

Ornest. An Eingel warrior; Badulf's second-in-command. Name origin: Old English *ornest* ("trial by battle").

Paul, Apostle. Paul (formerly Saul) of Tarsus, Christian missionary in the AD first century.

Peredur (PARE-eh-dur) mac Hymar. Hymar's son; Ogryvan's stepson; Gyanhumara's half brother. Clan: Argyll, Caledon. Nickname: Per. Name origin: Scottish Gaelic *pòr dùr* ("stubborn seed"). Legendary name: Sir Percival.

Piosan. Chief adviser of Clan Tarsuinn. Name origin: Scottish Gaelic *pìos* ("silver cup").

Rhys (HREES). Centurion in the Dragon Legion of Brydein, Gyanhumara's aide-de-camp. Clan: Argyll, Caledon.

Rionnach. Chieftain of Clan Tarsuinn of Caledon; husband of Dynann; father of Tavyn, Eileann, and Rionnag. Clan: Uisnathrean, Caledon. Name origin: Scottish Gaelic *rionnach* ("mackerel").

Rionnag nic Dynann. Youngest child of Dynann and Rionnach; sister of Tavyn and Eileann. Clan: Tarsuinn, Caledon. Name origin: Scottish Gaelic *rionnag* ("star").

Saigarmor. Caledonach warrior; Alayna's second-in-command. Clan: Alban, Caledon. Name origin: inspired by Scottish Gaelic *saighdear* ("soldier"), *mór* ("great"). Legendary name: Sir Sagramor(e).

Sgeir. Wise-woman of Clan Tarsuinn. "Sgeir" is an alias; her birth name is unknown. Name origin: Scottish Gaelic *sgeir* ("a rock in the sea").

Sian. Wise-woman of Clan Tarsuinn. "Sian" is an alias; her birth name is unknown. Name origin: Scottish Gaelic *sian* ("storm of wind and rain").

Tavyn mac Dynann. Oldest child of Dynann and Rionnach; brother of Eileann and Rionnag. Junior-grade officer (decurion) in the Brytoni army, commander of Second Turma, Manx Cohort. Clan: Tarsuinn, Caledon.

Terwyn. Captain of the guard at Dunpeldyr and Loth's primary adviser. Clan: Lothian, Gododdin, Brydein. Name origin: Welsh *terwyn* ("brave").

Urien (OO-ree-ehn) map Dumarec. Chieftain of Clan Moray of Dalriada, Brydein. Son of Dumarec and Wreigdda; husband of Morghe. Legendary names: King Urien, Uriens.

Uther map Custennin. Late Dux Britanniarum (succeeded Ambrosius). Ambrosius's younger brother; Ygraine's second husband; father of Arthur and Morghe. Latin name: Vetarus Aurelius Constantinus. Legendary name: King Uther Pendragon.

Venna. Late mother of Wat; Brytoni servant at Caer Lugubalion with whom Elian had enjoyed intimate relations, though she never identified him as being Wat's father.

Vortigern. Late Brytoni warlord who employed Saxon mercenaries against the Caledonians and Scots.

Wastad map Elian. Son of Elian and Venna; this is the adoptive name of the former Caer Lugubalion stable hand Wat. Nickname: Wart. Name origin: Welsh *wastad* ("level," "constant").

Wat. Brytoni stable boy at Caer Lugubalion. Nickname: Wart.

Wihtred (VIH-tred). An Eingel warrior; member of Badulf's unit. Name origin: Old English *wihtred* ("white counsel").

Willa (WEE-thlah). Nun at Rushen Priory.

Wlencing. Late West Saxon prince. Younger brother of Cissa; father of Ælferd. Historically, Cissa, Wlencing, and Cymen appear to have been sons of Ælle, though the latter two men rarely appear in Arthurian tradition.

Wreigdda (ooRAYG-thah) ferch Brychan. Widow of Dumarec; mother of Urien. Clan: Moray, Dalriada, Brydein. Name origin: Welsh ("good lady").

Yglais (ee-GLACE) ferch Gorlas. Second daughter of Gorlas and Ygraine; Arthur's half sister; wife of Alain. Clan: Cwrnwyll, Rheged, Brydein.

Ygraine (ee-GRAY-neh). Chieftainess of Clan Cwrnwyll of Rheged, Brydein. Widow of Gorlas; widow of Uther; mother of Annamar, Yglais, Arthur, and Morghe. Nickname: Ygrayna. Banner: ivory unicorn on crimson. Legendary name: Queen Igraine.

Ymyl (EE-meel). Manx fisherman. Name origin: Welsh *ymyl* ("edge", "margin", "border").

GLOSSARY

THIS APPENDIX INCLUDES place-names and foreign terms. Pronunciation guidelines are supplied for the less obvious terms, especially those of Brythonic or Scottish Gaelic origin. In the case of a term having multiple translations used in the text, the most commonly referenced term is listed first. Word and phrase origins and English translations are given wherever possible.

My choices of word selection, translation, spelling, suggested pronunciation, and the use of accent marks reflect an attempt to imply a "proto-language" to today's version, especially with regard to the Scottish-Gaelic-based words, compounds, and phrases. Terms identified as having a Pictish source are based on studies of Scottish place-names, since there are no known documents that were written in ancient Pictish. Brythonic-sourced words are derived from ancient Welsh literature, such as the *Mabinogion*.

Astute fans of the series may notice differences in spellings or pronunciations of some of the terms from those given in earlier installments. These differences represent updates in my research.

A Dubh Loch (Caledonaiche, "From the Black Lake"). The nickname Angusel gives himself as a poetic description of the condition of his soul; also a poetic reference to the Hibernian Sea. Origin: Scottish Gaelic *a* ("of" or "from"), *dubh* ("black"), *loch* ("lake").

Abar-Dùr (Caledonaiche, "Mouth of the Eternal River"). One of the ferry ports controlled by Clan Tarsuinn, located on the north bank of the Firth of Forth near present-day Aberdour, Scotland. Origin: proto-Celtic/Pictish *abar* ("river mouth"), Scottish Gaelic *dùr* *("stubborn" or "persevering").*

Abar-Gleann (Caledonaiche, "Mouth of the River Valley"). Site of Arthur's first battle as Dux Britanniarum, where he defeated the Caledonians, located at the eastern end of the Antonine Wall on the south bank of the Firth of Forth near the present-day town of Bo'ness, Falkirk, Scotland. This equates to the first of Arthur's twelve battles, the "mouth of the River Glein," recorded in Chapter 56 of the *Historia Brittonum* (written in the early 9th century). Origin: proto-Celtic/Pictish *abar* ("river mouth"), Scottish Gaelic *gleann* ("valley").

Add (ATH) Valley. Lands surrounding the River Add near Dunadd.

Adversary, the. Euphemism for Caledonach demon overlord, Annàm, and Satan.

Aífe (EE-fay). Scáthaichean demoness. In Irish folklore, Aífe is the twin sister and deadly rival of Scáthach. Given the other name associations and folkloric connections, for the purposes of this story I affiliate Aífe with the Scháthan ancient enemies, the Aítachaitais.

Aífhein (ee-FAY-an; Scáthaichean, "one who belongs to Aífe"). A Scáthaichean epithet roughly equivalent to "bastard" or "traitor." Also deliberately evocative of the present-day slang adjective, "f-ing."

Ainm (ah-EEM; Caledonaiche, "name"). Used as part of the sign-countersign codes in the Dragon Legion. This challenge is given to determine friend-or-foe status; the correct response is Latin rank, name, and unit designation as listed on the duty roster. Origin: Scottish Gaelic.

Aítachait (EEtah-kite; pl. Aítachaitais/eetah-KITE-iss, poss. pl. Aítachasan/eetah-KAHsan; Scáthaichean, "strife with Aífe"). Name applied by the Scáthan to the inhabitants of the western portion of Eireann that Latin-speakers know as Attacots, echoing for the

Scáthan the mythological Scáthach-Aífe rivalry. Origin: inspired by Scottish Gaelic *a'tachairt* ("occurring").

Ala (pl. alae; Latin, "wing(s)"). Cavalry unit usually consisting of five turmae, commanded by a centurio equo.

Alban ("The Wild People"), Clan. Caledonaiche: *Albainaich Chaledon* (poss. *h'Albainaich*; "of Clan Alban"). Member of the Caledonach Confederacy. The clan's name tracks to the ancient name for Scotland and is deliberately evocative of an alternate legendary name for Arthur's realm, "Albion." Banner: rampant white lion on cerulean blue. Cloak pattern: sky blue crossed with crimson and green. Gemstone: aquamarine. Name origin: inspired by Scottish Gaelic *am bàn* ("untilled") and *Albainn* ("Alba," "Scotland").

Albanach (Caledonaiche, "of the Wild People"; pl. Albanaich). Female version: *ban-Albanach*. Terms used by the Caledonaich to refer to one or more members of or items belonging to Clan Alban of Caledon. Origin: inspired by Scottish Gaelic *am bàn* ("untilled") and *Albainn* ("Alba," "Scotland").

Alexandria. City founded by Alexander the Great in 331 BC and currently the second largest in Egypt.

Al-Ilyah (Arabic). Moon god symbolized by the crescent moon, origin of the name "Allah."

Amadan (Caledonaiche; lit. "foolish man," colloq. "ass"). An epithet. Origin: Scottish Gaelic.

An tùs (Caledonaiche, "the anointing"). A Caledonach ritual most commonly used for ordaining priests (*tùs an sagart*, "anointing the priest"), it was also used in generations past for preparing warriors for an important battle (*tùs an gaisgeach*, "anointing the champion"). The ritual's primary component involves having the priest's or warrior's body painted with woad god-marks (q.v.) to invoke special blessings for the coming ordeal. A priest undergoing an tùs is anointed by his brethren priests. A warrior is anointed by his soul mate, and there may be a sexual component when the ritual functions as a farewell too. Origin: Scottish Gaelic *an tùs* ("the beginning").

Anderceaster (Saxon). Latin: *Anderida*. Saxon-controlled port on the Narrow Sea near the present-day town of Pevensey, East Sussex, England.

Angalar (poss. Anghalar, Caledonaiche, "(of the) Diseased Person"). Unflattering terms the Caledonaich apply to a single Angli individual. Origin: Scottish Gaelic *an galar* ("the disease"), *a'ghalar* ("of the disease").

Angalaranach (poss. Anghalaranach, pl. Angalaranaich, poss. pl. Anghalaranaich; Caledonaiche, "(of the) Diseased People"). Unflattering terms the Caledonaich apply to the Angli people. Origin: Scottish Gaelic *an galar* ("the disease"), *a'ghalar* ("of the disease").

Angli (Latin). Of or pertaining to the inhabitants of the eastern coast of Brydein.

Annàm (ahn-NAIM), Lord. Caledonach demon overlord; a.k.a. "the Adversary." Annaomh's twin brother; leader of the evil Samhraidhean of the Otherworld, symbolized by a pair of crossed bloody cudgels, sometimes with an ox skull displayed between them. Name origin: Scottish Gaelic *an nàmh* ("the enemy").

Annaomh (AHN-nuh), Lord. Caledonach supreme deity; ruler of the Otherworld and leader of the Army of the Blest, symbolized by the sun; a.k.a. Lord of Light. In Caledonach mythology, his evil twin brother is Annàm. Name origin: Scottish Gaelic *an naomh* ("the saint").

Antonine Wall, the. Latin: *Antoninorum murum*. Caledonaiche: *Am Balla Tuath* ("The North Wall"). Frontier fortification built in southern Scotland by Roman Emperor Antoninus Pius in the A.D. midsecond century. Extends from the Firth of Forth to the Firth of Clyde. Caledonaiche origin: Scottish Gaelic *am balla* ("the wall"), *tuath* ("north").

Aonar (EYE-nar, Caledonaiche). "Alone." Origin: Scottish Gaelic.

Arbroch (Caledonaiche, "Exalted Town"). Brytonic: *Ardoca*. Latin: *Alauna Veniconum*. Seat of Clan Argyll and home fortress of Gyanhumara and Ogryvan; Roman fort captured in the 1st century A.D. by the Caledonaich, located near the present-day village of Braco in Perthshire, Scotland. Caledonaiche origin: Scottish Gaelic *àrd* ("exalted"), *broch* ("burgh").

Arddwyn (ARTH-win; Brytoni, "thief"). Gawain's warhorse. Name origin: inspired by Welsh *ddwyn* ("thief"), with the *ar-* prefix added as a connection to Welsh *arth* ("bear" (animal)).

Àrd-banoigin (aird-ban-UH-ghin; pl. àrd-banoigainn; Caledonaiche, "exalted heir-bearer(s)"). The female member of the ruling family through whom the clan's line of succession is determined. Typically, the clan's chieftainess serves as àrd-banoigin while she is of childbearing age and passes this status to a daughter or niece when the younger woman reaches physical maturity. Origin: Scottish Gaelic *àrd* ("exalted"), *ban* ("woman"), *oighre* ("heir"), *gin* ("beget").

Àrd-banoigre (aird-ban-EEGH-ray; pl. àrd-banoigreann; Caledonaiche, "exalted heiress(es)"). The female heir of the àrd-banoigin and àrd-ceoigin. The àrd-banoigre may serve as clan chieftainess in the event that the àrd-banoigin is dead or incapacitated, upon ratification of a vote by the clan's elders and the chieftain. Origin: Scottish Gaelic *àrd* ("exalted"), *ban* ("woman"), *oighre* ("heir").

Àrd-Ceann Teine-Beathach Mór (aird-KAY-ahn TEE-neh BAYah-tahk more; Caledonaiche, "High-Chief Great Fire-Beast"). Since Caledonaiche has no word for "dragon," this is the closest that the Caledonaich can come to rendering "Pendragon" in their language. Usually, they don't bother. Origin: Scottish Gaelic *ceannard* ("leader;" I switched the suffix to a prefix for consistency with other invented terms), *teine* ("fire"), *beathach* ("beast"), *mór* ("great"). There is no word for "dragon" in Scottish Gaelic, either. The word *nathrach*, which is used in the "Charm of Making" by the characters Merlin and Morganna in the 1981 movie *Excalibur*, means "snake."

Àrd-ceoigin (aird-kayUH-ghin; pl. àrd-ceoiginich; Caledonaiche, "exalted heir-begetter(s)"). The consort of the clan's àrd-banoigin. Marrying the àrd-banoigin gives the man access to her wealth but does not automatically grant him the chieftainship of her clan. Modern analogy: Queen Elizabeth II's husband, Prince Phillip. Origin: Scottish Gaelic *àrd* ("exalted"), *céile* ("husband"), *oighre* ("heir"), *gin* ("beget").

Àrd-oighre (aird-OOreh; pl. àrd-oighreachan; Caledonaiche, "exalted heir(s)"). The male heir of the àrd-banoigin and àrd-ceoigin. The àrd-oighre may serve as clan chieftain in the event that the àrd-ceoigin is dead or incapacitated, upon ratification of a vote by the clan's elders and the chieftainess. Origin: Scottish Gaelic *àrd* ("exalted"), *oighre* ("heir").

Argaillanach (Caledonaiche, "of the Tempestuous People"; pl. Argaillanaich). Female version: *ban-Argaillanach*. Terms used by the Caledonaich to refer to one or more members of or items belonging to Clan Argyll of Caledon. Origin: Scottish Gaelic *ar gailleann* ("our tempest").

Argyll (AR-gayeel; "The Tempestuous People"), Clan. Caledonaiche: *Argaillanaich Chaledon* (poss. *h'Argaillanaich*; "of Clan Argyll"). Member of the Caledonach Confederacy. The clan's name tracks to the former County of Argyll, Scotland, though at this point in the story, the clan hasn't yet expanded in that direction. Banner: two silver mourning doves in flight, on dark blue. Cloak pattern: dark blue crossed with saffron and scarlet. Gemstone: sapphire. Name origin: Scottish Gaelic *ar gailleann* ("our tempest").

Army of the Blest, the. Caledonaiche: *Sluagh na Beannaich.* The host of dead Caledonach warriors whose souls reside in the Otherworld. Origin: Scottish Gaelic *sluagh* ("host"), *beannaich* ("to bless").

Attacot(s) (Latin). Scáthaichean: *Aítachait.* Name applied to one or more inhabitants of the western portion of Eireann.

Attacotti (Latin). Scáthaichean: *Aítachasan.* Of or pertaining to the inhabitants of the western portion of Eireann.

Aurochs (pl. aurochs). An extinct wild bovine species native to Europe, Asia, and North Africa that is the ancestor of present-day cattle. Their horns were similar in length to those of Texas longhorn cattle, though they typically curved inward. The last documented living aurochs, a female, died of natural causes in Poland in 1627.

Ayr Point. Northernmost Brytoni signal-beacon site on the Isle of Maun, now called Point of Ayre.

Badge. Rank insignia worn by members of the Brytoni army: a cloak-pin fashioned in the shape of the legion's symbol (e.g., dragon). Enlistees' badges are bone or hardwood. Officers' badges are wrought of different metals depending on rank and are ringed by green (infantry), red (cavalry), or blue (navy) enamel, or a combination thereof, to indicate breadth of command. If the officer is of the nobility, the badge includes a gemstone eye representing the clan's dominant color.

Bannock. Small, hard cake made from barley or oat meal and cooked on an open griddle.

Bárweald (Old English, "boar wood"). A forest lying about 2.5 miles south of Dunpeldyr that corresponds to present-day Bara Wood, East Lothian, Scotland. Name origin: Old English *bár* ("boar") and *weald* ("forest, wood, grove").

Bear of Lothian, the. Symbol of Clan Lothian of Gododdin, a rampant amber bear on forest green. Also called the Lothian Bear and the Amber Bear.

Belteine (bel-TEE-nay; pl. Beltean; Caledonaiche, "Passion Fire"). Brytonic: *Beltain*. Fertility ritual celebrated by non-Christian Caledonaich and Breatanaich culminating on May 1 with firelight activities that would make a Ròmanach orgy participant blush. Caledonaiche name origin: Scottish Gaelic *boil* ("passion"), *teine* ("fire").

Bian-sporan (Caledonaiche, "pelt-purse"). The accessory crafted from an animal's pelt collected during the deuchainn na fala rite, symbolizing a young warrior's passage into adulthood. Origin: Scottish Gaelic *bian* ("animal skin"), *sporan* ("purse").

Black River, the. Translated name for the Dhoo River, Isle of Man, UK.

Boar of Moray, the. Symbol of Clan Moray of Dalriada, a black boar on a field of gold; also referred to as "the Black Boar." Boar of Moray and Black Boar are also used as nicknames for Urien map Dumarec.

Bonding ritual. Caledonaiche: *dean am bann naomh* ("make the holy bond"). The Caledonach ceremony wherein the *àrd-banoigin* is tattooed with her consort's clan-mark and he with hers. Origin: Scottish Gaelic *dean* ("to make"), *am bann* ("the bond"), *naomh* ("holy").

Brædæn (BRAY-dane; Eingel/Saxon). Brydein. Origin: inspired by Old Anglo-Saxon *brædan* ("to extend"), with the modified second syllable to distinguish it from "Brædan."

Brædan (BRAY-dan; Eingel/Saxon). Of or pertaining to the Brytoni inhabitants of Brydein. Origin: Old Anglo-Saxon *brædan* ("to extend").

Bræde (BRAYD-eh; pl. Brædeas, Eingel/Saxon, "roasted meat(s)"). Slang terms the Angli and Saxons apply to one or more Brytons. Origin: Old Anglo-Saxon.

Braonshaffir (Caledonaiche, "A Drop of Sapphire"). Gyanhumara's sword, named for its distinguishing feature. Name origin: Scottish Gaelic *braon* ("a drop"), *shaffir* ("of sapphire," adapted from Latin *sapphirus* and rendered with possessive form (*sh-*)).

Brat (BRAHT; poss. Bhrata, pl. Bratan, poss. pl. Bhratan; Scáthaichean, "(of the) cheap cloak(s)"). Slang term for Brytons. Origin: Scottish Gaelic *brat* ("carpet"), also found in early literature

to identify a common article of outerwear clothing—hence my interpretation of "cheap cloak" as a racial slur.

**Breatanach (brayah-TAHN-ach; poss. Bhreatanach, pl. Breat-
anaich, poss. pl. Bhreatanaich; Caledonaiche, "(of the) Bry-
ton(s)").** Terms used by the Caledonaich to refer to one or more inhabitants of western and mid-Brydein; also may be translated as "(of
the) Deceiver(s)." Origin: Scottish Gaelic *Breatunnach* ("a Briton"),
bràth ("to deceive").

**Breatanaiche (brayah-tahn-EESH; Caledonaiche, "tongue of
the Brytons").** Term used by the Caledonaich to refer to the Brytonic
language.

Broch (Caledonaiche). A conical dwelling built partially un-
derground with one entrance, a top vent for hearth fires, and few or
no windows. The largest brochs have as many as three stories: the
lowest level is used for storage of raw materials and foodstuffs, the
ground level for working and entertaining, and the upper level for
sleeping.

Brogach (BROH-gak, Caledonaiche, "sturdy lad"). An endearment. Origin: Scottish Gaelic. The female version is *brogag*.

Brydein (Brytonic). Latin: *Britannia*. Caledonaiche: *Breatein*
(poss. *Bhreatein*, "(of) Brydein"). Britain, a.k.a. the Island of the
Mighty.

Bryton(s). Name applied to one or more inhabitants of western
and mid-Brydein.

Brytoni. Of or pertaining to the inhabitants of western and
mid-Brydein.

Brytonic. The native language of the Brytons, also known as
"Brythonic" or *P-Celtic* in present-day anthropological usage.

Cac. Brytonic: *cach*. Latin slang term for "dung;" see also *vacca
cac*.

Caer Alclyd (Brytonic, "Fort of Clyde Rock"). Caledonaiche: *Dùn
Bhreatanaich* ("Fort of the Brytons"). Brytoni-controlled fortress on
the north bank of the Firth of Clyde, home of Alain and Yglais, located
near the western end of the Antonine Wall in the present-day town
of Dumbarton, Dunbartonshire, Scotland. Caledonaiche name origin:
Scottish Gaelic *dùn* ("fortress"), plus my invented term, *Bhreatanaich*
("of the Brytons").

Caer Gwenion (Brytonic, "White Fort"). Latin: *Vinovia* ("the Ways of the Vintners," likely the name of the local tavern/inn when the fortress was built in the AD 1st century). Fortress controlled by the Brytoni clan Gwenion corresponding to what today is known as Binchester Roman Fort near Bishop Auckland, England. Home fortress of Melwas.

Caer Lugubalion (Brytonic, "Fort of Lugh's Strength"). Latin: *Luguvalium* ("Lugh's Valley"). Caledonaiche: *Dùn Lùth Lhugh* (doon LOOT hloo, "Fort of Lugh's Power"). Brytoni-controlled fortress near the western end of Hadrian's Wall, headquarters of the Dragon Legion of Brydein, located in what is now Carlisle, Cumbria, England. Caledonaiche name origin: Scottish Gaelic *dùn* ("fortress"), *lùths* ("power"), and my invented possessive form of the name Lugh, *Lhugh*.

Caer Rushen (Brytonic, "Rush's Fort"). Brytoni-controlled fortress near the southernmost tip of the Isle of Maun, located in present-day Castletown, Isle of Man.

Caerglas (Brytonic, "Green Fort"). Caledonaiche: *Dùn Ghlas* ("Locked Fort"). Brytoni-controlled fortress on the western end of the Antonine Wall that doubles as a garrison and headquarters of the Brytoni fleet, located in present-day Glasgow, Scotland. Caledonaiche name origin: Scottish Gaelic *dùn* ("fortress"), *ghlas* ("locked").

Caleberyllus (Latin, "Burning Jewel"). Arthur's sword, known through various sources as Caliburnus, Caliburn, Caledfwlch, and Excalibur. This name is my invention, derived from the Latin words *calere* (heat, origin of "calorie") and *beryllus* (beryl, a classification of gem) as a poetic description of the sword's distinguishing feature. Technically, a ruby is a cabochon, not a beryl, but I suspect that nobody was making that fine a distinction in the fifth century AD.

Caledàitan (Caledonaiche, "hard place"). A ferry port village controlled by Clan Tarsuinn on the north bank of the Firth of Forth that corresponds to present-day Kirkcaldy, Fife, Scotland. Origin: inspired by proto-Celtic *caled* ("hard") and Scottish Gaelic *àite* ("a place"). To speakers of modern Scottish Gaelic, the town of Kirkcaldy is known as *Cair Chaladain*, "Fortress of the Caledonians," though that name implies a much greater civic status than what I needed for the purposes of this series.

Caledon (poss. Chaledon; Caledonaiche, "(of the) Place of the Hard People"). The name the Caledonaich apply to their territory, encompassing what is now the Scottish Highlands and northern Lowlands. Origin: Pictish/proto-Celtic *caled* ("hard").

Caledonach ("Caledonian"), Caledonaich ("Caledonians" and "The Hard People"), Caledonaiche ("Caledonian language"), Chaledonach ("Caledonian's" or "of the Caledonian"), Chaledonaich ("Caledonians'" or "of the Caledonians"). Idiomatic terms of my own invention, based on Scottish Gaelic linguistic rules for indicating group membership (*-ach* (sing.) and *-aich* (pl.) suffixes), and the possessive form (*Ch-* prefix). Language designation (*-aiche* suffix) is my own invention.

Caledonach Confederacy, Caledonian Confederacy. Caledonaiche: *Na Cairdean Caledonach* ("The Caledonian Friends"). Caledonach political entity. Member-clans mainly consist of those living closest to Brytoni-controlled territories. Historically, the region of Caledonia may have been divided into seven major kingdoms, each with many client-kingdoms, and it most likely wasn't a united nation. Caledonaiche name origin: Scottish Gaelic *na cairdean* ("the friends"), plus my invented term, *Caledonach* ("Caledonian").

Caledonach law, Caledonian law. Caledonaiche: *Sgianan na Chaledonaich* ("Laws of the Caledonians"). Unwritten code memorized and recited by seannachaidhean, and administered by priests. Caledonaiche phrase origin: Scottish Gaelic *sgianan* ("knives"), plus my invented term, *Chaledonaich* ("of the Caledonians"). Although there is a word in Scottish Gaelic meaning "law" (*dlighe*), I opted for a more poetic approach.

Caledonia (Latin). The name that Latin- and Brytonic-speakers apply to the home of the Caledonaich, the region encompassing what is now the Scottish Highlands and northern Lowlands.

Caledonian(s). Of or pertaining to the inhabitants of the nation of Caledonia, terms used by Latin- and Brytonic-speakers.

Calends. The first day of any month on the Roman calendar—and the origin of the word "calendar." Origin: Latin *kalendae* ("the called"). From Wikipedia: "To find the day of the Calends of the current month, one counts how many days remain in the month, and add two to that number. For example, April 22 is the 10th of the Calends of May because there are 8 days left in April, to which 2 being added, the sum is 10."

Centurion. Latin: *centurio* ("century commander"). Mid-grade military officer; in Arthur's army, this is usually a century or ala commander, or commander of a garrison staffed with fewer than four centuries or alae. Badge: copper brooch with appropriately colored enamel ring around the legion's symbol.

Century. Latin: *centuria*. Infantry unit consisting of approximately 100 soldiers, commanded by a centurion.

Cernunnos (ker-NOO-nohs). Caledonian/Brytoni deity: Lord of the hunt, symbolized by a stag.

Chieftain's Rock, the. A tall, large, flat rock standing inside Dunadd's innermost defensive perimeter, inscribed with a series of notches, a boar, and the indentations of a basin and a footprint.

Clan-mark. Caledonaiche: *fin-cìragh* ("clan-crest"). A tattoo representing the Caledonach clan's symbol, usually painted with woad dye. A woman receives the clan-mark on her right forearm when she achieves the status of àrd-banoigin. During the bonding ritual, the àrd-banoigin receives her consort's clan-mark on her left forearm. Likewise the àrd-ceoigin is tattooed with her clan-mark, also on the left forearm. The clan-mark is a special classification of warding-mark. Origin: inspired by Scottish Gaelic *fine* ("tribe," fem.), *cìr* ("cock's crest," m.), *carragh* ("monument," fem.).

Clota. Caledonach/Brytoni goddess of wisdom symbolized by a leaping salmon.

Cohort. Latin: *cohors* ("company"). Military unit usually consisting of ten centuries or alae or combination thereof, commanded by a prefect (non-nobleman) or tribune (nobleman).

Coilltichean Chaledon (Caledonaiche, "Forest of Caledonia"). Vast wooded region north of the Firth of Forth through which Arthur's legion must march to intercept the Angli army. Though most of the military action occurs on the bordering plain near Dùn Fàradhlann, this corresponds to "Cat Coit Celidon," site of the seventh of Arthur's twelve battles as recorded in chapter 56 of the ninth-century work *Historia Brittonum*. Name origin: Scottish Gaelic *coilltichean* ("forest") plus my invented term *Chaledon* ("of Caledonia").

Comes Britanniarum (Latin, "Count of Brydein"). Female version: *Comitissa Britanniam*. The historic Roman army title was applied to the soldier who commanded all field action against enemy threats between the Antonine and Hadrianic walls. In Arthur's army, it applies to his second-in-command. Also can be translated as "Companion of Brydein."

Comites Praetorii (Latin, "Count's Guard"). The ala designated as the bodyguards of the Comitissa Britanniam or Comes Britanniarum, consisting of five 20-horse turmae. The unit is commanded by the Primus Eques ("First Knight"), equivalent in rank to prefect, who also commands First Turma. The subcommanders are Secundus Eques ("Second Knight"), Tertius Eques ("Third Knight"), Quartus Eques ("Fourth Knight"), and Quintus Eques ("Fifth Knight"), all equivalent in rank to centurion. Every other member is called an equitem ("knight;" pl. equites), and is an officer equivalent in rank to decurion. All members are selected based on recommendation and rigorous competition, and they usually serve for life, though they may be detailed to lead other units from time to time, especially as the need arises in battle. Competition (think "sports combine") to replace dead/injured members is held annually, at Easter, as needed. Colloquially, the unit members call themselves "the Companions," an alternate translation of Comites. This is deliberately evocative of the Round Table fellowship, but established by Gyanhumara, not Arthur.

Badge: bronze (Primus), copper (Secundus, etc.), or iron (Equitem) dragon, with red, green, and dark blue enamel ring.

Banner and shield: dark blue dragon rampant on gold.

Uniform: double-fringed, bronze-studded dark blue leather kilt; dark blue cloak, undertunic, and neck stole; dark blue leather boots; bronze, dragon-crested helmet; bronze, dragon-embossed greaves and forearm-guards; and torso armor with feather-shaped bronze scales.

Compline. The last of eight Christian canonical hours of the day, occurring at approximately two hours past sundown. Origin: Latin *complere* ("to fill up").

Constantinopolis. The Latin name of the ancient Greek city that is present-day Istanbul.

Corinth. A city-state on the Isthmus of Corinth, the narrow stretch of land that joins the Peloponnesus to the mainland of Greece, and one of the most influential cities of ancient Greece and Rome. It was visited by the apostle Paul in AD 51 or 52.

Council of Chieftains, the. Conclave of Brytoni chieftains that convenes to pass judgment on matters involving more than one Brytoni clan.

Crimson Eagle, the. Symbol of King Colgrim of the Angles, a crimson eagle on a white field.

Criòsdail (Caledonaiche). Christian. Origin: Scottish Gaelic.

Cùtorc (KOO-tork; pl. cùtuirc; Caledonaiche, "dog-boar(s)"). An epithet stronger than cù-puc, usually applied as a sexual slur. Origin: Scottish Gaelic *cù* ("hound"), *torc* ("boar").

Cù-puc (KOO-puck; pl. cù-puic; Caledonaiche, "dog-pig(s)"). An epithet. Origin: based on Scottish Gaelic compound *cù-muc* ("dog-sow"), with a change in consonants to make it sound more satisfying when spoken aloud.

Cwrnwyll (KEERN-weedl), Clan. Caledonaiche: *Càrnhuileanaich* ("The Rock-Elbows People"). Brytoni clan occupying the region of Rheged. I invented this clan name to be evocative of Cornwall, the region ascribed by tradition for Arthur's birth. The fact that it renders very nicely into Caledonaiche is something I didn't discover for almost 25 years. Banner: rampant ivory unicorn on crimson. Cloak pattern: dark red crossed with sky-blue and saffron. Gemstone: ruby.

Cymensora (Saxon, "King's men's shore"). A settlement of the South Saxons thought to correspond to present-day Selsey Bill, Sussex, on the shore of the English Channel. Referenced in the ninth-century *Anglo-Saxon Chronicle* as Cymenshore. The translation "King's men's shore" is my invention, inspired by the Saxon word for king, *cyning*, which makes sense as a garrison name.

Dalriada (Latin). Caledonaiche: *Dailriata* (poss. *Dhailriata*; "(of the) Necessary Meadow"). Political region in the northwest sector of Brydein consisting chiefly of the Kintyre Peninsula and western islands of Scotland plus the Isle of Man. At the time of this story, the Scotti incursions into this region were just getting underway, and historically the Isle of Man was never considered part of the later Scotti kingdom of Dál Riata. Caledonaiche name origin: Scottish Gaelic *dail* ("meadow"), *riatanach* ("necessary").

Dance of the Summer Wraiths, the. Caledonaiche: *Ruidhle na Shamhraidhean*. One of the Caledonach activities performed on Samhainn day, a precursor to trick-or-treating. Clan warriors dress up as either Lord Annàm and the Summer Wraiths to harass the feasters, or as Lord Annaomh and Army of the Blest to rescue them, symbolizing the triumph of good over evil. Caledonaiche name origin: Scottish Gaelic: *ruidhle* ("dance"), plus a term of my invention, *shamhraidhean* ("of the summer wraiths"), inspired by *samhradh* ("summer"), and *samhlaidhean* ("replicas," "metaphors," "ghosts").

Dance of the Virgins, the. Caledonaiche: *Ruidhle na Righinnean.* One of the Caledonach activities performed on Belteine night to invoke fertility blessings. Caledonaiche name origin: Scottish Gaelic *ruidhle* ("dance"), *na rìghinnean* ("of the young ladies").

Decurion. Latin: *decurio* ("commander of tens"). Junior-grade military officer, usually a turma commander. Badge: iron brooch with appropriately colored enamel ring around the legion's symbol.

Deuchainn na fala (Caledonaiche, "trial of blood"). The rite of passage for Caledonach warriors. Clad in a loincloth and armed with a dagger, the candidate is taken into the forest and charged to return in at least three days. Being early is taken as a sign of cheating and cowardice. Origin: Scottish Gaelic *deuchainn* ("trial"), *na fala* ("of blood").

Doves of Argyll, the. Caledonaiche: *Na Calmaig h'Argaillanaich.* Also Argaillanach Doves, Argyll Doves. Symbol of Clan Argyll of Caledon, a pair of silver doves in flight on a dark blue background. Origin: Inspired by Scottish Gaelic *na calmain* ("the doves" and rendered in the plural feminine form with the -*aig* suffix), and my invented term, *h'Argaillanaich* ("of Clan Argyll").

Dragon King. Eingel-Saxon translation of "Pendragon."

Dragon Legion, the. Latin: *Legio Draconis.* Northern Brytoni army unit, whence the term "Pendragon" originates. When Arthur took command after Uther's death, this was the only legion in existence—what was left of it.

Dubh-lann (doo-LAHN; Caledonaiche, "black-blade"). The ritual challenge to the clan's present or future àrd-ceoigin. By Caledonach law, the àrd-banoigin cannot interfere and must accept the winner as her consort, regardless of her personal feelings. Origin: inspired by Scottish Gaelic *dùbhlan* ("challenge"); compound of *dubh* ("black"), *lann* ("blade").

Dun Eidyn (Brytonic, "Fort of Eidyn"). Caledonaiche: *Dùn Éideann* (doon EE-day-ahn, "Well-Armed Fort"). Hill-fort on the summit of what is known today as Arthur's Seat, Edinburgh, Scotland, located on the south bank of the Firth of Forth. Site of the battle where, prior to the opening of *Dawnflight*, Uther was killed by King Colgrim and his invading Angli army, forcing Arthur to take command of the retreating Brytoni troops to prevent a rout. Caledonaiche name origin: Scottish Gaelic *dùn* ("fortress"), *éideadh* ("armor").

Dùn Fàradhlann (doon FAY-rajh-lahn, Caledonaiche, "Sword-ladder Fort"). A fictional hill fort corresponding to present-day Dunfermline, Fife, Scotland, and home fortress of Clan Tarsuinn, located three miles from the north shore of the Firth of Forth. Dùn Fàradhlann earned its name from the reputation of its early Caledonach occupants, who repelled invaders' ladders with vicious sword attacks. Name origin: Scottish Gaelic *dùn* ("fortress"), *fàradh* ("ladder"), *lann* ("blade").

Dunadd (doon-ATH, Brytonic, "Fort on the River Add"). Caledonaiche: *Dùn At* ("Swelled Fort"). Hill-fort near the town of Kilmartin on the Kintyre Peninsula in Argyll and Bute, Scotland, that is believed to have been the capital of the ancient Scotti kingdom of Dál Riata. In this story, it is the seat of Moray, home fortress of Urien and Dumarec. Caledonaiche name origin, which is the oldest written form of the fort's name: Scottish Gaelic *dùn* ("fortress"), *at* ("to swell").

Dunpeldyr (Brytonic, "Fort of the Spear"). Caledonaiche: *Dùn Pildìrach* (doon peel-DEER-ack, "Fort of the Turning Ascent"). Traprain Law hill fort near Haddington in East Lothian, Scotland, which serves as the seat of Clan Lothian and the home fortress for Annamar and Loth. Caledonaiche name origin: Scottish Gaelic *dùn* ("fortress"), *pill* ("to turn"), *dìr* ("to ascend").

Dux Britanniarum (Latin, "Duke of Brydein"). Caledonaiche: *Flath Bhreatein.* Roman military title applied to the commander of the legions stationed between the Antonine and Hadrianic Walls. Prior to the Roman military exodus from Britain in the early part of the 5th century, this force consisted of two legions. When Arthur took this job, approximately 80 years later, there weren't enough trained soldiers available to form a single legion. Badge: gold dragon, with a red, green, and blue braided enamel outer ring. Historically, this title was applied only to the commander of northern stationary defenses (i.e., troops guarding the Hadrianic and Antonine walls), and it was not a field command. My Arthur doesn't have that luxury. Caledonaiche name origin: Scottish Gaelic *flath* ("prince"), plus my invented term, *Bhreatein* ("of Brydein").

Eingel(s). Terms the Eingel people apply to themselves that are more Germanic pronunciations than the Latinized form, "Angli."

Eingelcynn (INE-ghel-kin, Eingel, "Angle-kin"). Also Eingelfolc (INE-ghel-volk, "Angle-folk"). Terms the Eingel people apply to their race.

Eireann (Scáthaichean, "Ériu's Head"). Ireland. Latin: *Hibernia*. Caledonaiche: *Airein* ("Men of the Plow"). Eingel/Saxon: *Æren* ("Brazen"). Caledonaiche name origin: Scottish Gaelic *airein* ("plowmen"). Eingel/Saxon name origin: Old Anglo-Saxon *æren* ("brazen").

Epona. Caledonach/Brytoni deity: Horse goddess symbolized by a prancing mare.

Falcon of Tarsuinn, the. Also Tarsuinnach Falcon. Caledonaiche: *A'Seabhag Tarsuinnaich*. Symbol of Clan Tarsuinn of Caledonia, an attacking falcon. Origin: Scottish Gaelic *a'seabhag* ("the falcon," fem.), and my invented term *Tarsuinnaich* ("of Clan Tarsuinn").

Fealty-mark. Caledonaiche: *dìleas-tì*. A scar on a Caledonach warrior's neck made by his or her sword wielded by the person to whom the warrior has sworn the Oath of Fealty. Origin: Scottish Gaelic *dìleas* ("faithful"), *tì* ("intent").

Feast of Christ's Passion, the. Easter.

Fenrir. A demon-wolf in Norse mythology and god of destruction.

Ferch (VERK, Brytonic). "Daughter of," followed by the father's name; e.g., Morghe ferch Uther.

Fiorth (Brytonic), the. Caledonaiche: *Ab Fhorchu* ("River of the Flowing Hound"). Firth of Forth, southeastern Scotland. Caledonaiche name origin: inspired by Scottish Gaelic *Abhainn Fhorchu* ("River Forth"), *forasach* ("forward," adj.), *cù* ("hound").

Fleet Commander, the. Latin: *Navarchus Classis Britannia*. Admiral in charge of the Brytoni war-fleet. Since the word "admiral" originates from Arabic, I considered it appropriate to employ a different title; technically, in Arthur's Roman-based military force, the fleet commander is equivalent in rank to a legate. Badge: silver dragon brooch with a blue enamel outer ring.

Geall Dhìleas (Caledonaiche, "Oath of Fealty"). See Oath of Fealty. Origin: Scottish Gaelic *geall* ("promise"), *dhìleas* ("of faithfulness").

Gododdin (go-DOTH-in). Brytonic: *Guotodin*. Caledonaiche: *Gò Do-dìon* ("Deceptively Difficult Defense"). Brytoni-controlled territory corresponding to modern southeastern Scotland and northeastern England. The Brytonic name is derived from the Latin name of the Celtic tribe inhabiting the area at the time of the Roman occupation, the Votadini. The Caledonaiche version implies that the region is deceptively well-defended. Caledonaiche name origin: Scottish Gaelic *gò* ("deceitful"), *do-dìon* ("difficult defense").

God-mark. Caledonaiche: *cìr na dia* ("crest of the god"). A tattoo, either permanent or temporary, representing one of the Old Ones, usually painted with woad dye. A warrior may receive many god-marks during the ritual of an *tùs*. A priest receives one god-mark during an *tùs* representing the god or goddess who has chosen him for special service, though he is expected to serve all of them during his tenure as priest. The god-mark is a special classification of warding-mark. Origin: inspired by Scottish Gaelic *cìr* ("cock's crest," m.), *na dia* ("of the god").

God-name. Caledonaiche: *darainm-diathan* ("named by the gods"). A nickname bestowed by Caledonach gods upon a worthy mortal. Origin: inspired by Scottish Gaelic *dar* (archaic word for "by"), *far-ainm* ("nickname"), *diathan* ("gods").

Gold Hammer and Fist, the. Banner of the king of the South Saxons, Woden's hammer and fist in gold on a field of black.

Green Griffin, the. Symbol of Prince Ælferd of the West Saxons, a green griffin on gold.

Gwenion, Clan (Brytonic). Brytoni clan headquartered at Caer Gwenion and occupying the plains region of present-day England that's due east of the North Pennines mountain range, approximately midway in latitude between York and Carlisle.

Hadrian's Wall, Hadrianic Wall. Latin: *Hadriani murum*. Caledonaiche: *Am Balla Deas* ("The South Wall"). Frontier fortification built in northern Britain by the Roman Emperor Hadrian early in the second century A.D. Extends from Wallsend on the River Tyne through Carlisle to the Solway Firth near Bowness-on-Solway. Caledonaiche name origin: Scottish Gaelic *am balla* ("the wall"), *deas* ("south").

Hafonydd (HAH-von-eeth; Brytonic, "riverside"). Caledonaiche: *Aodanninean ("rock face")*. Brytoni-controlled village along the

River Tyne that corresponds to Haddington, East Lothian, Scotland. Name origin: Welsh *hafonydd* ("riverside"). Caledonaiche name origin: inspired by Scottish Gaelic *aodann* ("the face"), *innean* ("rock, hill").

Hati. A demon-wolf in Norse mythology who is believed shall destroy the moon and help cause the destruction of the world; brother of Skoll.

Hauberk. Saxon chain mail shirt that reaches to midcalf.

Heather. One of the donkeys used by the nuns of Rushen Priory, named for the plant.

Hero's portion. A haunch of roast pork, offered before anyone else partakes of the feast's centerpiece entree. In ancient Celtic societies, a wrestling tournament between warriors was staged as the main entertainment, with the hero's portion given as the traditional prize since it was considered the best cut. This practice stood in contrast to contemporary Roman tradition, wherein military officers competed for the patronage of a wealthy potential benefactor or—as with the Comites Praetorii—advancement to an elite unit.

Hibernian Sea. Latin: *Mare Hibernium*. The Irish Sea.

Horse Cohort. Latin: *Cohortis Equitum*. Unit in the Brytoni army consisting of eight cavalry alae and no foot soldiers, formed as a result of the Brytoni-Caledonian treaty forged after the battle of Abar-Gleann. First Ala is comprised mostly of Brytoni horsemen; the remaining alae are comprised of Caledonians.

Ides (Latin). A Roman calendar term referring to the 15th of the months March, May, July, and October, and the 13th of all other months.

Ifrinn (EEF-reen; Caledonaiche, "hell"). In the Caledonach worldview, this is the realm of Lord Annàm and the Samhraidhean, as well as other malevolent spirits and demonic beings. Origin: Scottish Gaelic *ifrinn* ("hell").

Ironwort. One of the donkeys used by the nuns of Rushen Priory, named after the herb.

Laird (Scáthaichean, "Lord"). Honorific applied to the overlord of the Scáthaichean.

Lammor, Clan (Brytonic). Caledonaiche: *Làmanmhor* ("People of Great Hands"). Full Caledonaiche designation: *Làmanmhoranaich Srath-Chlotaidh Bhreatein*. Brytoni clan of the region of Strathclyd,

Brydein. Banner: emerald-green stag's head on silver. Cloak pattern: grass-green crossed with silver and black. Gemstone: heliodor. Brytonic name origin: inspired by the Lammermuir Hills of southern Scotland, where this clan is located. Caledonaiche name origin: Scottish Gaelic *làmhan mhor* ("of great hands"), i.e., craftsmen and -women; *Srath-Chluaidh* ("Strathclyde"), *srath* ("low-lying land near river"), and my invented term, *Chlotaidh* ("bank of Clota's River").

Lann-seolta (Caledonaiche, "blade-cunning"). The attribute possessed by Caledonach warriors who are particularly adept at predicting their opponents' moves in battle, especially in regard to swordsmanship. Origin: Scottish Gaelic *lann* ("blade"), *seòlta* ("cunning", "skillful").

Lavender. Medicinal and aromatic strewing herb.

Legion. Latin: *legio*. The largest unit in the Roman military infrastructure, usually consisting of six infantry cohorts and at least one cavalry ala, commanded by a legate. Technically, Arthur is *Legatus Legio Draconis* ("Legate of the Dragon Legion"), but his status as Dux Britanniarum is more descriptive and therefore supersedes the "legate" title, so I don't use the term "legate" to describe him in this text.

Liberation Night. Saxon term applied to the event marking their freedom from Brytoni rule under King Vortigern in the mid-fifth century A.D. This event is known to the Brytons as "Night of the Long Knives" because of the wholesale slaughter of Brytoni nobility as the two factions were feasting. Although Vortigern escaped, this event created a power vacuum in Brydein into which stepped Ambrosius and Uther.

Lion of Alban, the. Also Albanach Lion. Caledonaiche: *An Leóghann h'Albainaich*. Symbol of Clan Alban of Caledon, a white lion rampant on a field of cerulean blue. Non-Caledonians refer to it as the Alban Lion. Origin: Scottish Gaelic *an leóghann* ("the lion"), plus my invented term, *h'Albainaich* ("of Clan Alban").

Llafnyrarth (JHLAV-neer-arth; Brytonic, "Blade of the Bear"). The broadsword wielded by Chieftain Loth of Clan Lothian and his heirs, the first of the three great blades forged by Wyllan on the Isle of Maun. Origin: Welsh *llafn yr arth* ("blade of the bear").

Loki. The trickster god in Norse and Eingel/Saxon mythology.

Lothian, Clan (Brytonic). Caledonaiche: Clan *Lùthean* (LOOT-hay-ahn, "People of Power"); full designation is *Lùtheanaich Ghò Do-*

dìon Bhreatein. Brytoni clan of the region of Gododdin, Brydein. Banner: rearing amber bear on dark green. Cloak pattern: forest green crossed with dark blue and gold. Gemstone: amber. Caledonaiche name origin: Scottish Gaelic *lùths* ("power").

Lugh. Caledonach/Brytoni deity renowned for his strength, symbolized by a bull.

Mac (Caledonaiche). "Son of," followed by the mother's name; e.g., Angusel mac Alayna. Origin: Scottish Gaelic.

Machaoduin (mahk-EYE-dween; pl. michaoduin; Caledonaiche, "son(s) of the unmanned"). Scáthaichean: *o'neduine.* An epithet with obvious parentage connotations; can apply to jerks, cowards, the condemned, the exiled, and traitors. Female form is *nichaoduin* (pl. *naichaoduin*). Origin: Scottish Gaelic *mac* ("son"), plus my invented compound, *aoduin* ("un-man"), inspired by *ao-* (negation prefix), *duine* ("a man").

Macmuir (Caledonaiche, "Son of the Sea"). Gyanhumara's horse (white stallion), sired by Macsen.

Macsen (Brytonic, "Great One"). Arthur's horse (white stallion), named in honor of a predecessor of Ambrosius, Macsen Wledig ("Great Prince").

Mansio (Latin, "abode"). The inn reserved for use by high-ranking military officers and civilian dignitaries; most Roman fortresses quartering a half cohort or more had one.

Manx Cohort. Latin: *Cohortis Mavnium.* Unit of the Brytoni army stationed on the Isle of Maun consisting of one infantry century posted to Ayr Point (with the men from that century being rotated to guard the Mount Snaefell signal beacon, as well), two centuries at Caer Rushen, two centuries plus two cavalry turmae at Tanroc, and three centuries and three turmae at Port Dhoo-Glass.

Map (Northern Brytonic). "Son of," followed by the father's name; e.g., Urien map Dumarec. Brytons of southern clans use the variant ap, also in conjunction with the father's name.

Matins. First of eight Christian canonical hours of the day. Properly occurring at midnight, the prayer service is sometimes combined with lauds at dawn. Origin: Latin *matutinus* ("of the morning").

Maun. Latin: *Mavnum.* Isle of Man in the Irish Sea.

Melys (Brythonic, "sweet"). A mare at Caer Lugubalion used for courier duty. Origin: Welsh.

Mite. A fraction of a brass or bronze coin bearing about as much value as a penny does today.

Mo ghaisgich (mo HEYE-sitch, Caledonaiche, "my heroes"). A term of respect and endearment. Origin: Scottish Gaelic.

Mo laochan (Caledonaiche, "my little champion"). A term of encouragement usually applied to boys; female version: *mo laochag*. Origin: Scottish Gaelic, a diminutive of *laoch* ("hero, champion, warrior").

Mo sìorransachd (Caledonaiche, "my eternal love"). A term of endearment spoken to a woman. When spoken to a man, the phrase is *mo sìorransachan*. Origin: inspired by Scottish Gaelic *mo* ("my"), *sìorraidh* ("eternal"), *annsachd* ("beloved one," female form).

Móran (Caledonaiche, "The Many People"), Clan. Caledonach moniker for the Brytoni Clan Moray of Dalriada, Brydein, coined simply because there are so many of them. Full Caledonaiche designation: *Móranaich Dhailriata Bhreatein*. Origin: Scottish Gaelic *móran* ("many").

Móranach (pl. Móranaich; Caledonaiche). Of or pertaining to the Brytoni Clan Moray of Dalriada, Brydein. Origin: Scottish Gaelic *móran* ("many").

Moray, Clan. Brytoni clan occupying the region of Dalriada, Brydein. Banner: black boar on gold. Cloak pattern: black crossed with gold. Gemstone: jet.

Navarchus Classis Britannia (Latin, "Commander of the Brytoni Fleet"). The Brytoni fleet commander's official title, though Bedwyr seldom uses it.

Nemetona. Caledonach/Brytoni goddess of war, symbolized by a z-shaped spear bisected by a horizontal rod, said to drive a crimson chariot drawn by four winged, fire-snorting black mares.

Nic (Caledonaiche). "Daughter of," followed by the mother's name; e.g., Gyanhumara nic Hymar. Origin: Scottish Gaelic, contraction of *nighean mhic* ("young woman offspring").

Nones (from Latin *nonus*, "ninth").
1. A Roman calendar term referring to the ninth day before the ides, having earned its own label because it was the traditional day when debts were due for payment; the seventh of March, May, July, and October, and the fifth of all other

months. Though the term has fallen into disuse, the fifth of the month retains mention in lease payment clauses.

2. Fifth Christian canonical hour and ninth hour of daylight, around 3 pm.; origin of the term "noon."

Oath of Fealty, the. Caledonaiche: *Geall Dhìleas.* The rite wherein a warrior pledges loyalty to a warrior of another clan; precursor of the knighthood ceremony. If trust is an issue for the person accepting fealty, the rite can be used for execution. Origin: Scottish Gaelic. The person holding the sword asks, "*An dean thu*, [Name and Title(s)], *an Geall Dhìleas chugam*, [Name and Title(s)], *gus a'bàsachadh?*" (Literally, "Make thou, [Name and Title(s)], the Oath of the Faithful to me, [Name and Title(s)], until the dying?") The person swearing the oath responds, "*A chaoidh gus a'bàsachadh.*" ("Ever until the dying.")

Og (Scáthaichean). "Son of," followed by the father's name; e.g., Cuchullain og Conchobar.

Old Ones, the. Caledonaiche: *Na Déathan Sean.* Collective name applied to the Caledonach deities. Origin: Scottish Gaelic *na déathan* ("the gods"), *sean* ("old").

One God, the. Caledonaiche: *An Díaonar.* Caledonach term for the Christians' deity. God-name: One (Caledonaiche *H'aon, inspired by Scottish Gaelic a h-aon, "the one"*). Origin: inspired by Scottish Gaelic *an dia* ("the god"), *aonar* ("alone").

Optio (Latin, "assistant"). Lowest-ranking military officer, usually a centurion's clerical assistant, courier, or scout; this officer typically does not command other soldiers. Badge: iron legion symbol, no enamel on the ring.

Otherworld, the. Caledonaiche: *An Domhaneil.* In the Caledonach worldview, this is the realm of the Old Ones, analogous to heaven but with more traffic of mortals and spirits back and forth between both worlds. Origin: based on Scottish Gaelic *an domhan* ("the world"), *eile* ("another").

Pendragon, the. Brytonic: *Y Ddraig Pen* ("The Chief Dragon"). Latin: *Draconis Rex* ("Dragon King"). Caledonaiche: *Àrd-Ceann Teine-Beathach Mór* ("High-Chief Great Fire-Beast"). Honorific applied to the Dux Britanniarum, commander of the Dragon Legion.

Phalanx. A closely spaced, heavily armed, wedge-shaped military formation employed in charges for the purpose of opening a gap in the enemy's line. Tactical origin: ancient Greece.

Phalera (Latin, "ornament"). Term applied to a military accolade earned in battle. For an individual soldier, this is a bronze disc embossed with either the unit or legion symbol, which is worn on the breastplate only during parades. The unit citation is a much larger disc that is affixed to the standard's shaft.

Phalera Draconis (Latin, "Dragon's Ornament"). The highest award that can be won by any soldier of the Dragon Legion, a bronze disc embossed with a dragon.

Pict(s) (Latin, "Painted Folk"). Epithet applied by Latin-speakers to one or more inhabitants of Caledonia.

Picti (Latin, "of the Painted Folk"). Of or pertaining to the inhabitants of Caledonia.

Port Dhoo-Glass (Manx). Brytoni-controlled port named for its location at the confluence of the rivers Dhoo ("Black") and Glass ("Green"), present-day Douglas, Isle of Man. "Above the river called Dubglas" is the site of battles 2, 3, 4, and 5 of Arthur's twelve battles on the list cited in chapter 56 of the ninth-century *Historia Brittonum*. On my list, Port Dhoo-Glass is the site of battles 2 (in *Dawnflight*) and 5 (in *Morning's Journey*). Technically, Gyanhumara led #5, and Arthur was present only in its aftermath.

Praefectus Cohortis Equitum (Latin, "Prefect of the Horse Cohort"). Senior military officer commanding Arthur's only all-cavalry cohort. Badge: bronze brooch with a red enamel ring around the legion symbol.

Praetorium (Latin, "governor's residence"). The living quarters of the garrison commander; also may be translated as "palace."

Prefect. Latin: *praefectus.* Senior military officer; in Arthur's army, this is usually a cohort or garrison commander. Badge: bronze brooch with either a red or green enamel ring around the legion symbol, or both colors if the garrison also has a cavalry unit.

Prime. Third Christian canonical hour and first full hour of daylight, around 6 a.m. Origin: Latin *primus* ("first" or "chief").

Rasher (n.). A small serving of bacon or ham.

Rìbhinn-crann (HREEN crahn; pl. rìbhinn-chroinn; Scáthai-chean, "maiden-plow(s)"). Euphemism for the obvious male body part. Origin: Scottish Gaelic *rìbhinn* ("virgin"), *crann* ("plow", "mast").

Rioghail ("The Royal People"), Clan. Caledonaiche: *Rioghai-lanaich Chaledon.* Member of the Caledonach Confederacy. Banner: purple eagle standing, on gold. Cloak pattern: black crossed with pale purple and red. Gemstone: amethyst. Name origin: Scottish Gaelic *rioghail* ("royal").

River Add (ATH). The watercourse on the Kintyre peninsula that has lent its name to the valley and to the hill-fort Dunadd.

River Fiorth (Brytonic). Caledonaiche: *Ab Fhorchu.* Firth of Forth. See Fiorth, the.

Ro h'uamhasach (roh HWAH-wah-sahk, Caledonaiche, "the most terrible man"). Term applied to a Caledonach warrior fighting in the deepest throes of battle-frenzy; a berserker. Origin: based on Scottish Gaelic *ro h–uamhasach* ("very terrible," "very dreadful").

Ròmanach (poss. Rhòmanach, pl. Ròmanaich, poss. pl. Rhòmanaich; Caledonaiche, "(of the) Roman(s)"). Usually uttered in derision—though not always. These terms are also used by the Scáthaichean.

Ròmanaiche (roh-mah-NEESH; Caledonaiche, "tongue of the Romans"). The Latin language.

Rukh. Peredur's horse (bay gelding).

Rushen Priory. Christian women's religious community located on the eastern coast of the Isle of Maun, presided over by a prioress.

Sacred Flame, The. Also the Flame. Caledonaiche: *An Lasair Naomh.* Caledonach symbol of religious purity, analogous to Christian holy water. Origin: Scottish Gaelic *an lasair* ("the flame"), *naomh* ("holy").

Saffron. An herb that yields a yellow dye.

Samhainn (SOH-wen; Caledonaiche, "Summer's End"). Brytonic: *Samhain.* Harvest festival celebrated by non-Christian Caledonaich and Brytons on November 1. Name origin: Scottish Gaelic *samhainn* ("Hallowtide").

Samhradh (SOW-hrah; pl. Samhraidhean; Caledonaiche, "Summer Wraith(s)"). Evil resident(s) of the Otherworld; demon(s). In the Caledonach worldview, a warrior who dies dishonorably becomes a Samhradh, doomed to fight against the Army of the Blest for all eternity. Name origin: Inspired by Scottish Gaelic words *samhradh* ("summer") and *samhladh* ("ghost" or "replica").

Sasun (SAH-soon; Caledonaiche). Term referring to a single Saxon individual.

Sasunach (sah-SOON-nach; pl. Sasunaich, poss. Shasunach, poss. pl. Shasunaich; Caledonaiche, "(of the) Saxon(s)"). Terms applied by the Caledonaich to the Germanic inhabitants of southern Brydein. Origin: Scottish Gaelic *Sasunnach* ("English", "Englishman").

Saxon(s) (Brytonic). Of or pertaining to the inhabitants of the southern portion of Brydein; name possibly derived from their weapon of choice, the *seax*.

Scarlet Dragon, the. Standard of the Brytoni army, a scarlet dragon passant on a field of gold, very similar to the present flag of Wales; also referred to as "the Dragon." Can double as a nickname for Arthur, usually spoken by his enemies.

Scáth (SKITE; poss. Scháth, pl. Scáthan, poss. pl. Scháthan). Terms the Scotti people apply to themselves to demonstrate racial devotion to the warrior-goddess Scáthach. The Caledonaich use the terms "Scáth" and "Scháth" but follow their own rules for pronunciation and for indicating group membership. Whether or not this is the true origin of the term "Scot" and its affiliated words, I found the association far too tempting to dismiss.

Scáthach (SKY-ah). Scotti war goddess and Irish folklore character famous for being the warrior-woman who trained the mythological hero Cú Chulainn in the martial arts, and perhaps in "bedroom combat" as well.

Scáthaichean (skytah-KAYan; "Warriors of Scáthach"). Name the Scotti people apply to their race in honor of their warrior-goddess Scáthach. Also the term they use when referring to their language.

Scot(s) (Brytonic). Caledonaiche: *Scáth* (poss. *Scháth*, pl. *Scáthinaich*, poss. pl. *Scháthinaich*). Terms applied to the inhabitants of the eastern portion of Eireann.

Scotti (Latin). Caledonaiche: *Scáthinach*. Of or pertaining to the inhabitants of the eastern portion of Ireland.

Sea holly. A plant that can be used as an aphrodisiac.

Seat of Moray, the. Caledonaiche: *Cathair na Móranaich*. Clan Moray's administrative headquarters at Dunadd, Dalriada. Caledonaiche name origin: Scottish Gaelic *cathair* ("chair" and "city"), plus my invented phrase, *na Móranaich* ("of Clan Moray").

Seax (Saxon). War-knife, usually measuring 15–18 inches from point to end of hilt.

Senaudon (Caledonaiche, "Place of Charmed Protection"). Angusel's birthplace and Alayna's home fortress located in present-day Stirling, Scotland. Origin: inspired by Scottish Gaelic *seun* ("a charm for protection" and "to defend by charms").

Sennight. Measure of time: one week (contraction of "seven nights," analogous to "fortnight" being a contraction of "fourteen nights").

Seven Saxon Sisters, the. Brytoni drinking song that's not particularly flattering to Saxon women.

Sight, the. Otherwise known as Extrasensory Perception. This version manifests in prophetic visions and dreams.

Signifer (Latin, "standard-bearer"). The soldier charged with carrying the unit's banner—and guarding it in battle.

Silver Wolf, the. Standard of Cuchullain, Laird of the Scáthaichean, a loping silver wolf on a pine-green background; also referred to as "the Wolf." Sometimes doubles as a nickname applied to Cuchullain.

Sithichean (see-tee-KAY-ahn; Caledonaiche). Of or pertaining to any of the spirits residing in the Otherworld, good or evil.

Skoll. A demon-wolf in Norse mythology who is believed shall destroy the sun and help cause the destruction of the world; brother of Hati.

South Saxons. Term applied to the Germanic people living in the region now known as Sussex, England.

Stonn. Angusel's horse (gray stallion).

Stylus (pl. styli; Latin). Pen-like implement used for making impressions on soft clay and wax, usually fashioned of iron or hardwood.

Tabhartas bàs (Caledonaiche, "death offering"). In Caledonach culture, these are gifts to assist the dead on their journey to the Otherworld, which can consist of food, drink, flowers, jewelry, armor, weapons, or tools for the hearth and home. Origin: Scottish Gaelic *tabhartas* ("offering," noun), *bàs* ("death").

Tanroc. Brytoni-controlled fortress on the western coast of the Isle of Maun and site of the third of Arthur's twelve battles on my list (technically, Cai led this one in Arthur's stead), situated near the present-day town of Peel, Isle of Man, UK.

Tarabrogh (Scáthaichean, "Tara's Settlement"). Cuchullain's home fortress located at Hill of Tara, County Meath, Leinster, Ireland.

Tarsuinn (TAR-shoon; Caledonaiche, "The Crossing People"), Clan. Caledonaiche: *Tarsuinnaich Chaledon.* Member of the Caledonach Confederacy, so named because they run a large ferry business from several points across the Firth of Forth. Banner: gold falcon in flight, on azure. Cloak pattern: saffron crossed with blue and red. Gemstone: golden beryl. Name origin: Scottish Gaelic *tarsainn* ("across").

Tarsuinnach (Caledonaiche, "of the Crossing People"; pl. Tarsuinnaich). Female version: *ban-Tarsuinnach.* Terms used by the Caledonaich to refer to one or more members of or items belonging to Clan Tarsuinn of Caledon. Origin: inspired by Scottish Gaelic *tarsainn* ("across").

Trews. Loose-fitting trousers made of leather, wool or linen, worn by Brytoni men and by Caledonaich of both sexes.

Trìbruachan (Caledonaiche, "Three river banks"). Site of the seventh of Arthur's twelve battles. The name describes the confluence of two tributaries of the Dour Burn, which in turn empties into the Firth of Forth near present-day Aberdour. This site corresponds to the tenth battle cited by Nennius in *Historia Brittonum* ("Tribuit"). Origin: Scottish Gaelic *trì* ("three"), *bruachan* ("river banks").

Tribune. Latin: *tribunus.* In Arthur's army, this is a high-ranking military officer (usually a prefect) of noble birth. Badge: bronze brooch, with appropriately colored enamel ring and the clan's gemstone.

Turma (pl. turmae; Latin, "squad(s)"). Roman cavalry unit consisting of 10–30 horsemen, commanded by a decurion. In Arthur's army, the typical size averages 20.

Uisge (OOS-ghee; Northern Brytonic, "water"). A strong alcoholic beverage distilled from barley. I chose to employ a dialectic shortening of Scottish Gaelic *uisge-beatha* ("water of life;" i.e., whiskey) because humans during that era rarely drank unboiled water lest they run the risk of getting sick.

Uisnathrean (Caledonaiche, "The Water-Serpent People"), Clan. Caledonaiche: *Uisnathreanaich Chaledon.* Member of the Caledonach Confederacy based at Inverness, Scotland. Origin: inspired by Scottish Gaelic *uisge* ("water"), *nathair* ("serpent").

Vacca cac (Latin, "cow dung"). An expression of frustration. Origin: Latin *vacca* ("cow"), *cac* (slang term for "dung").

Valerian. Medicinal herb.

Vespers. Seventh Christian canonical hour, occurring at sunset. Origin: Latin *vespera* ("evening").

Warding-mark. Caledonaiche: *seunail.* A tattoo believed by Caledonaich to be a physical manifestation of divine protection. Origin: Scottish Gaelic *seun* ("a charm for protection"), *aileadh* ("mark").

West Saxons. Term applied to the Germanic people living in the region now known as Wessex, England.

White Horse, the. Symbol of the king of the West Saxons.

Wintaceaster (Saxon, "Market Castle"). Winchester, Hampshire, Wessex, England.

Wintaceaster Palace. Residence of King Cissa of the West Saxons.

Woad. An herb that yields a blue dye.

Woden. Eingel/Saxon deity; ruler and father of the gods. In their worldview, Woden's Hall houses the souls of dead warriors. "Woden's Day" survives in modern usage as "Wednesday." Also known as Wodan, Wotan, Odin.

Wyrd. The Eingel/Saxon concept of fate or destiny, believed to be unchangeable.

The Challenge Comic Book
Story by Kim Iverson Headlee
Art by Tim Shinn

Arthur's captor has challenged Gyan to a winner-takes-all duel for
the kingdom as well as his life. Now Gyan must face all her de-
mons—private as well as public.

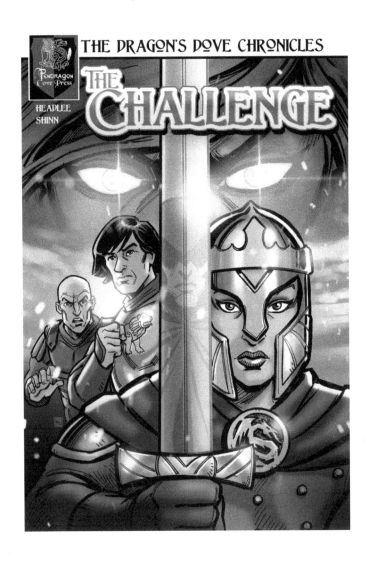

Interior Art

 Gareth	BEAR'S HEAD: original line art ©2014 by Jessica Headlee
Gawain	BEAR, STANDING, facing right: original line art ©2014 by Kim Headlee
Gull	TARSUINN FALCON: original line art ©2012 by Kim Headlee

All other character totems are line-art adaptations ©2012–2018 by Kim Headlee, based on photographs of the following Pictish stones found throughout Scotland:

Accolon	EAGLE: DETAIL on stone Inveraven 1, Moray
Alayna	CAT: DETAIL on the front of Meigle 5, Meigle Sculptured Stones Museum, Angus, Perth and Kinross
Al-Iskandar	Z-ROD, SIMPLE: Meigle 7 in the Meigle Sculptured Stones Museum, Angus, Perthshire and Kinross
Angusel	LION, STANDING: inspired by a detail on the side of Meigle 26 in the Meigle Sculptured Stones Museum, Angus, Perthshire and Kinross
Angusel	LION'S HEAD: inspired by a detail on the Daniel Stone, Rosemarkie, Black Isle, Easter Ross, depicting a lioness with a man's head in her mouth
Arthur	DRAGON, HORIZONTAL: the Dragon Stone, Portmahomack, Tarbat, Ross and Cromarty
Arthur	DRAGON, VERTICAL: detail on the front of stone Meigle 4, Meigle Sculptured Stones Museum, Angus, Perthshire and Kinross

Badulf	**LEOPARD'S HEAD:** detail on a silver plaque found in the hoard at Norrie's Law, Fife; the glyph's orientation on the plaque is vertical
Cai	**HOUND, WALKING:** detail on the Golspie Stone, Craigton 2, Highland Sutherland
Camilla	**GRIFFIN:** ADAPTED from a detail on the side panel of Meigle 26 in the Meigle Sculptured Stones Museum, Angus, Perth and Kinross; the glyph on the stone features a much fancier tail
Eileann	**HARP:** DETAIL on reverse of the Nigg Stone, Nigg, Easter Ross, Ross-shire
Eileann	**LADY HARPER:** based upon the male harper detail on the front of stone Monifieth 4, Monifieth, Angus, Perth and Kinross
Elian	**CRIPPLED BOAR:** the Dunadd Boar, Dunadd, Kilmartin, Argyll and Bute
Fergus	**TONGS:** DETAIL on the Abernethy Stone, Abernethy, Perth and Kinross; the glyph's orientation on the stone is vertical

Fioruisge	CAULDRON: DETAIL on the rear of Aberlemno 2, Aberlemno Kirkyard, Angus, Perth and Kinross; the glyph's orientation on the stone is vertical
Gawain	BEAR, WALKING: the Bear Stone, Scatness, Shetland Isles
Merlin	SALMON: DETAIL on the Golspie Stone, Craigton 2, Highland Sutherland
Morghe	V-CRESCENT: DETAIL on the Brough of Birsay Stone, Orkney
Niniane	DISC-CROSS: THE Dyce 6 stone, City of Aberdeen
Peredur	HORSE: THE stone Inverurie 4, Inverurie, Aberdeenshire
Urien	BOAR: THE Boar Stone of Clune Farm, Dores, Highland Inverness

About the Author

KIM HEADLEE LIVES on a farm in the mountains of south-western Virginia with her family, cats, fish, goats, Great Pyrenees goat guards, someone else's cattle, half a million honey bees, and assorted wildlife. People and creatures come and go, but the cave and the 250-year-old house ruins—the latter having been occupied as recently as the midtwentieth century—seem to be sticking around for a while yet. She has been a published novelist since 1999 and has been studying the Arthurian legends for half a century.

http://www.kimheadlee.com
https://twitter.com/KimHeadlee
http://www.facebook.com/kimiversonheadlee

OTHER PUBLISHED works by Kim Iverson Headlee:

The Challenge comic book, illustrated by DC and Marvel Comics artist Tim Shinn, e-book and print, Pendragon Cove Press, 2019.

Twins, the novella genesis of book 6 of The Dragon's Dove Chronicles, e-book and paperback, Pendragon Cove Press, 2017.

The Business of Writing: Practical Insights for Independent, Hybrid, and Traditionally Published Authors, e-book and paperback, Pendragon Cove Press, 2016.

Kings, a sword-and-sorcery crossover novella by Kim Iverson Headlee and Patricia Duffy Novak, e-book, audiobook, and paperback, Pendragon Cove Press, 2016.

The Challenge, a Dragon's Dove Chronicles novella, e-book, audiobook, and paperback, Pendragon Cove Press, 2015.

King Arthur's Sister in Washington's Court by Mark Twain as channeled by Kim Iverson Headlee, illustrated by Jennifer Doneske and Tom Doneske, e-book, audiobook, hardcover, and paperback, Lucky Bat Books, 2015.

Liberty, second edition, e-book, audiobook, and paperback, Pendragon Cove Press, 2014.

Snow in July, illustrated by Jessica Headlee, e-book and paperback, Pendragon Cove Press, 2014.

Morning's Journey, The Dragon's Dove Chronicles, book 2, e-book and paperback, Pendragon Cove Press, 2014; the 2013 paperback edition published by Lucky Bat Books.

"**The Color of Vengeance,**" a short story excerpted from *Morning's Journey*, e-book, audiobook, and paperback, Pendragon Cove Press, 2013.

Dawnflight, The Dragon's Dove Chronicles, book 1, e-book, audiobook, and paperback, Pendragon Cove Press, 2014; the 2013 paperback edition published by Lucky Bat Books.

Liberty, writing as Kimberly Iverson, paperback, HQN Books, Harlequin, 2006.

Dawnflight, first edition, paperback, Sonnet Books, Simon & Schuster, 1999.

FORTHCOMING:

King Arthur's Sister: The Once and Future Queen, the sequel to *King Arthur's Sister in Washington's Court*, Pendragon Cove Press.

Kings comic book, illustrated by Tim Shinn, Pendragon Cove Press.

Prophecy, the sequel to *Liberty*, Pendragon Cove Press.

Zenith Glory, The Dragon's Dove Chronicles, book 4, Pendragon Cove Press.

CPSIA information can be obtained
at www.ICGtesting.com
Printed in the USA
FFHW011607220119
50271429-55275FF